SCHIMMERT

JOURNEY TO SILENCE

Terry Lee Bowe

Family Leers-Westhovens from Meers, The Netherlands

Text copyright @ 2019 Terry Lee Bowe

Book design and illustrations by Rare Hare Creative

ISBN-13: 9781794391321

Acknowledgments

A special thanks to the loves of my life:

· Ruth Ann Bowe, my wife

· Nathan Bowe, my son, and his spouse, Rebecca Johnson Bowe

· Michael Bowe, my son, and his spouse, Alexis Fenton Bowe

· Alisha Smith Dumrongkietiman, my daughter, and her spouse, Victor Scott Dumrongkietiman

· Emily Smith Hoffman, my daughter, and her spouse, Jonathan Ryan Hoffman

· Audra Smith, my daughter

· Riley Jean and Sianna Quinn Dumrongkietiman, my lovely granddaughters

· George W. and Elsie Keeney; Frank and Marjorie Bowe, my grandparents

As a constant reminder, my life has been blessed and touched by thousands of people who I endeavor to thank, including:

· All of my friends from the upper Kanawha Valley, especially from my hometown, Riverside, WV

· My Cedar Grove High School classmates, particularly the graduating class of 1970

· My history department classmates from the West Virginia Institute of Technology

· My tight-knit, loving Bowe family from Riverside, WV

· Phyllis Ferrell and family from Riverside, WV

· George R. Feltner, lifelong friend from Cedar Grove, WV

· The Leers family from Meers, the Netherlands

· The Schrijnemaekers family from Schimmert, the Netherlands

· Karl and Agnes Trags and family from Kerkrade, the Netherlands

· Hans Reulein and family from Oettingen, Germany

· Dieter Welsch and family from Grobsolt, Germany

· My U.S. Army buddies who I served with at AFCENT, Detachment A, at Tapijn Kazern in Maastricht, the Netherlands

· The friendly people of Limburg Province in the Netherlands

· My fellow "Good Neighbor" State Farm Insurance agents and employees

· My former teachers and professors, all members of the world's greatest profession

· Kathy Nelson-Legg, Margaret "Peaches" Nunley, Kirsten O'Brien, Kimberly Young, and Carolyn Surbaugh, current and former office staff associates at my State Farm Insurance agency

· All of my wonderful policyholders who I have been honored to serve

Writing this book was more of a challenge than I initially imagined. Throughout the arduous process, I soon realized in order to complete my novel, I needed guidance, stimulation, and assistance from many talented individuals. From the bottom of my heart, a big thank you goes out to my faithful and diligent editors and my talented designer:

- Kenneth W. Barton, my lifelong friend, and former classmate
- Dr. Thomas J. Kiddie, Associate Professor, English Department at West Virginia State University
- Mickey Johnson and Fran Allred, retired newspaper editors from The Herald-Dispatch of Huntington, WV and current partners at weeditbooks.com
- Sheree Wentz, owner of Rare Hare Creative, designer, format specialist, and illustrator

1945 Photo of the Family Vroemen-Sijen
de Kling Road, Oensel (Schimmert) the Netherlands

From the Author

I had to write this book so I could scratch it off of my "things to do" bucket list. Deep inside I have always had a burning desire to interweave some of my favorite passions into the content of a fiction novel. Inspired and nurtured by childhood memories, I faithfully purchased tickets to my local movie theater where I watched hundreds of double-feature films starring famous actors like John Wayne, Jimmy Stewart, Gary Cooper, Kirk Douglas and Burt Lancaster or starlets such as Doris Day and Marilyn Monroe.

My friends and I would often escape to the dark confines of Palmer's Theater in Cedar Grove, West Virginia, where we became mesmerized to the influences of countless films of the day. Almost every Sunday afternoon, we sat there on the edge of our seats anxiously engaged in the middle of a wartime, gangster or cowboy gunfight or were touched to our core by a light-hearted romantic entanglement or comedy.

While Palmer's provided a happy diversion, I have always felt blessed to have been raised in a small, dirt-poor community in Appalachia. Riverside, my hometown of 200 people, was my whole world from birth to my late teens. As a young kid, the town's meager economic makeup and safe confines afforded me the opportunity to explore my surroundings with little or no adult supervision. I thrived in the environment and the freedom it gave me was liberating. I learned how to improvise in Riverside.

I was personally acquainted with everyone in town and encouraged by my working parents to explore. My buddies and I swam at our favorite Kanawha River swimming holes and interacted together playing pick-up sports, baseball being a favorite. For countless hours, we played tag, hide-and-go-seek, board games, rode our bicycles, explored the mountains, and built secret makeshift hide-away cabins. Mostly, we made our own decisions and were expected to entertain ourselves.

After finishing high school, I started college, was drafted U.S. Army at age 19, trained as a military policeman, ultimately landing at Maastricht in the Netherlands. To this day, I credit serving in the army as one of my greatest personal experiences. The opportunity was life-changing and being stationed overseas opened my eyes to other cultures. I was assigned to a NATO installation and worked with allied soldiers from several western European nations. To my delight, through two Dutchmen who worked with me at the base, I was introduced to the Leers family from the little Dutch village of Meers, to the Trags family from Kerkrade, and later, to the Schrijnemaekers from Schimmert. My newfound friends and their families gladly accepted me into their homes and exposed me to their unique Limburg way of life which I quickly came to enjoy and admire.

After returning home, I finished my college degree, married, became a father, divorced, remarried, and have worked as a State Farm Insurance agent since 1984. I have traveled extensively, often visiting World War II historical sites in Europe, and genealogy and discovery is still a passion. With my loving family's encouragement, my historical interests of the 1930s and '40s, and by using Limburg Province as an endearing setting, I was empowered to fulfill a lifetime vision. Hence, my book.

Dedicated to My Parents:

Raymond Lee Bowe & Rosalie Fay Keeney Bowe

Table of Contents

CHAPTER ONE
IT WAS A HOME RUN

I was anxious as I approached the Chicago Tribune's gothic office tower on the morning of April 24, 1936, a beautiful day in the Windy City. My best friend Al and I worked as reporters for the prestigious Chicago Tribune, which boldly and proudly proclaimed on its front page the slogan "World's Greatest Newspaper." Al was preparing to cover a Cubs game at Wrigley Field, and I was on my way to an 11 a.m. meeting with my supervising editor, Herman Kellmeyer. My hastily arranged meeting with Kellmeyer had been set the day before and he had hinted that he had to make an important decision that involved me.

I wondered, "What could possibly be so important that he urgently needed to see me?"

For months I'd planned to take that Friday off as a vacation day, and looked forward to an extended weekend helping my parents at their downstate farm. My mother understood when I telephoned her to explain that I may not be home for dinner as planned. She knew that I had no option when the boss said my presence at today's meeting was imperative and in the best interest of my budding career.

I was open to whatever was in the making for me that clear spring day, and, frankly, I had little to fear. I never thought about any consequences that could be in store. I didn't know, of course, that I was about to make a decision within the next 14 minutes that would change my life forever and ultimately fill my heart with endless joy and merciless pain. Those dual emotions would engulf my soul for the next nine years.

As with any decision, the final verdict can only be right or wrong.

Conversely, within a split second, a baseball slugger has to decide whether to watch that high fastball settle safely into the catcher's mitt and hope to hear the ump call, "Ball one," or to swing for the fences with everything he's got. Either of the batter's choices could end with a positive outcome. On the other hand ...

"Was I about to be faced with one of those quick decision making options?" I wondered.

I'd always envisioned becoming a famous newspaper writer. After all, I was working as a reporter for a top-notch news organization and had written some important stories, but who was I kidding to imagine that my dream could come true?

With only 11 minutes remaining before the meeting, I fantasized about whether a Pulitzer Prize might soon be within my grasp or whether the honor would have to wait for another day.

My dear mother, who was born in the Netherlands, passed on to me her motto she labeled her "Dutch touch," meaning someone who had a sense of bravado combined with a spirit of compassion. Whenever faced with adversity, she'd always raise her hands high above her head and shout, "Never fear the unknown." My indomitable mother nurtured my vision and would never allow my spark to extinguish. She believed in me and knew I possessed a risk taker's mentality. I was her only son, her everything.

The first sounds I remembered hearing as I walked into the building that morning came from the elevator operator shouting out his familiar directions, "Watch your step! Going up!"

I always greeted him with the same request: "Apostle's floor, thank you, Mickey," which he recognized instantly as the 12th. Our feisty five-foot-two squirt of a lift commander looked dapper as ever in his light-gray uniform, which resembled a bellboy's outfit, complete with red-striped pants legs and a spiffy flat-topped cap. He flirted with every single girl in the building, even though they always rejected his advances with laughter. They viewed his constant flattery as a joke. The many rejections, however, never stopped his frequent attempts at eliciting a "yes" from one of the young ladies.

"Joe," he told me several times, "those dolls don't know what they're missing. Just one date with ol' Mickey would make those dames realize Casanova had been right under their noses all along, and one day one of those lucky dolls is going to find that out."

I always agreed with Mickey.

Once the car was loaded and its passengers intimately squished together like a can of sardines, the metal doors closed tightly and we launched toward the heavens. Just 10 minutes before I was to learn of my fate, my heart was pounding faster than ever.

I noticed both my clammy thumbs rubbing against my index fingers as our pilot announced: "Third floor, advertising!" Then, a few seconds later, he repeated: "Watch your step! Going up!"

I wondered if that last phrase Mickey called out was some sort of a sign.

"Sixth floor, accounting! Watch your step! Going up!"

His caution to be careful was to be his recurring message on that unusually hot, puzzling day. As Mickey turned the brass operator's lever that guided the elevator to its destinations, my mind raced. My watch showed 10:51, just nine more minutes before Armageddon or Valhalla.

My parents saw the future in me, and I never wished to disappoint them. They had worked too hard for me to fail. They constantly reminded me that hard work, compassion for others, and a strong, solid character were the qualities of a man. Having faith in myself and my abilities, they counseled, would ultimately guide me in the right direction.

Nervous, I closed my eyes and heard my mother saying, "Home could be anywhere in the world. After all, it's the people, dear friends, and a loving family with little doses of the five senses that make that four-letter word so endearing."

Mother always told me Schimmert, her birthplace in Holland, was a special place. I always wondered if I would ever visit her old Limburg village. Most important, she insisted that the most precious ingredient of all could be waiting around any corner. That essential component, of course, was love.

The odd train of thought stopped dead in its tracks when the sluggish elevator doors finally opened on the 12th floor. I was the sole passenger.

Breaking with tradition, Mickey shouted with glee, "Apostle's floor, where the disciples toil. Watch your step! Next stop is the top floor where the gods work, live and play!"

Then with a laugh and a wink, he gently closed the doors. I took my first steps toward Kellmeyer's office with seven minutes to spare. As I pondered the possibilities of the meeting with my boss, I found myself peering aimlessly at my workplace.

Even though the big open space looked the same as always, my eyes fixed upon a flickering light dangling from the massive white ceiling. I knew the light that shone down from dozens of fixtures above was powered by huge electric generating plants fueled by enormous mounds of black Appalachian coal. I was fully aware of the dusty mining towns and the men whose backbreaking labor extracted the black treasure from the earth hundreds of feet below ground. I knew those coal miners worked daily in constant peril so we "city folk," as they referred to us, could give light to darkness. Back home in West Virginia, where we were from, my father, a former railroad engineer, had hauled that coal to similar power plants.

As I continued walking down the aisle, I was once again reminded by Mabel, my partner in creating my stories, and her identical roommates that the busy newsroom was alive with the never-tiring vibrations of beat reporters, copy editors, artists, and section editors buzzing about the immense space like honey bees, working diligently at their day-to-day grind. At my far right, two ticker-tape readers were checking the daily stock and commodity prices, energetic little machines continually spewing printed thin white paper strips loaded with the much-anticipated news of that day's trades.

I was astonished to see Mabel stoically sitting in the second row, waiting all alone and receiving no attention whatsoever. Her location was our special place to rendezvous, though we normally only allocated time to be with one another when I was in the midst of some deep thought. We'd been properly introduced on my very first day on the job at the Trib in 1934, and though I'd shared her with others since then, I'd been the most familiar with Mable for the past two years. She looked beautiful as always, and it was a rare day indeed to see her so quiet with nary a word pouring out. She and I'd spent many lonesome nights together, and I guess it would have been appropriate to say that she was one of my best friends.

Yes, my trusted ebony Underwood typewriter, "Ol' Black Mabel," a name that I had lovingly given to her, was certainly one of the most dependable ladies I'd ever met. She was perched atop my cluttered desk near the rear corner of the line but seeing her unattended was a bonus since I would need to use her again before I left the newsroom that spring day.

Intrigued when I went downtown that morning, I was impatient to speak with my edgy, domineering, but much-respected boss, who had summoned me to his office for the mysterious meeting. Beforehand, I'd been tipped off by a cohort who had heard a rumor that I may be in line for some yet unidentified, but coveted, assignment.

Upon reaching his two-paneled door, which bore his name painted on the fragile glass upper panel, I was reminded of my comparatively insignificant status by the constant sounds of clicks and dings from the ever-humming typewriters ringing in my ears. With some apprehension, I knocked on his office door and was greeted with a hearty handshake. That warm, but surprising, gesture should have been my first clue that something was up.

Kellmeyer's intense obsession with timepieces was no secret among his subordinates, and being prompt was a trait I knew he appreciated. I entered his domain wearing my best suit, meaning it was the only one of the three I owned that was freshly pressed. He, on the other hand, looked commanding as always at six-feet-two with his neatly trimmed gray beard and his Teddy Roosevelt glasses slung low on the bridge of his nose. His dark blue suit featured a vest with a slit that held his pocket watch, which was attached to a gold chain that dangled across his expansive belly.

"Grab a seat young man. I admire a fellow who's on-time and you're five minutes early, Mr. Fisher. I like that," he said wryly with a wink as he looked down at my cheap Timex wristwatch displaying 10:55 a.m. His much larger electric wall clock's second hand slowly circled its face, ticking to the beat of my heart as he continued.

"Can I get you anything, a cigarette or a cigar, perhaps, or maybe a shot of whiskey or a nice glass of wine since we no longer have to abide by that horrible, ill-advised Eighteenth Amendment. Prohibition. What a silly experiment that was!" he archly observed.

"No, thank you, sir. I'm OK," I replied, anxiously waiting to hear the reason for my strongly recommended and urgent visit.

"Well, Joe, I'm a man of few words, as you should know by now. How long have you been here with the Tribune now, one year?" he asked.

"Two, sir," I quickly responded.

"Oh, my, how time flies, Joe. I forget where you're originally from again, and, for the life of me, I can't recall where you went to college either."

His inquiry seemed a bit casual and showed little concern for my comfort as he gazed out his big glass window overlooking Chicago's famed Michigan Avenue below. Before I answered, he took a seat behind his impressive black walnut desk.

"I'm from Morgantown, West Virginia, and I graduated from West Virginia University in 1930," I answered.

"Yes, yes, I remember now, West Virginia, down in 'rebel' country. I always wanted to see your capital in Richmond where Robert E. Lee and Stonewall Jackson led the Confederates during the Civil War," he replied with a comment that got as much wrong as it did right.

He knew I would have to respond, and I did.

"Sir, Charleston is the capital city of West Virginia, not Richmond," I corrected him with little regret. "I think you may have us confused with Virginia. It's a common mistake. We Mountaineers usually don't take offense to the error.

"It was Virginia's folly for choosing the South's side, not ours," I said with a chuckle, assuming he was just playing games.

"Yes, yes, Charleston. Please forgive me, Mr. Fisher. Geography is not my strong point," he replied with a grin. "For some reason, I was under the impression that you came to us from Bloomington in downstate Illinois."

"That's true, sir, I did work for The Pantagraph. I first moved to Illinois after getting a job there after I graduated from college. My parents have moved there as well; they own a little farm." I explained.

"Ah, I see!" he acknowledged.

Before I could expand, his telephone rang. He apologized and motioned for me to stay seated as he took the call.

I graduated from college with a bachelor's degree in English and journalism. My studies also included a heavy dose of the classics, but my main interests were courses in journalism, editing, and advertising. Of course, English grammar was required because my goal was one day to become a writer for a metropolitan newspaper. My mentor in college was Dr. Perley Isaac Reed, an enthusiastic English professor who constantly stressed to his students the power of the written word. He had a passion for his students who wished to become newspaper reporters. With his steady guidance, I was fortunate to land my first job with the Midwestern, Illinois newspaper The Daily Pantagraph in Bloomington. I'd like to think that my writing skills landed me the job, more than Professor Reed calling in a favor to his friend, John Keeney, who was one of The Daily Pantagraph's editors.

In July 1934, another opportunity came my way. Keeney sent me to Chicago to cover a breaking-news story about crop prices and corruption plaguing the agricultural markets. It had been uncovered and chronicled by the Chicago Tribune a week earlier. While there, I met one of the Trib's city editors, who invited me to lunch. Afterward, he offered me a personal tour of the newspaper's headquarters. He took, it seemed, an immediate liking to me and, to my complete and gratified surprise, I returned home three days later with a job offer from the greatest newspaper in the Midwest.

After a weekend discussion with my parents and the editor of The Daily Pantagraph, we decided the unexpected offer was a challenge I should accept. Six days later, I found myself in Chicago working for the Tribune.

The decision had been made easier since my family had settled comfortably in Bloomington and the farm was up and running smoothly. The rich soil and hard work had produced a bumper crop the previous year, and projections were even better for 1935. That allowed Father to hire a replacement for me. Mother, my emotional inspiration and cheerleader, seemed happiest of all with the decision, and wholeheartedly supported my move. As she saw it, I was only two hours away and could still help them with the farm on most weekends.

"Please forgive the interruption," Kellmeyer said as he hung up the phone. "Now, back to the subject at hand. I'll be direct: I've got a job for you, Mr. Fisher. I need a couple of my very best reporters to take charge of a very important and pressing overseas assignment. Naturally, one of the names that immediately came to my mind was yours. By the way, I loved that follow-up story you wrote last week describing Al Capone's living conditions at the U.S. Penitentiary in Atlanta. I bet ol' Scarface wishes he'd paid his income taxes now. I'm sure you're aware, he was sent to the slammer by the Feds for income tax evasion."

He rambled on, demonstrating his knowledge of Capone's criminal history, but soon refocused on the business at hand.

"Originally, as you may have heard, our newspaper was not going to send any reporters to cover the Olympic Games in Berlin, but the management gurus from on high have now decided differently," he explained. "Since their decision was somewhat late in coming, the stay in Europe will have to be extended for several more weeks than we had hoped because of the difficulty in finding passage on a steam liner. Most have already been booked months ahead for the normal summer season.

"Now, with the games taking place this summer, the only tickets the travel agency was able to secure call for a three-month stay, which includes a few weeks before and after the games. The big bosses have given me the authority to make the final decision about whom to send, and I must say they are more than willing, in my estimation, to be quite generous with the arrangements for my ultimate selections."

"Sir, if I may interrupt, did you just say the Olympic Games in Berlin, Germany, and by any remote chance are you asking me if I'm interested in going?" I asked, eagerly awaiting his reply.

"Yes, yes, Mr. Fisher. Haven't you been paying attention?" he said rather curtly. "Why do you think I sent for you today? As I mentioned, we need a fine, experienced feature writer such as you to go across the Atlantic with one of our most competent sports scribes to report on this athletic event better and more authoritatively than those blowhards from The New York Times. Your duties would also include writing a few human interest stories with some articles about the host country thrown in for good measure. And of course, some dirt about those blasted Nazis. We'll wait to print the Nazi articles once you're back home, safe and sound.

"Do you get my drift, Joe?" he asked with a wink "Are you willing to go or not?"

"Of course, I'm interested, but it's so sudden, sir," I said, a little flustered. "I don't know what to say. I mean there would be lots of personal things that would have to be taken care before I could even begin to agree to accept such an assignment. I mean I have rent and utilities to pay here in Chicago and I'd need time to save some spending money. And, when I can, on most weekends, I normally help my parents on their farm, and I'm sure I'm missing some other expenses, too."

Kellmeyer, mustering as much understanding as his stern demeanor allowed, slowly nodded his head.

"Yes, I somewhat understand your predicament," he said, rubbing his chin and glancing toward the ceiling. "But trust me the newspaper is prepared to handle most of those concerns for you, Mr. Fisher. Would $2,000 be enough money to take care of your expenses here and your local transportation, food costs, hotel arrangements with possibly some additional funds left over to help your parents hire temporary help and pay for some of your other unanticipated expenses? The ship's tickets have already been purchased remember."

I did some quick mental calculations. Since I only spent around $26 a week for my shared apartment and food cost, I figured the proposed allowance would be no issue at all, especially since my annual salary was only $2,600 a year.

"Well, all that sounds generous indeed, sir," I said as I nodded my head, looking as if I were in agreement.

"Then it's a deal, Joe? But remember $2,000 was all I could squeeze out for you from accounting, so don't ask for any more money," my anxious supervisor said firmly, anticipating an affirmative reply from me.

"No, I understand, sir. The money allotment sounds fine, but am I to assume my traveling partner would also get the same amount?" I asked, hoping the right answer would make my decision easier.

"Of course, he'll get the same $2,000," he quickly, but calmly, shot back.

Without thinking further, I gleefully blurted out: "Count me in. I'll go, and I promise you, I won't let you down, sir!"

With that, my thoughts immediately shifted to who might be my traveling partner and when we might be required to depart.

"Who would be going with me, and what timelines are we talking about?" I nervously inquired.

"Well, let's see," he thought aloud, as he gathered up the ship's ticket folder lying on his desk and began reading.

"OK, the dates are here somewhere," he said as he scanned the boarding slip.

"Ah, yes, the ship leaves New York Harbor on May 28 and returns from Hamburg, Germany, on August 27," he said, waiting for my feedback.

"Sir, with all due respect, that's only 4 1/2 weeks away," I said.

"Mr. Fisher, you're a young man, not married with any children. I wouldn't expect that short timetable to pose any problems for you. Don't you agree?" he said in a firm tone.

"I guess not. You're right, sir. That short notice should present no issues for me."

"Now, about who would accompany you, I've been giving that question a little thought, Joe, and I was thinking about George Bowers," the burly editor said, checking my reaction to his proposal. "My pick would be George Bowers. I think he would be a good teammate on this definitive adventure of a lifetime. What do you think about him?"

"Well, sir, with all due respect, while George is certainly an accomplished writer and everything, he's quite older than me, and I'd be worried about the stress of traveling and lugging his heavy suitcases around Europe," I replied, looking for any excuse to avoid the prospect of Bowers becoming my partner.

"It likely would cause him a bit of wear and tear that may be difficult for him to handle. Besides, although George writes a few sports articles, he's more of a feature writer like me, not a full-on sports guy, by any measure.

"Sir, wouldn't it make better sense to send someone like Al Obermeyer, a young, proven sports writer, who also happens to speak German? He would be a big help with the language barrier, too," I suggested, hoping to dissuade Kellmeyer from saddling me with the older writer.

"Huh. I hadn't really given much thought about any potential language difficulties. So you think Obermeyer can handle the job, do you?" he asked, clearly interested.

"Yes, sir, I know he can and we're great pals as well, so, together, I assure you, we'd be a perfect match," I said, crossing my fingers and hoping that Kellmeyer would agree.

As we both paused for a minute, I thought to myself, there was no way I'd want to go if George Bowers was my partner for three whole months. The guy's a friend, but he's also a die-hard Republican who's still mad about Roosevelt's victory over Hoover for the presidency in 1932. Even though Hoover's policies had put our country in a horrible economic depression, George still complained about his candidate's failure to win a second term. He hated everything the Democratic Party stood for, and since chatting about politics would be one of our few common interests for discussion, I'd be afraid we might not always be polite and civil. History always repeats itself, so, hopefully, he'll be satisfied again with affairs of state in the future. But going with me on that trip? No way. Besides, he'd snore constantly and drink hard liquor to high heaven all night long. I've attended enough Cubs games with him to know his demeanor all too well when he's had one too many.

"I'll think overnight about Obermeyer as an option and let you know my decision by Monday morning," Kellmeyer said." In the meantime, if you see Al, ask him how he feels about the idea while I ponder your suggestion. Of course, I'll need to speak with his section editor, Mr. Dumron, to see if he can spare his absence."

As Kellmeyer twice slapped my shoulder on my way out his office, he looked me in the eye and said, "I picked you specifically as my top choice for this assignment because I know you're an up-and-coming, eager, trustworthy, dedicated young man with a bright future at this newspaper. The paper is counting on you to do a good job providing the Tribune with some exciting stories about the Olympics."

Without another thought, I enthusiastically shook Kellmeyer's hand, offered one last plug for Al to be selected as my traveling companion, and left happily with my emotions soaring.

Just like that, our short to-the-point meeting was over. My feeling was almost indescribable. It was as if I had just hit a Babe Ruthian grand-slam homer over the ivy-covered center field wall at Wrigley Field as my enthusiastic admirers waved feverishly while I rounded the bases.

Immediately, I rushed to my desk and called my buddy Al to see if he was free for lunch. He agreed to meet me in the lobby in five minutes for a quick bite since he needed to get to Wrigley to cover the Cubs-Pittsburgh Pirates baseball game that afternoon.

In the lobby from a distance, I noticed George Alfred Obermeyer III, or just plain Al to his closest friends, pacing in a small circle stopping only to tap his left shoe on the marble floor.

Uncharacteristically, he seemed slightly restless as all six-foot-two inches of him waited there, his ensemble complete with black wing-tipped shoes, a crisp white shirt, and a tailored gray suit he could ill afford. His ever-present freshly steamed fedora was in his right hand and a carefully folded white handkerchief peeked from his breast pocket. He was outfitted like one of those mannequins on the men's floor at Marshall Field's, one of Chicago's finest downtown department stores. Al loved compliments about his flawless appearance and his Nordic good looks. Along with his overabundance of self-confidence, those attributes assured him plenty of praise, especially from the ladies. He was funny as all get out, to boot.

Al was a single, 28-year-old, third-generation German-American from Madison, Wisconsin. He worked for the Tribune as a junior sportswriter. Mainly, he covered local and college teams and only occasionally the professional clubs, meaning the Cubs, White Sox or Bears. He didn't mind since college football was his favorite. He bragged nonstop about the Badgers from the University of Wisconsin, from which he graduated in 1930. He hated Notre Dame and the University of Minnesota and didn't have a whole lot of love for Northwestern either, although he attended most of their football games when they played at home in Chicago.

The first words out of Al's mouth were just what I expected: "Don't you realize a vacation day means you don't have to come to the office, you knucklehead? What in God's name are you doing downtown? I thought you'd be in Bloomington by now!" he said, puzzled by my presence in the building.

"Well, pal, that was the plan, but sometimes even the best-laid plans get a little side-tracked," I answered.

"What the dickens does that mean, Joey?" Al asked impatiently "Don't tell me those assholes canceled your vacation day."

"No, no, it was nothing like that," I told him. "I came to the office to meet Kellmeyer to discuss a little business trip and it could include you, too."

"Wait a minute, Joey. First, what the hell have you got me into, and, second, what do you mean it could include me, too? I can see that glint in your eyes. Tell me, you hillbilly, I don't have time to grab lunch and play games, too. Just give me the lowdown!" my eager friend begged.

"Al, ol' pal, you're not going to believe our good luck, and I'm certain Kellmeyer bought my story to bring you along for the ride as well," I said.

"Are you ready for the news? Brace yourself, my friend. In three months we're going to be seated at the opening ceremony of the 1936 Olympic Games in Berlin, Germany." I blurted out.

"Can you repeat what you just said? I must have been dreaming when I thought I heard you just say you and I are going to Germany for the Olympics." Al said.

"That's right, Al, you Germanic cheese ball. We're heading to the Olympics in four weeks," I answered.

"Wait a minute," he said. "In four weeks? I thought the games weren't until August, which is 12 or 13 weeks away, not four."

"You're right, my friend, but we're not going straight to the Olympics," I explained. "Our ship leaves New York on May 28, landing a week later in England. We can go to London and Paris, but then I want to make a long-overdue stopover for a few weeks in the Netherlands to visit some of my long-lost relatives who live in a little Limburg village named Schimmert. My family's from the town. It's the place where they lived before immigrating to the United States almost 40 years ago."

"Wait! Wait! Wait! How in the hell did you con the powers that be to give you all of that extra time in Europe to go sightseeing, you genius?" Al asked, wondering if my account of the trip might be a hoax.

"It's no joke, my ol' Wisconsin Badger from the frozen waters of Lake Mendota. I'll fill you in on the details when we have more time to talk," I said.

"Hey, Joe, I've got a few old relatives living near Cologne, Germany, as well. My dad corresponds with them regularly. When I tell him about all of this, he'll go bonkers," Al shouted.

"So will my mother and Grandfather Wilhelm," I said. "Neither of them has ever returned to their Dutch homeland, but constantly wish that I could go there someday, and now that dream is about to become a reality."

"Oh, my God, I've got to go on that trip with you, Joe. Do whatever you can to get me on that boat. This is a dream come true, a sportswriter's nirvana, the jackpot of all jackpots," he gushed.

We jumped up and down like a couple of teenage schoolgirls who'd just met Bing Crosby. After calming down, we talked for a few more minutes and gobbled down our lunches. Al left for the ballgame with a brand-new attitude and I headed back to the Tribune Tower with a new appreciation for my job and our employer.

Arriving back at the office, I hoped to talk with Kellmeyer about Al's positive reaction and wished to express again my strong desire for Al to accompany me to Berlin. But the boss had just left for his lunch meeting, which, I was told by his secretary, would take an hour.

Kellmeyer's lunch date was Jeffrey Dumron, Tribune sports section chief. They met at a diner down the street from the newspaper building.

"Well, how'd it go, Herman?" Dumron asked as Kellmeyer sat down and eyed the lunch menu.

"He bought it hook, line, and sinker," Kellmeyer said, swiping a hand across his brow in a gesture of relief.

"Fisher agreed to go without any argument?"

"None whatsoever. He was like putty in my hands," Kellmeyer boasted. "Perhaps the publisher will lay off me now after my first five preferences declined the Olympics job."

"You're so persuasive you should be in charge of sales or advertising. What did he say about George Bowers going along?" Dumron asked.

"Well, now, Fisher did have something to say about Bowers. He'd like Al

Obermeyer to tag along instead."

"Obermeyer? Is he nuts? Obermeyer would make a shambles of the whole trip. He's a womanizer and a party boy, you know," Al's boss said.

"He's a good sports writer, isn't he? You recommended that we hire him, remember?" Kellmeyer reminded Dumron.

"He is, and, yes, I did recommend him," Dumron agreed. "He's one hell of a writer, but he's still learning the ropes. I'm just now letting him cover a few Cubs' games to whet his chops a little. I'd have to think long and hard before letting him go abroad. He's just a young chick who thinks he's a rooster."

"I think you need to consider allowing him time to fly real soon. I don't want Joe Fisher changing his mind about going. I'm taking a chance on young Fisher. Can't you do the same with Al? I've taken enough grief from the men upstairs," Kellmeyer said.

"I see your point, Herman. OK, you don't have to twist my arm. I understand the situation," Dumron said reluctantly. "He can go, but promise me you'll remind him to be serious about this assignment, and that we insist on no funny business."

"Thanks, Jeffrey, I owe you one," Kellmeyer said as they shook hands.

Exactly an hour later, Kellmeyer was back from lunch. After exiting the elevator, he strode straight to my desk and informed me that the plan for Al to accompany me had been approved without having to wait until Monday for confirmation. At our earlier meeting, I thought I'd picked up a vibe from the boss's body language indicating that Al's selection would be wholeheartedly approved by his section chief, and my intuition was confirmed when the chief told me he had just had lunch with Dumron.

Later, we learned he had offered the job to several of the more experienced and married writers, but the official line was they'd turned down the assignment because of the short timeline or family concerns. Most likely their wives didn't want them to go overseas without them. So it was suggested by the editors that two single guys might volunteer for the assignment or else, although we didn't need a whole lot of persuasion.

No matter the circumstances surrounding our opportunity, we were soon to be off to Europe and the Olympic Games.

Soon after receiving the news I'd hoped for, I hopped in a Yellow Cab and made a beeline for Wrigley Field to tell Al the good news. The other reporters covering the game must have assumed we'd just won a million bucks as we yelled and screamed in unabashed excitement. It was a great day for the Cubs, too. Despite all of the commotion we caused up in the press box, the Cubs won the game that afternoon 6-1 with Lon Warneke pitching a complete game to complement his seven-hitter.

It was a day of celebration for sure. Before meeting Al at Wrigley, I had spoken to my parents, and they, too, shared in the excitement. During our call, I was reminded again of my core values, which I took to heart. My parents' reaction prompted me to sit down with Mabel again to type a few reflective notes of my own.

My mother often talked with me about the importance of taking chances and thinking unconventionally. She challenged me to be different and not to fear the unknown. Moreover, she encouraged me to embrace opportunities that would open my eyes to wonders beyond my wildest imagination. It was heady stuff, but I knew she desperately wanted me to chase my dreams and experience life and all its gifts. Pursuing that goal, especially as a young immigrant girl during the early 20th century and burdened by the weight of her own circumstances, had likely been too daunting for her.

Mother believed that life was a series of decisions that determine the paths we take throughout life. Sometimes we make good decisions and sometimes bad, but living life to the fullest extent possible, learning from our mistakes, and embracing the adventures in between, is the fabric that eventually defines us.

I would often catch myself following her advice without really thinking about it. By sheer coincidence, during an English class homework assignment as a sophomore in high school, Diana Fleshman, my teacher, introduced me to a simple lyric that perfectly cemented Mother's passionate vision. Outlined so masterfully in his thought-provoking poem, "The Road Not Taken," Robert Frost beautifully summed up the meaning of those choices in the last lines of his classic when he wrote:

> *Two roads diverged in a wood,*
> *and I took the one less traveled by,*
> *And that has made all the difference.*

I understood the symbolism of his poem had been considered many times by thinkers as cheesy fodder. But only after I had traveled almost halfway through life's journey did I realize we all face difficult choices accompanied by scores of twists and turns, many of which are beyond our control. Decisions made by strangers from other parts of the world can sometimes have tragic influences on our lives. When a border dispute leads to war, or when an economic or trade issue disagreement shakes up the world's stock markets, or when bizarre laws or restrictive court rulings are made, these can often wreak mayhem upon our own individual intentions. Choices made by our family and friends can alter our judgment or impact our future pathway, too. But I also came to understand that good luck and self-determination also play a role in our lives.

Such upheaval and uncertainty were prevalent during the turbulent years of my adolescence and lasted well into my young adulthood during the 1930s and '40s, a time when inconceivable events, such as Prohibition, a depression, and a second world war meant havoc, or worse, for so many. Living during that chaotic period also provided me with opportune choices that dictated the trail I was forced, and at other times blessed, to follow.

Yes, even finding love when not searching at all, uncovered another reason for one more fateful decision that would soon bring both immense joy and excruciating heartache to my life. Taking a prompt from Frost, I came to realize my journey through that period could have easily been wrapped up by replacing one simple verse of his epic with my own haphazard summation:

The road I was about to travel led me to her,
And that decision has made all the difference.

CHAPTER TWO
OUT WITH THE OLD, IN WITH THE NEW

That Friday, after Al and I had our little celebration at Wrigley, I dashed to Union Station, caught the rush-hour Alton Railroad passenger train, and headed south for the 3 1/2-hour ride to my parents' farm in Bloomington.

Graciously, Kellmeyer gave me Monday off as compensation for meeting him earlier that morning. I couldn't wait to see my family to share what details I knew about my upcoming trip. My grandfather Wilhelm planned to meet me at the train station. In the meantime, I leaned back in my comfortable seat and started reading a fresh copy of the Tribune as the telephone poles flashed by my window.

My formal name is Simon Jozef Wilhelmus Schrijnemaekers Fisher, but to Americanize my name, it was shortened to just plain Joe Fisher. My mother, originally from the Netherlands, called me Zef, the Dutch version of Josef. I'm actually only half Dutch by blood, but, according to my grandparents, I'm full Limburger. They took greater pride in hailing from the Dutch province of Limburg where my family originated than from being known simply as citizens of the Netherlands. So, naturally, my first memories revolved around a strong sense of Limburg culture.

The Netherlands, located on the western coast of continental Europe, is bordered by Germany to its east, Belgium to its south, and the North Sea to its north and west. It is divided into 12 provinces similar to our states.

The southernmost province is called Limburg, symbolized by the fearless lion on its flag. Stories about the province were a big part of my upbringing, even encompassing beloved tales of the unofficial national flower, the tulip.

Whenever I close my eyes and think of my dear mother, Rebekka Maria Sabien Schrijnemaekers Fisher, I can vividly picture her placing a perfectly shaped red tulip into a vase on our kitchen table. She so loved the color red, and every March when the tulips were in full bloom in her tenderly cultivated flower garden, she would be magically transported back in spirit to her native country and to her childhood home in the tiny Limburg village of Schimmert.

Though Mother was only 12 when she came to live in America in 1896 and took great pleasure in the fact that she had become a naturalized American citizen, she was proud to be Dutch and, in particular, a Limburger.

At bedtime, she would often fill my head with touching stories of her hometown, including tales of her school friends and her family. She also told me of her pet cow, Elsie. She always joked that having a pet cow was more practical than owning a dog.

"Cows don't bark or bite. They just keep the grass cut and provide fresh milk," she said.

Sometimes, however, I felt that she was tormenting herself because she'd often become glum when she reflected upon her beloved childhood memories.

Mother was especially close to her grandparents on her mother's side, Grootmoeder Stella and her Grootvader Willem Westhovens, as she referred to them. They died of pneumonia just a few days apart during the cruel Dutch winter of 1895, only nine months before Mother left Schimmert for America. I know those tragic events left her heartbroken. I believed she grieved for me as well, knowing that I would never receive a loving hug or a nod of encouragement from her adoring grandparents. It haunted her that she was not able to tend their graves after she left the Netherlands.

My mother was a positive person, affectionate and playful with a delightful warm smile. But some pain could not be hidden, even by someone as amazing as she. Her blue eyes would fill with tears whenever she spoke of her grandparents, but she assured me they were not sad tears but instead those of happiness. She often told me that she hoped I someday would get the chance to visit their graves, and, if I did, I had to promise her that I would place some red tulips where they rested. Of course, I always assured her that I would. Unbelievably, in a few weeks, that childhood promise would come true.

Mother had a special place in our backyard near a large maple tree where she pretended her grandparents' spirits resided. For her first birthday in Illinois, my father placed a large rock near that tree. Pops and I hollowed out a circular depression in the stone, about two feet in diameter and about 10 inches deep, and filled it with water. I remember we had to use a chisel and a hammer as we pounded and carved on that rock for hours. She called it her "fountain stone," and said it was similar to the one in her hometown that she had left years ago.

Mother religiously kept it filled with clean water so the birds could always have a fresh drink, and she always made sure flowers adorned that area. She would venture to her beloved spot whenever she felt the need to speak privately to her grandparents. Pops and I always respected her time there alone with her thoughts. Even as a boy I would tear up just imagining the emptiness she must have felt as she said goodbye to her family and friends for the last time. Sadly, Mother knew little of her father's parents because they had died of consumption before she was born.

My mother usually wore a big smile and filled her life and mine with a contagious joy whenever she reminisced about her youth in Limburg. I loved her wonderful stories and her colorful delivery. It seemed as if she wanted to make sure I knew every little detail of her past. Her storytelling painted pictures in my mind of the little farms in Oensel, of the monks and nuns of Saint Marie, of the caves and the castle at Valkenburg, and of the Sint Hubertus Windmill. Even though they were places I might never see in person, it pleased my mother that I knew they existed.

"Zef, over here," my grandfather shouted as I walked through the Bloomington train station. He'd been sitting on a wooden bench awaiting my arrival.

"Have you been waiting here a long time?" I asked.

"No, I just got here five minutes ago. Are you ready?"

"Yes," I replied as we walked into the darkness toward his black 1924 Model A four-door sedan.

"We're all very excited about your good news, especially your mother. Oh, do I have some great stories to tell you about Schimmert," he said, his face beaming.

"I'm not sure there's anything else to tell. I've heard about Schimmert and Limburg my whole life," I replied with a chuckle.

"Yes, I know, my boy, but you haven't heard everything, and it's my job to make sure you do!" he said, laughing as we sped through the night.

My Grandfather, Wilhelm Schrijnemaekers, was the reason my mother and my Grandmother Renee came to America in the late 1890s. My grandfather, Opa to me, was like so many immigrants from western Europe at that time. He wanted desperately to find his American dream. He was a tall, thin, educated man who possessed a full gray beard that reached down to his chest. I always enjoyed tugging on it when I was a child.

"Oma Renee would have loved to know you are going to our hometown. She loved you dearly, my son," Opa said.

"I know Opa, I miss her, too. She was the best grandmother. She's resting in peace back in Morgantown," I softly replied.

"Yes, I miss her so," her old partner lamented, teary-eyed.

"Do you realize it's been almost five years ago since we all moved out here to Illinois?" he said. "What a trip that was in '31, moving two households 600 miles with a 70-year-old man in tow."

"Yeah, I remember, Opa," I replied. "Thankfully, Father had that old reliable 1922 Chevy half-ton truck with the wooden flatbed and those rickety slats for sides. Pops drove that truck, Mother drove her 1930 Dodge DD four-door sedan, and you and I drove this Model A. How in the world did we manage to successfully load up all that furniture, with all those heavy wooden boxes, and then move everything in those three old vehicles to Illinois safely? I'm still flabbergasted that we did that!"

Bloomington was in McLean County in the heart of the most beautiful farmland I had ever seen. When I first moved there and began working for the local newspaper it was hardly my dream job. But it paid the bills, and my editors gave me the freedom to hone my craft. I wrote articles about accepted farming practices, robberies, telephone problems of rural customers, auto accidents, and even a story about employees who wore roller skates to speed up service at a new company headquartered in Bloomington. It was called State Farm Insurance.

As we drove through the darkness, I reflected on what I had left behind in West Virginia to take the job in Bloomington. That decision led to the loss of my college sweetheart, Kay Green. Oh, I dated Norma Lynn Maynor in high school, but I'm not counting her because she dumped me after we dated for only two months, opting instead for the captain of the football team. Kay, however, was my first love. She couldn't fully comprehend why I took the newspaper opportunity in Illinois. She was interested in marriage at the time. I wasn't.

Eventually, our letters became less frequent and our telephone chats became shorter and more argumentative until, finally, a letter arrived informing me that she wanted to see another guy she'd met at WVU. It was easy to understand why our courtship ended, so I focused on what my mother had always drummed into my head about seizing life's adventures and not looking back in regret. Her advice was sound; I moved on. But Kay was a keeper, and I did briefly wonder if I had made a mistake.

Mother heard the car as we pulled up to the house. Shouting for joy, she rushed to me with open arms and wrapped both of them tightly around my waist.

"I'm so happy for you, Zef. I always knew you would go to Schimmert someday, but so soon, I never expected that," she said as my father stood in the doorway in his bedclothes. He waved, called out a "Welcome home,

Joe," and shuffled off to bed.

"Your father may be too tired to hear the details of your trip, but I want to hear it all before we go to sleep," she said.

We talked until three in the morning before I finally dozed off on the couch.

Farmers get up and start moving early, and that time-honored tradition was also observed at our house. As we sat down at the breakfast table, I was enjoying one of Mother's tasty biscuit and bacon sandwiches when my grandfather placed a small box in my hand.

"I have been planning to give this to you for some time, my boy," he said. "It's a pocket watch that belonged to my father, your great-grandfather, Peter Schrijnemaekers. He gave it to me on my wedding day, and it's my most treasured possession. I want you to have it. Take it to Schimmert with you. It keeps perfect time and has served me well for over 50 years."

"Are you sure, Opa?" I asked. "It's a Swiss-made Jaeger-LeCoultre watch. The name's printed on the face, and I'm sure it's worth a lot of money."

"Who cares about the money?" Opa replied dismissively. "The watch now belongs to you, Zef! Give it to your son someday and pass its story on to him. I was with my father the day he bought it in Maastricht years ago."

He opened up a book and retrieved an old bent black-and-white photo of his father, Peter, and his mother, Maria.

"If you look closely enough, you can see this pocket watch sticking out of his vest. I handed it to him, just before the picture was taken," he said proudly.

"Wow, now that is special!" I happily replied to his approval.

Mother was standing nearby and spoke up.

"I have two things that I need to say about that. First, take the watch, Zef. Dad wants you to have it. Second, what if Zef has a girl? If so, does she get the watch someday, Father?" she asked in jest.

"Well, yes, of course. If Zef's son says it's okay, then he can give it to his second child, that little girl you so dearly want Zef to have. I assume you want him to name the girl Rosalie, too?" Grandfather said with a laugh.

"Why, you sly old goat! You know Rosalie would be my choice. Zef, your father and I always wished for a second child, one we could name Rosalie, but you were to be our only sunshine," she explained.

"Wait just a minute. You two are already naming my unborn children? Wow, then tell me, when am I getting married?" I chimed into the conversation.

"Oh, Joe, you're just acting silly now, but, wait, I want you to have something, too," she said as she reached into her apron pocket. "This is your Oma Renee's wedding ring. Dad and I talked this over this morning, and we hope someday you will place this ring on the finger of your lucky bride. Isn't that right, Father?" she said raising her voice so he could plainly hear.

"Of course, that's what we want, Rebekka, but wait for the right woman like I did, Jozef. Make sure she's the right woman."

"Oh, Father, he will. Zef will find the right girl. Of that, I have no doubt," Mother responded with a wink to me.

"Well, I guess I'm right. This morning's conversation does sound like you ol' critters are in cahoots and plotting to marry me off so I can produce some offspring as soon as possible," I joked. "I think I'll join Dad out in the barn where it's a little safer."

"Zef, I'm going to keep this ring with me until the happy day arrives, OK?" Mother shouted after me as I walked toward the barn.

"OK, but most likely you'll have it for a long time," I replied.

"If you take too long, I've got a few prospects for you," Opa teased.

My parents came to Bloomington to visit me in the spring of 1931 and fell in love with the fertile, flat farmland, which, my mother said, reminded her of Schimmert. When they returned home to Morgantown, they convinced my grandfather to move with them to Illinois. The timing made sense especially since Oma Renee and my father's parents had died a few years earlier.

Even though my grandfather had retired from WVU in 1928, he had never forgotten his original intention had been to go to the Midwest and start a farm when he, Oma Renee, and Mother left New York City in 1897. Although my grandfather was not physically able to handle the work required to operate a farm, he could rest assured that my father and mother were more than capable.

My father had attempted to run his parents' farm near Morgantown after they died. And for a few years, he and Mother managed that operation while he still worked for the railroad. He lost his job with the Baltimore & Ohio Railroad in 1929 because of the stock market crash, however, and he and his brothers sold the farm to a neighbor for half its true value right after visiting me in Bloomington that summer.

In September 1931 with the meager profits they made on the sale of Grandpa Fisher's farm, along with their own savings and with some additional financial backing from Opa, my parents, at $200 an acre, purchased a small, 37-acre farm that straddled Sugar Creek, just north of the city limits of Bloomington. With Father's knowledge of trains, he was able to land a good job repairing train engines at the Alton Railroad Repair Shops in town. He worked there for a few years until the farm was up and running.

Our farm sat less than two miles from the office building where I once worked. The property included a seven-room frame farmhouse, an outhouse, and two barns. It was located near the tiny campus of Illinois Wesleyan College, which pleased my grandfather. To everyone's relief, Father and I added indoor plumbing soon after their arrival.

I went back to West Virginia to assist them with the move. I used that rare opportunity at home to visit with my friends and family. After their belongings were loaded, we all paid a visit to Oma Renee's grave. She had passed away from pneumonia during my last year of high school. It was an emotional time, especially for my mother and grandfather. At her grave, they both cried like babies, so Father and I walked away after paying our respects to give them as much time as needed to say their goodbyes to their precious wife and mother. Sadly, it wasn't the first time the two of them had left a loved one behind.

My father was our family's pillar of strength. He was a tireless worker, and his intensity and optimism were unmatched. In my eyes, his only flaw was his constant smoking habit, which irritated my mother, too, especially at dinner time.

In short order, my parents and I got the farm in tip-top shape. After the second year, unexpected record crop prices gave us all comfort and provided my loving parents with a welcome boost. The extra money allowed them to hire another worker when I took the job with the Tribune.

That first Christmas in Illinois, Father surprised Mother with a hand-made gift. It was a wooden sign he'd whittled from an old oaken board he'd taken from his parents' farm in West Virginia. The sign simply had the word "Schimmert" carved on the four-foot plank, which he proudly placed for Mother over our barn door.

"Pops, did you know anything about the watch and the ring that Opa and Mother just tried to pawn off on me?"

"I sure did. I hope it works, too! You should know by now, your Mother and I have no secrets between us," he said.

"Geez, not you, too, Pops!" I said, shaking my head.

"Your family just loves you, Joe, that's all. We're so proud of you, son," Pops replied.

My father was genuine like that, a man everyone could count on for anything. I loved him dearly for his candor and honesty. He was as good as they come, and everyone who knew him felt the same way. He was a man of few words, but I had no doubt the people who were most important to him were my mother and me.

That evening, Mother invited the Magnuses over for dinner. They were our closest neighbors. Before their arrival, she and I wrapped our arms around each other's waists and strolled to her fountain stone as we chatted.

"Jozef, you're so fortunate. You're going to love Schimmert! I know you will! There is no place on earth like it. Maybe it's just a combination of the feeling, the culture, the farming lifestyle or something in the air, Zef, that makes it different. But, whatever it is, it gets deep into your bones.

"However, it's the silence of Schimmert that's so special. I can never forget the silence. I'm just so happy for you," she said as tears slowly rolled down her cheeks.

"The silence?" I asked. "What's so special about that? It's very quiet here, too. Listen! Nothing!"

"I cannot explain it, Zef, but you will understand what I mean when you are there. I go to bed early sometimes so I can close my eyes and dream about it," she said.

"You miss Schimmert, don't you?"

"Yes, always, but I know if I went back there to stay, I would miss being here, too. If I had stayed there, Zef, I would not have Raymond or you in my life. This is my home and I'm very happy here with my boys," she said.

"I think I understand. You know I will always consider West Virginia my home." I reminded her.

"I do, and I must tell you there will always be something special in your heart about those lush green mountains," she said, giving me a hug. "I miss those beautiful hills, too, you know."

"I know, Mother, I know," I said before kissing her cheek.

"I'm happy, Mother. I know I will love Schimmert, too," I reassured her.

She handed me two quarters and told me to drop one of the coins into our fountain stone and save the other to put into hers in Schimmert.

"Mother, let's throw this first one in together," I said.

"I wish for your health, your happiness, and your safe return," she declared.

"I wish for your health, your happiness, and your chocolate cake tonight," I said, laughing as we tossed the coin and watched it disappear into the water. My request put a big smile on her lovely face that matched the one on mine.

The weekend flew by too quickly, and I headed back to the city on the early Monday evening train. Before I left for Europe, I came back home every weekend. My parents said they were proud of me, but, in reality, it is they who deserved all the credit. They were without question the loves of my life.

CHAPTER THREE

ADVENTURE
TO DREAMLAND

I was never one to pass up a new learning opportunity, and tackling an adventure like this excited my spirit. Some of the guys at the paper thought we got the short end of the stick by having to travel all the way to Germany to write about some minor sporting competitions with foreign athletes of whom most Americans had never heard. But Al and I couldn't have been more thrilled. It was a rarity that such a chance for free travel fell into our laps, so we just ran with it and never looked back.

We were warned it would be wise for us to abide by any and all of the strict guidelines mandated by the Nazis to avoid any potential problems. We were nervously confident that we would be able to navigate our way through. Al had the ability to talk to anyone about anything and an uncanny knack for making his point without causing ill feelings. I took comfort in his ability to do that.

The weeks crept by until finally, our train was waiting on track number six at Chicago's LaSalle Street Station. It was 5:55 p.m., May 26. People were milling about, loading their luggage, kissing their wives and children goodbye, puffing on that last cigar, and getting ready to board our train to its destination, New York City.

Al, of course, was nowhere in sight.

"Where the hell was he? He's always late," I nervously said to myself as I paced the concrete platform. My worried thoughts collided with one another.

"Did that idiot oversleep?"

"Doesn't he know our train is scheduled to leave in five minutes?"

"Where is he, for God's sake?"

Suddenly I heard his familiar voice echoing through the station.

"Joe! Joe! Hold that train!" that slug yelled to me about 100 yards away. Huffing and puffing as he reached me, he said, "Joe, my boy, you weren't worried waiting here for ol' Al were ya? Don't panic Joey. You know ol' Al wouldn't miss this choo-choo for anything."

I rolled my eyes at him and reached down to grab my suitcase.

"All aboard, Joe, all aboard!" he yelled in my ear as he pushed me up the Pullman car steps.

"Geez, Al, pipe down, you're gonna give me a heart attack, you crazy Hun," I shouted.

Facing me and smelling of cigarettes and beer, Al put his left hand on my right shoulder and pinched my cheeks with the other hand. He was in pure ecstasy as the train whistle blew, and steam escaped the boiler with a soothing hiss.

"What a time we're gonna have, ol' pal of mine," he said, as we walked slowly through our coach looking for our row. I spotted our seats while simultaneously Al noticed a pretty blonde seated across the aisle from us. He gave her a wink and introduced himself while I wrestled the suitcases into the overhead bins. The guy thought all women adored him, so he insisted that I take the window seat while he sat adjacent to the aisle and across from that poor blonde.

"Yes, sir. We're going to have ourselves the time of our life. Wow!" he blurted out to the woman.

There was never a dull moment with Al around. I swear the man had never met a stranger.

He and I had been best buddies for more than two years, and during that brief period, I quickly learned that Al had three main loves: women, beer, and sports in that order. He was a swell guy and really one hell of a writer, too. Al was the best in my book.

Our train slowly rolled out of the station. The reality of our amazing situation abruptly kicked in as we found ourselves aboard New York Central's self-proclaimed "Most Famous Train in the World," aptly named the 20th Century Limited. I paused briefly to reflect and quietly whispered to myself, "What a time we're gonna have, indeed."

Finally settled in our coach seats, I cried out in glee, "Al, ol' pal, can you believe that our last stop on this train is Grand Central Station in New York City, almost 1,000 miles and 17 hours away? Gee, this is gonna be one hell of a ride across the good ol' U.S. of A."

"Yep, and the best thing about this trip, Joe, is we're not paying a dime for it," Al said, as we both broke out in laughter.

"Did you notice this train's engine? It's a Hudson and looks like something right out of a Flash Gordon comic strip," I said.

"Maybe this train is going to the moon instead of New York City," he deadpanned while rolling his eyes. We couldn't stop laughing about our good fortune.

"Three months to check out all of those European tomatoes. Are we gonna have a ball or what?" he laughed, as we each grabbed our bellies and continued giggling like a couple of little kids. Tears of joy were streaming down our faces. The other passengers must have thought we were crazy.

"Hey, Joe, listen to this," Al said as he started reading a brochure that was left on his seat.

"Heart to heart ... Overnight, every night ... rain or shine, fog or fair ... the 20th Century Limited links the heart of New York with the heart of Chicago. And this is swift, luxurious travel that you can depend on ... plan on, days in advance, 365 days a year. Eastbound or westbound, you can step aboard at the end of the business day. You can sleep soundly as the CENTURY speeds you through gentle water level valleys. And you step off, the next morning as the business day starts ... with energy at peak after your overnight vacation on the world's most famous train."

Al sighed as he reflected on the NYC's promotional puffery, then added an observation of his own: "The best part of that load of malarkey is the part about sleeping soundly."

I was a bit bewildered that Al had so quickly given up his feeble attempt to impress the lady sitting to his right. About 30 minutes later, our moods more moderated, Al pulled his hat over his eyes, hunkered down in his seat trying to get as comfortable as he could, and said to me yawning, "Goodnight, Joey!"

He dozed off as I stared out my window at the endless rows of corn stretching out for miles in the fertile fields. As Al napped, I thought back to my mother and the memories and stories she passed on to me of Schimmert. She was so happy knowing that her only son would soon be walking the same streets she had known as a child.

Just as I started to nod off, the conductor walked down the aisle shouting, "Tickets!" I quickly procured mine from my coat pocket.

"Al, Al, wake up," I said with a nudge. "Al, your ticket. Where's your ticket?"

With eyes still shut, his hands searched his body for his.

"Here you go, Mack," Al said as he lazily handed his train ticket to the conductor.

"Hey, boys, if you're hungry, dinner will be served in five minutes in the dining car three cars back," the conductor informed us.

"Thanks for the heads up, buddy," Al replied. "Joe, I could use something to eat. How about you?"

"Yeah, me, too," I responded.

The dining car was opulent and could seat 40 people for dinner. It was decorated like a fancy Michigan Avenue restaurant and fashionably trimmed in fine cherry veneer with lights that resembled mini chandeliers. There were two rows of tables so four people could sit on the left side of the aisle and two on the right. Each table was preset with fine porcelain china on white linen tablecloths. A finely woven carpet covered the floor and racks for coats and hats were mounted on the walls. The dining car attendants were all black men who wore white, long-sleeved shirts with bow ties and black pants. The conductor had suggested the chicken dish, and it proved to be a very good choice.

Shortly after dinner, Al yawned and said, as those droopy eyes of his slowly began to close, "Joe, I'm beat. It's time for me to hit the hay."

"You must have had a rough time last night, ol' boy! I hope that dame was worth it! What was her name?" I said, chuckling.

"One was Erma, the other..... Josephine, I think," he casually said.

"Oh, Joe, you know me. I never kiss and tell. Besides, they both, er ... well, at least one of them might want to see ol' Al again when we return. If only I could remember which one," he laughed.

"I'm sure she'd be better off if she had never laid eyes on you, you beer-drinking Hun," I answered.

"What's the number of my bunk?" Al asked.

"You mean berth?" I replied.

"Yes, smarty pants, berth!" Al yawned again.

"You're in berth 3B, on the top, and I'm right below you, so no snoring or any funny business with any dames tonight," I joked.

"Dames? Are you kidding? I'm lucky to have strength enough left to climb that silly ladder to my berth, Joey," Al replied.

"See you in the morning, Sweetie Pie Joey, and a pleasant good evening to you, too, honey!" Al cracked as he nodded to the pretty blonde he'd briefly pursued.

The porter, who had heard us bantering, rolled his eyes as Al walked to the end of the car. I stood in the aisle planning to follow him but had stopped to gather my luggage, forgetting for a moment that his new blonde friend was next to me. Without thinking, I shouted, "Hey Al, remember that dame you spotted when we first boarded the train? The one you winked at, remember? I guess I can tell you now, she winked back at me."

I sensed someone near me and turned to look. The blonde gave me the nastiest stare I've ever seen. So much for opening my big mouth.

Once in the sleeper car, we climbed into our berths and bedded down. It felt good to stretch out, but as tired as I was, I couldn't fall asleep. All night long, I had a rough time in the sack. I literally tossed and turned or bounced and rolled with every movement of the train. I eventually resigned myself to listening to the clattering of the wheels, the polka-rhythm jerking of the train, and the loud snoring that surrounded me. But I consoled myself with wonderful thoughts of new adventures that surely lay ahead.

Will Uncle Wouter and Uncle Karl be happy to see me? What will their children think of this distant Yankee relative they know nothing about? How many people in Schimmert will still remember my grandparents or my mother? First thing, I'm going to visit Mother's grandparents' gravesite, just as I promised her. Then, I'll see her old church, her old farm ...

"Slow down, Joe, slow down," I mentally cautioned myself. "You'll see it all in due time. Better get some shut-eye; you'll need to be refreshed and ready to go when the 20th Century Limited glides into New York City in the morning."

Finally, as the wheels of the train speeding along the tracks hummed a mechanical lullaby, I dozed off.

As the night passed, our train steamed through Toledo, Buffalo, Syracuse, and Albany. At daybreak, from out of the blue, I heard Al's happy voice: "Wake up, Joe. We're almost in NYC. The time for cutting those zzzz's is over, kid. We're going to enjoy ourselves in this city today. And, tonight, we're gonna sow some oats on Broadway, my friend."

"Yeah, yeah, you crazy Hun, NYC," I replied, still only half awake.

When we entered the main concourse of Grand Central Station, I understood immediately why they called it grand. I had never seen such a train station in my life. It would have seemed more appropriate to call the place a palace because of all of the marble and ornate glass work.

"Al, we've only got one day in town. Do you really think we can see it all in one day?" I asked.

"I don't know, Joe, but they're sure as hell going to know that the boys from Chicago have been in town after tonight," he said.

"Oh, no, Al. Now, remember we've got a ship to catch tomorrow," I reminded him.

"Yeah, but that's tomorrow. Who's worried about tomorrow today? Joe, you only live once. The way I've got it figured, since we've only got one day here, we've got to pack a lifetime of memories into the short time allotted. Follow my lead, buddy," Al ordered as he lighted his cigarette and inhaled.

When we hit the pavement outside the terminal's doors at 89 East 42nd St., I gleefully cried, "Well, I wonder if the Yankees are playing in the city today? Maybe we can catch a ballgame before we leave town?"

"Are you crazy or something, Joey? We're in New York City, my friend. To hell with baseball! We need to have a little fun tonight. Like I said a few minutes ago, pal, just follow my lead," Al said and flagged down a cab.

Professional baseball was king during the 1920s and '30s. Babe Ruth was just about every American kid's hero. I had always hoped to see him play in person, but, sadly, never got the opportunity.

I once, however, saw a doozy of a game with some of my college friends. We took a train to Pittsburgh on June 13, 1927, to catch a ballgame between the Pittsburgh Pirates and the Brooklyn Robins.

Funny how a certain date sticks in one's mind, but that day was special. Not only did I go to a Pirates game, but that magical day was noteworthy for another reason. A crowd estimated at more than 4 ½ million people filled the streets of New York to cheer for Charles Lindbergh, American aviation hero, who was the first person to fly solo across the Atlantic Ocean. The parade down Fifth Avenue was all over the radio and newspapers that day. I never understood the fuss for just flying a plane over the ocean. June 13, 1927, was more important to me because it was game day. The sound of the home plate umpire yelling, "Let's play ball" was all I wanted to hear that sunny afternoon.

The Pirates' stars in '27 were brothers, Paul and Lloyd Waner, patrolling the outfield and Pie Traynor at third base. The Pirates won the game that day 4-3. Paul Waner, the National League MVP that year, hit a home run in the only game I ever witnessed in person at Pittsburgh's Forbes Field.

The Pirates went on to win the National League pennant in 1927, but lost the World Series to the New York Yankees and their famed Murderers Row lineup, which included sluggers Lou Gehrig and the great "Bambino," Babe Ruth. Game four of that series, a 4-3 victory by the Yankees, was decided when the winning run was scored on a wild pitch. It was the only time that had ever happened in a World Series game final. The Yankees' star player, "The Babe," had a legendary year and amazingly stroked 60 home runs. Incredibly, he hit six more homers that season than the entire Pittsburgh team. Still, "The Babe" did not win the American League Most Valuable Player trophy that year. It was awarded instead to his teammate, Lou Gehrig, who hit 47 home runs and had an eye-popping 175 RBI's.

I don't know or remember half of it, but somehow we managed to see most of New York City in one exhausting day and one drunken eventful night. We went to the top of the Empire State Building, all 102 floors. We visited Yankee Stadium but didn't go inside. We saw the Chrysler Building, Central Park, the Brooklyn Bridge, and, of course, Broadway. Oh, did we see Broadway? I don't think we missed one bar along the Great White Way.

I'd be surprised if there were any beer left in that town after that night. I lost count of the broads that Al and I kissed.

He was having a blast as always, and he constantly screamed over and over all night long, "This is going to be a night to remember!"

My head pounded, my clothes reeked of beer and smoke, and my eyes were bloodshot, but I thought, "What the heck, I'm young, it's New York City," and, as Al repeatedly said, "You only live once."

We finally stumbled into a little all-night grease joint on the corner of 58th and Broadway. How we got there only the good Lord knows. Al grabbed about 30 minutes of shut-eye in our booth while I, after drinking my fifth cup of coffee, just sat there slumped over with my head resting on the table.

As the sun pierced the tiny diner's front window, I suddenly remembered the ship.

"Whoa," I shouted with an obvious slur as I shook my liquored-up traveling companion.

"Al, Al," I screamed. "We've got to get a move on buddy!

"We've got a boat to catch!"

CHAPTER FOUR

STEAMING ACROSS THE OCEAN BLUE

Thursday, May 28, had finally arrived, and I found myself standing on Pier 56 in New York Harbor. I got my first look at the SS New York, a German ocean liner of the Hamburg-America Line. It was the biggest ship I had ever seen, and Al and I would soon be boarding her. The word "Welcome" was written in three-foot-tall letters on either side of the gangway connecting the ship to the dock. The boat's hull was painted black on the bottom half and white on the top, with the two smokestacks dressed out in those same colors with two red stripes circling both.

The first Nazi swastika flag I had ever seen was billowing above the ship's superstructure on that breezy, clear morning. Before boarding, we were met by two German and two American officials. They checked our passports and marked our names off the passenger manifest before inviting us up the gangway. I was so excited that my hands were trembling as I took in my new surroundings.

The lifeboats were perfectly aligned like soldiers on both sides of the vessel. The tiny tugboats looked like toys floating next to her hull. Once on deck, I overheard one of the officers' mates saying that it would take four hours to load all passengers and their luggage. In the meantime, one of the ship's beautiful hostesses welcomed everyone aboard with an invitation to visit the promenade deck, whatever that meant, where refreshments were being served before departure.

Al and I instead chose to walk around the impressive ship to explore her in all of her glory. The deckhands wore sharply pressed black uniforms in contrast to our rumpled attire. But I'd bet we had a lot more fun than they did last night. Hundreds of sturdy wooden lounge chairs were perfectly aligned on the teak light-stained decks. Looking down from the outer top observation area, it looked as if we were 10 floors or more above the ship's waterline.

In the distance, my eyes caught a glimpse of the brick immigration processing buildings on Ellis Island. I stood there frozen in awe in the midst of the magnificent harbor, mindful that my own family's American experience, along with millions like them, began at the gates of that entry point. It was almost impossible to describe the thrilling sensation I experienced as I stared at the inspirational Statue of Liberty, standing stately on her own regal island.

"Just think, Al, my family's American adventure started right here in New York. They landed at Ellis on April 15, 1896, a date that has been pounded into my memory by my Grandfather Wilhelm," I reminisced with a sigh.

"Yes, my friend, it's also a pity to think of some whose dreams was dashed here, too," Al sadly responded. "The unlucky ones were sent back home if they were sick or diseased."

"My grandfather once told me they struggled after arriving and lived a bare-bones existence in the slums of New York's Queens Borough," I explained. "Luckily, my grandparents quickly realized that city life in that hell hole was not what they had bargained for and briefly considered returning to Europe after only one year. They had left Holland with dreams for a better life for themselves and for their only child. Determined to plant their stake somewhere else, my grandparents left the city without hesitation, deciding instead their future lay far away from the unforgiving streets of the big city.

"They boarded a train with only the essential items they could carry and headed west," I continued. "At first, they were just looking for some land in the Midwest that had a landscape similar to the homeland they had left, rural and flat. They sought a friendlier place where they would feel comfortable, someplace where a good family could put down solid roots."

"Well, even the best-laid plans don't always fully come to fruition, but theirs came close. Morgantown, West Virginia, was certainly not even remotely flat, but the town contained everything they had been longing to find. It was peaceful, calm, and friendly and turned out to be just perfect for them."

"I think my family's experience was similar," said Al. "They came from Germany with nothing but a dream, too. They had very little cabbage in their pockets, but they also were determined to make a much better life for themselves here. I know I joke a lot, Joe, but freedom? I don't take that for granted. Thank God our families had the grit and the foresight to embark upon these shores."

Simultaneously, we placed our hands over our hearts as we stared at the statue of our lady of freedom. At that moment, we were humbled as we gazed upon her regal copper figure, both fully understanding the symbolism that she so proudly represented.

"In high school, I had a class called 'Problems of Democracy' where the teacher insisted that my classmates and I memorize the inscription engraved on the bronze plaque mounted inside the pedestal at the base of the statue," I told Al. "We thought it was silly then, but now it takes on a new meaning,"

Gazing across the harbor at the statue, I began to recite poet Emma Lazarus' famous verse:

"Give me your tired, your poor,
Your huddled masses yearning to breathe free,
The wretched refuse of your teeming shore.
Send these, the homeless, tempest-tost to me,
I lift my lamp beside the golden door!"

"Those words are beautiful!" I marveled as Al listened intently.

"You know, purely by accident, Dr. J.K. Barton, one of the professors at West Virginia University who became a dear friend to our family, sat next to my grandfather on that train from New York," I said. "The professor was on his way back to college to start the new fall semester, which was beginning in a couple of weeks. During their conversations, the professor learned that my grandfather spoke several languages.

"Grandfather Wilhelm was fluent in Latin, German, French, Dutch, and English. Dr. Barton told him he knew the university was looking to hire someone with his language skills. His new friend agreed to introduce him to the president of WVU, and the rest, as they say, was history."

"Just pure luck, my friend! Your grandfather was at the right place at the right time," Al declared.

"Just like us, pal. We were at the right place at the right time, and now we're on our way to one hell of an adventure," I gleefully responded.

Exploring further, the whole exterior of the ship was spotless. We were surprised when we opened up one of the interior doors and were greeted by several large connecting parlors, each furnished with comfortable couches and cushioned chairs with plush carpet on the floors.

On one of the coffee tables was a copy of The Motion Picture Herald dated May 28, 1936, the day we set sail. The front cover featured photos of Norma Shearer and Leslie Howard. The promotional caption read, "The world is waiting for Norma Shearer and Leslie Howard in 'Romeo and Juliet.' Never in the history of Metro-Goldwyn-Mayer Pictures has there been so much interest by press, public, and exhibitors during the course of production as is happening with 'Romeo and Juliet.' To the famed producer, Irving Thalberg, go the honors for bringing to the screen with tenderness and reverence William Shakespeare's imperishable love story."

We chuckled at that load of malarkey.

Moving forward, we clumsily walked into a dining room that boasted patrician red-flowered carpeting and white, cloth-covered round tables that were precisely arranged with fine china. The seats were fabulous, fit for royalty. Several elegant chandeliers were spaced evenly across the 10-foot, white coffered ceilings. The walls were decorated with rich woods and covered with fine oil paintings depicting ships at sea or beautiful coastal landscapes. There was no doubt we had stumbled into the first-class dining room, obviously not meant for Al and me. It was there that we discovered a written post that spelled out the required dinner dress code that must be strictly observed by all guests. Suit and tie would be the mandatory dress for men and Sunday best for ladies and children.

Even though both of us were dead tired, we located the common showers and toilets on our deck. We also found our dining area filled with tables with seating for eight, but still decked out with white tablecloths, suitable for third-class passengers like us. Still, it was very fancy by our standards. The ship offered other fine amenities as well: three bars, two dance floors, stages for entertainers, a play area for children, barber and beauty shops, a gaming room, a huge kitchen called a galley, a smoking room adorned with opulent wooden paneled walls, a parlor for ladies only, a small library for reading, and an altar for prayer. The ship was equipped with electric lighting and sleek staircases. Altogether, it was too much luxury for a couple of bums like us, we looked forward to enjoying it during our days at sea.

The deck plan book stated Capt. J. Wagner would be at the helm of the SS New York. The book described the ship as 645 feet long and 75 feet wide at its greatest point and built in Hamburg, Germany, in 1926 by the renowned shipbuilders Blohm & Voss. The ship's top speed was 20 knots, which allowed it to cross the Atlantic in only seven days. She could accommodate 976 passengers with a complement of 422 officers and crew.

Our first port of call would be Cherbourg, situated on France's Normandy coast. It was a man-made harbor and its construction began in 1783 during the reign of France's King Louis XVI. The harbor was 150 miles west of Paris, but only about 90 miles south of the Port of Southampton in southern England, where we would disembark the morning after the Cherbourg landing. The ship would then steam on toward its final destination, Hamburg. After the Olympics, Al and I planned to spend a day or two in Hamburg before heading home on August 27 aboard another Hamburg-American ship, The Deutschland.

Finally, we made it to our stateroom, which slept four people and was only eight feet wide and 12 feet long. Our accommodations were tourist class, but we could hardly complain, especially with the Tribune footing the bill. We hoped our prospective roommates would not show up to share our cramped little compartment. Our room was divided into two distinct spaces, a set of metal bunk beds and two small wooden lockers on both sides with a tiny sink under the porthole. It was tight, sufficient for sleeping and nothing more.

After we finished unpacking our suitcases, we heard a knock at our door. To our chagrin, our bunkmates had arrived. "Four guys crammed together in this little box for seven days," I thought to myself. What an experience this voyage was going to be.

"Welcome, boys, come right on in and make yourselves at home. Our maid and butler just left, by the way, so there'll be plenty of room for you good fellas in our spacious luxury suite," Al deadpanned.

"With the four of us standing here at the same time, even a sardine can has more space," I chimed in.

"By the way, where do you fellas call home?" Al asked.

"We are home. We're from the city, right here in New York City," one of them answered.

"Oh, no. My worst nightmare. Seven days cooped up with two Yankees, Dodgers, or Giants baseball fans. By the way, I'm Al and this is Joe. We're from Chicago, so you guys must certainly understand our dilemma here," he said with a laugh.

"I'm Jonathan and he's my brother, Herbert. Nice to meet both of you. With you boys being from the Second City and all, we trust you aren't packing any heat. I'm sorry, we're both Yankee fans. Too bad for the Cubs, though. That was tough losing that series last year to Detroit 4 to 2."

"Just so you understand, in last year's World Series both of us rooted for the Cubs against the Tigers," Herbert added.

"Yeah, don't remind us of that one or the 4-0 beating that your Yankees put on the Cubs in '32," I replied with a good-natured growl.

"And please don't hold it against us for loving sweet Lou Gehrig and our new rookie outfielder, Joe DiMaggio," Herbert said.

"Agreed, but watch out this year for the White Sox. Remember, we've still got our star player ol' Luke Appling and manager Jimmy Dykes. Those fellas may have something up their sleeves for you guys this year," Al joked, as he gave them both a hearty handshake.

Jonathan and Herbert Engel were in their early twenties, born and bred in New York City, and children of German immigrant parents. They were on their way to London to assist some of their relatives in getting to the United States. The four of us spent most of the voyage together. They were both great guys who had little love for the Nazis, which seemed odd because of their family's Prussian heritage. But, as we all became a little better acquainted, Al and I came to a clearer understanding of the source of their discontent.

In fact, on our first evening at sea, the four of us witnessed an ugly episode involving a young Polish couple. We were on the rear deck lying on some lounge chairs, as were 30 or so other passengers. A deck attendant walked by and passed out woolen blankets to any passenger who requested one. The Polish lady asked for one, but she was ignored by the worker who accommodated other passengers instead. The husband approached the attendant and politely asked again for a blanket, but was also refused and told they were not meant for Jews. Without hesitation, Jonathan immediately confronted the attendant and demanded one of the woolen blankets. After a tense moment, he was provided one, which he promptly handed to the Polish lady. Under the glare of harsh stares, the German attendant stalked away.

The dinner atmosphere on our second night at sea was also fraught with a sense of uneasiness on the part of the Engels. The moment we took our seats, the brothers pointed out some irregularities that they felt were obvious. They had concerns about the uniformed staff, some of whom, they surmised, were most likely Nazi officials aboard to gather information about some of the passengers. They asked if we had noticed the framed Time magazine cover of Adolf Hitler on the wall behind the purser's desk where we had picked up our cabin keys. They insisted that even some of the paintings depicting fit, blue-eyed, blond-haired German men and women were hung to emphasize the Nazi ideology of Aryan superiority.

"Hey, you guys, I'm superior. Just look at this handsome, chiseled hunk of a man with my blond hair and blues eyes. Who wouldn't love a face like mine?" Al quipped, attempting to lighten the mood a little.

"Yeah, a mug only a mother could love," I said.

Our feeble attempts to change the tone of the conversation failed to humor the Engels.

Just then, one of the ship's crew members suspected by the Engels of being a Nazi official came over to our table.

"I trust you gentlemen are enjoying yourselves this evening?" he asked in a welcoming tone.

"Yes, thank you," we all replied in unison.

"Good, good," he beamed. "The menu tonight features some of our finest German dishes prepared with exceptional care by our superior chefs for the delight of our distinguished American guests."

Al smiled broadly and offered a warm handshake to his new German pal.

"That will suit us all just fine, for I assure you, sir, all of the gentlemen at this table have a superior appetite for some good grub tonight," Al said, displaying his high-wattage charm.

"Yes, yes, quite humorous," our greeter replied, somewhat rattled by Al's informal response.

As our overly attentive host left our table, the Engel brothers broke out into laughter and suggested that Al should never walk the deck alone or veer too closely to the ship's railings. They half-jokingly suggested he may at some point be tossed overboard into the middle of the ocean by his new friend.

Our dubious German buddy was correct about the food though. Our menu selections for the evening were certainly not our everyday fare. They included Russian caviar, Soup a la Reine, roast turkey with chestnut stuffing, potato croquettes, assorted cheeses and cookies with fresh fruits, and everyone's favorite, mocha, a strong Arabian coffee loaded with caffeine, which ultimately led us all to a very restless night.

As the evening progressed, the Engels told us in passionate detail of the horrific treatment that Jewish citizens in Germany were suffering under Hitler.

"Haven't either of you heard about the 'Jewish Laws' or 'Nuremberg Laws' decreed by Hitler?" Herbert asked.

"Jewish and Nuremberg laws? What are you talking about?" I said. "Yeah, I've seen a few newsreels and read a few newspaper articles about the Nazis boasting how Germany has gone through an economic miracle since Hitler took over. Some writers have even suggested that President Roosevelt modeled parts of his New Deal public work programs after Germany's, using them as a blueprint for putting our own people back to work."

"Hold your horses, guys," Herbert said earnestly. "There is a big difference in the USA's approach compared to what's going on in Germany!"

"Specifically, we don't have some repulsive laws that require Jews to wear the Star of David on their clothing to disclose their religion," Jonathan broke in. "We don't put up warning signs in the windows of Jewish-owned businesses or station Brownshirt stormtroopers in front of shop doors to deter potential customers from entering. We don't beat or harass Jewish children, teachers, and professors for going to school or wanting to teach."

"Does that really happen in Germany?" Al asked.

"That and a lot more, my friend, believe me," said Jonathan as he continued. "You should hear what my uncles, who left the Fatherland a little more than a year ago, have experienced. They and their friends have gone through pure hell, guys. They were forced to leave their jobs teaching physics and chemistry at the prestigious Technical University in Berlin after working there for over 15 years.

"They were evicted from their family home and were not even allowed to take their personal belongings with them, other than a few suitcases when they departed Germany for England in 1935. It didn't even matter that they both faithfully served as loyal military officers in the Kaiser's army and were highly decorated combat soldiers during the Great War. They were still forced to leave their beloved homeland despite the family's dutiful service to their country going back centuries."

I attempted to switch gears and change the topic in hopes of lightening the mood. "After all," I told myself, "we're on paid vacation."

"Did any of you guys see the movie 'Anything Goes' with Bing Crosby?" I asked.

"No," all of them responded at once.

"Well, ironically, this movie takes place on an ocean liner with Crosby attempting to save Ida Lupino, his co-star, who he thinks has been kidnapped by some bad guys. Well, the movie ends in Southampton, England, the same port in England where we're going. Isn't that an odd coincidence? We're on an ocean liner, and we're going to Southampton. Amazing!" I gushed.

"Slow down a little, Joe," Al said. "Let me get this right. Ida Lupino was on a ship and in distress? Well, if that babe is still in Southampton and in need of a real man, ring her up and inform her that George Alfred Obermeyer III is on his way to rescue her from ol' Bing. She's a doll, all right."

"Whatever, Al. Ethel Merman also liked Bing in that movie," I joked.

"Wait just a minute," Al interrupted. "Ethel Merman may still be waiting in Southampton, too? You can have her, Joe, but lay off of Ida. She's all mine," he insisted as he shook his finger at me.

The four of us had a hearty chuckle at the exchange.

The jovial mood ended quickly, though, as Herbert returned to the subject of the Germans' harsh treatment of Jews. "Over 200,000 Jews have left Germany since 1933, and more are hoping to leave."

"I didn't know about all of that," replied Al, shaking his head.

"So that's why you fellas are going to London to help your uncles?" I asked. "Such a sad story. We wish you guys all the best."

Herbert continued: "Many Jews have been forced to vacate their homes and businesses, some owned by their families for generations, for little or no compensation. They are forbidden to marry or even date a 'superior' Aryan partner. Jews are not allowed to hold any political office, have any governmental job, or even perform on stage or in a movie."

Understandably, neither Jonathan nor Herbert wished to reveal that they were Jewish onboard a Nazi-controlled ocean liner. They insisted that Al and I vow not to divulge that bit of private information, and we kept our promise. We were disheartened to hear this information on such a beautiful, calm night as we steamed across the Atlantic, now armed with a slightly different outlook after our exuberant last few days.

Our remaining days at sea were fun and relaxing, and we avoided political topics, discussing only sports, travel, and women. Fortunately, Al managed to avoid from getting thrown overboard.

CHAPTER FIVE
LONDON TO PARIS

Southampton is a natural harbor developed by a railroad company and located 75 miles southwest of London. Our ship anchored about a mile from the docks, and we tendered to shore 20 minutes away aboard speedy wooden motorboats. Each boat held 12 or so passengers, and the uniforms worn by the three-man crew reminded us of those worn by Chicago cops.

It was Wednesday, June 3, at 1:34 p.m. when we first set foot on foreign soil, having declined the opportunity to go ashore in Cherbourg. The weather was as I imagined: a cool 50 degrees Fahrenheit with light rain. Welcome to England!

The tender's captain recommended a local boarding house as a convenient place to spend the night. From the outside, the house was a drab little place, but it was close to the docks, clean and comfortable.

After a rather restless night, I dragged myself out of bed while Al was still sleeping like a baby. We had agreed to get together with the Engel brothers at 7:30 to catch the morning train to London. Around 6 a.m., as Al continued snoring, I packed and quietly crept down the tight, little wooden stairs with my old leather suitcase in one hand and a cloth duffel bag in the other.

The owner of the inn greeted me with my first hot cup of Earl Grey tea, a type named after a former prime minister. We talked for a bit, but even though we both spoke the same language, I had a difficult time understanding most of what he said. He kept referring to me as his mate, bloke, or Yank. I simply called my friendly host just plain buddy. After an hour of listening to stories from his army days during the Great War, Al and the Engels finally entered the downstairs parlor.

Soon after we said our goodbyes to the talkative innkeeper, we stepped outside our boarding house onto the cobblestone walkway. We were met by a rare sunny day on our way to Southampton's Central Train Station only 10 minutes away. We purchased our tickets and soon boarded our train for the three-hour trip to our destination, Waterloo Station, located in the heart of historic London.

In mocking fashion, Al greeted people with a "Tallyho, ol' chap" or repeated the words "Bloody hell" over and over and then laugh every time he'd utter the English terms. I'm sure the people we encountered thought he was loony and, possibly, a bit rude.

The lush countryside was dotted with small farms and quaint villages with many of the older homes topped with thatched roofs. When we got closer to the city, it looked similar to the outlying areas of Chicago or New York. From the comfort of our train compartment, we noticed cars driven on the left-hand side of the road and passed a surprising number of horse-drawn carts and carriages. We all agreed driving in England would present us with major challenges.

We were excited and flush with energy as our train came to a stop at Waterloo Station. The four of us had developed an American brotherhood that none of us wished to see end so soon. Jonathan and Herbert invited us to have dinner at their uncles' apartment, and we gladly accepted. We agreed to meet on Friday evening at 6:15.

During the next few days, Al and I acted like two lucky men on the verge of knighthood. We did some touristy things such as visiting Buckingham Palace where Al insisted on speaking with King Edward VIII. The king was at one of his country estates that day, according to the palace guards, thank God!

Nineteen thirty-six became known as "The Year of the Three Kings." King George V died in January 1936. His son, King Edward VIII, who was known as a ladies' man, then ascended to the throne. He had fallen in love, however, with Wallis Simpson, a married American woman, who became his mistress. The English despised her, even more so after she divorced her second husband and accepted King Edward's proposal of marriage. But the British people would not accept her as their queen, so King Edward VIII abdicated his throne in December of that year in favor of the woman he loved. His brother King George VI then became the third king in less than one year.

We rode double-decker buses, little black cabs, and the subway, or, as the British call it, "The Underground or The Tube." We visited Big Ben, Westminster Abbey, Piccadilly Circus, Hyde Park, the Tower of London, and the world-famous British Museum. We even said hello to Lord Nelson at Trafalgar Square, and, drunk as hell, stumbled across London Bridge as we sang the verses of a familiar childhood tune, "London Bridge is falling down, falling down, falling down. London Bridge is falling down, my fair lady." Trust me, it felt like it was falling down or at least shuddering that night. And what a night! In just seven days, we attempted to drink a pint of ale in every pub in jolly ol' London. And we damned near succeeded!

In keeping with the German obsession with being punctual, we arrived at the Engels' front door as scheduled. The night we had dinner was the only one during our short stay in Britain's capital city that we stayed completely sober. The uncles spoke little English, but Al, Jonathan, and Herbert acted as interpreters during the meal and throughout the evening. Speaking with the Engels' uncles only compounded our confusion about what was happening in Germany, and made us feel a little more uneasy about going there in less than two months.

The uncles, Salomon, and Julius Engel, could best be described as two intelligent, distinguished gentlemen who were both very accommodating and gladly opened up to us about their perilous flight out of their beloved homeland. The uncles told us they had been beaten and threatened by the Brownshirt thugs called the SA, or Nazi paramilitary, who attacked them because they were Jews. They were saddened by the anti-Semitic views that currently gripped their homeland and worried about the harsh suppression of their religion. They denounced the dangers of the rigid Nazi-themed educational regimentation required by Hitler's regime for all students, from kindergarteners to college graduates.

Because of their scientific backgrounds, they were able to obtain visas to come to England in March 1935. They traveled first by train from Berlin to Bremerhaven where they boarded a ship to Southampton.

Julius spoke in German as Herbert interpreted.

"Herbert and Jonathan gave us a little background that you young men are writers for the Chicago Tribune. That's impressive, I must say. Before you go to Germany, I hope you will go with an open mind. Undoubtedly, you've heard many conflicting stories about my homeland.

"I don't want you to think that every Christian or nonreligious German is evil. I am thankful to say they're not all Nazis. In fact, very few are National Socialists. The vast majority of Germans are wonderful, kind-hearted, and Godly people. I might add our non-Jewish friends tried their very best to help us, and most of them did so at great peril to themselves and their families," Julius said.

Salomon expanded upon Julius' gratitude for the help they had received.

"Yes, that's true. We will forever be grateful to them and will always consider them our good friends. But most Germans are just afraid to speak too loudly against Hitler's regime for fear of retribution from the Gestapo, the hated Nazi secret police."

Julius resumed, recounting fondly his former job and co-workers.

"We loved our jobs at the university and valued the interaction we enjoyed with our dedicated and brilliant colleagues. The faculty was top notch, and the laboratory research projects we worked on were fascinating and challenging. We miss our friends there and our wonderful students, too."

"We both pray that someday after all of the Nazi madness ends, we can go back to Germany and live again peacefully in our Berlin home," said Salomon, reiterating his brother's nostalgia for home.

"Although America is our preferred destination, Berlin will always be our home. As Julius said earlier, please don't blame all Germans. You will meet many wonderful people during your travels to our beautiful country. I only warn you to be careful when dealing with the Nazis. Be polite and don't do anything stupid," he warned.

They emphasized that Jews were constantly berated by the Nazi press. According to them, the state-controlled media blamed the Jews for everything from Germany's capitulation that ended the Great War to the unfair terms of the Versailles Treaty demanded by the Allies to humiliate the Germans, to the stock market crash in 1929, which caused unprecedented inflation of their currency and made the Deutsche Mark almost worthless.

"How can all of that be the fault of the Jewish people?" Julius plaintively asked. "Germany has a population of 65 million people, and the Jews make up only 500,000, and, since Hitler rose to power, almost one-third of them have left the country."

They described how propaganda, promoted by the Nazi press and supervised by Reich Minister of Culture and Propaganda Joseph Goebbels, labeled Jewish citizens as "Untermenschen," sub-humans. They also expanded on their fears of the organized military-inspired torchlight processions whose Brownshirt participants marched through the streets chanting and singing about despicable Jews. The fanatical members of that paramilitary organization were the same tormentors who burned books, not only those penned by Jewish authors but also by any writers who opposed their anti-Semitic doctrine. They told us that after the Nazis came to power, all labor and trade unions in Germany had been banned.

"Every worker was required by law to join the DAF, an acronym for the Deutsche Arbeitsfront, or German Labor Front in English," Herbert said, translating his uncles' somber message. "Union leaders who had opposed that mandate were sent to concentration camps for re-education, so little opposition existed. Millions of fine German workers are now busy working in factories all over the country rearming Germany's military. Now, I hope you better understand what is happening in Germany under the leadership of Der Führer, who, my uncles fear, will someday bring a new war to all of Europe."

"I pray to God that cooler heads will prevail, and that a war like the one your uncles fought in will never happen ever again, my friend," I said.

All nodded their heads in agreement.

We said our goodbyes, and even though we might never see each other again, we had become friends with the Engels for life.

We left the Engels' apartment in a hopeful state of mind, wishing success for Jonathan and Herbert's mission to get their uncles safely to America where they would have a chance to flourish without fear.

Reflecting on the evening as we made our way back to our hotel room, we knew how blessed we were to be Americans. Even with all of our country's social and economic problems, we realized how lucky we were to possess the most precious gift of all — freedom.

After a few days in London, we boarded a train to the Port of Dover on the east coast of England facing the English Channel. Once we settled into our train seats, Al started to sing very quietly. Before long, he had everyone in our coach joining him. At the top of our lungs, we sang Shirley Temple's "On the Good Ship Lollipop," "Cheek to Cheek" by Fred Astaire, "Happy Days Are Here Again," by Leo Reisman & His Orchestra, Marian Anderson's "He's Got the Whole World in His Hands," nursery songs, and we finished by singing English songs I had never heard. It was a welcome diversion from the previous night. God love that crazy Al!

From Dover, we took a three-hour passenger ferry to Calais, France, where we planned to catch another train to the capital city of Paris. Gazing upon the white cliffs of Dover as we pulled out of the harbor was an amazing sight.

"By my calendar, I'm only six days from seeing Schimmert for the first time in my life; I still can't believe all of this is happening!" I thought to myself.

We arrived at Calais at 2 p.m. on Friday, June 12. Within 45 minutes of disembarking, we were on a train heading to Paris, just five hours distant. Since our train's carriage car was mostly filled with Frenchmen, the language barrier prevented Al from conducting another sing-a-long.

As I tried to get a little shut-eye, however, he came up with more bizarre ways to occupy our time.

"Joe, who do think is better looking, Jean Harlow or Jean Arthur?" he asked.

"Really, now as I'm trying to sleep, do you have this obsession with women named Jean?" I asked. "Well, if I must answer, I'm more of a Carole Lombard or Betty Grable man myself. I'm a leg man, Al, plain and simple. A leg man."

"OK, smarty pants. Who's the better actor, Randolph Scott or Gary Cooper?" he asked.

"Neither. I more favor Errol Flynn or Cary Grant because they always get the beautiful dames at the end of the movie," I replied.

A little perturbed, Al persisted with the inane discussion.

"OK, Joe, one last chance to redeem yourself. Who's funnier, Laurel and Hardy or the Marx Brothers?"

"Al, my friend, from the cold and cheesy North, I can't believe those were your only two options, and, once again, I'll have to pick neither. The Three Stooges or Buster Keaton. Any of those funny guys will suit me," I shot back.

"OK, Joe, I may have to concede that one. Buster Keaton would be my choice, too, once I think about it," he reluctantly agreed.

"Al, just in case you intend to play another game of trivia during this trip, I prefer Betty Boop, Popeye the Sailor, and even Ol' Mickey Mouse over Scrappy and Crazy Kat, just saying," I laughed.

"I give up, you Flying Dutchman. Go fly a kite or something, you little piss ant," cracked Al as he punched me in the arm.

Around 8 p.m., our train pulled into the Gare de Nord, one of Paris' six famed main transit train terminals. From June 12 to June 16, we were in Paris, the City of Lights, or, as Al kept calling it, Ol' Gay Par-ree.

We found a hotel near the station with an elevator so tiny, only one person at a time could squeeze into it. Our room was just as small, barely large enough for two, and our toilet and shower were inconveniently located three doors down the hallway. We made do, however, and settled in for the evening. The next day, we made the typical tourist rounds and rode the crowded Metro to visit the world-renowned Louvre Museum, Montmartre, the Arc de Triomphe, the ruins of the Bastille, and the Dome des Invalides, which housed the tomb of the infamous French general and dictator, Napoleon Bonaparte.

The next three days we divided up the city and visited the Paris Opera House, strolled one of the most famous boulevards in the world, the Champs-Elysees, cruised on the Seine River, prayed at the Notre Dame Cathedral, rode the glass-windowed elevator to the very top floor of the Eiffel Tower, and walked down its hundreds of steps. We spent hours watching people in several of the city's fabulous parks. The Jardin des Tuileries was our favorite. We dined at sidewalk cafés and spent an evening at the Moulin Rouge. Paris' most famous nightclub featured nude dancing girls, and a lighted windmill perched on its roof. Al insisted, and I agreed, it was an evening well spent. But seeing that windmill made me eager to get out of Paris; I yearned to be on my way to Limburg to see a real one. I was tired of big cities. I was looking forward to seeing some beautiful farmland.

On our last day, we took a 30-minute train ride to the Palace of Versailles southwest of Paris. The palace was by far the most opulent in France and featured huge, immaculate gardens and fountains. The main structure was comprised of more than 700 rooms, including the magnificent Hall of Mirrors, made famous as the place the Treaty of Versailles was signed, officially ending the Great War. It was the former residence of France's kings during the Golden Era of the French monarchy. Its most famous residents included kings Louis XIV, Louis XV, and, lastly, Louis XVI, who, along with his wife, Marie Antoinette, was beheaded by a mob on the bloody guillotine during the French Revolution in 1793.

As our train rolled through the French countryside on our journey toward the Dutch city of Maastricht, we could still see signs of the ghastly, deadly trenches of the Great War. I pondered all of the senseless wars fought on the European continent from the conquests of the Romans legions, the

Viking raiders, Charlemagne and Napoleon, and the German Kaiser of the Great War. Consequential battles raged from Waterloo to Verdun with millions of casualties and pointless deaths throughout Europe's bloody history. To an American, it seemed that the European kings and empires loved war. They fought over insults to royal families, land, language, and religion, which seemed even more perplexing considering they were all Christian nations. How silly and difficult it was to comprehend.

CHAPTER SIX
LIMBURG WONDERLAND

Finally, on the evening of June 16, our train eased into the rail station at Maastricht, the old capital city of Limburg province. We stayed the night in town, and the next day I said goodbye to Al as he continued to Cologne, where he planned to visit relatives. We decided to meet there on July 24 to begin our original mission, writing articles for the Tribune about the Olympics from Berlin.

Many Americans, when they think of the Netherlands, expect to see windmills dotting the landscape, beautiful fields of colorful tulips, and man-made dikes holding back the North Sea. They anticipate men in wooden shoes the Dutch call "klompen." They also expect to see them wearing dark pants and white shirts under matching double-breasted short coats, suspenders, and loose, red neckties, topped off by traditional Dutch caps. Americans imagine seeing women decked out in long, layered, fluffy dresses with aprons tied at the waist and pointed, starched, lace bonnets.

The vast majority of the people in the Netherlands dress, however, just like us with maybe a little less flair. In fact, the majority of Americans may be surprised to learn that the Dutch share many of the same conveniences that people in the United States enjoy. The major difference is many Dutch homes and buildings in the picturesque cities and towns have been around for centuries.

The next day as I stepped onto my bus, I noticed all the sliding-glass windows were wide open in an attempt to defeat the smoldering heat of the day. The interior of the small vehicle was charmingly spartan in comparison to those of Paris or London. The only other passengers were two nuns clothed in traditional habits complete with full-length black tunics and coiffed veils. Their unique outfits were adorned with customary silver crosses dangling on modest black cords hanging from under the white wimples covering their necks. Additionally, they each wore a silver band on their left hand, indicating they had taken their vows pledging perpetual service to their Lord, and attached to their aprons were rosary beads.

I attempted to strike up a friendly conversation with them, and the one named Sister Truus gladly obliged. I told her a snippet of my tangled story, and I was thrilled to hear that they both personally knew my Dutch family and remembered my grandparents and my mother. The sisters beamed bright, happy smiles and seemed overjoyed about my family ties to their hometown and my visit.

When I first saw the name Schimmert scrawled across a wooden signpost pointing the way to my destination, a huge lump formed in my throat. I felt my heart starting to pump faster, and my soul filled with anticipation as my eyes yearned to take in all of the things Mother had passed down to me. As our driver sped along a dusty single-lane dirt road, I marveled at the tidy little farms and admired the neat rows of crops positioned endlessly in the rolling meadows. I was in awe of the tall trees that stood as if in military formation dividing still more lush green fields sown with stalks of wheat and barley. People riding bicycles appeared everywhere as I stared in wonder at the houses decorated with colorful flowers nestled neatly in their window boxes. But, most of all, I enjoyed the smell of crisp, glorious, fresh, country air.

As my heart beat ever faster, Schimmert, I thought, was just like Mother had described it to me. Gazing from my bus window, had it not been for the cars and trucks that occasionally passed us, I imagined an idyllic setting from the early 18th century. The sublime surroundings were just perfect, and I experienced sheer elation and exhilaration. To my delight, I glanced upon an actual windmill churning in the distance. As our bus turned around a corner, my eyes glanced at the Water Tower, and as we turned still another corner, the Sint Remigius Church steeple came into view. Near the church, we came to our last stop. I gathered my belongings, shook the bus driver's hand, and after years of anticipation, finally stepped upon the charmingly tattered cobblestone and gravel streets of Schimmert.

As tears of joy streamed down their heavenly rose-colored faces, my two travel companions gave me several big hugs and kissed my cheeks repeatedly to properly welcome me to their hometown. Our pleasant conversation continued as they insisted on escorting me to my Uncle Wouter's farm. I knew Mother would be overwhelmed with delight when I told of that first unexpected, but wonderfully warm greeting.

As we walked closer towards Klein Haasdal where Uncle Wouter Schrijnemaekers lived, Mother's frequent narratives of Schimmert seemed to burst out before me like a cork pried from a good bottle of wine. The aroma of fresh sunflowers filled the air, and they were stacked in such a pattern that nary a one stood out of place. Many of the residents lived in quaint, but sturdy, tiled-roofed houses. Most of the nicer brick homes boasted stout wooden doors, and many had large barns attached to the rear of the dwellings. Directly behind their houses, cows roamed the fields where farmers and laborers worked. Young children laughed and played in the streets while others jumped rope or chased one another as kids did everywhere.

It was odd to notice more horses and pigs than cars or people. Hundreds of chickens roamed their front yards, sometimes spilling freely into the roads while others scattered lazily, unfazed as we strolled by. Rabbit coops and clotheslines were a common sight.

There were a few shops mixed among the cottages: a bakery, a butcher shop, a cobbler, and, of course, the Sint Remigius Catholic Church. At that moment, it felt to me as if Schimmert were like an earthly purgatory that men and women should experience before stepping through the gates of heaven.

I observed the women who lived there were very industrious, too.

When they weren't baking fresh bread, making cheese, churning apple butter, or caring for their children, they were conscientiously sweeping the sidewalks in front of their houses, or polishing their windows to a brilliant shine. They also herded sheep and carried water pails that dangled from ropes, perilously balanced on wooden poles perched across their shoulders.

My grandfather Wilhelm had a brother Wouter, or Walter in English, still living in Schimmert. Uncle Wouter was 16 years younger than my grandfather. He was married to Ria, his much younger, tiny, adorable, always smiling wife. They had two sons, Math, spelled like the short for arithmetic, and Ralf. They also had two daughters, Kiki and Judy. Wouter was only nine years old when his father, and my great-grandfather, Peter died. Following that tragedy, Wouter and his mother, Maria, lived an uneasy life for a while. To make matters worse, shortly before Peter died he lost his textile business in Maastricht after declaring bankruptcy.

My great-grandmother Maria remarried and continued to reside in Klein Haasdal, one of the little hamlets of Schimmert, with her new husband, Jules d'Leers. Jules, who had no children of his own, treated Wouter as his son. Maria died of consumption only two years after marrying Jules. Wouter, who was just 12 when his mother died, continued to live with Jules. Upon Jules' death, his little farm in Klein Haasdal passed to Wouter.

After the initial surprise of meeting me, the next few days went very well at Uncle Wouter's home. I was welcomed warmly and soon realized our mutual love of sports helped solidify our relationship. His interest in the upcoming Olympics only strengthened our bond.

My uncle and I, along with his sons, were able to listen to the Joe Louis-Max Schmeling heavyweight fight on the radio on June 19 before a sold-out crowd at Yankee Stadium in New York City. There was national pride on the line. Louis was considered the unquestioned favorite as he entered the ring with a perfect record at 27-0. Schmeling was the German heavyweight world champion from 1930 to 1932, but he was 30 and thought to be well past his prime. He was an obvious underdog in his scheduled 15-round matchup with Louis.

Louis, 22, and ranked as the No. 1 contender for the heavyweight title, did not consider the German a serious threat. But Schmeling proved he was more than up to the task. Before the match, Schmeling had dutifully studied Louis' style and trained extremely hard, under the tutelage of his Jewish trainer. Schmeling knocked out Louis in the 12-round upset, but returned to Germany denied a chance to face titleholder James J. Braddock as international opposition to Nazism grew. Hitler was said to be overjoyed with Schmeling's triumph, which the Nazi press celebrated as proof of its ceaseless ideological propaganda campaign supporting its claims of Aryan supremacy.

After breakfast the next morning, we were still debating the surprising outcome of the previous night's fight before Uncle Wouter and his children peeled off to attend to their farm chores. Of course, I offered to help, but Uncle Wouter would have none of it. He insisted that I was a guest in his home and no guest of his, family or not, needed to work while on holiday. Not wanting to offend him, I decided to walk to Uncle Karl's farm on de Kling Road. After 25 minutes, with written directions in hand, I assumed I had arrived at Uncle Karl's property.

The house standing 100 yards in front of me with the attached barn in the rear was exactly as Uncle Wouter described it in great detail. I saw a young boy who looked about 10 years old heading toward the barn and watched him open a side door and step inside. I tried to get his attention, but to no avail. I moseyed over to the door and knocked on it. No one answered, so I gingerly opened the door and walked in uninvited.

"Is anyone home?" I called, but no one responded.

Two large doors on the back of the barn were open, so the interior was well illuminated by sunlight. As I moved closer to the first stall, I noticed the boy was busily grooming a horse, unaware that I was standing only a few steps behind him. I slowly meandered toward him to introduce myself and had just begun to speak when suddenly the barn door burst open, and in walked a striking, 20-something beauty.

I'll never forget my reaction the first time I saw her slender frame draped in that long, drab, brownish-colored dress. Her hands and face were splattered with mud, and she was wearing equally soiled black boots. Her long brown hair was covered with a ragged green scarf, but, for some inexplicable reason, the dingy first image she projected seemed strangely appropriate. My presence obviously startled her, and she gracefully looked down at the straw-covered floor as I continued to gaze at her.

Her head rose slowly and her eyes locked with mine to reveal the most heavenly, radiant blue eyes I had ever seen. For a second, she froze, as did my breathing. I softly said hello, and she tenderly responded in kind. I quickly apologized for unsettling her with my awkward presence.

"I'm sorry, I startled you," I said nervously. Of course, by her facial expression, I realized she had no idea what I had just uttered.

"Het spijt me," I sputtered, unsure if my halting Dutch conveyed my apology.

She flashed a stunning smile and replied with a simple, "OK."

For one of the few times in my life, I was at a loss for words.

"Hello, my name is Joe Fisher. I'm from America," I squeaked.

She squarely looked at me as she continued to walk slowly around the barn seeming to search for something other than me to focus upon. Our eyes remained glued to one another for what felt like minutes. Then she looked away for a brief moment, which gave me an opportunity to gather myself. I extended my right hand to shake hers, but, to my surprise, she curtsied to me as if I were royalty.

Still bowing, her tender voice broke the silence: "My name is Sterre. I am Sterre," she said haltingly.

"Sterre," I slowly repeated. "That's such a beautiful name.

"I am so happy to meet you, Sterre, but please don't bow to me. I'm just plain Joe from West Virginia, from America. Honey, trust me, no one ever bows to a West Virginia Mountaineer," I said with a silly laugh.

She just stood there with an indifferent look on her face.

After a few minutes of polite banter, she told me the correct way to pronounce her name. To spell her name phonetically, it should be broken down into two syllables and spelled Stair-ree, which would also be the proper way to pronounce her name in English. In Dutch, Sterre means star. No matter how you say it in any language, the name Stair-ree could easily be used to describe one of the most beautiful creatures in the universe.

Still somewhat distracted, I clumsily asked, "I was looking for my Uncle Karl, Karl Westhovens. Is he here?"

"No, he does not live here. He lives just down the road," I was stunned to hear her say in almost perfect English. I placed my hands on my hips and started to laugh at the prospect of being able to easily communicate with her.

"You speak English very well," I said. "I was worried I might not be able to talk with anyone here who would understand me."

She motioned for me to stop and asked me to speak more slowly so that she could better understand what I was saying.

"I speak a little English, but you must talk slowly, OK?" she requested.

"OK, I understand. Sorry."

"Do you know Karl Westhovens?" I asked unhurriedly.

"Yes, I know him. He is a friend of my father and lives nearby. Did you say he was your uncle?" she asked.

"Yes, my uncle. Well, he is my grandmother's brother, so he is not my real uncle. But really he is my mother's uncle, and that would make him my great uncle. Understand?" I said awkwardly.

"Some I understand, and some not," she said, laughing a little. "I can take you to his house if you would like. It's only a few minutes away by walking."

"Great, I mean, OK. I would love to walk with you anytime, I mean that's so nice of you to take me right to his house, which is right down the road, and even though you must have other work to do, you still are so sweet to offer to take a stranger from America to meet his long-lost uncle, even though he is not lost. He lives here in Schimmert, I hope," I rambled on, flustered by the girl's generosity and beauty.

She just smiled at my awkward behavior.

As the unexpected pressure subsided, I calmed down as she led me toward Uncle Karl's farm. I was hoping his farm was farther down the road than she originally indicated. I was captivated by my gracious and charming guide.

Even though the muddled conversation was somewhat difficult, I learned a lot about her on our little jaunt. I found out that she was a school teacher at a local elementary school and taught children between the ages of 10 and 12. She was also a seamstress, having learned the time-honored trade from her mother, who had acquired some formal training in her youth. I learned that Sterre lived with her father, Paul Trags, and two younger brothers, Jim and Arjan, on their family's farm on de Kling Road at Oensel, a small northwestern district of Schimmert. She told me she attended Sint Remigius Kirk te Schimmert, the same church my mother went to as a child, although Sterre said the church my mother knew was replaced by a new building erected on the same spot in 1926.

I also learned she had the most soothing voice, and I was a little more than saddened when our brief journey ended and we said our goodbyes. I told her I enjoyed meeting her and thanked her for helping me. Then I nervously asked if I could seek her advice and expertise if I needed any Dutch-to-English translations in the future. I was thankful for her agreement, and she then went about her business. I watched her walk away as I shook my head and sighed. And, yes, she did look back a time or two and even waved at me. I, of course, waved back. After meeting Sterre, I knew it was indeed a wonderful day to be in Schimmert.

Uncle Karl, my Oma Renee's younger brother, was as shocked as Uncle Wouter to see me on his doorstep. He lived on his farm in Oensel with his only son, John, who was a tall, hearty fellow of 37. He was not the most handsome guy on earth, but strong as an ox and completely devoted to his father. His mother, Ceciel, died from complications during her second pregnancy. The baby was born prematurely and also didn't survive. John was only 10 when the tragedy occurred.

Uncle Karl was a typical Limburg farmer, a self-assured, hard-working man who dedicated his life to farming, followed his heritage, and devoted his soul to the land. He was 61, but could easily pass for someone in his mid-forties. He stood six-feet-four and wore a long, thick, black mustache streaked with silver that matched his full head of hair. His property had been in his family for well more than 250 years. He was the sixth generation of Westhovens to call the farm their home. It was a beautiful piece of flat farmland that was separated from Sterre's family farm by a fenced five-acre plot where a neighbor's horses grazed.

Uncle Karl was amazed that anyone from America would come to visit his family, especially someone related to them. From his front yard, I noticed a windmill in the distance. I wondered aloud if it was the same one my mother spoke of so fondly, and he assured me it was. He graciously welcomed me into his home and though I was still somewhat fatigued, he asked me to tell him everything about my mother and my grandparents.

My mother was born and lived on his family's farm for her first 12 years. Uncle Karl took me upstairs to the same bedroom where she was born. Tears rolled down my face when he described the glorious event that occurred where I now stood. He, John, and I talked well past midnight as I was besieged with question after question and answered them all as I struggled to keep from dozing off. With my stamina fading, my uncle put me up for the night. I requested to sleep in the room that used to be my mother's. He, of course, insisted upon it. Oh, how I prayed that night and so wished Mother could witness the smile on my face as I lay there staring at the ceiling in her old room. It was magical.

The next day John was eager to show me how hard it is to work and live on a successful Limburg farm, not fully understanding that I'd performed that type of labor most of my life. We hammered shoes on their horse,

Riny. We fed cows, chickens, and pigs. We repaired fence posts and dug a ditch to help channel water to the fields. For the evening meal, we picked some beans, tomatoes, cucumbers, and carrots and gathered potatoes from their vegetable garden to complement the local horse meat dish that we prepared called zoervleis. I found the meal quite tasty when marinated in apple syrup, a favorite Dutch sauce, and still better when served with a slice of gingerbread called ontbijtkoek.

CHAPTER SEVEN
STERRE TUGS AT THE HEART

I was exhausted that night as I fell upon my bed. I decided to make a surprise visit to Sterre's home the next morning, and just after daybreak, I casually approached her farm. As I walked closer, I peeked through the fog that eerily blanketed the surrounding fields and noticed her saddling a big brown mare.

"Goedemorgen," I greeted her in Dutch.

"Please let me help you. I love horses," I said as I hurried to her side.

"Oh, thank you, Joe. I can always use some help with this stubborn horse. My four-legged Princess Ellen is always a little difficult in the morning," she replied with slight irritation.

"Sounds like Princess Ellen behaves a little like my Opa Wilhelm before he eats his breakfast," I said in jest.

After we finished wrestling with her stubborn horse, she invited me into her kitchen where she offered me a cup of hot Pickwick tea served with a warm slice of Limburgse vlaai, a fruit-filled pie covered with a lattice crust that is uniquely a traditional southern Dutch treat.

"That's the best pie I've ever tasted, Sterre. Did you make this delicious confection?" I inquired after the first bite.

"Of course, I normally make all our meals every day. Father and the boys have their daily chores, and cooking is one of my many duties," she explained.

"I understand. I'm from a farming family, too. In addition to cooking, what other duties do you have around here?" I asked.

She seemed slightly surprised by my interest.

"Well, let me see. I do many things. I clip my father's and my brothers' hair, I milk the cows and feed them along with our horse and the pigs. I gather the eggs, clean and sweep the house, work in the barn, tend to the garden, sew, pick vegetables, run errands, and, in my free time, I love to read and paint. But usually, I only get to enjoy those hobbies during the winter," she said as she counted off her duties on her fingers.

"Oh, I almost forgot. I also shovel horse and cow manure," she sighed, holding her nose and pretending to mock a foul smell.

"Other than that, I teach children to read and write when school is in session," she proudly proclaimed.

"Do you ever have any time just to have a little fun?" I asked coyly.

"I assume your fella must be a little sad with your not having a lot of free time to be by his side," I said cautiously, hoping she'd say a fella didn't exist.

"Fella? What does fella mean?" she asked, looking confused.

"Fella, oh, that means a man, your boyfriend, your steady guy. Someone who looks like you must have a fella," I replied.

"Oh," she laughed, "there is no fella. I don't have time for another man. I'm raising three already, and they require all of my undivided attention."

After the awkward exchange, I knew she could sense by the relieved look on my face that I was intrigued by her. I noticed that same look in her eyes. There was no question in my mind that it was one of those tongue-tied moments like the kind Clark Gable and Claudette Colbert shared in the movie "It Happened One Night." In their hit feature film, the two Hollywood stars were obviously infatuated with each other as they attempted to get to know one another better in that little cottage with just a rope-suspended sheet separating their beds. Just like Gable, I was attempting to win her over.

Changing the subject, I noticed a painting of a ship's captain hanging on the wall. As I pointed to it, I asked, "Did you paint that portrait?"

"Yes, I did when I was 12 years old," she replied a little embarrassed by the thought as she continued. "It's of Holland's most famous admiral, Michiel de Ruyter. Do you know of him?"

"No, I never heard of him, but he must have been one fearsome naval officer," I replied. "I can see by that look on his face."

"He was the leader of the king's fleet and won sea battles in the 1600s against the English, French, Spanish, Portuguese, and Swedish navies," she answered, providing me with a brief Dutch naval history lesson.

"You're very talented, and your artwork is amazing, especially considering that you painted it when you were so young. Do you have any more paintings?" I asked.

"I kept just a few small ones up in my room, mostly of Father and Mother and of one of Ellen and our dogs. I do have a big book with some of the sketches that I have drawn over the years. Most of them I don't think are very good, but Father seems to enjoy them, and Mother loved them. They, of course, were not art critics, just doting parents," she said, blushing before her beautiful face revealed a smile.

"I understand, but I would love to see them someday. I admire anyone with a talent such as yours," I told her, as she blushed.

She handed me a piece of Kleure black licorice candy as we walked through the rear door on our way back out to the yard. It was the most disgusting object I had ever placed in my mouth, but I ate the entire thing out of respect for my gracious hostess. For the rest of my stay, whenever offered any more of that foul-tasting treat, I politely declined.

"I was hoping you could carve out a little time for me, to show me some of the exciting attractions of Schimmert," I suggested nervously.

"Schimmert?" Sterre fired back at me, astonished by the request. "Exciting attractions? We only have the Water Tower and the church. Otherwise, only farms, animals, and people."

"I can't believe that. For instance, look right over there," I declared as I pointed to a windmill standing on Schimmerterweg Road about a mile away, facing the morning sun. "Now that's a sight that few Americans ever have an opportunity to witness!"

"You don't have windmills in America, Joe?" she asked a little confused.

"Of course we do, but none as majestic as that one. I'd be honored if you would be so kind to show it to me today, please," I begged. To my good fortune, she agreed, but only on one condition: I had to agree to ride double on horseback with her at the reins of Princess Ellen. Without hesitating, I happily accepted her offer.

Not only did we visit the Sint Hubertusmolen Windmill, but Sterre gave me a tour complete with a verbal history as we climbed the wooden stairs all the way to the top. As we stood there looking out a window, I reflected: "I'll bet my mother and my grandparents once stood here, right where we are now standing. I am finally getting to relive my mother's dream! She had always wished for me to see her hometown, and now I'm lucky enough to be here in person with the most beautiful girl in Schimmert."

A little startled by my brashness, she humbly answered, "First, Joe, I am not the most attractive girl in Schimmert, and, second, I'm just a plain girl from Oensel, nothing more."

That clear understatement notwithstanding, I insisted that she show me more of the village.

As we bounced up and down on her mare, Sterre purposely alternated the pace by bringing ol' Ellen to a full gallop and then to a slower lope. I think she was testing my riding skills. Little did she know that I had been around horses my entire life. She playfully teased me and bestowed upon me a new nickname, Cowboy Joe. I liked my new moniker, but not as much as I enjoyed her spirit. Before we departed that afternoon, I managed to procure a little more time to be with her the following day.

The next day, once the morning chores were finished, we rode bicycles into the countryside and eventually stopped beside a small stream that she called the Kleine Guel near the village of Valkenburg. We sat down on the lush green grass and watched in silence as the small, muddy stream flowed past. I took the liberty of brushing her long brown hair with my hand and began to recite to her the beginning of a mushy little tune written by American composer, Irving Berlin.

"Heaven ... I'm in Heaven ..." I started, but before I could finish the first verse, she screamed.

"Joe! I know that song, I know it! It's from the movie 'Top Hat' with Fred Astaire and Ginger Rogers," she gushed, smiling from ear to ear.

"Yes, that's right, from the movie 'Top Hat.' You know that movie?" I asked, a bit astonished.

"On my birthday last month, Father surprised me and my brothers and took us to a movie theater in Maastricht to see this motion picture. It's the only movie we'd ever seen, including my Father. Oh, and I loved every second of that movie, the dancing, the singing. I had never experienced anything like that in my life," she raved. "I tried to sing the songs as we rode the bus returning from Maastricht, but I could not remember the lines, but I do remember, 'Heaven ... I'm in Heaven,' " she gleefully said.

"Do you remember any more of the song? Please, Joe, try to remember," she asked.

"Well, I know a few more lines, but, remember, I'm not the best singer in the world. I'll try my best for you, Sterre."

Then I began to sing,

"Heaven ... I'm in Heaven ...
And my heart beats so that I can hardly speak ...
And I seem to find the happiness I seek ...
When we're out together dancing cheek to cheek."

"That's it, Joe! Can you sing it again, only slower, so I can learn all of the words? Please, for me again," she adoringly requested.

Of course, I sang it over and over and each time I finished the song, she asked for one more performance. I couldn't refuse her even though my rendition was a bit amusing compared to Astaire's. We sang that tune so much that I felt a little like I was Fred singing with joy to Ginger.

We continued our pleasant journey by visiting the small Limburg resort town of Valkenburg, just a short distance south of Schimmert. The village, settled by the Romans more than 2,000 years before, featured ruins of an old castle perched on a hill overlooking the town. It was built with a soft marl stone where thousands of visitors' names had been carved over the preceding centuries.

An impressive system of caves had been tunneled into the hills that surrounded the ancient town, and we decided to explore one called the "Fluweelengrot," or "The Velvet Cave," dug during the 11th century. Upon entering, I couldn't help but notice many elaborate, hand-painted and carved murals that adorned its 10-foot-high, pliable-stone walls. With my pocket knife in hand, I, too, joined thousands of our predecessors and carved our names along with the year. When I finished, the permanent impression simply read, "Joe and Sterre 1936." The clumsy creation was surrounded by an eight-inch-square border.

The old medieval village made it easy for me to imagine damsels in distress being rescued by brave knights in shining armor. But there was little to fear in Valkenburg on the bright sunny summer day when we visited. The tourist town was overrun with visitors who filled its many small hotels and dined or enjoyed the multitude of restaurants and bars that lined her cobblestone streets.

I saw Sterre every day after that. I masterminded numerous excuses just to be by her side. There was no question that I was more than smitten.

As I had pledged to my mother, we visited my great-grandparents' gravesite. I shared with Sterre the promise I had made to my mother that I would place a tulip upon their graves in her memory, and, with Sterre's assistance, my mission was successfully accomplished. She provided the red tulip out of respect for my mother, even though they had never met. The very instant Sterre placed that red flower into the palm of my hand, I knew something special was happening. When her gentle, soft fingers touched mine, and I looked into her enchanting blue eyes, I knew I was a goner, but fought to keep my raging emotions in check. I spent those precious next few weeks working with her as well as with my uncles on their farms. The two of us made a determined effort to carve out special time so we could be together.

Over the coming days between frequent rainstorms, which were prevalent in the country, Sterre and I visited her school. We talked about my family life back in America and my career as a newspaper writer. She constantly quizzed me about all things American. She loved our movies, music, and dancing. As a teacher, she was especially interested in hearing about my education and our school system. Where most school districts in America are publicly funded, Limburg's school system is primarily operated by the Catholic Church with little government assistance. Our conversations veered in many directions, often resembling a strange history lesson.

"Were you aware that the Dutch once owned New York City and had settlements all around the area before the English took control later in the 1600s?" she asked. "Even your President Roosevelt is of Dutch ancestry!"

"I knew that Miss Smarty Pants, but were you aware his cousin Teddy Roosevelt was a descendant of the Netherlands, too, as was one of our older presidents, one Martin Van Buren? And he, my dear Sterre, spoke your language as a child before learning English later in his life," I playfully replied.

Continuing the conversation, she cheerfully informed me that Harlem is named after a Dutch city near Amsterdam, the word Yankee is frequently used by the Dutch to describe Americans, and that Knickerbocker is Dutch as well.

"That's pretty funny," I told her. "Now we crazy Americans use the name Yankee as the nickname of one of our favorite baseball teams. Even an odd little city called Hackensack got its name from the Dutch as well as three boroughs in New York, Brooklyn, Staten Island, and the Bronx. And if you push me even further, I can tell you that back in the 1600s, New York was originally called New Amsterdam and that its former Dutch governor, Peter Minuit, as legend tells us, bought, or should I say bamboozled, Manhattan Island from the native Indians for a few beads valued at less than $25.

"I love history, my darling Sterre!" I informed her as we both laughed about all the funny historical facts and tidbits we had just recited.

On the other hand, I became engrossed in everything Dutch, more specifically, everything about Limburg and especially her. I told her how I enjoyed Droste's Chocolate Cocoa, which came in a red tin container, decorated with a painted picture of a Dutch nun. A cup of hot chocolate made with their cocoa mix along with some Dutch mints and sugar cookies called stroopwafels became my favorites. I especially liked De Ruijter's Orange Sugar Hail, a sweet breakfast sprinkle, but not Douwe Egbert's coffee. The coffee was filled with so much caffeine that I could put it in my car and use it for fuel. Even when watered down, that stuff could redden the eyes and, jokingly I told Sterre, "grow hair on your chest." I much preferred a tasty Brand beer, one of the many fine beers brewed in Limburg, especially when served with a Frikandel Speciaal, a local sausage delight similar in shape to a thick hot dog wiener. Two days earlier and to my complete satisfaction, Judy, Uncle Wouter's daughter, grilled one of those succulent delicacies especially for me. I loved the taste, especially when doused in curry sauce imported to the Netherlands from the country's Indonesian colonies.

I quickly came to admire the Dutch and their attention to detail, from the locally produced Maastricht China to the expensive hand-painted Royal Delft De Porceleyne Fles coffee mugs and teapots, right down to the Mosa ceramic tiles that covered their floors. Some families I visited served soup in wooden bowls, which I found odd. I must report, however, that their light brown toilet paper felt like coarse sandpaper. That's one thing I'll further leave up to the imagination and won't miss in the least.

Yes, it rained a lot, but it was also the essential ingredient that kept the country's landscape so abundant and green. I wanted to learn everything I could about Sterre and her homeland, and the wet weather or a good party seemed always to encourage the discussion. One of those rainy evenings, I was at her house when the radio was tuned to a German broadcast, and her family listened attentively to every word spoken by the Nazi Fuhrer, Adolf Hitler. He was spewing propaganda, boasting about the greatness of his accomplishments and those of his Aryan "Master Race," my hosts interpreted for me.

"Aren't you all just a little fearful of his rhetoric?" I asked, curious about how they regarded his swagger. "I mean, the German border is only a few miles east of here, and he marched his troops into the Rhineland just four months ago! The Saarlanders voted last year to be reunited with Germany after being occupied by the Allies after the end of the Great War. To me, the chancellor of the Nazis seems somewhat a braggart and possibly a warmonger. How do you all feel?"

"The Netherlands is a neutral country, we're peaceful, so why should our country be fearful of the Germans?" Sterre's father, Paul, calmly answered, I thought, to settle his children. "We are of little importance to any of the great powers."

"Hitler, I agree, appears boastful, and since the war ended, he blames the Jews for all of Germany's problems. But he has put Germans back to work, and most of them seem to be very happy with him and his Nazi Party. Really, we Dutch have nothing to worry about, Joe. Who knows? Hitler may be voted out of office in their next election!"

After a pause, Sterre continued her father's train of thought.

"Joe, the Dutch do not pose much of a military threat to anyone. In that regard, we're like the Swiss. We share a common border with Germany, and we've had no major problems. Don't worry, Joe, we're safe here in Limburg. I'm sure you know that many people here speak German as well, and we stay abreast of what is going on there. Most of what we hear on the radio or read in Limburg's Dagblad newspaper appears to be positive."

"Well, I hope you're right for your sake," I said fretfully as her father left us to tend to his cows. "I'll get a better feel about the Nazis when I'm in Berlin in a few days. Maybe then I can learn to share your optimism."

Sterre found this an apt time to change the topic.

"The winter is a wonderful time to be here," she said. "In the winter, all of Limburg celebrates Carnaval, or, as we call it in Limburgish, Vastelaovend, and everyone eats and celebrates to their heart's content."

The beginning date of the Catholic-inspired festival changes from year to year but is normally held in February or March. Carnaval starts six weeks before Easter Sunday and is a pre-Lent celebration, one last hurrah before the austerity of the six weeks of Lent.

"The villages and cities have parades where almost everyone dresses in a costume and participates in the merriment some way or another. The fun lasts for weeks and many of the businesses close, but never the bars since there is a lot of drinking during Carnaval. I know you would love it, Joe," she declared.

"It sounds a little like the Mardi Gras party they have in New Orleans. Believe me, after Prohibition ended in the U.S. in 1933, the beer flows freely at home, too," I explained, to a confused Sterre.

"Prohibition?" she asked.

"Oh, I'm sorry, I should explain," I said, looking at her blank stare. "The sale of alcohol was illegal in the United States from 1920 until 1933, and that period was called the Prohibition Era."

"You mean no one could purchase liquor?" she asked, shocked.

"Well, not legally, but you could buy all you wanted illegally and many people did. That's why that crazy law was repealed. Do you understand?" I asked.

"Yes, but no. It sounds like everything is OK now. Is that so?" she asked.

"Yes, all OK!" I indicated by flashing a thumbs-up sign.

The conversation continued.

"Oh, Joe, I wish you could have been here at the beginning of June for Schimmert's Kermis Festival," Sterre said wistfully. "You would have loved it."

"Wait, my mother told me a little bit about the Kermis Festival. I remember her telling me all of the children follow the priest in a parade through the village with a band dressed like toy soldiers playing music."

I was unsure of my description and looked to Sterre to see if I had been accurate.

"Well, that's almost correct, but here in Schimmert, it's a very special holiday. You see, the entire village gets involved," she explained. "All of the children who are seven years old dress in white linen clothing and are led in a procession through town by our priest. Following him are the nuns, then the Montfort students, next are the little children and the town band, and lastly the parents, grandparents, and siblings of the seven-year-olds. The parade goes to all five of Schimmert's hamlets and stops at each of the little chapels where the children and the priest say a few words before the town festival commences at their school.

"The festival always involves music and games and the whole town participates. Each family of a special seven-year-old child decorates their home with flowers or garlands and spells out the child's name on a banner then places it on their front door.

"Our town's band is also very special. The members range in age from as young as nine to age 70 or older. Father plays the trombone and has performed with our band since the age of 12. He wears his brightly colored toy soldier uniform proudly, too!" she explained with a bright smile and a wink in reference to my earlier comment.

"You're right! I would have loved to see that parade. I played the saxophone in my high school band," I told her. "The first song I learned to play was an Austrian tune, Edelweiss."

"Really Joe, you need to practice so next year you can come back and be in our Kermis Festival and play alongside Father," she insisted with another big smile.

"I'd love that Sterre, I'd really love that."

"Do you hope to have children of your own someday, Sterre," I abruptly asked.

"Well, yes, I would hope to have a little boy or girl of my own someday, but I don't know if that will ever happen, Joe," she answered awkwardly.

"You would be a wonderful mother. I know that for sure," I reassured her. "You're going to make some fella a very lucky man someday. You deserve nothing but the best, and I'll bet you'll have five or six children, maybe more!"

She seemed amazed by my declaration.

"Well, that's not possible," she replied. "I'm 22 and getting a little old for that. Besides, it takes two people to make a baby, and there is only one of me.

"You know we have a time-honored tradition here. When the time comes that a child's pacifier is no longer necessary, its mother will place it in a shoe and replace it with a piece of special chocolate."

She demurely handed me a piece of her freshly handmade chocolate before asking about my plans for fatherhood.

"What about you, do you want children?"

"Of course, but there is only one of me, too. But if I ever did ask someone who'd be crazy enough to marry me and be the mother of my children, I would hope she'd be someone like you Sterre," I replied.

For a brief second, she looked a little anxious and began to blush. She seemed somewhat uneasy but pleased with my bold statement. It was one of those moments in which I felt we both wanted to be closer, and I seized upon the unspoken hint. But as I leaned in for a long overdue kiss, we were interrupted by Arjan, who had entered the room eager to show us a newborn calf in the barn. I gently reached for her hand, and we shared a forlorn look as we walked away unfulfilled.

Most evenings, Sterre, her brothers, and I would play table games or cards such as Keezbord, in which the playing cards describe the players' movements, or Sjoelbak, which is a small wooden version of shuffleboard. But my favorite game was Mens Erger Je Niet, literally translated as Don't Get Worked Up Guys. It was a maddening game that held true to its funny name.

Before play began, Sterre and her father prepared some local dishes to feast upon. They made knakwoorstjes (little sausages), kaasblokjes (cubes of cheese), borrelnootjes (mixed cocktail nuts), or bitterballen (deep-fried meatballs), which were even more delicious when dipped in warm applestroop (apple syrup), a favorite Dutch staple.

The conversation on one of those game nights focused on the differences in the way the Dutch and Americans celebrate Christmas, specifically the time-honored traditions of Ol' Saint Nicholas.

Arjan asked me curiously, "Joe, what do Americans call Sinterklaas?"

"Oh, you mean, Santa Claus! We call him Jolly Saint Nick and Santa Claus. He sports a long white beard and comes from the North Pole riding his sleigh pulled by eight flying reindeer," I informed him.

"Wait, Joe, you're talking too fast for me to understand, but did you just say that he comes from the North Pole on a flying sled pulled by flying reindeer?" Jim asked incredulously.

"Well, that's just silly. Everyone here in Limburg knows that Sinterklaas magically comes from Spain on a boat and once on land rides a white horse to all of the villages along with his little black assistant, Zwarte Piet, who passes out kruidnoten to waiting children who line the streets. Zwarte Piet also leaves gifts in burlap bags for children on December 6."

Proud of his explanation, Jim thrust out his chest and nodded in agreement with all but me.

"No, no, no," I insisted, "How can he be magical getting off a boat and riding a white horse? Our Santa Claus can fly through the air in his sleigh and deliver gifts to all of the children in the world in one night, on December 24, Christmas Eve! The children leave treats of milk and cookies as a snack for ol' Saint Nick.

"Who in the world is Zwarte Piet and what are kruidnoten?" I asked with a confused look.

"Joe, in English, Zwarte Piet means Black Pete, and kruidnoten are small gingerbread cookies," Sterre explained.

"OK, I still have no idea who Black Pete is, but I do get the kruidnoten,

I guess," I said as I continued. "In addition to bringing gifts, Santa Claus fills our stockings with candy, nuts and little surprises. The stockings are laid under the tree or hung from the fireplace mantle by the family earlier. There is no way that Sinterklaas can do all of that by horseback.

"Now, try to top that," I said smugly.

"In America, Christmas Day is celebrated on the 25th and the gifts are opened that morning, and the family enjoys a big meal together usually in the late afternoon or for dinner."

"I assume you are now finished gloating, Joe?" Sterre asked as she crossed her arms in amusement and confidently began making her case.

"I can easily top your story. Our tradition of Sinterklaas is much older than your Santa Claus. First of all, Sinterklaas has been coming to the Netherlands since the Middle Ages, and he doesn't wait until December 24 to deliver his gifts. As Jim said, he does that on December 6 in Limburg. The children leave him carrots and some sugar for his horse. Then they carefully take their shoes and place them near the door so Sinterklaas can fill them with goodies.

"So, Joe, my dear fella, Sinterklaas was here centuries before your Santa Claus. Case closed!" she laughed triumphantly. "Besides, the American Santa came from Dutch roots brought to America by Dutch settlers many years ago, so without the Dutch, you Americans would have no Santa Claus at all."

She concluded her argument and waved a finger in my face.

"Your point is well taken! Well, I guess you win your case by default, my dear Sterre, but would you agree that our Santa Claus might be more magical than yours since he can squeeze his fat body down countless chimneys while carrying millions of gifts in one tiny sleigh? He can fly, for God's sake! Doesn't that count for something?" I pleaded.

"OK, Cowboy Joe, we'll concede yours may be a little more magical, but our Sinterklaas wins on tradition. Agreed?"

I gave her that point as we all laughed together.

That conversation ended with Sterre and her brothers playfully humming an old Dutch Christmas carol called "Zu Zijt Wellekome" or "You Are Welcome." Her father watched our debate with good humor, but I could sense he felt that Sterre and I were becoming much more than mere friends.

That night, Sterre wanted me to tell her father and brothers why my family moved to America, and a little about my parents.

"Well, guys, do you want the short version or the long version?" I asked, hoping for the latter. Of course, they insisted on the longer one.

"OK, please interrupt me if it gets too confusing," I asked.

"Now this will be a mouthful, I'm warning you. My grandfather Wilhelm's father, Peter Schrijnemaekers, once owned and operated a successful textile business called Maastricht Textiel-en Productie, located just a few kilometers from his family's country home near Klein Haasdal. My grandfather studied languages at prestigious Leiden University at the insistence of his father, who valued a good education."

"Your grandfather went to Leiden?" Paul interrupted. "It's one of the best universities in the Netherlands, you know."

"Yes, I've heard that many times," I said. "My Oma Renee's and my Uncle Karl's father, Frans Westhovens, was the bookkeeper at Maastricht Textiel-en Productie and was also a close friend of my great-grandfather, Peter, his employer. Frans Westhovens, as you are aware, lived on his family's farm with his wife, Phyl, where their son, my Uncle Karl, currently lives."

"Do you all still understand this?" Sterre asked her family as she translated my dialogue. They were fine with her interpretation.

"Through the friendship of Peter Schrijnemaekers and Frans Westhovens, their children, my Opa Wilhelm, and Oma Renee met and later married. My grandparents had known one another since early childhood. However, the familiarity with each other's families led to their romance even though my Opa Wilhelm always insisted my Oma Renee chased him. He said she could not resist his good looks and charm. Who knew under that big beard he now wears once stood a handsome man!" I said with a grin.

"Now I understand it better, Joe," Paul said. "I knew your great-grandparents and your grandparents."

I nodded in Paul's direction and continued the tale.

"Unfortunately, my great-grandfather Peter's textile business fell upon hard times and the business closed in 1882, soon after my grandfather Wilhelm completed his university studies. My great-grandfather Peter lost everything, including his family's home and farm and died in Klein Haasdal in 1883, just a few months after my grandparents were married. Opa Wilhelm and Oma Renee moved in with her parents, the Westhovens, on their small farm on de Kling Road at Oensel. My mother was born at that farm in 1884."

I went on to share with the Trags family that my grandparents struggled during that period. Oma Renee attended to her sickly mother, Phyl, and helped her father and younger brother Karl with their farm while Opa Wilhelm tutored children from some of the wealthiest families of Maastricht and also helped with the farm. My mother told me countless times that life was very difficult for them during that period.

I looked at Sterre, Paul, Jim, and Arjan to make sure they were keeping up with the story. I seemed to have captured their attention so I plowed ahead.

"After Oma Renee's parents died, the pathway and their dream of going to America became a reality. Oma Renee's younger brother Karl, newly married to his wife Ceciel, who my Oma loved as a sister, inherited the family farm as was the Dutch custom. Unselfishly, Karl helped his only sister, my Oma Renee, finance her family's journey to America."

"Yes, I know your story so far, Joe, Ceciel's death during childbirth was tragic," Sterre's father acknowledged. "Like I said, I remember them and your mother. Both your mother and grandmother were beautiful young ladies, too. I know that for sure because I never forget a beautiful girl!"

The family laughed with appreciation at his admiration for the appeal of my mother and grandmother.

"Please go on, I like your history," Arjan encouraged me.

Everyone focused on my words as I kept going.

"Well, after living in New York City for a year, they moved west, and my grandfather Wilhelm, fortunately, found a job as a language professor at a university in Morgantown, West Virginia, and worked in a profession that he dearly loved. He, my Oma Renee, and my mother came to love Morgantown. Maybe the place would not have been every immigrant's American dream, but it was theirs. Grandpa Wilhelm's job at the university provided stability, and the academic atmosphere added a smidgen of prestige to the family.

"My Oma Renee was the polar opposite of my mother. She was reserved, a little passive, but very protective of my mother. She had a tougher time adjusting to the dramatic lifestyle change that was America in the early 1900s, but ultimately she came to feel more comfortable and slowly made the transition to her surroundings and her new home in Morgantown. The community opened its arms and welcomed my family wholeheartedly. It was almost heaven for them!

"My mother developed many friendships and attended Morgantown High School where she met and fell in love with my father, Raymond Lee Fisher, who was a year older. My father never graduated from high school, but my mother did with the class of 1902, a rarity for a young woman during that era. My father's parents were farmers, too. They owned a small farm of mostly mountainous terrain, about two kilometers north of Morgantown.

"Father's oldest brother, George, worked as a train engineer for the Morgantown and Kingwood Railroad, a newer spur line that mainly hauled coal and timber out of West Virginia's hills to the industrial cities of Pittsburgh and Cleveland. The M&K, as Uncle George called it, connected to the much larger Baltimore & Ohio Railroad at Morgantown. Uncle George encouraged my father to quit high school when he was only 17 because he wanted Father to work with him on the railroad and because it paid good money at the time when good-paying jobs were hard to obtain.

"Initially, both of my mother's parents were opposed to the idea of my mother marrying my father. They felt he was not up to the high standards they had envisioned for their only daughter's future husband. Reluctantly, they gave their blessings, and my father and mother were married on July 23, 1903, at the Wesley United Methodist Church in Morgantown. I was born exactly five years later on the same day in 1908. July 23 was always a day we reserved for a big celebration in our household. A few years after I was born, my father took a different job with the much larger B&O Railroad and trained to become an engineer like his brother George.

"My childhood in West Virginia was typical but very fulfilling. My parents emphasized the importance of studying hard and making good grades, to be a hard worker and respectful of my elders, to trust in the good Lord, and to be thankful for our health and our many blessings. At Morgantown High School, I was in the honor society, marched and played the saxophone in the band, and played baseball for the Mohigans, which was the name of our school's Indian tribe mascot. My favorite passions were baseball, hunting, fishing, camping out with my friends, and, of course, writing.

"While in college, to gain writing experience, I worked for free at a local newspaper called the Morgantown Post. They let me write a few sports articles, usually just high school stuff, but I loved it. No doubt, working at the Post whetted my appetite to follow an academic path that would hopefully lead to a job as a newspaper reporter."

"Are the women teachers single like here in Limburg?" Sterre suddenly asked.

"Of course not," I answered, a little confused.

"In Limburg, if a female teacher marries, she will most likely lose her job," she explained. "I don't like it, but it's true."

"I've never heard of such a thing," I replied. "So, you're telling me that you could lose your job if you got married someday?"

"I have a solution for you, Sterre," her brother Jim said with a chuckle.

"Just never get married, and you will always have a job teaching."

I decided that this might be a good time to change the awkward topic.

"During summer breaks in high school and college, I would help my Grandfather Fisher on his farm. I was fortunate to work there occasionally with my father or one of his four brothers, Preston, Leonard, Alfred, or Tom, but always with my grandfather, Frank."

"It's good, honest work to be a farmer, Joe!" Jim added enthusiastically.

"I agree, Jim. Working the farm with my family taught me all I would ever need to know about hard work. Eventually, my grandfather came to trust me enough to operate his tractor, which was his pride and joy. My main job with the tractor was cutting hay and storing it in his barn to feed his cows during the harsh winters we usually experienced in northern West Virginia. During those summers, I learned valuable lessons about hard work and discipline and all of the intricacies one needed to be a successful farmer. Mostly, I just loved the good times working alongside my grandfather and my father.

"After I finished my college studies, I landed a job at a newspaper in Bloomington in the state of Illinois, which is located about 800 kilometers farther west of Morgantown. My parents, along with my Grandfather Wilhelm, later moved to Bloomington where they now own and live on a small farm. I helped them with the move. Then two years ago, I was hired at my current job as a newspaper reporter with the Chicago Tribune, so I now live in Chicago. I know that was a long-winded story, but I hope it helps you understand better a little something more about me," I said.

"That was an interesting story even if I only understood about 25 percent," Paul said to everyone's amusement.

"Oh, Father, I will interpret for you tomorrow everything Joe said," Sterre promised as everyone headed to bed for the night.

CHAPTER EIGHT

COULD IT BE LOVE?

Early the next morning, as the two of them sat at their kitchen table drinking cups of hot tea, Paul began questioning Sterre about her relationship with me.

"Sterre, I have been carefully observing the way you and Joe look and interact with each other," he inquired with concern. "Is there something I should know, something you want to confide in me about? After all, any good father should always know when something is bothering his beloved daughter.

"Your blessed dear mother would most likely have been the person you wished to speak with about this sort of thing, but, unfortunately, she's no longer with us. But, remember, she still peers down on us from heaven above, my dear."

Surprised by her father's questioning, she quickly attempted to dispel his concerns.

"Oh, yes, Father, I know she is looking out for all of us," Sterre replied as she crossed her heart. "Well, to answer your anxieties, I do like Joe. He's different, Father. He's a good man like you, and he cares about people. I know Mother would have liked him. She could tell if a person had a good character, and I know you see that in him, too, don't you Father? You can tell Joe's a good man, too, can't you?"

Her question was posed with a little apprehension, but with the hope that her father might agree.

"Yes, I can see that, but how do you really feel about him?" Paul inquired, wanting to learn more. "I notice a lot more than you give me credit for, and I see something different in your eyes when you're with him. The boys and

I talk about how happy you appear to be when Joe's around here."

Sterre looked gratefully into her father's eyes and let slip without realizing what she was uttering: "I know Mother would have loved him, too!"

Paul immediately noticed her exuberance and questioned the word she had just spoken. "Loved! Did I hear you correctly? Did you just say you love him, my dear Sterre?"

With that unexpected revelation, she quickly put her hand over her mouth, closed her eyes, and started slowly nodding her head. "Did I say it, Father? Did I say, love?"

She then blurted out in sheer joy, "Father, I love him. I love Joe! I know it's been only four weeks, but I know in my heart that I love him. How did you and Mother know when you were falling in love? I want to hear that story. Please tell me!"

Sterre waited eagerly for her father's reply.

"Well ..." Paul began, still somewhat in shock. Sterre rose from her chair, sat down beside him, and put her arms around his neck as she did as a little girl needing fatherly reassurance and comfort.

"Ah, I fell for your mother when I was just 16 and she only 15," he confessed. "We were still teenagers when we married just three years later. Your sweet mother, Marjo, was the most beautiful woman I had ever seen until you came along, Sterre."

"Oh, Father, you're incorrigible. I remember very well how beautiful Mother was, and I saw how much you loved her. Please go on," she pleaded.

"I had known her my entire life, and we were childhood friends, and she was definitely the prettiest girl in the village. All of the boys liked her. She only lived a thousand meters away, you know, on Langstraat, and we went to church together every Sunday. One Sabbath day, we were walking home with some friends when one of them whispered in my ear that your mother liked me. I couldn't believe that she liked me. Me, for goodness sakes. She could have had her pick of any boy she wanted, you understand.

"Well, hearing that from her friend was like music to my ears. For some crazy reason, I walked right up to her, and, on impulse, I kissed her on the lips right in front of everyone. You should have seen her eyes. She was stunned, but flashed the most wonderful smile I'd ever seen. That's when I fell in love with your mother. I knew instantly!"

He smiled broadly and sighed as he recalled the moment.

"For months after, every time I was in the same room with your mother, my heart would flutter like a sail in the wind! I knew! Yes, I knew!" he remembered as he squeezed Sterre's quivering hand.

"Ah, you were quite bold in your youth, you tiger," Sterre teased with a little giggle.

"Have you told Joe how you're feeling?" Paul asked.

"I haven't told Joe anything, but my heart flutters, too. I can hardly wait until it's time to see him. I can't seem to get him out of my mind. I'm so confused. I've never experienced feelings like this before! I don't know what to do! He's leaving in a few days," she said with disappointment.

"He's an American. He lives in Chicago in the United States. What am I thinking, Father? I can't leave my family, not you, Father. I don't know what to do. I cry myself to sleep every night."

The two of them sat there for several more minutes holding onto one another, without uttering a word.

I, too, was in the midst of my own personal predicament. I'd spent the last 28 days in Schimmert and had only 7 more to go before I had to leave for the Olympics. Covering the games was my obligation, my profession. Falling for a Dutch girl named Sterre was unexpected. I was an emotional wreck, fighting an internal battle with my feelings.

"This cannot be happening!" I muttered to myself over and over, but I ultimately knew I could not control my heart. After all, I understood that it's nearly impossible to deny the heart what it desires. I finally came to that painful conclusion and realized even with all of the unimaginable obstacles before me, I had to tell her how I felt.

I desperately needed to talk to someone. That night Uncle Wouter provided a sympathetic ear.

I had been alternating between his and Uncle Karl's homes for the last month. Uncle Wouter was quiet, but a man of substance, an intelligent man even though he had only finished high school. He was well read, a trait he shared with my Opa Wilhelm.

One sultry summer evening, while his children were listening to their favorite mystery radio show, Uncle Wouter and I were alone in his barn. Uneasily, between sips of a warm locally brewed, Gulpener beer, I began to speak. Leaning against the open barn door, I surveyed the endless lush fields that surrounded us as I watched the sun sink on the distant horizon. Uncle Wouter walked over and placed his hand on my shoulder.

"You seem to be lost in the silence, Joe," he declared as we scanned the orange sky. "It's so easy to get lost in a beautiful sunset like that, isn't it?"

"Yes sir, it's very easy to get lost in many things here in Schimmert," I slowly responded using my best West Virginia southern drawl. "Mother predicted I would come to appreciate the silence here."

"Yes, I understand, and it's free to enjoy the calm especially by someone with a heavy heart. You're worried about leaving her in a few days, aren't you, Joe?" he inquired in a comforting tone. "An old farmer and father can sense these things, you know."

"Well, if you must know the truth, yes, I am thinking about her. She's all I think about these days. Initially, coming here I never expected anything to happen like this, but thinking about Sterre is driving me crazy, Uncle Wouter."

"It's driving me crazy!" I repeated emphatically.

"Does she feel the same way about you?" he asked.

"I think so. No, I hope she does," I responded.

"My son, it's just a natural thing when a man like you meets such a wonderful female companion like Sterre. I can easily understand why it must be so very troubling considering the two of you live in different countries and were raised in dissimilar cultures."

He conveyed the message with heartfelt sympathy.

"That's a big problem, and I have no good solution for it either. I can't think that far ahead right now. I just know the way I feel about her, and I'm just so confused. Do you understand my dilemma? If so, I could use some immediate help."

I hoped that he might have a simple solution for my complex predicament.

"I only know that when a man is lucky enough to find the right woman for himself, logic does not always matter. If Sterre is meant for you and you for her, then the good Lord above will find a way. He will guide you both and make a solution possible.

"Just two years ago, I had a similar talk with my daughter, Judy. She told me she was in love, at only 16, mind you. She was in love, she told me over and over. Well, it was true. I could see it in her eyes and in the eyes of her young man, Lukas. They loved each other. I realized that someday they would be husband and wife. It's never the right time, my boy. When you know, you know, and I can see it in your eyes, Joe. You know," Uncle Wouter reasoned.

"You're a wise man, Uncle. Yes, you're right, I do know," I replied with solid Limburger logic.

After church services ended on July 19, that last Sunday before I had to leave for Berlin, Sterre and I wanted to spend the rest of the day together. Excited, she insisted on taking me to a place we had not yet visited. She told me she had been saving her favorite spot in Schimmert for last, and wanted to show it to me before my departure.

We walked toward a clump of trees at the back border of Uncle Karl's property. As soon as we reached the area, we began clearing some tangled vines, and once the overgrowth was cleared, she pulled away a few small tree branches that had been hiding a large gray rock. As soon as I saw it, I put my hand over my mouth and shameless tears of joy filled my eyes. Astonished, I was certain Sterre's secret place was the same sacred fountain stone that my dear mother had described to me many times.

"This is my mother's fountain stone," I exclaimed. "Look, there's a small pool of water in the middle of that stone just like Mother described it to me. This is it! This is it!

"How long have you been coming here?" I eagerly asked.

"I've been coming here ever since my mother brought me here when I was just a tiny girl," she said. "We shared this place together as our own special little hideaway. She never brought my brothers here. This was our special place where only she and I could share our secrets and make our memories. We discussed our dreams just like the ones my mother shared with her best childhood friend."

I interrupted her with a question the answer to which I hoped I already knew.

"Who was your mother's best friend, Sterre?" I asked.

"My mother so loved her best friend," she continued. "She was a little girl from Schimmert who left with her parents for America when she was only 12 years old. She was a cherished friend who my mother never forgot. Her name was Rebekka Maria Sabien Schrijnemaekers.

"That's right, Joe. Your mother was my wonderful mother's best friend," Sterre proclaimed as she spoke, her lips trembling.

Sterre's mother Marjo died in 1935 in a senseless accident when the horse she was riding was spooked by a honking horn from a passing automobile. The horse reared, causing her to plummet to the ground where she broke her neck and suffered a fatal head injury. She died in her husband's arms just minutes after the fall. The official medical report ruled that she died from a brain hemorrhage. The report, however, did little to lessen the devastating loss that her husband and children suffered.

Sterre then reached into her purse, opened a faded letter, and handed it to me to read. The letter was dated May 17, 1933, and was addressed to Marjo Trags. I immediately recognized my mother's handwriting.

As I finished reading the letter, Sterre walked over and stood in front of me. She placed my hand in hers as I spoke with my voice quivering.

"Most of the letter was about me. Mother had written about how proud she was of me and my accomplishments. Mothers exaggerate a bit, you understand!" I chuckled.

"Amazingly, Mother mentioned in this letter her deep desire that I would someday come to Schimmert to meet Marjo and her family, and especially her daughter Sterre. Can you believe this? It's unbelievable! I knew Mother wrote letters to her brother Karl and to Uncle Wouter's wife, Ria. She mentioned some of her friends to me over the years, but I didn't realize her friend Marjo was your mother."

Sterre, too, was excited that our two mothers' dreams had indeed become a reality. She moved closer as she spoke.

"I stand here now with you, Joe, with my new best friend, a man from America who I have unexpectedly and happily fallen madly in love with. I don't know how you will react to what I have just revealed, but I know only how my heart feels, and I know without question that I love you, my dear Cowboy Joe."

Speechless for a second, I had just heard the three most magical words that I had longed to hear from the most wonderful person on the face of this good earth. The thrill of truly being in love shot straight to my rapidly beating heart. Sterre stood before me with her eyes closed and her head lowered, trembling as I gasped, searching for the appropriate words to respond to her revelation.

"I fell in love with you the very minute I first laid eyes upon you, my lovely, darling Sterre," I candidly burst out.

She raised her head and opened her star-struck eyes in joy and rushed into my waiting arms. We kissed, we hugged, we cried, in pure elation and joy. We were hopelessly in love!

Before leaving, I reached into my pocket and pulled out a quarter bearing the likeness of George Washington that Mother had given to me weeks before with a heartfelt request that I was about to fulfill. With Sterre's approval, I happily dropped the coin into the still, cool water. Our mothers' wishes had come true and, unbelievably, ours, too.

I was ecstatic in the days that followed our commitment to one another. We used our rapidly fading time to be with each other constantly. On July 23, all of my uncles and their children, Sterre's family, several nuns and Father Peter from the Catholic church, and a few of their personal friends surprised me with a party on my 28th birthday. It was held at Uncle Karl's barn. I was reminded again that news traveled fast in a small town when Sister Truus approached Sterre and me to congratulate us on our newly forged relationship. She wasn't the only one to do so. Sterre's best childhood friend, Kelly van Dyke, and another friend, Tiny Jergens, congratulated us as well.

The celebration was somewhat like ones held in America, except I had never tasted so many wonderful Limburger vlaai pies in my life. We ate moorkop, a pastry filled with whipped cream; nonnevot, another sweet pastry that translates hilariously to nun's butt; and koude schotel and hazarensalade, two local salad dishes. Everyone made me feel as if I were a beloved member of the community, not simply a traveler passing through town.

Sterre pulled me aside and presented me with a most special gift. She gave me her silver Christ cross to bring me good luck. Her mother had an identical cross that Sterre now wore. Every time I looked at my cross, I thought of her. I would treasure that precious gift for the rest of my life and realized its special powers had been at work since the day I arrived in Schimmert. Everyone in the room knew instantly that she and I were the lucky ones that day.

I dreaded to see Friday, July 24, draw closer, but it now was upon us, and I knew I had to face it head on and stay strong. The morning fog still lingered as the sun was just starting to peek over the horizon. I had trouble sleeping the night before and had risen early, planning to be at Sterre's doorstep as she awoke. My suitcase and duffel bag were packed and sitting by Uncle Karl's front door.

That afternoon I was to meet Al at Cologne's Hauptbahnhof, the city's central train station, but all I could think about was Sterre. My heart broke every time I contemplated the unpleasant thought of leaving her in just a few short hours. The pain was nearly unbearable.

As I opened Uncle Karl's front door, I was elated to see Sterre pacing in his front yard. I rushed to her, took her in my arms, and kissed her like never before. When my lips pressed against hers, I sensed her despair, which raced through my soul as well. Without uttering a single word, we continued to hold tightly to each other as tears flowed down her lovely cheeks. Talking at that moment was unnecessary. We both fully understood what was happening and loathed the prospect of not knowing what would be in store for our relationship.

"I will come back," I promised her again and again. Every time I spoke those words, it reminded me how difficult that might be, but I knew I had to find a way. Something wonderful had happened to me in Schimmert, something that I had never expected to experience there. I was hopelessly in love! For some strange reason, it felt as if it were the most maddening emotion ever. My head was spinning, and my heart was beating so fast I feared it might burst right out of my chest. I realized I had to be strong for Sterre, so I focused all of my remaining attention that dreadful morning on her. She was distraught. I could clearly observe the sorrow in her pale blue eyes and felt her pain in the touch of her shaking hands.

"Smile for me," I said.

"OK," she replied simply as she regained her composure.

"I will wait for you, my dear Joe. I promise. I've never felt this way about anyone in my life, and yet I barely know you, and that's what's so crazy about everything. Am I going mad or something?" she asked with a confused stare.

"No, Sterre, I don't understand what is happening to us either. All I know is that I've never been happier in my 28 years. I know without a doubt that I love you, my darling, with all of my heart. I can't explain it, but I know it is true," I insisted.

"Me, too, Joe, I know I love you, too," she said softly.

"We will find a way. Please trust me, we will find a way," I reassured her.

As we waited for Uncle Karl to drive us to the train station, we walked down de Kling Road to gather our racing emotions. We needed a brief time just to laugh a little and allow our minds to roam to a better place. On our way back to the farm, I noticed Uncle Karl standing next to his truck smiling at us as we trudged ever closer to him.

"Ready, Joe, my boy? And goedemorgen to you, too, sweet Sterre. You come with us as well today?" he jokingly asked in his broken English with a hearty laugh and a wink.

"Yes, Uncle Karl, you know very well I could never leave this place without her by my side," I sheepishly replied as we all laughed, fully knowing the answer to his foolish question. I then reached for Sterre's hand and helped her up into the cab of the truck.

When we reached the Maastricht train station, I knew I would be leaving her from that majestic light brownish brick building all too soon. Uncle Karl unloaded my baggage so I would not lose a precious second of time with Sterre. I barely remember walking through the station. My attention was elsewhere. I gazed deeply into those big blue eyes and saw my own reflection as she stared back. It was as if her eyes were a razor slicing its way directly into my broken heart. I took a long look at her and impulsively, but tenderly, began to sing softly into her ear.

"Heaven ... I'm in Heaven ... And my heart beats so that I can hardly speak ... And I seem to find the happiness I seek ... When we're out together dancing cheek to cheek."

She flashed a bright smile but continued to cry. I knew without question that Sterre felt exactly the same as I.

"Do you dance like Fred Astaire as well?" she kidded.

"Ginger, give me your hand, and I will boogie-woogie with you until the cow jumps over the moon," I responded while attempting to lighten the mood as another gorgeous smile appeared on her lovely face. The silly ploy worked!

While in the midst of a long kiss, the train slowly began to pull away from the station's platform. I did not want to leave her but knew I had no choice.

I leaned in for another kiss and repeated several times, "I will be back, I promise, my love. I will be back in three weeks."

I quickly shook Uncle Karl's hand and left him standing alone while Sterre ran along beside me as the train continued to move. Recklessly, I hopped aboard the train's carriage steps still holding her shaking hand for a final squeeze. I did not move an inch and never looked away. All I could do was lovingly stare at her now reddened face while she waved frantically, left behind and weeping at the far end of the platform.

As the train gently rolled down the tracks, both of us cried out over and over again, "I love you, I love you" until our images faded from one another and our voices could no longer be heard.

CHAPTER NINE
BERLIN OR BUST

My trip from Maastricht to Cologne that morning was like a daydream. I remember changing trains in Aachen, but, otherwise, the entire ride was just a blur. Aachen was located just a short distance over the Dutch border from Maastricht and was the first large German city that I'd ever seen. It was famous for being the imperial capital of the Holy Roman Empire under Charlemagne, who was the first recognized emperor of Western Europe after the Romans.

All I could think about was Sterre, and every few minutes I would catch myself wondering where she was at that very moment. I wished, of course, that she was with me.

I vaguely remember the German train conductor asking for my ticket and passport once we crossed the border into his country. Directly behind him, a man in a military uniform gave me the once-over. His English was difficult to understand, and he peppered me with questions. He wanted to know where I was going, who I was planning to visit, why I was in Germany, what I was scheduled to do, and when I expected to leave. I kept saying to him, "I'm going to the Olympics," but I don't think he believed me.

As the train pulled alongside the concrete platform in Cologne's Hauptbahnhof, the main rail terminal, I hardly noticed the bright sunlight shining through the iron-and-glass roof. I was concerned that Al might have forgotten our meeting time. Our arrangement was to meet between 1:00 and 5:00 p.m., or as stated on the schedule 1300 and 1700 Greenwich Mean Time.

Even though ol' Al was full of German blood, being timely was never his strong suit.

"Oh well," I muttered to myself as I ate lunch while waiting. Even though I understood little German, I still enjoyed listening to the hordes of people as they passed my table. When I became tired of sitting, I walked outside the station's front doors and discovered the crown jewel of the city's skyline standing just a few hundred feet away. I gazed at Cologne's impressive, twin-towered Cathedral Church of Saint Peter, a medieval Gothic church on which construction began in 1248, a mere 244 years before Christopher Columbus sailed for the Americas.

It was 4:15 p.m. when I finally spotted Al coming through the entryway at the far end of the massive train station, looking like he owned the place and strutting with a woman on each arm.

When he saw me he began to yell, "Hey, Joey, Al's got a present for you. Do you like them blonde or brunette? It makes no difference to me which one you choose, you know, because I love them both."

"God save me!" I sighed barely audibly, before taking a deep breath. We shook hands and hugged as if we hadn't seen one another in years, although it had been only a few weeks.

"Al, I don't know how you could ever top that entrance, you crazy Hun," I said.

"Joey, over here they refer to me as Herr Alfred, right, fräuleins? That's German for a young, single lady, Joey!"

"Jawohl, Herr Alfred," they replied.

"Aren't they two beautiful dames, Joe? We've had a ball over here in 'Der Fatherland.' The beer is even beautiful over here, and the fräuleins are a little friskier, too, if you know what I mean, Joey," Al said with a wink.

"How much time do we have, Joe? Enough time for a beer or two with these two cuties before we depart for Berlin?"

"Yeah, Al, whatever you say, a beer or two sounds good. Our train doesn't leave until 7:45, but you know the Germans, 7:45 means 7:45. You'd better have at least one foot in your train car, or you'll get left behind," I deadpanned.

After a couple of hours of fun with his two flirty female companions, we said our goodbyes and rushed to the train station's track number three.

At 7:40 p.m., we boarded our train for Berlin and settled into our compartment, which had two rows of cushioned bench seats facing each other. Each row held three adults comfortably with storage racks above for luggage. At exactly 7:45, as stated on our ticket stubs, our train departed Cologne. We were scheduled to arrive in Berlin at 6:02 the next morning with two stopovers to change trains, one in Hannover for two hours and the other in Potsdam for an hour and 45 minutes.

We were excited about the Olympic Games and talked incessantly for the first hour or so about the stories we intended to write and the unique angles we wished to create so our readers back home would feel as if they were sharing the seats right beside us at the events. We talked about the athletes we hoped to interview as well as the storylines we proposed to explore. We also intended to write a few columns about our personal adventures while traveling abroad.

Overwhelmed by our own laughter, Al and I pretended to practice our acceptance speeches for the Pulitzer Prizes that we would win for our exceptional writing skills. The more silly ideas and accolades we fancifully envisioned, the more we realized how ridiculous we had been for even dreaming that a Pulitzer would ever be in the cards for two young Chicago Tribune scribes like us. Still, we had a fun time acting out our phony fame.

My enthusiasm waned as I started thinking about Sterre. I was uncomfortable at first to speak to Al about her. I kept trying to gauge how he would react. Would he label me crazy, or would he help me figure out a way to solve my seemingly impossible dilemma? My mind was swirling, but I knew I had to break the news to him sometime, somehow. With the two of us trapped alone in our tiny compartment, I thought what better time and place than now? Besides, he was my best friend, and even though Al was Al, I valued his honest opinion.

I decided to just blurt it out: "Al, I've got something that I have to tell you before I explode."

"Yeah, what's her name, Joey?" he astutely replied.

"What makes you think it's about a woman, big shot?" I quickly responded, a little unnerved by his correct assessment.

"When a man is as nervous as you've been since we met in Cologne, I figured, what else could it be? Remember, this is ol' Al, your best pal, you're talking to, and don't forget, I can read you like a book. When a man has his brain focused on a dame, he gets a little flustered like you are right now."

"Tell me I'm wrong, Joey! I knew right away something was up when you rejected my offer about taking one of those fräuleins off my hands back there at the train station. This girl who's gotten into your head must be some broad for you to turn down the juicy offer I made you with those two girls. Now, with all of that drama out of the way, tell me everything and don't leave out any details, Casanova," he finished with his eyebrows raised.

"You think you know everything, don't you?" I shot back.

"I know women, and this one must be special because I can tell she's got you by the horns, including the one between your legs, I'll bet," he said as he laughed out loud.

"Well, first of all, first of all, well, first of all," I stuttered, "you're right, you silly Hun. She's got my mind all scrambled like a bunch of eggs in a skillet. I don't know what to do, Al! Have you ever seen me in such a fix? I'm going back to the United States in a month and may never see her again after that. What was I thinking?"

"I've never met anyone like her, Al. She's beautiful, kind, thoughtful, caring, and just perfect. Oh, my God, Al, she's perfect!" I said with a tortured look on my pitiful, troubled face.

"Perfect! Seems to me like you just described a Girl Scout, Joe! Oh, no, oh, no, are you in love with this gal, Joe?" Al asked, shaking his head in disbelief.

"Frankly, Al, to be honest, yes, I am in love with Sterre. I love her, Al. I know I do. It's real love, Al, the kind you can feel in your bones, in your soul," I said, baring all to my best friend.

"Sterre! What kind of name is that? Real love? I've never had any experience with that emotion before, Joe. I don't have a clue how to help you with any of that," Al continued with his questions. "I mean, I can see it in your face, my friend. You really are in love, Joey, I guess!

"I knew I should have stayed with you in Sillymert, and then none of this would have happened! I would have taken care of you," he said.

"Skim-mert, Skim-mert, that's how the town's name is pronounced, Al," I corrected him in frustration. "The name means 'to shimmer or to shine'. Legend has it that ol' Charlemagne himself loved the place so much that he supposedly name the village, Schimmert. And I didn't need anyone to take care of me either. It's just inevitable, my friend, you know, boy meets girl and all of that stuff."

"Whatever," he conceded. "We've got a problem to solve, ol' boy. Man, do we have a problem to solve! We need to wrap our heads around this situation and analyze the circumstances to come up with a logical conclusion, and we will, Joey. I promise you that. We will. But, first, I'm just going to close my eyes for a few hours to clear my mind of any distractions."

Al leaned back in his seat and closed his eyes as our train made another station stop.

A short time later, our compartment door opened, and in walked a beautiful blonde who appeared to be in her twenties. Al perked up very quickly, of course, and immediately began tending to her every whim. He neatly stacked her luggage and then stood holding her hand like a gentleman while insisting she takes the seat beside him. He initiated a long conversation with her right away, zooming in like a hawk in search of its prey. She went by Agnes, I gathered from their conversation in German. She held Al's full and undivided attention for the rest of our trip to Berlin.

I ended up being the one who tried to get some rest, but enduring thoughts of my enchanting lady from Limburg constantly interrupted my attempts to catch a little shut-eye.

"So, this is what love is all about," I asked myself, grinning as I tried my best to doze off.

Before we departed the train station in Berlin, Al secured a lunch date with Agnes. She agreed to meet him in two days at the famous Café Kranzler on Unter den Linden Boulevard in the Mitte district of the city. She invited me to join them, but on cue with a nudge from Al, I politely declined the invitation. I took the hint and naturally figured Al would prefer lunch be only for the two of them. Three people, I realized, would be one too many. Nonetheless, I marveled at the tried-and-true techniques that he so successfully deployed with unsuspecting members of the opposite sex. For the rest of that day in Germany's capital city, I referred to him as Don Juan Obermeyer.

As soon as we stepped onto Berlin's streets, Agnes noticed that Al and I seemed lost and in urgent need of a little help. She flagged down a taxi and directed the driver to take us to a part of town where she knew a local family that owned a boarding house. To our relief, she also hopped into the cab. With her persuasive powers, the innkeeper agreed to put us up throughout the games, but at an insanely inflated price. Without hesitation, Al and I quickly agreed to take the room, especially since it was being paid for by the Tribune.

The quaint, little boarding house was located on KluckStraße, just south of the Tiergarten, the city's largest park, near the center of Berlin. It was only 2 ½ miles from Olympic Stadium, which we would be visiting many times during the next few weeks.

We shared a room in the house owned by Dieter and Gitte Heinz and their fluffy German rex bred cat, Raquel. They were a fun-loving couple and were extremely accommodating to Al and me during our three-week stay. They weren't Nazis, but instead a warm-hearted, loyal German couple who were just trying to make ends meet. Dieter had served in the German army as an infantryman and fought in the trenches of Belgium and France during the Great War. He was proud of his military service and, as we later learned, a decorated soldier. He'd been awarded the Iron Cross, one of Germany's highest military honors, for his bravery during the war. He displayed his treasured medal, mounted in a picture frame that was proudly perched on their dining room mantle for all visitors to his inn to admire.

The stage was set for the start of the 11th Modern Olympic Games in Berlin on August 1. In German, it was referred to as the Olympische Sommerspiele 1936. In 1931, the city had been awarded the privilege of hosting these games over Barcelona, Spain.

Ironically, on July 26, just nine days after Spain's Civil War began and only five days before the opening Olympic ceremonies, Axis Powers Germany and Italy agreed to send military equipment and supplies, including air support, to General Francisco Franco, the right-wing Spanish nationalist rebel leader, in his fight against the Republican democratic government. The buzz spread quickly all over town that Sunday morning about Germany's decision to support Franco, but eerily the unsettling decision had become an afterthought by evening mealtime. The Olympics dominated talk among ecstatic Berliners that late July and no civil war in Spain was going to dampen excitement over their vibrant city's hosting of the games.

Early the next day, writers representing most of the world's major newspapers received press passes that would allow them access to the major Olympic events, including the opening and closing ceremonies, which were expected to be spectacular. The Germans had gone all out in preparing the city in hopes of impressing the whole world that would be watching and listening to the much anticipated athletic events.

We decided to give the U-Bahn, Berlin's subway, a whirl and took the underground railway to the Charlottenburg section of the city where the Olympia Pressehauptquartier (Olympic Headquarters for the Press) was located. After getting our press passes, we were each given a medium-sized, zippered, leather briefcase loaded with maps of the city, including a detailed description of the Olympic Stadium complex, along with a schedule of events plus bus and U-Bahn routes in German and English.

The packet also listed the locations of the best restaurants, movie theaters, and clubs with intricate descriptions of the best shops. The officials told us that we could even request an interpreter, if necessary. We sat through a short lecture for reporters that outlined where the press corps was to be placed at each venue for the finest views of the events. In addition, we were shown the top places to interview the athletes before and after their competitions. After a half day of listening to the informational seminars, we quickly bolted from the place to take in the sights and sounds of Berlin.

The entire city sparkled. It was clean, right down to the trolleys, taxis, double-decker buses, and subways. That German efficiency that I'd often read about was on full display. The dynamic city was on the move as construction cranes and scaffolding arose in every direction across the capital's skyline. The wide streets and tree-lined boulevards were perfectly aligned, nary a bulb out on any of the metal-cast lights perched on precisely straight lamp posts. The town was adorned with Nazi Party flags on every major building and monument, all draped in the now familiar black swastika symbol within a white circle surrounded by a red background.

I got a little homesick when I spotted a Coca-Cola ad that read, "Ein Volk ein Reich ein Getrank Coke ist es," which Al translated for me: "One People, One Nation, One Drink, Coke is it." It felt a little awkward to see that truly American iconic logo plastered on a sign that featured not only the Olympic rings, but also the Nazi eagle grasping a victory wreath with the swastika etched inside.

People were smartly dressed and appeared very upbeat, and they all happily offered instant assistance when asked. I didn't know what to expect when I first set foot in Berlin, but I was pleasantly surprised by the German hospitality. Many people seem to be wearing some sort of uniform, and everyone else looked as if they were donning their Sunday best. I saw adults and children wearing black uniforms, gray uniforms, blue uniforms, brown uniforms, and an array of other colors.

Young boys in groups similar to our own Boy Scouts marched around everywhere in their brown shirts and short black pants, and they always seemed to be singing an upbeat marching song. The young men were called "Hitlerjugend", or, in English, Hitler Youth. Almost everyone seemed to be wearing a swastika armband on their left sleeve, and I never witnessed so much saluting in my life.

The shops and street vendors offered an odd assortment of souvenirs all bearing some sort of Olympic theme. They sold decorative plates, watches, clocks, rings, ashtrays, necklaces, lapel and coat pins, cigarette lighters, little Nazi flags, postcards of famous German athletes, and, lastly, keepsake photos of Adolf Hitler in various poses, which giddy purchasers gobbled up quickly. Al and I purchased our share of souvenirs as well.

Though I had originally declined to meet Agnes for lunch, Al persuaded me to join them out of pure guilt, and I reluctantly agreed to tag along. It was almost 1:30 in the afternoon before we arrived at the front door of the Cafe Kranzler. We eventually found Agnes, sitting at a table for two sipping on what she said was her third cup of tea. The well-known cafe, along with many of the city's most hallowed structures, including the Berlin Cathedral, was conveniently located on the most famous boulevard in the city, the Unter den Linden. The landmark road was named for the thousands of linden trees that lined its sidewalks.

Hanging high on the impressive government buildings located on both sides of the broad boulevard was a multitude of red Nazi and Olympic flags, some as long as 30 feet. The Kranzler featured local German delicacies with seating for dining inside or outside. If guests wished to sit outside, they could choose either a table on the sidewalk in front of the main entrance or one on the second-story balcony. Regardless of their decision, customers in both locations enjoyed a bird's eye view that was a perfect spot for people watching.

"Doll, sorry we're late, but believe me when I say Joe and I tried everything possible to get over here as fast as we could. And, by the way, you look terrific, baby," Al greeted her and planted a smooch on her right cheek.

"She looks great, doesn't she, Joey?" Al asked.

"Yes, my dear, you do look beautiful. Agnes, I'm Joe. I hope you remember me from the train?" I said.

"Sure, I do, Joe, from the train on Saturday and also from the boarding house. Of course, I remember you, Joe. My memory is not that bad!" she pointedly replied.

Just then, Agnes looked at Al and, without saying a word, clearly indicated with her body language that she wasn't overly pleased that ol' Joe was there for their lunch date, which, she correctly assumed, was made for just the two of them.

Al explained that he couldn't bear leaving a lost puppy like me alone in such a big city. But soon after his lame excuse, I was laughing and joking with her like we were long-lost school chums.

I could tell Agnes was a swell girl. She elegantly wore her chic blue dress and her stylish high heels with a touch of class well beyond her years. Her blonde hair and blue eyes fit the bill as to what a beautiful German woman should look like. Without question, she was a knockout, and Al, I could tell, was totally enamored.

After a few drinks, the conversation turned political.

"Joe, I sure have learned a lot in the short time we've been in Europe, especially here in Germany. Have you ever seen a place so alive, yet so well organized? Even the trams and buses run on time. The women are gorgeous. I mean just look at Agnes. Boy, she's something else," he gushed.

"The new roads are magnificent, too. Back in Cologne, my uncle let me drive his car, and I headed straight for a newly built section of the Autobahn, Germany's new four-lane highway system now under construction across the country. You can get anywhere fast driving on those roads, and everyone

I've spoken to gives Hitler the credit for getting them built."

"There seem to be plenty of jobs, too. I passed thousands of people working on bridges, surveying and laying out new roadways. They were cutting through solid rock mountainsides with handheld hydraulic jackhammers, chopping down massive trees, and moving dirt with gigantic steam shovels. They loaded the debris onto dump trucks or small trains and moved it elsewhere to be used as fill material. Believe it or not, I even saw thousands of laborers digging with mere picks and shovels on the autobahn and other building projects.

"Joe, my relatives are excited by promises from Hitler about every German family owning their own car in the near future, too. They called these yet-to-be-built cars Volkswagens, or 'people cars.' They can be paid for in advance by purchasing stamps and once your stamp book is full, you get a car. Supposedly, Hitler admired automaker Henry Ford back home, and was impressed by his assembly-line production methods."

Al paused momentarily in his praise of German innovation, giving me a chance to make an observation about what we had learned earlier from the Engels.

"That all sounds well and good, Al, but what about what we've been hearing about the way the Nazis are treating the Jews and other groups that oppose their ideology," I said. "Remember what the Engel brothers said to us on the ship and their uncles reiterated to us in London?

"Haven't you noticed the signs that say 'Juden Verboten' on the shop windows, at movie theaters, and even in the parks? The Nazis purportedly locked up anyone who opposed them such as communists, Jews, or leaders from rival political parties. We've both heard the rumors about forced labor camps in beautiful Germany."

"Yes, of course, I've heard those rumors, too, but maybe that's all it is, Joe, just rumors," Al offered with raised eyebrows.

"Think for a minute, Joe," Al continued. "I've been in Germany a little longer than you, and I'm no expert, mind you, but let me tell you what I've learned. First, the average German is not a member of the Nazi Party; most are just good people like you and me who only want a better life for their families. Second, the people I've spoken with have told me that after the Great War, their country faced starvation and massive inflation, and more than six million Germans were put out of work during the depression. Finally, they say the Nazis have reversed all of that prior negativity, and now most of the people here seem to have embraced that new energy by displaying some hope. They see positive results with all of the new jobs that have been created. Just two weeks ago, I took a boat trip down the Rhine River Valley, and even I was amazed."

Al continued without pause, "The bustling river valley was bursting at the seams with commercial activity, with hundreds of boats and barges floating on the river and trains running along tracks on both sides of its banks. They were constantly streaming past. I saw trucks and ships filled to the brim with coal, steel, and manufactured goods. People were visiting old medieval castles atop vineyard-covered mountains that stretched from their peaks down to the valley floor. The roads were full of vehicles of all types, including horse-drawn wooden wagons full of vegetables or hay. Workers were in the fields harvesting their crops."

"Everywhere, boys dressed in lederhosen and little girls with pigtails carrying leather backpacks strapped to their shoulders were happily going about their business. Their well-built, half-timbered houses were neat and tidy with no slums in sight."

"The shops and street vendors were teeming with customers, and smokestacks at factories were belching smoke. I passed marching bands and parades and noticed those same Nazi flags on buildings and poles everywhere I traveled. And would you believe this, Joey? They started this holiday public service organization for workers called 'Kraft durch Freude,' in English, 'Strength through Joy,' where they and their families can enjoy discounted or free vacations and cruises. They even set up free public concerts and sporting events for them as well. Isn't that incredible?"

"Al, that sounds a little like what the Roman emperors did to control the masses back during their ancient empire days, but with no gladiatorial contests and less violence, of course," I cracked with a grin.

"Funny, wise guy!" he fired back.

"Haven't you noticed all of the soldiers milling about?" I asked. "They appear everywhere -- on trains, at train stations, at hotels, on street corners and cafés and bars, just everywhere. That's something we don't see in Chicago or New York, and I hope we never do."

Al nodded slowly, grudgingly conceding my point.

"I've noticed the military presence all around, too, but it seems from the naked eye that Hitler's dictatorship must be working here in Germany, 'Ein Volk, ein Führer, ein Reich,' " he reasoned. "You know I'm all about our democracy and the all-American way of government, Joe, but our way of managing things is relatively new to these European countries. Most of them, until just recently, has been ruled for centuries by monarchs and kings."

The time to change the conversation was signaled by a Black Forest cuckoo clock mounted high on the café's wall that began to chime. Agnes had been sitting there quietly pretending not to understand a word of our discussion, but I felt she may have been too afraid to enter any political talk concerning the Nazis in such a crowded public venue. After all, Nazi informants could be anywhere, and she well knew it.

Across the street from our cafe, we observed a group of marching teenage girls all wearing blue skirts with white blouses filing past on the wide boulevard. All of them were singing happily in unison as they paraded by in perfect step.

"Agnes, I've noticed these girl groups all over Germany. What are they called, and why are they always marching?" Al inquired. "They seem too young to be in the military."

"You are right," she replied. "They are not in the military. They are young girls between 14 and 18 years of age. They are members of the Bund Deutscher Mädel in der Hitlerjugend, or, for short, the BDM."

"The what?" I questioned.

"In English, the name would be The League of German Girls or Maidens in the Hitler Youth," she readily explained. "You will see the BDM all over Germany in almost every town and village. Girls can first join the Jungmädel, or Young Girl's League, as early as the age of 10 and then the BDM upon reaching age 14. It's the only organization for girls in the country allowed by the government.

"I would have joined the BDM myself, but was too old to be a member when they first organized. I would have loved to have been one of those lucky girls," she sighed.

"The girls look so happy because they are serving our country, and they are learning how to be wonderful mothers and homemakers someday. They learn about sewing, cooking, and many other lessons such as how to care for babies and even learn some farming techniques. They are taught to be obedient through sports and exercise and participate in swimming, gymnastics, hiking, running and all types of fun athletic games. They also attend classes where they are taught how to be proper German ladies."

She added with pride that the BDM gave all young girls a sense of purpose, and belonging to an organization bigger than one's self-taught them the benefits of camaraderie and of self-sacrifice for the common good of all Germans.

"You said all girls. Can Jewish girls join?" I asked.

"No, they are forbidden. The Nazis say the Jews will never be allowed to be members since they don't have the racial purity or pure Aryan blood required for membership," Agnes explained.

"Racial purity! Aryan blood! Who in this world gets to decide who is pure?" I thought to myself as we abruptly ended the conversation.

That night, we hit more than our share of bars at the infamous Berlin nightclubs on Friedrichstrasse, which was like New York's Broadway and was alive with music and dancing. The area's clubs showcased staged acts such as acrobats, comedians, singers, or contortionists and, of course, scantily clad showgirls were featured at almost every establishment. The city was filled with outdoor cafés and bars, and beer flowed everywhere as good cheer and laughter spilled out into the streets well into the night.

Berlin was a festive place, and I realized how lucky I was to have been handed this gig. Still, there seemed to be an uncomfortable sensation amid all the orderly precision. The undercurrent was so thick, one could almost cut it with a knife. It felt like the good-natured excitement and enthusiasm were a little too well rehearsed, even fake.

"But surely every German could speak freely and voice their own opinion. Or could they?" I wondered.

Over the next few days, Al spent almost all of his waking hours with Agnes while I kept busy planning which events to see and even wrote a few short stories and had them wired to the Tribune, using my name and Al's as authors since he was preoccupied.

I explored Berlin as a star-struck tourist. I visited Brandenburg Gate, the impressive imperial Roman-columned gate and the most distinctive monument in the city, featuring "Quadriga," its stone-carved goddess of victory perched atop the building driving a chariot pulled by four charging horses while in her right hand she held a shaft topped by an eagle. The fierce bird was clutching a wreath circling an iron cross symbolizing Germany's defeat of France and her armies led by General Napoleon Bonaparte in 1815. I saw the ruins of the German capital building called the Reichstag which was almost completely destroyed by a mysterious fire in 1933. I toured the palatial residence of Stadtschloss, which was the royal residence of former Kaiser Wilhelm II before he was forced to abdicate his throne in 1918 after Germany's defeat in the Great War. The palace stood across the street from Lustgarten Park, one of the city's finest. I also rode a small passenger boat down the Spree River and went to the Zoolog Garten, the city's magnificent zoo.

I watched the changing of the guard in front of the air ministry building and rode trains on rails situated high above the crowded streets on elevated metal girders similar to those found in Chicago. People danced and bands performed on concrete dance floors at outdoor cafés and in venues all over the city's fabulous parks. In one, I noticed sophisticated women were smoking cigarettes attached to elongated ivory holders seemingly oblivious to their status and between puffs, they sporadically sipped sparkling white Mosel or Riesling wines from their long-stemmed glasses.

I took so many photographs of bronze statues and monuments dedicated to former Prussian leaders and war heroes depicting past military triumphs that I lost count. The most impressive site was the Column of Victory surrounded by avenues teeming with traffic. The column was built to depict Prussia's crushing victory over France in the Franco-Prussian War of 1870. I took an electric trolley car over to Potsdamerplatz, which was Berlin's equivalent of Times Square in New York City. I spent almost an entire day there sitting on a park bench, taking in the enthusiastic atmosphere that captured the glimmering German capital city in expectation of the Olympic Games.

Circular billboards about 10 feet tall were plastered with posters featuring the face of Hitler or Olympic events, and men walked around selling newspapers and magazines from wooden racks attached to leather hangers resting on their shoulders. The traffic-congested streets were filled with Mercedes-Benz and BMW automobiles, crowded buses and trolleys, horse-drawn carriages, bicycles, and an odd assortment of motorcycles, some accessorized with three wheels or sidecars.

Lastly, I enjoyed taking a bus ride about 15 miles southwest of Berlin to the cool, clear waters of Wannsee Lake. Once there, I took an afternoon dip as I watched hordes of giddy teenagers and people of all ages and sizes frolic on its beaches covered with white sand imported from the Baltic Sea. I tasted every variation of the local cuisine listed on the German-language menus, from sauerbraten and swinebraten to bratwurst and sauerkraut and huge salty pretzels. I loved them all, especially the apple strudel and the Berliner Pfannkuchen, a deep-fried pastry similar to our doughnut. I was thoroughly enjoying Berlin.

Although the mood in the city was festive and gay, in the back of my mind my inner thoughts were somewhat tainted as I repeatedly remembered the dire warnings and terse comments echoed by the Engels in London. Their precautious descriptions painted a darker picture of Germany complete with a more sinister undertone of their uncle's Berlin hometown.

Flashes of their alerts seemed unfounded until we witnessed the aftermath of a brutal beating when we passed a crowd on the street who had witnessed a disturbance. According to Agnes, an old Jewish couple had wandered into a restricted area where they were previously told by the authorities to avoid while the Olympics were being conducted. For no apparent reason other than unintentionally ignoring a posted sign directed at Jews, the pair was thrashed by a young group by Nazi thugs, who after the assault, stood nearby boasting of their vicious attack.

Thankfully, some older Germans attended to the old couple and appeared shocked and shaken, as were we. Al and I were both appalled but felt helpless. Our attitudes towards the Nazis, however, took a nastier turn after that unfortunate incident. Despite the economic progress and optimism we witnessed, we slowly began to realize that Nazi doctrine based upon fear and ignorance had an evil grip on the thinking and politics of the nation. We were perplexed and expressed our thoughts to each other in disbelief.

We questioned, "How could such an educated and progressive country blindly follow such harsh leaders?"

CHAPTER TEN
OLYMPIC GLORY IN THE NEW REICH

Al and I made our way to the first day of the games via the U-Bahn, arriving at the Olympiastadion subway station. Before entering the arena, we spotted a crowd making a fuss about something a few yards from a side entrance to the stadium. The milling spectators were getting a rare close-up glimpse of Hitler's personal Mercedes-Benz 770/W07 automobile. The 770 was a black-and-chrome, four-door convertible that featured the familiar Mercedes emblem signifying power and wealth perched atop its large impressive chrome radiator. Lined up neatly in a row behind his vehicle, stood four Mercedes-Benz G-4/W31 behemoths used mainly by Hitler's security detail. The parade vehicles were painted light gray with black fenders and rear wheel wells that bore two uniquely designed twin rear axles. The vehicles were over 20 feet long and each weighed more than 8,000 pounds.

The front passenger seat of Hitler's car could be folded, which allowed the Fuhrer to stand while the vehicle was in a parade. Twelve soldiers guarded the vehicles and each man was decked out in a black uniform neatly trimmed in silver. The elite unit was called the Schutzstaffel (protection squadron), but better known simply by their initials as the SS. They stood stoically beside each corner of Hitler's personal car. The SS men each carried a dagger with the case attached by a silver mesh lanyard to their black belts, which featured large silver buckles. A Luger pistol was secured inside a black leather holster and carried on their right side. They all wore gleaming, knee-high, black jackboots with their pants legs tucked inside. The red Nazi armband was proudly placed on their left sleeve, and their hats bore the German eagle with the infamous death's head pin depicting a skeletal skull. The vehicles and the so-called "storm troopers" made a strong statement to everyone who saw them, including Al and me.

My first sight of the newly constructed Olympic Stadium was overwhelming. I had never experienced an arena that magnificent. It boasted a seating capacity for 100,000 spectators, but when we entered it and saw every seat filled to capacity, the sudden rush of adrenaline was awe-inspiring. It was built in a circular fashion with the top portion cut out on one section only. The Olympic Flame was to be lighted near that open-ended area about two hours after the opening ceremony began. The flame itself came directly from Mount Olympus in Greece, site of the first ancient Olympics, and was relayed by selected German citizens to the torch-lighting pedestal erected at the stadium. For the first time, the games were being televised on a limited basis and shown in theaters throughout Germany via a new technology developed by the German Broadcasting Co.

Flags from all 49 countries represented at the games were placed around the top of the stadium with the five linked Olympic ring flags peppered among them. Behind the torch cauldron, outside the open part of the arena, stood two huge white-marble columns each 200 feet tall and about 50 feet apart. Between them were 10-foot-tall linked Olympic rings showcasing the international Olympic symbol, which could be seen easily by everyone in the stadium. The magnificent spectacle was best witnessed from the massive German airship Hindenburg, which flew majestically above the arena. It was a setting fit for the gods.

Once the crowd was seated, Hitler entered the stadium to a thunderous roar amid a sea of disciples, all recognizing him with the Nazi salute.

"Sieg Heil, Sieg Heil, Sieg Heil," they screamed over and over again for several minutes in his honor. As a gesture of goodwill, Hitler accepted a gift. It was a small olive tree from the first marathon winner of the Modern Games, a Greek runner, Spyridon Louis. The Führer later said a few words to open the games to more rousing cheers.

Suddenly, thousands of white pigeons were released. As the birds circled overhead, cannons were fired, which caused the poor birds to have a release of their own, and, not surprisingly, they splattered the crowd below. Even though the birds' mishap interrupted the formality of the event, the now-smelly stadium was filled with laughter and good cheer from the flabbergasted audience.

To signal the opening of the competition, 100 trumpeters began to blow their horns. Then, the teams, consisting of 3,963 superbly trained athletes, 331 of them women, paraded in order behind the flags of their respective countries. The countries marched in one by one led by Greece, aptly honored as the country where the first ancient games had originated 2,700 years earlier. There were no Olympic Games from the fourth century AD until they were revived again in the 19th century. Athens, Greece, was selected to host the first so-called Modern Games in 1896.

It was customary as each team approached the host country's reviewing stand for the flag holder to momentarily dip his or her country's flag. The flag bearer from the United State refused in defiance because of Hitler's harsh treatment of the Jews and others who opposed him. Before the games, America's Olympic Committee agreed not to dip the flag to Hitler at either the Winter or Summer games in 1936. (In 1940, Congress passed a law making it illegal to dip our country's flag for any person or object.) After presenting the flags, all of the teams settled into the infield area surrounded by the running track where the track and field athletes would perform during the games.

Finally, Fritz Schilgen, a German 1500-meter runner who had been chosen to be the final torchbearer, entered the stadium. He carried the flaming torch with his right hand and stopped for a brief moment at the top of the 100 or so steps before him. Amid thunderous applause, he descended the steps and ran halfway around the track then up another 100 steps at the open part of the arena. Then, he stepped in front of the cauldron, held up the torch, pointed it to the sky above, and, finally, used the blazing symbol to light the Olympic

Flame, which represented the light of spirit, knowledge, and life.

A choir started to sing composer Richard Strauss' "Olympic Hymn" over the loudspeakers, backed by the Berlin Philharmonic and the National Socialist Symphony Orchestra. It was all very impressive. The whole event was filmed for posterity by the famed German female cinematographer, Leni Riefenstahl, who in 1938 released her epic "Olympia" about the Nazi-inspired spectacle.

Of the 129 events at those games, none spoke louder and meant more to the United States than the four gold medals earned by Jesse Owens, who won in each of the events in which he competed. As a black athlete from Alabama, it was a miracle that he was even allowed to compete for his country, considering the segregation policies and racial laws in the USA during that period. Prior to the games, however, he was the world record holder in the 100- and 200-meter dash and in the long jump. Keeping him out of the Olympics would have been an outrage.

Owens did not disappoint the crowd. First, he won the 100-meter race on August 3 and the 200-meter event on August 5. But perhaps his most memorable medal was in the long-jump competition on August 4. Al and I were lucky to be in attendance for the occasion. In that memorable event, Owens mistakenly took what he assumed was a practice jump and only leaped a short distance. But to his surprise, the jump was officially counted as his first of three allotted attempts to qualify for the finals. In his second attempt, he committed a foul for crossing the designated starting line at the beginning of his jump. Before his last jump, his German counterpart and most feared competitor for the prized gold medal, Luz Long, his country's record holder, advised Owens to start his jump a few inches behind the starting line to avoid another foul that would have eliminated him.

Owens, it was reported, took Long's advice and qualified easily for the finals, beating Long to win the gold medal. Long placed second in the event and won the silver medal. To Hitler's displeasure, Long gave Owens a congratulatory hug after the finals as a show of sportsmanship. Owens won his fourth gold medal in the 4x100-meter relays when track coach Dean Cromwell inserted him and fellow sprinter Ralph Metcalfe into the relay squad, replacing sprinters Sam Stroller and Marty Glickman, the only two Jewish American athletes on the entire team's roster. Cromwell never explained his decision to replace the two runners. Owens and his teammates won the relay race and set a new world's record. For his heroics, Owens became the most popular athlete of the Berlin Games and single-handedly shot down Hitler's Nazi theories and claims of Aryan superiority.

Long and Owens remained friends and wrote to one another after the Olympics and through the beginning of the war that followed. Long was killed fighting for the German army against the Allies in Sicily in July 1943. Later in life, Owens honored his German friend by attending the wedding of Luz's son, Kai Long, and served as his best man.

Earlier, in February 1936, Germany had also hosted the Winter Olympics in Garmisch-Partenkirchen in the German Bavarian Alps. Twenty-eight countries sent teams, and only 646 athletes competed. Surprisingly, little Norway captured the most medals, winning 15 of the 51 awarded, including seven gold medals. Germany and the USA won a total of six and four medals, respectively.

Sonja Henie of Norway won the gold for figure skating, her third such victory in a row, beginning with the 1928 Winter Games. For her triumphs, she became the darling of the winter sports competition and a favorite of Hitler. He invited her to come to his retreat at Berchtesgaden near the Olympic venue in Garmisch. Her acceptance of Hitler's invitation prompted bitter denunciation by the Norwegian press. Once her skating career ended, she came to the United States and became a film star when she signed a long-term movie contract with 20th Century Fox in Hollywood.

The games were about to end, but I didn't want to miss the finals in the rowing competition because the American men's eight with coxswain team consisted solely of student-athletes from the University of Washington. It was an amazing story. Just getting to Berlin to compete in the summer games was an accomplishment. The people of Seattle raised money to pay for the team's expenses, or those boys might have just sat at home and listened to the race on their radios. The fellas were all from the state of Washington, and most came from working-class backgrounds. They had won the right to represent the United States in the Berlin games by beating several elite Ivy League teams in American Olympic qualifying races.

At the Olympic preliminary race on August 12, they had set the world record in the 2,000-meter men's eight with a time of 6:008. I knew I had to be there to witness the finals on August 14. The competition was held at the Berlin-Grunau Regatta Course on the Langer See, a river-lake on the Dahme River, which flowed into the larger Spree River a few miles away. The German and Italian teams were the favorites, but the British team, made up mainly of alums from Cambridge and Oxford universities, also had plenty of experience and couldn't be counted out.

The Führer and some of his top ministers, including Hermann Goering and Joseph Goebbels, were in attendance. I was told by fellow writers that the University of Washington team, even with its impressive preliminary victory, had very little chance of winning a medal in its first international competition. The writers claimed the favored teams were holding back during the preliminaries with anticipation of rowing their best in the finals, and that the young Americans didn't have the experience necessary to win.

I nervously attempted to find a place to sit. The boys from Washington had a reputation for starting slowly and finishing with a flurry, but I wasn't convinced that would be a good strategy for that day's race. I missed the qualifying races, but couldn't wait for the event to begin. Six teams were vying for the gold medal in the finals. The American team was positioned in lane six and faced a strong wind that could prove to be a problem. The other teams were Great Britain, Switzerland, Romania, Italy, and host Germany. The start time was 6 p.m.

A new acquaintance, Bill Henry, a sports writer for the Los Angeles Times, as well as a sportscaster for CBS Radio, had been sent to Berlin, like me, by his employers. I had met Bill earlier at an agenda meeting for the 700 or so journalists assigned to cover the games. The German press corps and broadcasters had been especially hospitable and helpful in every way. The host country built a new shortwave broadcast center that was expected to reach a worldwide radio audience of more than 300 million listeners.

Bill was a swell guy, a professional scribe who had also covered the 1932 games in Los Angeles. He told me he was going to broadcast the rowing event since our boys from the Northwest made the finals. He was the main reason I got to witness the event in person. He got me tickets, so there I sat waiting for the race.

I knew almost nothing about rowing, but looking at the huge crowd, estimated to be around 75,000 spectators, I was excited for the race to begin. The frenzied, virtually all German throng lined both sides of the course, and they all expected another rowing victory for their country. After all, the German teams had won five of the six gold medals already awarded for rowing events. They had won the single sculls, the coxless pairs, the coxed pair, the coxless four, and the coxed four. In the double sculls, Great Britain had won the gold, and the Germans had settled for the silver. The USA had won only one medal up to that point in the rowing events, a bronze that Daniel Barrow had won in the single sculls. Although I knew very little about the sport, that crowd had me roaring like a lion.

It was only 10 minutes before the start time, and I was jockeying to see between the people standing in front of me for a decent glimpse of the course. People were shouting, saluting, screaming at the top of their lungs, jumping, and pushing. And in that crazed audience, I assure you, many were more than a little tipsy. Remember, we were in Germany where the "giggle water," or strong hearty beer, frequently had top billing. There was a whole lot of giggle juice flowing in the venue on race day.

Then, Hitler made his appearance in his simple dark gray uniform proudly displaying his Iron Cross won for his bravery on the Western Front during the Great War. In unison, the possessed swarm of spectators shouted ear-numbing enthusiastic cheers. As he slowly made his way to the VIP viewing stand, thousands of the faithful extended their right arms high into the afternoon sky in the now-famous Nazi salute to their beloved Führer. He appeared in good spirits, smiled a lot, and frequently acknowledged his adoring following with half-hearted salutes.

The multitudes spontaneously erupted again and began screaming, "Heil Hitler" and "Mein Führer," which echoed from one side of the river venue to the other. The sound was deafening. I thought, regardless of one's political views. That event, with that crowd noise, was the ultimate highlight.

It was three minutes to race time, and the crews were getting into their boats. I glanced at my program that listed the American team roster as Don Hume, George Hunt, John White, Gordon Adam, Charles Day, Roger Morris, James McMillin, and Joseph Rantz with little Robert Moch as the coxswain, the participant who sits in the rear of the shell and yells instruction to the crew through his megaphone. The German team members all stood erect in their shell with the swastika symbol emblazoned on their uniform shirts. In unison, they flashed the Nazi salute toward the viewing stand and their dictator.

The crowd then responded with more deafening roars of "Sieg Heil," "Heil Hitler," and "Mein Führer."

The spectators were in a frenzy for a race that would last only six minutes. I didn't understand it, but I loved it!

Before I realized it, all six teams had their boats lined up in their starting positions awaiting the start judge to give the signal to begin the race. The anxious crowd quieted and became glued to the start flag. Suddenly, the flag dropped, and they were off! The crowd reacted in unison and started a seat-jarring chant of "Deutschland! Deutschland! Deutschland! Deutschland!"

The Americans' boat, "Husky Clipper," named after their university's mascot, started slowly as anticipated. As expected, the German, Italian, and British crews took the lead going into the first 500 meters.

"What's wrong with our boys? They're already falling behind again," I screamed. "Come on boys, come on, you can do it!"

The constant chants of "Deutschland! Deutschland! Deutschland" became even louder as the Germans gained and trailed only the Italian team at the halfway 1,000-meter mark. To hell with Deutschland, I thought, as I yelled at the top of my lungs, "Go, go, USA! Faster, faster, boys!"

Then, the USA crew picked up the pace. Moch was straining his vocal cords to the maximum, but I wondered, "How could his team hear him with all of this noise?"

"Go, boys," I yelled louder. "Five hundred meters to go!"

I couldn't judge what place our boys were in from my vantage point. People were screaming wildly. They were jumping higher and higher and pushing in hopes of gaining a better view. Women were perched on the shoulders of men and men on shoulders of other men. It was, without question, the most exciting thing I had ever witnessed in my life!

Then, suddenly, the race was over.

"Who won? Who won?" the crowd wondered in anticipation.

A nervous sensation overwhelmed the venue. There was a momentary pause, and then the announcer's voice crackled over the loudspeakers and then a second pause, which felt like minutes. Everyone was anxiously listening for the final results.

In shock, the speaker's voice clearly blared: "The Americans first at 6:25.4, the Italians second at 6:26.0, and the Germans third at 6:26.4." Our boys had won the gold medal by a mere sixth-tenths of a second.

"Can you believe that race?" I screamed in pure elation to no one in particular. Holy cow, those hotsy-totsy German tomatoes were crying, and a few of them fainted around me. Me, I was in heaven.

I began shouting, " USA, USA, USA" with a few "Hail Roosevelt" cheers thrown in just for good measure. I jumped for joy and hugged anyone near me.

A few minutes later, my new heroes slowly rowed back toward the grandstand and began to wave to their emotionally sapped audience. The crew beamed wide smiles and its members were greeted with a heartfelt standing ovation from the German crowd, which by then had overcome its shock and was enthusiastically clapping for the Americans. Hitler seemed unimpressed, but he did manage token applause for the victors. Our boys looked as exhausted as was I. Whew!

Then, in an instant, Sterre's face flashed before my eyes. I wished more than ever that she were by my side to witness what had just occurred. I wanted her beside me to share my joy. I couldn't seem to get her out of my mind. Somehow, I knew right then that I had to get back to Schimmert to see her before I boarded my ship for home on August 27, less than two weeks away. It was too little time as I realized I'd be stuck there in Berlin for a least three more days until August 17, and the wait was torturous. I started to process my countdown -- three days in Berlin, at least two days' travel time to Maastricht, and from there to Hamburg where my ship would depart. I needed more time, I thought nervously, even insisting to myself that I'd walk the last 50 miles from Maastricht to Schimmert if I had to.

I was that desperate. I guessed that I'd be lucky to have a week left to see her. I then pondered, why I was even thinking about changing my original plans to see the Alps before meeting Sterre. But deep down my heart knew the answer: I had to have just one more glimpse of her. I convinced myself it would help make some sense of my hopeless situation. I feared I would never see her again. Was I driving myself crazy? I wondered.

As I sat in my seat, I suddenly realized I had a story to write and needed to get it wired to the Trib while everything was still fresh in my memory.

Meanwhile, once the boat was secured back at the dock, with the boys still seated in their shell, a large victory wreath was placed upon the shoulders of the first rower, and after 15 seconds or so, he passed it back to the person sitting behind him and so on, so each eagerly waiting teammate had his turn. It was a moment fit for a conquering hero. A Caesar. Every guy was grinning from ear to ear, enjoying that magical moment with his hands held high in total disbelief and happiness. Yes, America, the gold medal was ours, thanks to our heroes from the state of Washington. In need of a scoop, I instinctively rush over to the dock and got some good quotes from the crew before they were mobbed by their adoring fans.

Lastly, in what felt like a gesture of good sportsmanship, "The Star-Spangled Banner" was played, honoring our boys in their moment of glory during the medal ceremony. The pro-German crowd readily gave the Nazi salute with their right arms stiffly stretched skyward, seemingly in tribute to our lads' victorious triumph.

After an hour-long wait in the middle of all of that commotion after the race, I knew that catching a bus or trolley back to the city was going to be almost impossible. Abruptly, Bill popped into my head.

"Where the hell was Bill?" I frantically wondered as I worked my way over to the radio broadcast booth, hoping that my new friend might help out a fellow writer in desperate need.

I was relieved when I spotted Bill across the crowded media room, which was buzzing with chatter. Finally, I got his attention, and he and I both rushed toward each other, bumping into people standing in our paths. I reached out to him in what I anticipated to be a handshake. Instead, he grabbed me, picked me up off the ground, and spun me around in pure exhilaration. Bill, had been broadcasting the event live to his radio audience in the United States and was thrilled and beside himself with delight. What an unbelievable day that was for him even though his listeners back home had to stay up well past midnight to hear the surprising victory.

"Have you ever seen anything like that before, my boy?" he exclaimed. Connecting with Bill saved me that day; the man sure had some clout. In a ruse, he somehow convinced two German motorcycle patrolmen that I was an important American diplomat who urgently needed to return to the city posthaste. Thanks to him, I got back to the city in no time on the back of a motorcycle with a police escort.

I finished what I had considered one of the best accounts I had ever written about any event. My story was loaded with background information, some enthusiastic quotes from the crew, and some behind-the-scenes tidbits accompanied by facts and statistics. It was full of the whos, whats, whens, wheres, whys and hows that Professor Reed, my old mentor from WVU, would have been proud to see. It was a great day to be a newspaper writer. I bet the editors at the Chicago Tribune were glad that they had had the vision and the wisdom to send ol' Joe Fisher to Berlin after they read that article. Was my story of that day equal to sportswriter Frederick T. Birchall's account of the 1936 Olympic Games opening-day ceremony that he penned for The New York Times? Hardly, but that guy is a genius. Next morning though, I was still giddy.

Other highlights of the games were the additions of basketball, handball, and canoeing as first-time medal events. The American team won the gold in basketball and Marjorie Gestring won for the USA in springboard diving, which made her the youngest person ever to win a gold medal at any Olympics. Germany, however, won the most events of any country, capturing 89 medals with the United States coming in second with 59. In all, American athletes won 24 gold medals, led by Jesse Owens with four. Other fellow countrymen of note who won gold were Glenn Edgar Morris of Colorado in the decathlon and John Woodruff in the 800-meters competition.

The wonderful and magical Berlin Olympic Games of 1936 provided Al and me all the suspense, drama, and excitement we could have asked for. The material we gathered permitted us to pen some fantastic stories with a few interesting tidbits thrown in to keep our editors satisfied, and, hopefully, our newspaper's readers in Chicago entertained. We both thoroughly enjoyed every second of our time in Germany's capital city.

Even though I had fun in Berlin, I took the time to send Sterre a letter or a postcard every day. I wanted her to know that she was always on my mind.

The Summer Games' closing ceremonies on August 16 were a blur to me. Yes, it was wonderfully orchestrated with all the pomp one would expect from the Germans. The teams all marched into the stadium again, but this time in the darkness of the late evening. The flag bearers all dipped their flags, save for one. The choir sang inspiring music. Hitler and his entourage stood at the viewing stand and presented the Nazi salute to the adoring crowd. The Olympic flag flew proudly with it's symbolic, five linked rings of blue, black, red, green, and yellow on a white background that represented at least one of the colors found in every nation's flag. The now familiar coupled rings were proclaimed as the official emblem of the modern Olympic movement and first used during the 1920 Games in Antwerp, Belgium.

On cue, fifty or more massive searchlights circling the stadium were simultaneously switched on. Their striking white beams raced skyward through the low hanging clouds causing an awe-inspiring reaction from the stunned crowd.

At last, the final curtain call of the magnificent spectacle ended when the Olympic flag was lowered from its staff as the announcer called upon the youth of the world to assemble once again in 1940, only four years hence, in Tokyo, Japan. Of course, no one knew that a devastating war would prevent the next scheduled games from ever happening. So, in Berlin, the once brightly burning Olympic flame was extinguished.

On August 17, Al and I left town on the 6:14 a.m. train heading west toward Maastricht. But the departure wasn't without drama. Al had stayed up far too late the previous night with Agnes, and she had to almost drag Al to the station. To my surprise, he wasn't drunk, but more forlorn than I had ever seen him. I almost had to pry him from Agnes' arms to board the train. I knew how he must be feeling as he left her crying at the train station platform. I put my arm around him in a display of support and gave him a friendly nod of sympathy. He just sat there quietly in our compartment lost in his thoughts. I didn't utter a word or interrupt him in his moment of obvious sorrow.

After about 45 minutes of aimlessly staring out our window, he finally opened up a little.

"Joe, life can be so unfair sometimes," he said, snapping his fingers as he contemplated the perceived injustice of his current situation. "I mean, I meet a girl like Agnes, and just like that, she's gone! I may never see her again, Joe. She's there, and I'm not, and I know I will probably never lay eyes upon her beautiful face again, and that's downright unfair, my friend.

"I'm hurting, Joe. I'm really hurting! I guess now I understand a little better how you must feel, Joey, about Sterre. I mean, sometimes I wish I had never met Agnes. Then I wouldn't feel like this. But, man, Joey, Agnes is one of a kind. She's so lovely, caring, and sweet, and she was great in the sack, too," he disclosed with a sigh followed by a chuckle.

"She sounds like a Girl Scout to me," I laughed to lighten the mood.

"Girl Scout? Oh, you got me on that one, Joey," he shot back with a smile.

"She could do things that ol' Al had never experienced before, but she was still classy, Joe, if you know what I mean. She was so elegant, yet she had that fire about her that men like me can only dream about. I hope someday, somehow, she and I meet up again. I'd like that, Jocy. I'd really like that," he said with another long sigh.

I looked at Al with a sheepish smile and said, "Al, I never thought I would ever see you in such a tizzy about a dame. But you're crazy about Agnes. I can hear it in your voice."

"These European girls are something, aren't they?" Al said wistfully. "There's some sort of sophistication in her beauty yet an air of sweet innocence that surrounds her. And you must see in Sterre that same characteristic of innocence and beauty, yet, as you say, elegance. Man, are we two suckers for love or what?"

"Welcome to my world, Al," I said.

"Joey, ol' pal, I'm not sure if mine is love or lust!" he proclaimed playfully.

We laughed heartily as I welcomed back the Al I knew. We both slept soundly practically the remainder of our journey as our train rolled through the blissful German countryside.

Al wanted to spend a few more days in Cologne with his relatives or most likely with those two young ladies I'd met who were so infatuated with him a few weeks ago. But, with the inner pain he was suffering by leaving Agnes behind, maybe having a little fun with those girls from Cologne was just what he needed.

We agreed we'd meet up again on the afternoon of August 23 at the train station in Maastricht. I gave him addresses for Uncle Karl and Uncle Wouter in the unlikely event that we missed one another, but I assured him I would be at the station to welcome him to Limburg and Schimmert.

CHAPTER ELEVEN
SCHIMMERT
FOR A SECOND GO

It was 5 p.m. August 18 and I had a nervous feeling when my train pulled into the Maastricht station. Impatient, I leaped from the train while it was still moving. So quickly, in fact, that I forgot my luggage. Like a madman, I had to run back to retrieve it before the train moved out. I found it still on the rack above my compartment seat.

With my belongings secured, I walked briskly down Stationsstraat, located directly in front of the train depot. I dodged several Sparta and Batavus mopeds on the busy street that connected the train station to the Maas River 300 meters away. At the river, I crossed the oldest bridge in the Netherlands called Sint Servaasburg and maneuvered my way to the Vrijthof, the city's most prominent and charming square. One side of the square featured the impressive old churches of Sint-Jans and Sint Servatius, and beside them stood the Militaire Hoofdwacht, built as a barracks for the city's military guards in the mid-1700s.

Maastricht's famous cobblestone plaza was bounded on the other three sides by grand old buildings with dates from the 16th and 17th centuries carved into their stone and brick facades. A large gazebo for musical events sat directly in the middle of the square. I waited there restlessly before catching a ride on the last bus headed to Valkenburg, which was in the general direction of Schimmert.

It began pouring rain when the bus finally completed its 30-minute route to the medieval fortress town, but the foul weather was of little concern because I knew it was only a short walk to Sterre's arms. I trudged up the hill on Nieuweweg Road with my drenched bags in tow and my sights on her house on de Kling Road in Oensel. When I got within view of the Tragses' farm, Sterre's brothers ran out to greet me even though it was still heavily raining. I was so soaked that my shoes literally disintegrated during the downpour.

Once inside their home, I expected to find Sterre but was told she wasn't home. She had agreed to care for the baby of a sick girlfriend whose husband was out of town for the evening. I wasn't surprised because of Sterre's reputation for aiding a friend in need, especially since she had no knowledge of my hurried arrival. Even though my inner feelings were crushed, I fully understood her absence.

Paul offered me a bed for the night, but I politely declined. Once the rain subsided, I walked to Uncle Wouter's. As soon as I opened his door, I was inundated with questions about the Olympics. His sons, Math and Ralf, peppered me with questions about the games and were glued to my every word as they listened intently to my commentary.

"Was Jesse Owens the fastest man you'd ever seen?" Ralf asked excitedly. Before I could answer, Math chimed in, "He's so fast you couldn't beat him in the 200-meter race if he was running and you were on your bicycle, Ralf!"

I responded with a boisterous laugh and said, "There is no question in my mind that Jesse would easily win that race, even if Ralf was on a motorcycle."

Everyone laughed.

Uncle Wouter grumbled a little and asked, "Joe, did you see Adolf Hitler, and, if so, what did you think about him?"

"Well, I did see him on three different occasions," I said, "at both the opening and closing ceremonies and at the scull racing event. I was not close enough to talk with him, but I got within 50 meters of him at the finals of the scull competition, which was won by the American team," I beamed.

"Could Hitler beat Jesse Owens in a race?" Ralf joked.

"Maybe if he were shot from a cannon," I suggested with a chuckle.

Uncle Wouter's girls, Kiki and Judy, marveled at my stories and seemed more interested in who had the most handsome athletes.

"Do the girls in Berlin act as we do?" Judy asked. "Do they wear the same style of clothes?"

Kiki, only nine years old, asked, "Did you go to see any lions or elephants at the Berlin zoo?" She wondered if I had missed them, and giggled when she asked if I had missed Sterre. She loved the stuffed monkey that I brought back for her.

I was delighted to answer every question and was thrilled that they were all so interested in my experiences. We talked late into the night. When the questions finally ended, I fell into my bed exhausted, but thankful.

The next morning, I darted out Uncle Wouter's door and rushed over to Sterre's farm at breakneck speed on Ralf's bicycle. As soon as she spotted me, she came running. I leaned the bike up against a fence post and charged into her waiting arms. After a long kiss, we just stood and hugged each other for several minutes. When I gazed into her eyes and saw that radiant smile upon her face, I knew I was exactly where I needed to be.

Once inside her home, I had nearly the same conversations with her family as I had had at Uncle Wouter's the night before, but I didn't mind the questions. We were so happy to be with each other once again.

Normally, Sterre would have been busy working on the farm, but her father and brothers were well aware of our predicament and fully understood that I would be leaving her for America in just a few days. So they insisted that she and I spend the next several days alone while they worked the farm without her. I could tell her father was very concerned, but I knew he loved Sterre and wanted only happiness for his only daughter. Paul and I had become friends, and he knew my intentions and feelings for his daughter were sincere.

During my absence, I'm sure she questioned the absurdity of our romance, as did I. Honestly, I tried to rationalize the situation, but to no avail.

"How in the world could any of this unbearable madness come to any logical conclusion?" I had repeatedly asked myself. As crazy as the maddening scenario appeared, I knew the exhilarating emotions I was feeling weren't just a casual infatuation.

"No, sir, it was 100 percent pure, committed, punishing love," I rationalized. Even though my mind told me that the impossible predicament I had gotten myself into could never work out between Sterre and me, my unwavering heart constantly worked to convince my brain that it could. From one minute to the next, I questioned my tangled sanity and thought of new obstacles and new solutions.

"For God's sake, I'm American and she's Dutch, and we live thousands of miles and an ocean apart. I live and work in Chicago, Illinois, and she lives in Schimmert in Limburg with a tightly knit family that depends on her. How did I get so blindsided so quickly? Why did my lonely heart lead me to her? Why?"

I fought with my raging emotions and demanded answers from my tortured soul.

But when I looked at Sterre, all of my doubts instantly disappeared, and I drowned helplessly in those glistening blue eyes. Holy cow! Truth is truth and facts are facts, and I'm in love! No question about it, and God forgive me now but come hell or high water, we will find a way, somehow, some way! I reasoned in that perfect moment of determination.

Sterre hugged her father and each of her brothers, and I shook all of their hands before we left to travel around the area by bicycle. The two of us left alone during that time was just what the doctor ordered.

Both of our Dutch-made bicycles were the standard black Gazelle brand, manufactured by Rijwielfabriek in Dieren, according to the metal labels attached to the front of the bikes. The ladies' version that Sterre rode featured a removable woven straw basket, a metal sprocket chain guard, a bell on the handlebars, and leather mudguards covering the top portion of the rear wheel. My bicycle, called the Gazelle Cross Frame, was essentially the same as hers, but slightly larger with an added metal bar welded across the middle of the frame that included a headlight and white tires compared to her black ones. It was the best-built bicycle I had ever ridden and pedaling it was smooth and easy.

"I love to ride my bicycle," she said. "Just about everyone here rides one, from children to grandparents."

"I enjoy it, too, but I don't ride much living in Chicago. Too much traffic," I replied.

"The bike I'm riding once belonged to my mother and, before her, my grandmother. I rode it 35 kilometers every day to Maastricht and back when I was in training to become a teacher," she proudly told me.

"Wow, most people in Chicago don't ride that much in a year," I responded to her amazement.

We were finally in a position to get reacquainted and enjoyed the sunny day and each other's company. First, we decided to concentrate on Schimmert once again. We rode by the now familiar landmarks including the Water Tower, the Sint Remigius Church, and the Montforten Seminary. Then, we stopped at each of the four little chapels consisting of the Mariakapel in Kruis, the Mariakapel in Op de Bies, the Hubertuskapel in Groot Haasdal, and the Sint-Rochuskapel in Klein Haasdal. Oensel, with its wrought-iron cross, was the last of the five hamlets that formed the village of Schimmert. Sterre provided a little history of each as we visited them.

"I know we have only spoken briefly about our religious beliefs, and I want you to know before you answer, I love you regardless of your faith, but are you Catholic?" she delicately asked.

Smiling, I replied, "Yes, in some sense, but my father is not. His family is all Protestants, Methodist to be exact."

"Methodist?" she asked, shrugging her shoulders. "What is a Methodist?"

"Well, it's similar to Catholics, but their church services are not as formal, and they don't have a Pope, priests, or nuns, but they all believe in God just like the Catholics," I explained. "My mother's family, of course, was all Catholic. But when my grandparents came to the United States, they didn't attend church services regularly, maybe once a month or so, but went to Mass on all special occasions like Christmas. So I answered your question with a 'yes' since I was officially baptized in the Catholic Church back home in West Virginia where I was born. However, I rarely attend church services now."

"Almost everyone around Schimmert goes to Sint Remigius, you know, especially with the Montfort's presence in our village!" she said. "But if we are together, would you be OK with me attending a Catholic church?"

"Of course it would, and I'll go with you, too. I went with you every Sunday when I was here earlier, and I'll be by your side this Sunday as well," I reassured her.

"That pleases me, Joe, and I want you to understand that I respect all religions, including the Methodist," Sterre happily replied to my relief.

Continuing on our bicycles on a wooded road called Kleverstraat in the Groot Haasdal section of Schimmert, we stopped pedaling, and she grabbed my hand and led me down a small pathway. To my surprise, we came upon a small cemetery that contained four tombstones.

"Do you know the people who are buried here?" I asked as we gazed upon the stones,

"No, this is an old Jewish cemetery. Can you read the writing? It's in Hebrew," she said.

"I wish I could, but, no, I can't," I replied.

"Well, on the other side of the stones, the words are in Dutch, and this one states that David Caen was born on the 11th day of August in 1815," she read as she pointed to the words with her finger.

"Eighteen-fifteen?" I quickly responded. "That was the year the French dictator General Napoleon Bonaparte was defeated at Waterloo in Belgium by combined British, Prussian, Dutch, and Belgian forces. I even visited Napoleon's tomb a few weeks ago when I was in Paris. The French army's defeat changed the course of history and some of the borders in Western Europe as well, including Limburg Province. David

Caen, buried here, lived through the aftermath of all of that as did David Benedik, Jacob Caan, and Caroline Caan," I said as I read the names on the other tombstones.

"Rarely does anyone visit here anymore, but sometimes I come and place some flowers on their graves. These people were more than likely born here and raised their families here years ago, and they probably had a hard life during that tumultuous time. Their graves deserve respect. Father visits my mother's grave every Sunday. I can't imagine her grave being abandoned someday," she said sadly.

"I agree, my dear, I agree. Thanks for bringing me here," I said as we held hands and slowly walked away.

Our next stop was another cemetery called Paterskerkhof. It was the final resting place for the Patrons Montfortanen (priests) and the Daughters of Wisdom (nuns) in the hamlet of Op de Bies, where more than 200 members of the Schimmert-based religious order were buried. It was a sacred place for Sterre since one of her uncles had been a priest and was buried there.

The farms and fields that surrounded Schimmert once again looked as if they framed a perfect picture of serenity, just as my mother had described them to me when I was a young child. Every person we passed waved as we rode by, and many stopped us to share a story or two or to thank Sterre for some kind deed she had done for them. I could tell she was respected and loved by everyone in town, and why not? She was perfect and I knew how lucky I was to be in her presence even though my time with her would end much too soon.

Throughout my first day back we relished each other's company and basked unashamedly in the pure joy of the moment. We talked very little about our situation and mainly focused upon the present. To talk about all of our problems or worry about future challenges to our relationship would have ruined the atmosphere. We both wanted our minds to be united happily as one, and, on that beautiful summer day, they were.

As we continued our jaunt, I asked her, "Besides farming what other jobs are in Limburg?"

"Coal mining, mostly," she replied without much hesitation. "DSM, meaning Dutch State Mines, is headquartered in the city of Heerlen, not far from here. Many men work in the coal mines from all over southern Limburg. In addition to Heerlen, there are mines near Schinnen and Geleen, and even more in Kerkrade near the German border. The mines have created other jobs in Limburg as well. Some of the local railroads and the recently completed Juliana Canal were built here in Limburg mainly to haul coal. There are a lot of other companies here that support the industry. There are machine shops and electric power stations that employ thousands of Limburgers."

"What a coincidence," I told her. "I grew up around coal mining in West Virginia. There are mines located all over the state that also support thousands of families. My own father once worked as a railroad engineer, and he hauled tons of coal out of the hills back home. That's one more thing we have in common, and I never would have guessed that it would be coal mining."

I chuckled at the many things we shared in common despite the vast distance between our homes.

"Every time I think of a coal mining town, I remember this little town back in West Virginia called Riverside," I said. "Just like Maastricht is the capital of Limburg, Charleston is capital of West Virginia. When I was in college at West Virginia University, I once went to Charleston in October of 1929 to write a story for my school newspaper. I was covering a football game between WVU and Washington & Lee College in Virginia, a game, which, by the way, we won 26-6. Oddly enough, that day was exactly 10 days before the big stock market crash on October 29, 1929, that started the economic depression we're still experiencing. Some high school buddies and I drove almost eight hours through a raging downpour to see that game.

"Initially, the game was our focus, but we also went down there to visit an old high school friend of ours who was attending New River State College in nearby Montgomery. All four of us landed in this little town called Riverside where we got a room for the night in a dumpy boarding house that sported a Mail Pouch Tobacco sign painted on one side of the tattered two-story wooden building just a few feet off a dusty two-lane road. The town itself was nothing but a two-bit, dirty, hellhole of a place situated between two other seedy towns called Glasgow and Hugheston with London just beyond. Other than the boarding house, there were only a few houses, a couple of beer joints, which you would call bars, and river locks built in the 1880s to assist boat traffic on the Kanawha River that flowed through the town.

"This place was so rough, one of the bars was called the Bloody Bucket if you can imagine. Well, sure enough, we were in that two-bit tavern when a fight broke out between my friends and some of the local coal miners who frequented the bar. Before we knew it, beer bottles were flying everywhere. To my misfortune, one of those miners planted a Black Label beer bottle right on my noggin and knocked me out cold," I said, recalling the pain as I pointed my finger between my eyes. "Those coal miners back home were as mean as hell and tough as nails.

"So, when anyone mentions coal miners to me, all I think about was my massive headache after that night in Riverside."

"Our coal miners are never so violent," she responded in shock. "They are good men, husbands, and fathers."

"Ours is, too, but, as I said, some of ours were as mean as wildcats, but most were as gentle as sheep as well," I assured her. "But on a Saturday night after downing a few cold beers, the former description best suited them."

The next day, we took a bus to Maastricht. The old city had been settled by the Romans more than 2,000 years before and changed hands many times, coming under rule by Germanic tribes, the Holy Roman Empire under Charlemagne, Spain, France, Belgium, and, finally, the Netherlands. Around 65,000 residents called Maastricht home in 1936 with 80 percent of them Catholic. The city center was surrounded by remnants of solid stone medieval walls, quarried throughout the centuries from the nearby hills of Saint Pietersberg, which overlooked the ancient city.

A 500-foot-long, 15-foot-high wall with a round tower called the Onze-Lieve-Vrouwewal faced the Maas River and featured the Helpoort, meaning Hell's Gate. It wrapped around a corner just 50 feet from the tower. The Helpoort was the oldest city gate in the Netherlands, dating back to 1229, stated the sign carved in wood and placed over its stone arched entrance.

We walked through the Stadspark, the largest city park in town. It was framed on one side by a massive wall that stretched for a few thousand feet and followed a little stream called the Jeker. Jutting out every so often along the wall were circular stone escarpments to better view any approaching enemies.

I was stunned as we approached a statue in the park that commemorated one of my childhood heroes, Frenchman Charles Ogier de Batz de Castelmore, or Comte d'Artagnan, who was killed in Maastricht during the Dutch-Franco War in 1673. Better known in western literature by simply d'Artagnan, his adventures were immortalized as a captain of the French guard. He was praised in Maastricht as the dashing leader of his fictional famous sidekicks, Athos, Porthos, and Aramis, better known as "The Three Musketeers" in Alexandre Dumas' literary masterpiece.

We spent two hours or so in the park feeding the ducks and birds as we discussed my life as a writer for the Tribune and my living arrangements in Chicago. She was most interested in learning about my childhood in Morgantown and the adventures I'd experienced. She hesitantly asked about my former girlfriends. Of course, I was truthful with her and told her I'd had only one serious relationship and that was in college. It ended with me moving to Illinois to take my first newspaper job in Bloomington.

I explained that later I'd been romantic with a few women, but nothing too serious. She nonchalantly said she understood considering I was a 28-year-old man. She told me several men had attempted to win her affections, but, until me, she'd had no serious relationships either, especially after her mother's death. Since then, she had devoted her life to the care of her father and brothers. She shared a close bond with her mother that I understood soon after meeting her. I knew she cherished that relationship and that it was dear to her heart.

Sterre described her mother in the most loving of terms, and I could tell her spirit was still alive in the depths of Sterre's character. Even though we tried to avoid the obvious, most of our discussions thereafter focused on our future.

Of course, my immediate plan was to return home to Chicago to continue my career with the Tribune, but now that goal seemed trivial. I knew my future lay in the loving hands of this lady who would soon be miles away from me. The solution to our dilemma appeared to be unsolvable; she, with her commitment to her family and I with mine and my job. I, of course, hoped she would come to America. On the other hand, she hoped that I would prefer to live in Schimmert.

I reasoned with her on several occasions that people from all over the world emigrate to America to search for their dreams or to seek their fortunes. It was not the other way around. She reluctantly agreed with my argument, but I fully understood that family ties were more dear to her heart. I'd bet good money that we hashed that issue over more than any other, and even on the day I left Schimmert for home, our romantic fate was still unclear. There was no question that we were sure of our love for each other. Thank God for that! That fact was the lifeline that carried us through the ordeal that we had no idea at the time would soon challenge our very beings.

As we continued to ride our bikes through the park, we traveled along a portion of the medieval wall and came upon Tapijn Kazern, a military barracks, and headquarters for Dutch soldiers based in the city. Earlier some of the soldiers from the small installation had been walking behind us. After they turned to walk down another street and were out of our sight, she told me they that had whispered some flattering remarks in

Dutch about her which she ignored. I hadn't a clue about what had been said or I would have defended her honor, but she just brushed off their immature behavior and laughed at their childish comments.

On our way to the city's center, simply called the Centrum, stood a stately town hall administration building called the Stadhuis, which also featured the Markt, an open-air market where fresh produce and fruits were sold every Saturday and Sunday. But my favorite place in the city was a little square called Onze Lieve Vrouwegplein, or Square of Our Dear Lady. The tree-shaded square was about 150 meters long and 100 meters wide and dominated by the twin towers of the Basilica of Our Lady, a Protestant church near the shopping area of the old walled town.

In addition to the church and quaint shops that surrounded the area, the square was dotted with wooden benches, wicker tables and chairs where locals could visit or relax over a warm cup of tea or coffee. The Jekerkwartier, as the ancient district of the town was called, was noted for its slick cobblestone and brick streets. As we pedaled down one of its streets called Stokstraat, it became apparent that it painted a picture of what I had always dreamed a typical European lane should look like. The curvy road was uniquely Limburg in character. It boasted old stone or brick buildings that housed colorful flowers shops, a butcher shop with fresh meats hanging in its windows, and vendors pushing wooden carts and selling all types of items, including fruits and vegetables.

Busy deliverymen unloaded a variety of goods from horse-drawn wagons as well as from a few odd-looking motor vehicles. An assortment of motorcycles and bikes sped by us, including Dutch-made Sparta and Eysink bikes. A vast array of aluminum radio antennas decorated many of the rooftops.

An underground maze of tunnels extended several hundreds of meters under the serene ancient city of Maastricht, which was sliced through its center by the meandering Maas River. The river's source began high in the French Langres Plateau, flowed through France, Belgium, and southern and central Holland, and finally emptied into the North Sea. The city made a lasting impression on me. I'd never experienced such a beautiful old municipality and looked forward to learning more about its history.

About four o'clock, we parked our bikes beside a large tree and shortly after found ourselves standing on the Sint Servaasbrug Bridge with my arms wrapped around Sterre. We watched the dark gray waters of the Maas flow beneath us as we held each other tightly. My heart was pounding as was hers. She leaned in and kissed my neck and then whispered softly in my ear that she loved me.

"I don't want this day to end," I told her as I wiped away a few tears gently rolling down her face.

She agreed and asked suggestively, "What should we do?" Both of us understood the obvious answer.

There was no denying the sexual tension between us had been bubbling to the surface all day. Nervously, my eyes roamed the streets that paralleled the river's banks until they spotted several hotels lining a street known as Kesselskade. Without pause, I suggested an option. "Well, I can think of several things that I would love to do with you, my darling." I arched my eyebrows while at the same time I pointed out to her several of the overnight establishments facing the Maas. I could tell from her surprised yet seductive eyes that she was open to the suggestion.

"A hotel! I'm a little fearful of that," she said, "but I know what we both must be thinking about the prospect."

Consecrating our relationship was a serious matter, yet the thought was more than a little exciting.

"I think we have been dancing around the issue, but you must know I've been thinking about it, too," she said. "I love you, Joe, and it's a normal feeling to have for two people in love. I know you would like that to happen, but I want you to know, so do I. Time is short, too short. I know you feel it is time and I realize it, too," she gently replied as she snuggled closer to me.

"Are you sure, my darling?" I asked as she closed her eyes, lightly bit the bottom of her sumptuous ruby lip, and slowly nodded her head in agreement.

Boldly, she then grasped my hand and led me in the direction of the inns. We stopped three times along the way and kissed as I searched her facial expressions for any doubts, but saw none. Before we entered one of the hotels closest to the bridge, I looked into her eyes and told her again how much I loved her.

I secured a room, and we walked up the steps with no luggage. We were followed by the disapproving expression of the gray-haired lady innkeeper. The wooden door of our room bore the number seven, a lucky number for Americans, which was certainly true that early sultry evening.

"I've never been with a man before, Joe," she said tenderly. "This moment is something I've fantasized about my whole adult life, and I'm so happy you're the man I get to share this tender moment with, my love. I'm so happy it's with you, Zef," she said, whispering my childhood nickname.

I affectionately held her in my arms and watched in an old ornate wooden framed mirror hanging on the wall behind her our reflection as we embraced.

I carefully unbuttoned her white cotton blouse as she pressed ever closer to me and caressed my hips with her hands. Her striking blue eyes were sharply focused, and staring deeply into mine. As her garments fell to the floor, I gazed in awe at her perfect, firm breasts.

Carefully, she pulled my shirt slowly over my head after unfastening only the top two buttons. I unzipped her skirt as she pushed my pants down, and soon we both stood naked beside the waiting bed. Our bodies melded in anticipation, our hands searching and clinging, but I could see a slight shadow of apprehension cross her face. I could feel her body tremble, but nevertheless sensed her excitement with every passing moment.

To calm her, I whispered reassuringly in her ear, "Remember, we love each other my darling. I will stop at any time you ask. We will be bonded for life after this night, and I don't want you to take that statement lightly. Take comfort in the fact that I will love you for the rest of my life!"

I held her tightly in my unflinching arms to reinforce my commitment.

Our lips met passionately but tenderly, and we lay down onto the bed and slowly slid beneath the soft cotton sheets as our warm bodies pressed closer together. As the heat intensified, nature soon took control.

Later that evening, we loaded our bicycles onto the last bus to Schimmert and within 10 minutes of taking a seat, Sterre fell asleep with her head resting on my shoulder. It was clearly evident why we spent the entire next day alone in Maastricht.

The day was magical. We could hardly wait to explore each other again and soon found ourselves snuggled together for a second time after checking into our familiar room number seven. Minutes after making love for the third time that afternoon, we lay in our warm bed in total bliss. The top of her head was nudged against my chin as she slowly twisted her mother's cross, which was dangling from a silver chain wrapped around her neck, while I was lying flat on my back with my head on the large fluffy pillow. We kissed more times than I could count as we both looked forward to more in the future. In the tender moments that followed, she asked about my mother and reflected upon her own.

"Mother would have loved you, Joe, I know she would," she said. "I hope someday soon I get the chance to see Chicago, and the hills of your childhood home in West Virginia, and your family's farm in Bloomington, too."

"My dear, you're going to see it all with me, I promise you that. We're going to see it all together," I replied with a sigh.

"I want to meet your mother and father. I hope they like me," she said.

"They will love you without a doubt, Sterre," I reassured her.

"What do you think about a diary?" she suddenly said.

"A diary? You mean a book where we write our private thoughts down on paper?" I asked skeptically.

"Yes, I want to know your every thought, every day," she said excitedly. "Then, each month we can send that month's pages to each other so we can keep abreast of what each of us is thinking. What do you say about that, Joe?"

"It's unconventional, but I agree. I must warn you in advance, however, my writings may be quite repetitive since only you will be in my thoughts! A diary! That's a great idea!" I happily concurred.

That evening we bumped into Sterre's best friend, Kelly van Dyke, who was standing at a bus stop near the bridge. Kelly had been in Maastricht shopping and accepted our invitation to accompany us to the train station to meet Al.

Right on time, we met Al at the station as I had promised him days earlier. Before shaking my hand, Al passed by me and with open arms made a beeline for Sterre, who was standing a few feet behind me.

"Now that I've seen this beautiful lady, I fully understand what all of the fuss was about! I hope you're Sterre, honey. If not, what are you doing tonight?" he coyly asked followed by his big laugh.

"I'm Sterre," she replied with a giggle.

"Of course, you are. Ol' Al was just joking with you, doll," he declared.

He turned to me and yelled, "And how's my best pal, Joey? Is everything OK? Are you ready to head back home to the good ol' U.S. of A.?"

"Hold your horses, Al. Would you be in any hurry to leave someone like her?" I replied as I gazed upon my love.

"I guess not. I see your point, Joey. She's a real gem, a real looker for sure if I ever saw one," he beamed.

I introduced Al to Kelly, who seemed a little shy compared to Al's big personality. But soon after their introduction, he worked his magic and had Kelly won over. He became fixated watching her roll a cigarette by hand, which she expertly did in her first attempt by using one thin white cigarette paper and a local Dutch brand of tobacco called Drum. It was a time-honored task that many Limburgers frequently performed throughout their day.

When she finished, he asked, "Can I give one of those a try, Kelly?"

It was entertaining watching him attempt the tricky maneuver and more fun studying an older lady waiting nearby for a train who was amused by Al's fumbling effort. The woman ended his frustration by graciously giving him a hand. Then, she kindly patted Al on the head and left abruptly, shaking her head in bewilderment as Al took his first puff of their creation. The expression on his contorted face was priceless, and we all laughed heartily to his delight. I decided that it was a good thing he wasn't using the stronger Van Nelle blend of tobacco. Who knows what his reaction would have been?

Al proved once more that he could be the life of any party with his good-natured attitude and witty charm. Finally, after more than a few laughs, we all rode the bus back to Schimmert. Al continued his comedy show at Sterre's home. After too many beers, Sterre and Kelly started singing some old Dutch children's songs. One was titled "Alles in de Wind" ("Blowing in the Wind") and our personal favorite was called "Katje poesje Nelletje" ("Kitten-pussy Nelly").

Al and I countered their effort with our own hilarious rendition of a few of our childhood melodies. I vaguely recall our version of "She'll Be Coming 'Round the Mountain," which never sounded so pure. The fun lasted well past midnight. Earlier that evening, I thought, what a sight to behold: My best friend and I thousands of miles from home in a foreign country with my girl and her best friend. It was sadly unlikely that we would all be together again in the same room for the rest of our lives.

But Al and Kelly hit it off and their new-found infatuation kept them occupied and out of our hair for the remainder of the stay in Schimmert.

I'd packed my suitcase the night before our departure and filled it with mementos that would remind me of Sterre. I had cardboard beer coasters from Dutch brands Amstel, Heineken, Brand, Gulpener, and Alfa Brouwerij with a few German ones, too, such as Oettingen, Löwenbräu, and Erdinger threw in for good measure. One of the coasters from Belgium was unique since the beer was brewed by Cistercian Monks at an abbey called Val-Dieu. I even stuffed in a still full green flip-top bottle of Grolsch beer.

Among my dirty clothes, I crammed in candy wrappers, small cheese boxes, cigarette cartons, a small Zaanse clock, several Dutch guilder coins, a deck of playing cards, which bore their queen's likeness, and a few tins filled with Gustaf's Black Licorice for the family back home. I also packed one of Sterre's small paintings she had given me depicting several old men sitting at a table dressed in their finest 16th-century costumes. It reminded me of a Dutch Masters' cigar box top.

One of my most treasured prizes was a black beret that I carefully tucked away among my belongings. Sterre had worn it recently, and she lovingly presented it to me as a gift, which made the cap even more special. It carried the sweet scent of her soft, silky hair. Lastly, for good luck, Sterre's brothers, Jim and Arjan, gave me a Dutch 10-cent guilder coin with a likeness of Queen Wilhelmina. I carry it in my billfold to this day.

That last evening was torturous, but we tried our best to keep the mood light and playful. We played some cards and shared dinner with her family. Then, as if on cue, everyone departed the room, leaving Sterre and me to spend our last precious hours alone. We talked and kissed as the candle sitting on the table slowly burned down ever closer to its base.

As the night passed, unplanned and spontaneous, I got down on one knee, reached into my pocket, and pulled out a 1936 American Indian head nickel, the only coin I had that bore that year. The proud Indian's face was on one side of the coin with the date and the word "Liberty" just to the right of his nose. On the back, the western plains buffalo had "United States of America" written above the animal's back and the motto of the USA, "E Pluribus Unum" (Out of Many, One) below that. The words "Five Cents" were spelled out just below its feet. As kids, my friends and I would make jokes about the "teat" proudly dangling beneath the buffalo.

As Sterre stood above me and looked down at my anxious face, I began to speak:

"Since meeting you, my life has been transformed forever. I can't imagine spending the rest of my life with anyone but you by my side. I consider myself to be the luckiest man in the world.

"I need you, Sterre! I love you, Sterre! Will you marry me?" I simply but nervously asked.

Breathless, as she stood quivering, I pressed the coin into her palm as an expression of my love as she shouted out repeatedly the one word I longed to hear: "Yes! Yes! Yes!"

Over and over again she screamed those words to my joy and happiness.

I promised her a more formal proposal when we got together again, but she said that wouldn't be necessary. She said she would cherish her special nickel forever.

Then, she gently whispered into my ear, "Heaven, I'm in Heaven!" Our special moment could not have been more perfect.

Al was speechless for once as my entire Limburg family, including my uncles, their children, Sterre's family, and friends, Sister Truus, even Father Peter, greeted us that last morning in Schimmert to wish us a safe journey home to America.

Later, in Maastricht, I had to gather all of my inner strength to keep my heart from breaking. I could feel her pain as she wept with Kelly by her side, her arms around Sterre, as they stood alone on the platform after we boarded the train. Memories of her standing there in tears as the steam engine pulled away from the station would haunt me. As I settled into my seat, Al and I spoke very little on the way to Hamburg. I just wanted to fall asleep and dream of her.

Diary: August 26, 1936
My first entry. Sterre, I will always love you!

CHAPTER TWELVE
BACK HOME IN THE GOOD OL' USA!

Arriving in Hamburg later than planned, Al and I hurriedly boarded the SS Deutschland as scheduled. Thinking back, our sea voyage and the train trip back home to Chicago with a stopover in Bloomington to visit my parents seemed like a blur.

Having some of our Olympic athletes and coaches onboard the ship allowed Al and me to have exclusive access to many enthralling, behind-the-scenes stories. Getting a few scoops for the Tribune during the week-long sea crossing helped take my mind off Sterre and gave me pause to consider my strategy moving forward.

During the short visit home, I had a long-awaited, eye-opening discussion about Sterre with my parents. Even though I was a grown man, a little family wisdom went a long way to help ease my weary soul. Mother was especially pleased to hear about my unexpected romance, and whenever I failed to fully explain the little details about my new courtship, she'd quiz me about any tantalizing tidbits I was willing to offer. Her enthusiasm for our happiness was infectious.

When I finally returned to Chicago, I moved back into the boarding house that I shared with three other friends. Two of them were junior accountants who worked for Sears, Roebuck & Co., and the other was a young distribution supervisor for the Tribune. After a few days back on the job, I slowly settled into my normal routine. Strangely, it felt as if the memories I'd just experienced at the Olympic Games had just faded away. My mind was elsewhere.

As for my friends in Chicago, all eyes were glued to the bigger story of the moment: The mighty Cubs were in the race to win the National League pennant. The baseball team was led by its second baseman, Billy Herman, who batted .334 and by pitcher Tex Carleton, who went 14-10 during the '36 campaign. But it was not to be the magical finish that Cubs' fans had hoped; they ended the season tied for second with the St. Louis Cardinals, five games back of the New York Giants, who went on to represent the league in the World Series.

After the high expectations of a baseball championship faded, I found the courage to explain my complicated situation concerning Sterre to my editors and was surprised by their amusement. After hearty congratulations, they agreed to allow me to work as many extra days as possible so I could save money to pay for her passage to America to visit me and, hopefully, make plans for our wedding.

Grandfather Wilhelm also offered me a little financial help for Sterre's arrangements. My grandfather reasoned he could not just stand by and witness my anguish without taking some action. Besides, he could not wait to meet my sweet Sterre from his beloved hometown.

It took nearly 10 lonely months of sheer heartache until Sterre's difficult preparations were at last finalized. She'd only been out of the Netherlands once in her life, and then only to Belgium, just 15 miles from her home. She was scheduled to leave the Port of Rotterdam on June 9, 1937, for a 40-day trip to the United States. Her arrival in New York was set for June 16. The voyage to America and back home aboard the SS Volendam of the Holland-America Line called for 14 days to crisscross the Atlantic. Her itinerary called for two additional days for train travel from New York to Chicago and back which left only 24 days for us to spend some time together.

I looked forward to showing her Chicago before a visit to my parents' farm in Bloomington. Without her knowledge, I had arranged to accompany her on her return to New York and planned to interrupt the train ride back with a two-day side trip to the lush green hills of my beloved childhood home. I desperately wanted her to experience in person the mountainous valleys I roamed during my youth, the beautiful place where I was born and raised, West "By God" Virginia!

Luckily, I had kept in touch with Jonathan and Herbert Engel, the friends I'd met last year when we traveled together to Europe aboard the ocean liner, SS New York. The guys graciously offered to meet Sterre at the harbor's dock in New York and personally accompanied her to Grand Central Station where she boarded the train to Chicago.

When she stepped off the train at the LaSalle Street station, I eagerly greeted her with a long-delayed kiss and a bouquet of a dozen of Chicago's finest ruby-red tulips. My buddy Al had made arrangements with Darrell Ferrell, one of the Trib photographers, to take a picture of the reunion. Darrell later presented each of us with a framed copy as keepsakes.

Sterre was happy to finally see me, but jokingly informed me upon her arrival that she had feared I wouldn't be on the terminal's platform to meet her. Relieved after seeing my cheerful mug, the fear that she might have to fend for herself in a foreign city with very little money soon faded. Exhausted from her long journey, there was no fooling around on the night of Sterre's arrival. She collapsed on my bed and quickly fell fast asleep.

The next day, we made a speedy tour around town. I took her to the Navy Pier, and we strolled through Lincoln Park and along Lakeshore Drive so we could talk about our future. She was astounded by the tall buildings and huge department stores that dotted bustling Chicago's skyline and amazed by the heavy traffic and gigantic mansions that lined her busy streets. They were sights she'd never before experienced.

Later, I introduced her to some of my friends at the Tribune. My boss, Herman Kellmeyer was among them, and he made a lasting impression.

"My dear, first, I'm honored to meet you and pleased to welcome you to Chicago. I feel partially responsible for getting you two lovebirds together. You see, I handpicked Mr. Fisher to go on that Olympic trip last year. All I expected were a few sports stories, not him bringing back a lovely bride such as you, my dear!" he gleefully, but a bit deceitfully, declared.

"Sir, I need to remind you that the wedding has not happened just yet."

"Oh, well, you'd better keep a close eye on this beauty, Joe. I may take her off your hands if you're not careful," he joked.

That day she also met my co-workers Kathy and Kirsten in advertising, Kim in the mail room, Margaret in layout as well as Howard in the sports department, and, of course, Sterre was reacquainted with my ol' pal, Al. They were my closest friends at the Trib and with whom I ate lunch almost daily.

Al invited us to dinner the next evening to introduce us to Ruth Ann, his new girlfriend. She wrote a gossip column for one of our rival newspapers, the Chicago American.

As we walked through the door of the restaurant, I could tell that Al was a little uncomfortable, but it was soon obvious to everyone he was enamored with Ruth Ann. When his new gal left the table to freshen up, he gave Sterre and me a few rules to follow.

"Please agree with everything she says, don't ask her to explain anything to you in detail, and please don't ask her to write anything down on paper because, if you must know, her handwriting is atrocious," Al warned us.

"Be prepared, it will take her 15 minutes or more just to order, and she'll insist on a comment from our waiter about every dish on the menu. But, otherwise, she's a doll, and I know you'll love her," he teased.

"Al has told me all about your romance with Joe. I think it's so exciting and intriguing," Ruth Ann said to Sterre upon her return.

Over the course of the evening, the two women talked for hours, and it appeared a new friendship was developing. Only one glitch occurred in our otherwise wonderful dinner engagement, and that happened when Ruth Ann asked a simple question of our unsuspecting waiter.

"Please tell me what looks good on the menu for this evening." Ruth Ann demanded. The answer to that one question took 21 minutes.

Al said, "I told you so," as the three of us had a hearty laugh while Ruth Ann and the waiter conversed. Even with her quirky nature, it was clear that

Al was in a serious relationship, and we could not have been happier for him.

The next three weekends Sterre and I found ourselves on Mother and Pop's farm. They immediately fell in love with her and were charmed by her calming presence, and infatuated by her inner and outer beauty. A strong bond formed between my mother and Sterre within minutes. I knew it would.

"Mrs. Fisher, I brought you something from Schimmert that I thought you might enjoy," Sterre said as she handed my mother an envelope filled with some black-and-white photos of Schimmert.

"They include ones of your uncles, Karl and Wouter, their children, my father and brothers, Sister Truus, several of the small hamlet chapels, the current Sint Remigius Church, your old school, and the Water Tower."

Mother held Sterre's hand as they paused to discuss each photo.

Opa Wilhelm was also very excited to see the pictures and commented about every setting depicted. All was calm until Mother saw the last photo. It was an image of her treasured fountain stone. When she saw it, she broke down in tears and was joined in her joy by Sterre and Opa as they all hugged and cried in the middle of our living room.

"Oh, my God!" Mother cried out in delight over and over again. More hugs followed. It was a touching moment.

"Marjo, your dear mother, told me in her letters that she took you to our special place many times," Mother recalled. "As children, she and I would go there to play. We'd make silly wishes and dream about being princesses and other far-fetched fun things."

"Yes, Mother told me those stories, and I shared some of them with Zef last year when I took him there," Sterre replied proudly.

"Ah, yes, he told me, dear, and I love that you call him Zef. That's a special name only we girls get to call him," Mother responded with a gleeful wink.

"Zef told me about that day and added some lovely details, too," Mother continued. "You see, Sterre and Zef, Marjo's and my wishes did finally come true. Just looking at the two of you, so happy and so in love, you're living proof that our dreams were fulfilled. Isn't that right, Raymond?"

Mother looked to my father as he sat in his favorite chair with his ever-present cigarette in hand.

"Of course, you're right, my love," Pops said. "We are all very happy about Joe and Sterre. After dinner, Sterre, I want my dear Rebekka to show you her fountain that Joe and I made for her shortly after we moved here. We hammered on that rock for days to give her a duplicate of the one in Schimmert. Take that photo with you when you go out back to see hers and let me know how it compares. From the day Rebekka and I met, I've heard many tales of that magical fountain stone."

Pops looked at Sterre before chuckling and giving her another welcoming wink. She had won Pops and Opa Wilhelm over the minute I told them that I was in love with her.

"Mother, you're getting a little too dramatic, maybe, but I certainly agree that I'm a very lucky man to have both of my precious girls together in the same room," I said with a wide smile on my face.

"Now you beautiful, lollipops, what's for dinner?"

"In honor of Sterre's visit, we're having some all-American fare tonight: a thick, tender steak, some fresh vegetables and potatoes, homemade bread, and a fresh apple pie that's still baking in the oven. I picked the apples this morning for the occasion. Does that sound good, my son?" she asked.

"No, Mother, that does not sound good. It sounds great. Pops, Opa and I will be at the table with fork and knife in hand ready to eat as soon as it's ready, I can assure you of that, dear Mother," I said in jest.

As I expected, each day my family became more smitten with Sterre and she with them. Her visit to our farm could not have been more perfect. It was easy for everyone who met her to tell that we were meant to be together, a fact that I'd known since the day I first saw her back in Schimmert.

I desperately wanted to marry her in Bloomington, but Sterre, with Mother's support, wanted to wait until June 1938 to exchange our vows in Schimmert. My father said by waiting, my mother would have an opportunity to return to her homeland to attend the ceremony. Over my objections, they all concluded that it was perfect timing for my mother to visit Schimmert to see her only son standing proudly at the altar of her hometown chapel to marry his beautiful bride. Besides, Sterre had always dreamed of having her wedding day in front of her family and friends at her church. With the odds stacked against me, I reluctantly agreed.

To our disappointment, the time Sterre was with us in America flew by. Before I knew it, we found ourselves on the train heading east toward the hills of West Virginia. Our visit to my childhood home was short and sweet, but, to my joy, Sterre fell in love with the charming place at first glance.

A little less than two months after Sterre left the United States to return to Holland, I revisited West Virginia to attend a funeral that I'd hoped would never occur. Our family was rocked by the news that my beloved Grandfather Wilhelm had died of a heart attack on October 3, 1937, while visiting his old friend and colleague, Dr. J.K. Barton, in Morgantown.

My grandfather Wilhelm had traveled by train to Morgantown to view the glorious golden autumn leaves. It was only fitting that his life ended in his beloved second home. Thankfully, we were able to bury him beside his devoted wife. My Oma Renee was the one true love of his life. I knew my mother was deeply saddened by his passing, but she also took great comfort in knowing that her parents were reunited side by side at their final resting place in West Virginia.

Weeks later, Mother found in Opa's chest of drawers a life insurance policy that he had purchased from his State Farm agent when he first arrived in Bloomington. In addition to the proceeds from his policy, he left Mother an inheritance that more than paid for his funeral expenses with a small amount left over for her.

But just a month before Mother and I were scheduled to depart for Holland and my wedding, Father suffered what was described by his doctor as "a mild stroke." I had planned our voyage on the brand-new SS Nieuw Amsterdam so Mother would have the luxury of traveling home aboard a Dutch vessel. The massive ship had just completed her maiden voyage and began full service between New York and Rotterdam in May 1938.

Sterre's stunning hand-made wedding dress, sadly, had to be stored away for another day. Her father, Paul, had paid for the delicate material and the good Sister Truus and Sterre's best friend, Kelly, painstakingly, took three months to carefully stitch the beautiful fabric together. When finished, the dress was dazzling, perfectly fitting for my future bride in every way and defined by the two seamstresses' astute attention to detail.

The news about Pops was devastating, however. Mother could not leave Father during his crisis, and neither could I. Sterre fully understood after I explained the situation. I canceled our tickets and used the money to help pay for Father's medical expenses. Shortly after, I decided to leave my job with the Tribune. My place was back in Bloomington helping my parents run the farm. Mother faithfully attended to my father's care and couldn't handle the operation of the farm by herself.

Father partially recovered after a few months and was left with a slight limp. He joked that it gave him even more character. As he grew stronger, Mother took a job with State Farm.

George J. Mecherle, the company's founder, met my parents at a church function one Sunday afternoon and offered Mother a job on the spot after learning of Father's condition. She gratefully accepted and began working immediately. Her first duties required her to learn how to roller skate since her job as a mail clerk required speed and dexterity to deliver the office mail between departments. The extra money she earned certainly helped. As Father continued to get better, the farm did as well. Our fall harvest was our best since moving to Illinois. So much so, that we were able to hire two additional workers to help us carry on while Pop's recovered.

Because of our good fortune that year, and my father's improved health, I was able to schedule another voyage to Holland. This time I was going alone since Mother refused to leave my father's side. With their full blessings, however, I planned to leave for Holland with Oma Renee's wedding ring in-hand to marry my sweetheart.

At their urging, I purchased an open-ended, round-trip ticket on the first ship I could. I booked passage on the French-built SS Normandie, which at the time was the largest cruise liner afloat and the flagship of France's passenger fleet. The ship's route was between New York and Cherbourg. From there, I could easily catch a train to Maastricht. The earliest booking I could secure was for Sunday, October 1, 1939, which allowed me to work on the farm during part of the autumn harvest.

Some unexpected good news also occurred during that time. I was blessed to be the best man at Al Obermeyer's wedding in Chicago on June 30, 1939. The Friday night service at Old Saint Mary's Church on Michigan Avenue was a doozy. The sanctuary of the big church was filled to near capacity with Al's old college chums and his family members who had come down from Wisconsin to celebrate. His sisters, Fay and Phyllis, loved a good time, just like Al, and they danced to every song. And, boy, could those two sisters put away the booze.

They, along with Ruth Ann's party-loving big family, were all raring to go led by her parents, Lester and Mary, her rowdy brothers Bill, Bob, and Mark, and her spirited sister, Vicky. Al's many acquaintances from the Trib filled in the leftover spaces. It would have made a lot of sense to have hidden the booze away from that crowd that evening, but all went well for everyone. Except for Vicky, who, I learned later, came close to relieving herself in an elevator after drinking one too many.

The Tribune published a nice feature story written as a favor by yours truly, accompanied by a picture of the bride and groom plastered on the front page of section C in its Sunday edition. It showed Al and Ruth Ann sipping from champagne glasses after a toast from Al's father, Virgil.

But the peace and joy in another small part of the world was shattered on September 1, 1939, when Nazi Germany invaded Poland, its eastern neighbor. That set in motion a chain of events felt around the globe and ushered in what would soon become known as World War II.

Immediately after Hitler's armies rolled across the Polish plains,

England and France declared war on Germany, honoring their alliance with the Poles, and soon after several other countries followed. My cruise liner, the Normandie, was seized by U.S. authorities on September 3 and was mothballed at Pier 88 in New York Harbor where the majestic ship remained until ravaged by an accidental fire in February 1942.

Soon after the invasion of Poland, passenger ship transport to Europe became extremely limited and a travel voucher difficult to obtain. When American government officials started warning our citizens not to travel to Europe by ship, tickets became virtually impossible to secure. No other safe means of transport existed. After much haggling, I received a refund for my ticket, which was of little consolation. I needed to be with Sterre. Our romance had been put in a state of limbo with no apparent quick solution to our horrible dilemma.

We could never have imagined in our wildest dreams that our plans would be interrupted by a maniacal tyrant, who was hell-bent on making the world his own. Our last kiss at Pier 39 in New York Harbor in the summer of 1937 seemed destined to be the last one ever between me and my true love.

When the hostilities began, neither the United States nor the Netherlands was at war. Our countries had not bought into the madness and the bravado. I prayed that cooler heads would prevail.

Italy and Germany had signed a military alliance in May 1939 called the "Pact of Steel," and England and France were allied and supported Poland's sovereignty.

After the Polish invasion, the armies of Italy and Germany expanded their aggression and Japan continued its conquests in the Far East. As the newsreels gravely featured one Axis Power's brutal act after another, the world soon learned to despise those warmongering countries even more. I blamed the Nazi and Fascist sons-of-bitches for causing my pain and blocking my path to Sterre's arms.

Diary: September 9, 1939

I'm angry at you for not marrying me while you were in the United States two years ago. I know all of the reasons you went back to Schimmert, and your decision was the correct one, but it's so difficult bearing this pain alone. I'm angry!

With little hope of soon reuniting with Sterre, I helped my parents operate our farm and wrote a few feature articles for the Bloomington newspaper, biding my time with little to no contact with Sterre. I wrote letters to her almost daily, but most came back posted as undeliverable. Our mailman even felt my agony.

The most innocent of situations would remind me of her. As a distraction, I took my parents to Chicago in March 1940 to spend a weekend away from the farm and to ease the disappointment of being without Sterre. Al and Ruth Ann graciously invited us to stay at their home. Our discussions danced around the conflict and my desperate plight. But, somehow, we muddled through talking about their honeymoon during dinner. Seeing the happiness that my best friend was experiencing helped ease my pain, but reminded me of my loss.

On our last night in the city, we all went to see my parents' favorite actor Clark Gable in his new movie, "Strange Cargo." Gable's character, Verne, struggled with being jailed and his timing at finding his true love, Julie, played by Joan Crawford. Just like Gable's Verne, I suffered from my own internment, a mental pain that kept me separated from Sterre. And just as Sterre waited for me, Crawford's Julie agreed to wait for Verne until he was free.

For me, the movie represented one of those defining moments. I could not get Sterre out of my thoughts, and it was beginning to affect my mind and health. My friends and parents knew it, too. I realized I had to change my attitude. From that day on, I changed direction and decided to focus my energy on positive things. My newspaper articles reflected my new optimism. I knew I would somehow find a way into Sterre's arms again and vowed to anyone who'd listen that I would never give up on our reunion or love.

CHAPTER THIRTEEN
TRAPPED IN THE EYE OF THE STORM

Any hope for peace ended on May 10, 1940. The invasion of the Dutch homeland started on the same day that Winston Churchill was named the new British Prime Minister. The former First Lord of the Admiralty succeeded Neville Chamberlain, who 19 months earlier had miscalculated his adversaries and incorrectly boasted to the British people by declaring he had helped achieve "peace in our time" after his "Munich Agreement" meeting with Hitler and Italy's dictator Benito Mussolini on September 30, 1938.

For the Dutch, the thought of peace had long faded from memory. On that fateful Friday, the might of Germany's powerful Wehrmacht Army was poised just a few kilometers inland from their common border awaiting orders to begin the attack. At precisely 4 a.m., their Panzer tanks swept across the flat plains of the Netherlands. A terrible darkness like no other before befell the helpless, little peace-loving nation. Schimmert was not spared the indignation and fear that comes with war. Its citizens didn't know then, but the nightmare their country was facing would last for almost five long years.

There had been rumors weeks before that the Germans had been massing troops near the nation's common border, but the Dutch felt they had little to fear since Holland was a neutral country and posed no military threat to Germany. So, why would Hitler attack them? The shock of such an event ever happening was unthinkable.

On that sunny clear day, Limburg felt the sting of hundreds of military vehicles from Germany's Army Group B. For the first time, the people of Schimmert heard the rumble of the Wehrmacht's tanks and listened to the roar of distant bombardment emanating from over the horizon. The sky was filled with screeching dive bombers, and the blasts of their bombs could be heard well into the night and throughout the next day. For several days thereafter, thousands of Hitler's soldiers and mechanized vehicles hurried through the tiny villages of Limburg eager to enter the fray.

After the initial assault, additional German support troops followed on bicycles and motorcycles while others rode on horseback. Horses also pulled wooden carts and wagons loaded with supplies. There was an odd assortment of trucks, the larger ones carried boats or pulled massive artillery guns. The last group of infantrymen that passed through Limburg's villages merely walked.

The people of Schimmert were told to stay inside their homes and off the roads, and warned not to interfere in any way with the German advance. Many of the town's citizens wept in stunned disbelief as they watched the endless procession from their front doors and windows. Unbelievably, some locals flashed the Nazi salute with their arms outstretched and offered the enemy soldiers drinks of water, or worse, spoke words of encouragement. A few waved small Nazi flags and cheered seemingly in joy as their beloved town and country were being violated.

"How could some people from our village be so treasonous, so disloyal to their friends and neighbors?" Sterre, clearly shocked, asked her father.

"Traitors!" he answered in anger.

"Who could they trust?" they wondered out of fear and sadness.

"Oh, my God, Father, what is to become of us, our family?" Sterre pleaded with her father, searching for answers.

"How can we endure this horrible catastrophe?" she questioned.

"Don't you worry, my children, we'll all be OK," Paul reassured his family, although the quiver in his voice betrayed his apprehension.

During the night, the bombing continued uninterrupted. Fortunately,

Schimmert was spared that horror. Sterre, fatigued and lying in her bed under her covers, thought of the frightened innocent victims being killed as she hugged her pillow and wept softly. Nobody in the family slept that dreadful night as heavy trucks and soldiers kept filing past the front of their house.

"Please, God," she prayed with little conviction. "Please help and protect our family and friends."

Wondering what might happen to them was exhausting. Battling the frightening thoughts racing through her mind was even more terrifying than the reality of her country's desperate situation. Her father tried his best to comfort his family, but his words of encouragement rang empty as the days wore on.

"Just wait and see," he reassured them over and over.

During the Great War, Holland had remained neutral and had hoped to continue that status, but that faint possibility was now shattered. From the onset, the Dutch military leaders fully understood it would be virtually helpless in any fight with the Germans. But still, with incredible odds stacked against them, the Dutch soldiers fought bravely.

When the war began, the Netherlands had a very small army that consisted of only 20 army battalions. Most of the troops were poorly trained and equipped with light weapons. The air force was almost nonexistent as was the navy with just a few warships in active service. Essentially, the peace-loving Dutch were totally unprepared for the onslaught that was happening before their very eyes.

Maastricht was overrun within a few hours. The Dutch garrison stationed there managed, however, to destroy some vital bridges that spanned the Maas River. But, German army engineers built new pontoon bridges within hours and began pouring men and materiel forward toward the Belgian border and their main target, the fort at Eban-Emael on the Albert Canal. The battle at Maastricht claimed 47 Dutch and an estimated 150 German soldiers as casualties.

The fortress of Eban-Emael was built after the Great War and was considered by many to be impregnable. But it was captured and destroyed by the Germans within two days. After landing, specially trained airborne assault troops focused their attack on what proved to be the most vulnerable section of the fortress, the rooftops. With unprecedented speed, by using high explosives and flamethrowers, the airborne troops efficiently defeated the fortifications defenses and disabled its massive artillery gun emplacements. It was one of the few times that gliders and airborne troops had been deployed in warfare, preceded only by other similar German units that were successfully dropped into Denmark and Norway just one month before.

From the air, the Nazi Luftwaffe with its Junkers JU-87 Stuka dive bombers, fitted with their screeching sirens howling as they descended, wreaked havoc as their bombs rained down upon the helpless Belgian reinforcements who were attempting to relieve the battered fort's defenders. The swift surrender of Eban-Emael was a devastating blow to the morale of the western allies of Belgium, France, and Britain, whose stunned troops were in total disarray and retreating on all fronts as their front-line positions became ever-more vulnerable.

Early one morning, just days after the hostilities began, the Trags family nervously tended to their animals and their routine farm chores. Sterre was in the house when she saw eight German soldiers riding in a truck stop their vehicle near the family's front gate. The men quickly got out of the vehicle and scattered in front of the house. Her legs started to shake a little when she heard a knock at the front door.

As she opened the door, an officer loudly said in German, "Heil Hitler! My name is Lieutenant Mueller. Who owns this house?"

Still trembling and in shock, all Sterre heard was "Heil Hitler." Oddly, the first word that came out of her mouth was "goedemorgen."

He asked again but more harshly: "Again, who is in charge of this property?"

"My father," she told him.

The impatient lieutenant insisted that she summon her father immediately. He was well dressed in a spotless black uniform and wore black boots that came almost to his knees. He remained on the first floor, which contained an open living space including the kitchen and a small bedroom located in the back, while two other soldiers ran up the stairs to the bedrooms.

"Komm raus! Komm raus!" (Come out! Come out) they screamed.

Sterre told the lieutenant that no one was upstairs, but he did not reply. He just stared at her.

Without warning, Paul walked into the room through the back door and was quickly apprehended by two soldiers.

The officer then confronted her father and read loudly to him from a piece of paper written in Dutch:

"By proclamation of the general staff of German Armed Forces now occupying Limburg province, all residents over the age of 16 living in Schimmert and the surrounding villages are hereby ordered to attend a town meeting on Sunday, May 19th at 12:00 (noon) at the Sint Remigiuskerk in Schimmert. Your attendance at this meeting is mandatory. There will be no exceptions to this order."

"Understood?" he shouted.

Sterre's father nodded in agreement.

The lieutenant came to attention, clicked his heels, shot his right arm into the air, and shouted sternly, "Heil Hitler." He strode out of the house as his men hurriedly followed in strict military order behind him. The soldiers quickly proceeded to a neighbor's house, just down de Kling road.

Two days later, at Schimmert's massive Sint Remigius Catholic church, which sat squarely in the center of the village, the devastated residents were greeted by a German military band playing marching songs as they filed past and entered the church's main sanctuary. Once inside, they saw a German army captain standing smartly dressed at the altar in front of 30 or so rows of wooden pews. The town's priest, Father Peter, stood behind the captain along with several other German army officers of various ranks. Beside them sat village officials.

The sisters and monks of the Montfort's religious order, Saint Maria, were seated on benches in the front rows with 40 or more seminary students located behind them, each with their hands folded in their laps and their heads tilted downward looking at the cut-stone floor.

Sint Remigius, the town's sacred place of worship, seemed at first to be a strange setting to listen to the humiliating terms of the nation's surrender. Days earlier the Luftwaffe's brutal air assault on the Dutch port city of Rotterdam killed as many as 1,000 inhabitants, and the Germans threatened more devastating bombings to other major cities if the Dutch kept resisting. Because of the pressure, government officials reluctantly agreed to halt the hostilities on May 14, only five days after the invasion of their homeland had begun.

The military marching band, which had previously been playing in front of the church, was now standing at attention just to the right of the altar. The mood was surreal and somber. Most townspeople in attendance were confused and demoralized, and the subdued expressions on their faces bore witness to that stark fact. All the available seats were filled, forcing others in attendance to stand in the aisles.

Precisely at noon, the heavy doors on the building were closed with a loud thump that echoed throughout the massive church's sanctuary. The whole space fell silent, and, for a brief moment, only the sorrowful sounds of a few women softly weeping could be heard.

The band's field commander raised his baton and signaled its musicians to begin playing. The first song played was "Das Lied der Deutschen," the German national anthem.

As the music ended, the captain shouted, "Heil Hitler," unsettling most people in the crowd who sat in stunned silence, dazed by the helpless circumstances in which they found themselves.

But the most disturbing moment came when the traumatized audience helplessly observed a few of their neighbors and friends willingly and wholeheartedly offering the Nazi salute and deliriously applauding as they joined their conquerors in shouting, "Heil Hitler."

"Traitors among us," Sterre thought as her heart sank with alarm.

Paul and Sterre sat listening in anger as the captain began to speak. He was difficult to understand because he was using a combination of German and Dutch. While clenching her fists and grinding her teeth, she focused on every word that the man uttered so she could later clearly relay them to her father, who understood very little German.

First, the captain read the same proclamation, word for word, that the other officer had recited a few days ago in their home. Then, oddly, he thanked the Dutch government for ending the hostilities to avoid more tragedy for the sake of both their nations even though more than 10,000 Dutch soldiers had senselessly been killed or wounded defending their homeland.

Sterre silently prayed that their sacrifice would not be forgotten.

The captain rambled on, declaring that little would change for them. The people of Schimmert, who loved their country, knew better.

"You can expect your lives to continue as before with just a few necessary required modifications," he insisted as he shared that the German people valued their close friendship with their Dutch neighbors.

"All German troops will treat you and your property with respect," he assured his audience. And he warned that during the occupation cooperation and the restoration of order would be in the best interest of all involved.

He ended his disturbing speech by rattling off a list of 12 mandates:

A 9 p.m. curfew would be strictly enforced.

*Within three days, all guns, ammunition, and any sharp weapons
such as swords, hatchets, and axes, even family heirlooms,
must be collected and delivered promptly to the St. Maria School,
which would serve as the temporary headquarters of the military
administration until complete order was restored.*

*Proof of personal identification must be present on all citizens at
all times with the exception of children under the age of 16.*

*Absolute cooperation with no interference would be expected
from every citizen.*

*A complete list of all residents living at one's property must be
delivered within three days to the headquarters. The list must
include full names with dates of birth, religious preferences,
address, occupations, skills, and a description of all vehicles
and animals owned.*

*All shortwave radios must be turned over to the authorities
within three days. All other radios must be registered.*

*A temporary travel ban would go into effect immediately. No one
will be permitted to travel more than three kilometers from home
except for those with occupations classified as essential, such as
nurses, doctors, coal miners, utility and factory workers, or
others as approved by the military administration.*

*All non-essential traffic of any kind would not be permitted on all
highways and roads until further notice, meaning no motorized
vehicles of any kind, no horses or horse-drawn carts or wagons*

with the exception of bicycles, emergency vehicles such as ambulances, and public transportation vehicles.

Unless permitted by authorities, telephone use or riding a train or bus would not be permitted.

Any and all complaints or questions must be presented to military administration headquarters where a resolution or final verdict will be determined by occupation authorities.

Any form of armed or violent resistance that resulted in death or injury to any German soldier would be punishable by death.

Anyone caught violating the mandates would face harsh punishment as deemed appropriate by the military administration.

As the captain finished his list, Paul gently reached for Sterre's hand, put his warm fingers on top of hers, rubbed them softly, and looked straight into her eyes. He gave his daughter a reassuring fatherly look while nodding his head that all was going to be OK. She felt his confidence and thought if only she had his strength. She loved him now more than ever.

Before the meeting ended, other German officers presented to the stunned audience more obvious lies and false promises. Limburgers prayed that night, hoping that the allied armies or politicians could somehow end the madness.

Before the war, the Netherlands had many private radio companies that controlled radio signal frequencies and transmissions in the country. Those companies required their customers to pay a monthly subscription fee in order to have their radios directly wired to a provider, but only three or four channels could be heard on the system. After the German occupation, all of the private radio providers were nationalized and brought under the jurisdiction of the PTT, the Posterijen, Telegrafie & Telefonie, or in English, the Postal Telegraph & Telephone. This was done to centralize all radio transmissions, which allowed the Germans to better control the news broadcasts that they produced. They, of course, blanketed the airwaves with propaganda and biased programming.

Most Dutch families that owned radios used their own antennas, however, and were able to tune into many more channels than the direct-wired systems allowed, including the British Broadcasting Company (BBC). Starting in July 1940, just two months after Holland's surrender to the Germans, the BBC began broadcasts directed to the Netherlands in their native Dutch language and called it Radio Oranje. The Dutch government in exile in London managed and produced the content for the shows, which provided factual news and information that their countrymen trusted and could depend upon. Radio Oranje could be heard on the airwaves of the BBC for 15 minutes every evening starting at 9:00 p.m.

Shortly after Radio Oranje began its broadcasts on the BBC, all Dutch citizens were ordered to deliver even their home radios to the German authorities. The Trags family had two radios but decided to turn in only one and hide the other, even under the threat of severe punishment including death. The family felt there was power in knowing the truth, and wholeheartedly believed that understanding would ultimately help the Dutch resist their oppressors. Most Dutch citizens covertly and regularly listened to Radio Oranje and were loyal to their queen. They believed in her messages of hope and encouragement. It was through the broadcasts that the Dutch learned to their relief that Queen Wilhelmina, along with more than 4,000 Dutch military and government personnel, had escaped to England aboard a British vessel.

"Long live the Queen," they prayed.

Sterre and her younger brother, Arjan, tied the Phillips Superinductance 634A radio to the rear rack of Sterre's bicycle. Initially, typical standard radios were not required to be turned over to the authorities, but their powerful Phillips model was, due to its clarity and strong reception. The radio had special significance since it was a Christmas present for their mother from Sterre and her brothers. They had worked and saved for six months to pay for the luxury.

"Remember the smile on Mother's face when we gave her this radio? Who would have ever thought it would end up being taken from us by German soldiers?" Arjan said dejectedly.

"As depressing as that may sound, Arjan, in a strange way we're fortunate Mother is not here to see what is happening to us, to her friends, and to her beloved Schimmert," Sterre declared with a sigh, reflecting on her mother's tragic death five years earlier.

"Instead, remember the good fun we all had huddled around this radio under our blankets listening to music and our favorite mystery broadcasts. Can't you remember Mother making vegetable soup, and Father letting us have a little sip of his beer?"

"Yes, I remember, but it still makes me sad, no, mad, to give Mother's radio to those Nazis," Arjan said angrily.

"I know it makes you sad, but erase those bad visions from your mind and think only positive thoughts," Sterre said. "We are all still together, and we shall all stay together through this ordeal as a family. Father believes it, and I do, too, and so must you. Now, get back to the barn and help Father with the chores. Tell him I will be back in an hour or so, OK?"

Arjan watched her pedal down the narrow de Kling Road until she was out of sight.

As she turned onto Hoofdstraat in the center of Schimmert, 10 German soldiers who were gathered there started to stare at her and some made improper comments as she rode past them. Without warning, one of the soldiers, a Corporal Max Warner, lurched out into the street in front of her bicycle, startling her and forcing her to stop.

"Is there anything I can do for you, my dear?" he asked with a leer.

"I would be more than happy to help you do anything, and I mean anything," the smug soldier said slowly as he started a visual inspection of her body while she nervously stared straight ahead, never making eye contact with him. Though he had been in town only a few weeks, rumors of Cpl. Warner's rudeness, especially among women, had been circulating. His buddies started laughing and were having great fun watching Sterre's uncomfortable predicament.

She motionlessly sat on her bike in silence as the other soldiers surrounded her. They, too, began pelting her with inappropriate suggestions. Suddenly, an officer screamed out from the front steps of Sint Remigius Church, and all of the soldiers quickly came to attention.

"Hauptgefreiter Warner, explain to me what is going on here immediately!" the officer demanded as he walked briskly over to the group. "Well, corporal, speak up!" he ordered again harshly.

"Nothing, sir. We were just having a little fun with the fraulein. That was all, sir, just having a little fun," he answered uneasily.

"As I recall, you men were supposed to be helping push that stranded truck out of a ditch just down that road," the captain said, pointing down Montfortstraat.

"All of you, free that truck and then report back to your quarters. Now!" the captain bellowed.

The corporal responded in a loud voice, "Jawohl, sofort Capt. Welsch," as all of the soldiers signaled with the Nazi salute and then marched away without uttering another word.

"I don't want to hear about any of you men bothering this woman again, and that especially applies to you, Cpl. Warner. Do you understand me?" the officer shouted to the men as they marched away.

"Ja, Mein Herr," they all said in unison.

The corporal, however, cursed the captain under his breath with his fists clenched in rage.

Then, Welsch turned to Sterre and kindly said, "Please accept my sincere apology for the rudeness of my men. I promise you that it will not happen again, Fraulein. My men get a little anxious when they see such a beautiful woman like you, you must understand. I beg of you, miss ... miss?" he inquired, waiting for her to say her name.

"Trags," she answered politely.

"Miss Trags, you must have a first name as well, I presume," he calmly inquired.

"Sterre," she reluctantly responded.

"Ah, yes, Sterre. What a lovely name for such a lovely lady. If you should ever have any more difficulty with any of my men, you have my permission to report it to me personally, and I assure you I will take care of any concerns promptly. Would that be agreeable to you, Miss Trags?" he asked solicitously.

"Yes, captain, thank you. May I continue now? I must turn my radio over to your authorities as ordered," she replied.

"Of course, you may continue, Miss Trags, by all means. And I trust the rest of your day will be of a more pleasant nature," he said as she graciously nodded her head and rode off.

Welsch stood completely still as he watched her pedal down Montfortstraat. One of his lieutenants, who had been standing in front of the church observing the two from a distance, walked over, stood next to his superior officer, and offered him a cigarette, which the captain declined.

As the lieutenant pointed in Sterre's direction, he slowly remarked, "She is one beautiful woman, wouldn't you agree, sir?"

"Yes, I do agree, my friend. She's certainly a beautiful woman. Find out where she lives, lieutenant. I may need to pay Miss Sterre Trags a little visit in the near future," he mused suggestively.

After riding a short distance with her back now opposite the captain's, her hands started to shake, and her blues eyes began to well with tears. Panic filled her soul when she thought about what had just happened.

"Maybe this nightmare was going to be more difficult than I had imagined," she thought.

She understood that she needed to be more cautious and aware of how to avoid contact with any German soldier. To avoid alarming her father or brothers, when she returned home she did not mention the incident. During their evening meal, however, she did suggest that all of them should keep a low profile in any future interaction with soldiers.

She explained that the family needed to be respectful and act politely when confronted by German troops even though their pride may be at stake. The tactic was not shameful but actually cunning, she reckoned. She justified her suggestion since the family's goal needed to be avoiding danger in order to stay together. Sterre's family agreed that it was one of the survival tools they would deploy during the occupation.

Arjan ended the conversation by shouting, "All for one and one for all, just like 'The Three Musketeers!' Maybe we should consider the Trags family 'The Four Musketeers,' " he quipped, eliciting laughter from everyone.

Shortly after, things seemed to settle down in Limburg. But German troops and military supplies kept pouring across the border, as reports from the Nazi-controlled news outlets pointed toward a smashing victory, culminating with the account of the shocking retreat of the French and the British armies and their frantic evacuation at Dunkirk.

Welsch, who was obviously smitten with Sterre, visited her home on several occasions. He usually brought food or wine and stayed to talk longer than necessary, which made her family uneasy. But they politely listened to the captain's inquiries and stories. Though his actions appeared sincere, his presence placed them in an awkward position among their neighbors. His visits were unsolicited, but his presence and their courteous behavior toward the captain kept Cpl. Warner far from Sterre.

In the limited confines of Schimmert, the people abided by the 12 mandates outlined in the proclamation issued at the beginning of the occupation. But they were dismayed further when the jurisdiction of those

demands fell under the control of the hated Dutch Nationaal-Socialistische
Beweging, the NSB. Just when they hoped for some sort of normalcy from
the appalling war, the despised, fascist NSB swooped in with its black-
uniformed thugs pretending to be policemen. Those home-grown Nazi
traitors terrorized their Dutch brethren in ways that were both surprising
and harsh.

The NSB was founded in December 1931 in Utrecht, a Dutch city
of 160,000 inhabitants, 45 kilometers southeast of Amsterdam. One of
its founders, and later the group's detested political leader, was Anton
Adriaan Mussert. He was considered a Dutch fascist who modeled
his radical movement in the Netherlands after two of his inspirations,
Mussolini and Hitler. At first, the NSB even allowed Jews to become
members, but, after 1936, the party changed that policy and adopted a
more anti-Semitic view.

The party had minor political success in the mid-1930s, gaining two
Senate seats in the Dutch Parliament and garnering 8 percent of the vote
in the national election of 1935. But by 1939 it received only 4 percent of
the votes. Initially, Mussert had hoped to gain control of the Netherlands
by political means, but the government did not allow NSB Party members
to be civil servants, and church leaders and other political parties strongly
opposed them.

When Germany invaded Holland in 1940, the NSB became the only
political party permitted in the Netherlands; all other opposition parties
were disbanded. Of course, the NSB was propped up by the Germans as a
puppet government with the real power placed in the hands of Germany's
handpicked Austrian Nazi, Arthur Seyss-Inquart, who became the much-
hated Reich Minister of the Netherlands. Later during the war, he became
a virtual dictator over the Dutch.

The NSB's powers were limited to lower governmental and civil
service matters, and although Mussert was named "the leader of the
Dutch people," in reality his title was just an honorary farce. By 1941,

the NSB grew to more than 100,000 members, including thousands of Limburgers and their children, who were recruited to join the Nationale Jeugdstorm, a Dutch youth organization modeled after the Hitler Youth.

By 1943, many of the male members of the NSB were organized into the Landwacht and used as glorified policemen to control the Dutch population. Later, as many as 7,000 of them fought alongside the Germans on the Eastern Front against the Russians as members of the Nederlandsche SS. By September 1944, most of the hated organization's leaders had fled to Germany, and the party ceased to exist. In May 1945, the NSB was outlawed, and just days after the war's end, Mussert was arrested and executed by the Dutch after his pleas of mercy were rejected by Queen Wilhelmina.

The occupation, now going into its 15th week, was becoming routine. Sterre was swiftly riding her bicycle in an attempt to finish some errands and planned to visit a friend's mother who had wished to speak with her. On the way, she stopped at the intersection of Kruisstraat and Trichterweg at Mariakapel, a small four-by-four-meter chapel in the hamlet of Kruis, one of the five small sections of the town that constituted Schimmert.

The tiny chapel was built of brick with a large arched entrance and two small windows on both sides. A large cross rested atop the structure. She entered the small building as she frequently did and sat alone on the sole wooden pew. In complete silence, she reminisced for about 20 minutes about her mother and pleaded to her Lord for the safety of her family.

I learned later, much later, that I was always on her mind and in her prayers. She had received no news from me since May when the Germans occupied her country. She agonized, wondering if she would ever see me again, but vowed, as always, to stay true to the promises she made to me. Our separation was, now approaching four long years. She regretted, of course, the situations that had kept us apart before the war and fondly recalled her visit to America to see me and my family in 1937. I had sent money and arranged for her passage, but a week before her scheduled departure, her father broke his leg and dislocated his shoulder when he stumbled and fell from the roof of their house while attempting to make a repair. Even though her father and brothers insisted she should still go to America, Sterre only agreed after assurances from her family that they would take good care of her father while she was gone. She reluctantly left Holland under those circumstances.

She realized while sitting in the small chapel, neither of us had had the foresight to predict the present circumstances. She smiled when she remembered how quickly our bond formed and marveled at how strong her feelings and love for me still were. Despite the appalling situation, she still remained committed and hopeful, even though dire circumstances beyond our control prevented our reunion.

Our harsh and painful separation began, in large measure, as a result of the Nazis' ruthless invasion of Poland. Germany's military inflicted horrific carnage upon the Poles, who were dramatically outmanned and outgunned, and ended after a few weeks. The attack was preceded by years of continental turmoil.

After the armistice in 1918 that ended the Great War, Germany's western territories bordering France, the Saarland and Rhineland, were demilitarized and occupied by French troops as agreed upon by terms of the 1919 Treaty of Versailles. In January 1935, Saarland was allowed to vote on its national destiny and decided overwhelmingly to be reunited with Germany. In March 1936, German troops marched unopposed into the Rhineland, occupying its former territory. The Germans were greeted by cheering mobs.

On March 12, 1938, the Nazi state aggressively annexed its southern German-speaking neighbor, Austria. Later in 1938, Germany insisted the last territory it desired was the Sudetenland, which bordered eastern Germany and was part of the nation of Czechoslovakia. The Nazis claimed the German-speaking population living there was being persecuted and tormented by the Czechs. In an odd settlement called the Munich Agreement, British, French, German, and Italian representatives granted Hitler and Germany the Sudetenland. Even though the Sudetenland was Czechoslovakian territory, ultimately that country had no voice in the decision. Once again, in front of delirious, cheering crowds, German troops marched into Sudetenland in October 1938 without opposition.

In March 1939, Hitler broke the agreement and invaded the entire country of Czechoslovakia without fear of any military response from Britain or France.

After the invasion of Poland, Americans citizens were cautioned about traveling abroad, especially after England and France declared war on Germany on September 3, 1939, in support of their ally. Neither Allied power declared war on Soviet Russia, which also had attacked Poland in the same month as Germany. Previously, the two dictators, Germany's Adolf Hitler and Soviet Russia's, Joscph Stalin, had signed an agreement in August 1939 called the Nazi-Soviet Non-Aggression Pact. After that agreement, Germany and Russia felt empowered to attack and divided Poland between themselves without fear of each other militarily intervening. Russia's assault on Poland commenced on September 17.

Even though the United States had declared its neutrality shortly after Poland was invaded, Sterre realized soon after that any chance of me traveling to Europe to marry her had slipped away.

After the war began, European countries that operated cruise ships stopped their passenger service to the United States. American ship operators also experienced dramatically decreased bookings as cancellations from leery passengers increased, making it difficult to operate profitably. Ship owners also were fearful of an accidental or deliberate torpedo attack such as that suffered by the British ship SS Athenia when she was sunk by a German submarine with 300 Americans onboard, coincidentally, on the same day, Britain declared war on Germany.

While Sterre was sitting by herself, lost in her thoughts, she heard the roar of a motorcycle and realized the engine had come to a stop. She turned around and saw Capt. Welsch walking toward her. His tailored uniform was immaculate, and he looked intimidating wearing his shiny black boots. He lit a candle and placed it on the altar and then motioned with his hand for permission to sit down beside her. It was an awkward moment, but she had little choice. She nodded her assent.

"Do you come here often?" he asked.

"More than I used to come," she answered truthfully. "It gives me some peace to be here alone with my thoughts."

"Ah, alone, my dear Sterre. It is never a good thing for a woman as beautiful as you to be alone, especially now. Don't you agree?" he inquired.

"I enjoy being alone. It helps me to contemplate why men with power feel the need to have more power regardless of the consequences and pain it causes for so many innocent people," she said cautiously but firmly.

"I certainly understand your sentiments and see why you would feel as you do. If I were in your position, I'm sure I would feel the same way. But we Germans cannot forget the suffering our people had to bear from our defeat in 1918," he lamented.

"We fought runaway inflation, starvation, unrealistic reparations, high unemployment, and corruption, and my country almost stumbled into civil war, all due to the Jews and our corrupt former political hierarchy, backed by the French, British, and Americans if you fully believe Hitler," he explained with little conviction.

"So does that justify why your country would invade mine even though the Netherlands never wanted war? We only desired to be neutral as we were in the Great War. I don't understand war, and I hope I never do," she said.

After their exchange, they both sat there in silence pondering their next words. She wondered: Had she overstepped her boundaries? Was he going to arrest her for speaking so frankly?

Then he broke the silence: "Sterre, I realized you do not know me very well. I am a German military officer, as was my father. He was a major in the last war, and my grandfather served as a colonel during the Franco-Prussian War in 1870. Because of that respected tradition, I will serve my country with honor under any circumstances. The men in my family have always been proud Prussian officers trained as loyal and trusted members of the regular German army. I have never been accused of being a Nazi, nor will I ever become one in the future.

"Just so you know, I've had several Jewish friends throughout my life, and I'm saddened by what has become of them. Why just a few days ago, I was in Maastricht and witnessed an SS lieutenant kicking an old Jewish man in the street. Even though I outranked him, I'm helpless myself when attempting to interfere with the SS. I tried, but the lieutenant abruptly warned me to stand back and reminded me that the man he had kicked was nothing more than a filthy rat who was infecting the Fatherland. I am a Prussian and a father foremost, and a German second, but never a Nazi, never an SS man, Fraulein. Do you understand me?" he said with a stern, but moderate tone.

"I think maybe I do," she answered softly.

Changing her tone, she asked, "You said you are a father. How many children do you have?"

"One, a girl named Daisy," he responded.

"Daisy, like the flower?" she inquired.

"Yes, her mother loved that flower, and I'm home so rarely that I just agreed to let my wife, Sophie, select the name even though it is not a German name by any measure."

Suddenly and deliberately, the captain boldly placed his hand on top of hers. Visibly shaken, Sterre's initial reaction was discomfort, yet she remained motionless as he began to speak.

"I understand this may be awkward for you, but you must have realized by now that I have strong feelings for you, my dear," he said.

"I don't quite understand what's happening. I've done nothing to warrant, or invite, your attention," she muttered as she shook her head in bewilderment.

"You're an officer of an invading army and a married man as well. Please believe me when I say I appreciate your standing up and protecting me from that aggressive Cpl. Warner, but you and I can never have more than an innocent, harmless friendship formed during a troubling time."

"Well, I must say your description of our relationship seems a little harsh. If I were not married, would there be any possible chance for you and me?" he pressed. "I haven't been so charmed by anyone in my life until I met you."

Fearing an intense and possibly upsetting reaction, Sterre reluctantly told him that she loved another man, an American, named Joe.

"Perhaps I should tell you that I've done some investigating of my own and tell you that I've heard rumors about you and him. You met him years ago, I understand, but things must be different now," he said. "England will soon be defeated, and America is not even in the war and poses no threat to Germany. In reality, the likelihood of your seeing your American friend again would seem to be extremely remote. Someone as enchanting as you should never be without a strong male companion."

Perplexed, Sterre felt ambushed by his bizarre behavior and nervously peered into his eyes.

"It just occurred to me that I don't even know your first name," she said.

"Petri, my given name is Petri Hans Welsch," he replied in earnest.

"Petri, when was the last time that you saw your wife and daughter?" she asked.

"It's been a very long time since I've seen them. It was the year before the war began. I had planned several visits home, but before I was able to go, I was sent to Poland and now I'm here." He lamented.

"So, it has been almost two years," she calculated.

"Yes, almost two years," he shrugged.

"Can't you see, Petri, you don't really want me. You want them. You miss your wife and young daughter." She said softly.

"It only stands to reason why you are so lonely. Believe me, I fully understand how hurtful that raw emotion feels. Anyone who's been separated from their family and loved ones for such a long time would most likely be in search of affection," she reasoned.

"If your wife and daughter were living nearby and you were able to go home to them every night, you wouldn't have the slightest interest in pursuing a relationship with me," she reassured him.

Sterre had sensed his infatuation weeks ago but wanted his interest to go no further and felt the need to be direct.

"Captain, I'm flattered by your startling words, but please don't take what I am about to say the wrong way. You see, there can never any romantic feelings between us, for that matter, between me and any other man. I love Joe. I promised him that I would wait for his return, and I will. Forever, if necessary."

"Truthfully, didn't you make that same promise to your wife and child?" Sterre questioned.

Surprised by her candor, he had nonetheless wanted a clarification of their relationship. He respected her honesty and had even suspected her likely rejection of his unsolicited advance.

"Well, my dear Sterre, you're a wise and candid woman. I trust you will not blame a lonely man for trying. Your Joe is a very lucky man indeed," Welsch said dejectedly. "Please forgive my indiscretions, and rest assured, I will make no further mention of our encounter."

Then, he slowly rose, kissed her hand, and walked away.

Still, she was not fully certain about his sincerity, and she prayed for his understanding. She knew that all Germans were not Nazis, but still hated what their military and their fanatical policies had done to her country and to her beloved Limburg. Still, she did owe him some gratitude since it was he who had ordered Cpl. Warner to stay away from her and her family.

Sterre's friend, Tiny Jansen, had not been so lucky, however.

The skies had turned gray on that cool October day when Sterre left the chapel and hurried uneasily to the home of her friend's parents as she had earlier planned. Tiny was not at home when Sterre arrived. Tiny's mother quickly closed the door, led Sterre into the kitchen, and offered her a seat at the table.

"I must speak in a hurry to you about a frightful and serious matter that has happened to our family and our dear Tiny," Mrs. Jansen said anxiously.

"I can tell something is bothering you. Is it something that I can help you solve?" Sterre asked.

"Solving this problem may be impossible, but my husband won't talk about it, and I don't know where to turn," she said in anguish. "That's when I thought of you, Sterre. Can you talk to her? She needs to confide in a good friend like you, my dear! I know Tiny has always looked up to you ever since you two were little girls in school.

"I don't know any other way to say this, but, first, I need a promise that you will not mention what I am about to tell you to anyone, including your father. Promise?"

"I promise with my heart and to my Lord, I will not speak of this to anyone," Sterre agreed.

Mrs. Jansen burst into tears as she blurted out Tiny's dilemma.

"She's with child, and the father is a German soldier named Cpl. Max Warner!" she cried out.

"Cpl. Warner?" Sterre exclaimed.

"Yes, do you know him?" Mrs. Jansen asked urgently.

"No, not really. I ran into him a while back, but I do not know him," Sterre said with alarm.

"He denies that he's the father and refuses to acknowledge her in any way," Tiny's mother declared with embarrassment.

"Our family had even placed a German flag from the window of our home when their soldiers came here. The man has been welcomed into our home on several occasions. Most all of our neighbors and friends look at us with disgust now ever since the occupation. How do you think they will think of us when they find out that Tiny is pregnant and the father is a German soldier? For God's sake, my husband's grandfather was a German you know."

"I know you must be worried, Mrs. Jansen, but I promise, I will say nothing about our conversation to anyone, and I promise you that I will speak with Tiny as soon as possible," Sterre told her.

She left the Jansen home in shock and she sped home on her bicycle.

Two days later, Sterre talked to Tiny and offered her comfort, but realized at the same time she needed to keep her distance from her troubled friend to protect herself and her own family. Later, Sterre learned from Tiny that she had resolved her dilemma and had had a terrifying self-induced abortion with the assistance of her mother's nurse relative. Tiny almost died as a result.

The tragic episode gave Sterre one more reason to despise Cpl. Warner.

Only months after the initial invasion which began in May of 1940, the resulting momentum of Germany's military power proved to be enough to rout the armies of France and Britain and forced their eventual evacuation at Dunkirk. The war in the west appeared to be over. The air assault against Britain, according to German radio reports was going well and they felt Britain would soon sue for peace. Germany appeared to have finally gotten its long-sought revenge for the alleged Jewish betrayal that preceded its surrender and defeat in the First World War. The Germans believed they had evened the score by nearly destroying the armies of two of their bitter foes, who, the Nazi faithful believed, had inflicted upon their country the majority of the perceived injustices of the Treaty of Versailles of 1919.

Since war erupted, and after only a little more than 10 months of fighting, the Nazis had conquered and gained complete control of most of western Europe, including France, Denmark, Norway, Belgium,

Luxembourg, Austria, Czechoslovakia, Poland, and the Netherlands. The Germans repeatedly boasted over the airwaves with detailed accounts of their military victories and presented the image of being invincible. All of that bravado seemed entirely believable during the bleak fall and winter of 1940.

CHAPTER FOURTEEN
I'M IN
THE ARMY NOW

The United States was thrust into the war shortly after the empire of Japan's dastardly and deliberate surprise attack on our naval base at Pearl Harbor, Hawaii, on December 7, 1941.

I enlisted in the U.S. Army on July 2, 1942, in Bloomington and was sent directly to Fort Benning, Georgia, for basic training. The deployment was my first step in becoming an Army officer. Because of the massive number of recruits, the army needed thousands of junior officers in leadership roles. Since I had my college degree, my recruiter told me I possessed the qualifications required to be an officer candidate. I was agreeable since giving orders sounded much better to me than taking them.

My first impression of Fort Benning was the massive size of the base. In acreage, it was bigger than Bloomington with a population seven times greater than my Illinois farming community.

Our accommodations were woefully spartan. The wooden two-story barracks had been hastily constructed and had two open floors with bunk beds situated on either side and a single aisle cutting through the center. Tidy wooden footlockers sat at the foot of each bed with metal lockers for uniforms placed at the head.

The infamous latrine was at the far end of the first floor, which featured seven commodes in a neat row against one wall. There were no privacy dividers. On the opposite olive green-painted wall hung seven matching white porcelain sinks with accompanying framed mirrors. Everything we needed to start the day fresh and clean was located in that dimly lit open room that measured about 30 by 24 feet.

Attached to that unassuming space was a shower room with four water heads on both sides of the gray enamel spray-painted concrete walls and four drains embedded in the masonry floor.

Training in the Deep South in summer's suffocating, smoldering heat was torturous. When fully dressed out, we donned heavy woolen, long-sleeved fatigues and uncomfortable, ill-fitting leather boots. Our military gear included a heavy metal helmet, backpack, rain gear, utility belt, canteen, trench knife, and an Army-issue Garand M-1 rifle strapped over our shoulders.

It rarely rained that summer, and the dirt roads we marched on would stir up fine dust that was strangling. Our throats dried up, and the sweat burned our eyes as we ran in perfect formation through the Georgia pines on our way to becoming soldiers. I recalled never doing so many push-ups, sit-ups, and chin-ups or running so many miles in my life. We learned how to fire, clean, disassemble, and reassemble our M-1s blindfolded. We dug trenches with our utility shovels and learned how to throw hand grenades, maneuver at night with a compass, and use a bayonet. We became proficient in the art of hand-to-hand combat.

Of course, as future officers, we learned how to lead our men and to take charge when necessary. We were taught military protocol and learned the proper way to present ourselves to our men and superiors like the dignified American officers and gentlemen we were training to become.

Even though we'd been selected to become officers, our initial tutelage was conducted under the watchful eye of a non-commissioned taskmaster appropriately given the descriptive title, drill sergeant.

In the sparkling mess hall, there was a sign that hung over a table where metal dining trays and utensils rested. It simply read: "Take all you want, but eat all you take." We did just that and our platoon's Drill Sgt. Larry Hoffman enforced that rule to a T. As soon as we rushed through the chow line and sat down at a table, he would walk up and down the aisles screaming at the top of his lungs in his high-pitched voice.

"I want to see a fork in one hand and a knife in the other, and I'd better see sparks flying off of that metal plate as you gobble down Uncle Sam's free chow. Do you understand me, soldiers?" he'd bark.

We would all reply in unison by shouting out at the top of our lungs, "Yes, drill sergeant!"

Occasionally, someone would slip and answer, "Yes, sir," which would straightaway cause the ol' sarge to pop a few veins in his neck. After hearing what he interpreted to be an offensive reply, he would immediately hurry over to the man, place his face within inches of the offender's, look him squarely in the eyes, and snarl for a brief moment. Then, as the soldier would try his best not to laugh, sarge would bellow at him:

"I'm not an officer, soldier! I work for my damn money! Don't ever make the mistake again of embarrassing yourself like that in front of these men! Understand, trainee?"

Although we were exhausted every night, before we could go to bed, the barracks had to be cleaned, according to Hoffman's high, impossible-to-meet standards. No matter how hard we tried, he never seemed satisfied with our efforts. That bulldog required the blankets on our beds to be pulled so tightly that a dropped quarter should bounce into the air. All of our military gear had to be lined up just so, and anyone who didn't meet his expectations brought the sarge's crudest form of retribution upon himself and often the entire company. His personal favorite form of punishment made him drool when he could burden any of us with dreaded KP duty. Woefully, I learned the hard way the initials were short for "kitchen police," and we all hated that agonizing job.

Another reprimand inflicted as a penalty was late-night fire watch duty. That required a man to stay awake for an hour during the night before waking the next offender to take his place. All of the men tried their best to avoid, at any cost, either of those two feared punishments. Getting a good night's sleep was the best reward we could earn. During basic training, we were always tired, and having any chance for some extra shut-eye was always welcome.

By late October, after completing 17 grueling weeks of infantry officer training at Fort Benning, I became a newly commissioned second lieutenant in the U.S. Army. Along with my recently appointed fellow officers, one of our first assignments was to observe the 117th Infantry Regiment's training exercises. Normally, the 117th was attached to the 30th Infantry Division, headquartered at Fort Jackson, South Carolina, but the entire regiment was temporarily moved to Benning to learn the art of constructing and securing Bailey and pontoon bridges.

During a training exercise, units of the 117th built a footbridge across a small stream. That's where I first met 1st Lt. Nathan Johnson of Lexington, Kentucky. He was assigned to the 105th Engineer Combat Battalion, which was also a support unit of the 30th Division. He and two companies of his battalion were there to help supervise the men of the 117th during the bridge-building phases of the maneuver.

We formed a close bond from the start, especially with him hailing from Kentucky and me from West Virginia. He was an outdoorsman like me, so our friendship was easy and natural. He had graduated four years before with a degree in civil engineering from the University of Kentucky. He was posted to the 105th to help train the men to assemble bridges and in road construction. He and the men of the 117th Regiment trained at Fort Benning until the end of February 1943. After that, the unit was transferred to Camp Blanding, Florida, where they re-joined the entire 30th Division for additional tactical training.

To fill the urgent manpower need, officers deployed to bases all over the country. At Johnson's suggestion, I requested a permanent placement with the 117th Infantry Regiment. Subsequently, I left by train on my way to Fort Blanding on March 15, 1943, just in time for the beginning of another round of the south's tropical summer heat that I had come to despise. After reporting for duty, I was lying on my bunk attempting to grab a few minutes of shut-eye before the evening chow when suddenly I recognized a friendly voice. It was my buddy, Johnson, who had stopped by the barracks to give me a hearty welcome on my first day in camp.

"Welcome to sunny Florida, my friend. Here!" he said as he threw a couple of the 30th Division's insignia patches onto my lap.

"After you get these sewn on, you will officially become an officer of the Old Hickory!" he beamed. And to officially dedicate that time-honored distinction, he pulled out a bottle of Wild Turkey 101 from behind his back and poured us both a shot.

"Wow, that's some good whiskey," I said, squinting after downing that first drink.

"Whiskey?" Johnson declared with his eyes widening. "Boy, in this here bottle is some of Kentucky's finest bourbon. Only a hillbilly would drink whiskey."

"Well, please forgive me, "Colonel" Nathan Johnson, sir, but I am a hillbilly from West Virginia and proud of it, too, but for the moment I will surely agree with you. This ol' country boy loves the taste of that fine smooth Kentucky bourbon," I responded with a drawl in my best southern accent.

We toasted my improvised dialect as we downed the second shot.

The next morning I reported for duty bright and early at 7 sharp. I was assigned to 2nd Platoon, Bravo Company, 2nd Battalion, 117th Infantry Regiment of the 30th Division. Most of the men of the 30th came from either the state of Tennessee or the Carolinas. But with the United States at war for just more than a year, our ranks were filled with soldiers from all over the country, and I was honored to be among them.

When I walked into Company Commander Capt. Kevin Pachol's office, I wanted to make a good first impression, so I wore my newly pressed uniform and freshly polished boots. To my chagrin, the captain was not one bit impressed by my appearance. Just the opposite. He looked straight into my eyes with anger in his.

"Attention!" he screamed harshly as he circled my clueless figure.

"Lt. Fisher, I presume! I have half a mind to kick you out of Bravo

Company on your very first day," he barked, giving me a nasty glare.

"First, you're late. Bravo Company's platoon commanders meet here at this HQ every morning at 6:15, promptly! Second, the very first thing I noticed about your uniform is that it is devoid of the Old Hickory insignia patch, which should be a total humiliation to you and is certainly an affront to your fellow officers serving in this hallowed company. Why ol' Andrew Jackson himself, the namesake of the 30th, would roll over in his grave over the insult that you have displayed here today."

Suddenly, he stopped his tirade for a brief second and pointed with a wooden baton he was holding to the other lieutenants standing 25 feet away, staring and shaking their heads in disgust.

Then, his barrage started again.

"Third, and most importantly to a man, I and all three of your fellow platoon officers standing here only drink Jack Daniels Old No. 7, and we, sir, understand that you prefer a Kentucky bourbon called Wild Turkey instead. Well, what do you have to say in your defense, Lt. Fisher?"

Astonished, my mouth sprang open as all of them, including Pachol, broke out in laughter and reached to shake my hand with tears in their eyes. I would have loved to have a picture of my face at that moment.

"Lt. Nathan Johnson. Why that son-of-a-bitch, he staged all of this, didn't he?" I asked with a smile. "Boy, do I owe that Wildcat one helluva payback! A hillbilly never forgets a trick like that one, you understand. We get even!"

Just then, from an adjacent room, one of my favorite new songs started blaring from the radio sitting on 1st Sgt. Jack Reese's desk. It was Glenn Miller's band playing along with the Andrews Sisters singing the catchy tune, "Don't Sit Under the Apple Tree." The second line of the lyrics declared, "with anyone else but me." I knew it sounded crazy, but every time I heard that song, I would instantly think of Sterre, which inspired me to write a note in my book later.

Diary: March 16, 1943

I listened to a song today that reminded me of you. I remember the day we were together laying in the tall grass beside the Geul River almost seven long years ago. That image of you will never fade from my heart! Please, I beg of you, my love, as the song says, "Don't sit under the apple tree with anyone else but me!"

Pachol patted me on the back and informed me that he was from the south side of Chicago, and seemed pleased when I told him I used to work for the Tribune and that my parents lived in Bloomington. Pachol's family had emigrated from Poland to the United States during the same period my family left the Netherlands,

One of the other officers in the room was 1st Lt. Ernie Demler. He hailed from Pittsburgh, and we immediately hit it off with my Pirates baseball and Morgantown connections. He had graduated from the University of Pittsburgh, but I promised not to hold that against him. I also told him this year WVU intended to reverse the 11-game winning streak that the Panthers had been on against the Mountaineers.

1st Lt. Willy Taylor of Grand Rapids, Michigan, was a nice guy who loved baseball and blondes, hence his nickname "B Squared." Last to introduce himself was 1st. Lt. Wayne Buffam, born and raised in Portland, Oregon, who fancied himself an actor and was fascinated by everything to do with the movies. After handshakes and laughs, we toasted each other with a shot of Jack Daniel's Old No. 7.

The officers of Bravo Company formed a bond that morning that would last a lifetime. The rest of the day was spent touring the facilities at Camp Blanding. It was even more rustic than Fort Benning, but I realized my job, no, my sole duty, was to get the men in my platoon battle ready and not to complain about the limited accommodations.

At 6 the next morning, I eagerly sat at our HQ building waiting for my fellow officers. Pachol was first to meet me, and later he accompanied me to the company's barracks where he introduced me to the 2nd Platoon. The men weren't expecting me, but I soon discovered a mix of diverse characters who hailed from all over the country. Among them were sergeants Bill Ford of Illinois, Rocky Rucker of Texas, and Murel Wilson of Pennsylvania; corporals Willy Lanham, Stephen Edwards, and Myron Auxier, all of Tennessee, Grady McKnight and Doug Winfree, both of North Carolina, and Basil Stallard from Virginia; privates Fred Burke and Marty Holiday of Minnesota, Junior Krause of Wisconsin, Shepherd Green of Florida, Bob Frazier of Massachusetts, Kermit Puckett of Ohio, Phyle Briles of Oklahoma; and 22 other raw recruits fresh out of boot camp.

The enlisted men found themselves under the direct command of a novice citizen soldier from West Virginia with less military training than most of them had, with the exception of Privates Green and Puckett. Just as I, most had patriotically volunteered for service within days of the attack on Pearl Harbor and all were willing to die for home and country. It was my job to see that they didn't.

I pushed the men hard and trained them relentlessly with the intent of having them operate like a well-oiled machine. I attempted to treat everyone fairly but quickly came to understand that was a challenge when dealing with young men loaded with testosterone. Life in the Army wasn't all work and no play; we had our fun times, too. But at the end of the day, it was understood that soon we may all have to depend upon each other for our very survival.

During the next several weeks, I attempted to get to know each man a little better. Rucker was first up.

"So, you're from Texas, sergeant?" I asked.

"Yes, sir, from Fort Worth near the stockyards," he proudly responded.

"Is it true that everyone from Texas likes to ride horses and lasso bulls?" I asked in jest.

With a sheepish grin, he declared, "Well, sir, that just ain't rightly so. Most of the folks in Texas are tough as nails, though, including me! I've been in the Army for going on 14 years now. It's like a second home to me. You'll never have to worry about me; I know what Army life is all about, sir. But since this war started, a man with any good sense probably would have high-tailed it to Mexico or someplace else. But as you'll learn, sir, ol' Sgt. Rucker was never known as a man with a lot of brains between his ears."

We both laughed.

"Sergeant, you've been in this man's Army a lot longer than me, and I don't have any doubts you know a lot more about how things should be done around here, especially when it comes to training these men for combat. I'll need to lean a little on your experience if that's OK?" I requested as I looked him in the eye.

"You see, I'm not one of those officers who thinks he's a know-it-all, I'm happy knowing I have an ol' veteran like you to help me make our platoon first-rate," I explained, hoping to earn his trust.

Thank you, sir, I appreciate that. Like I said, sir, you'll never have to worry about me, and I'll help you all I can. I've got one more question that's been on my mind though.

"You're from West Virginia, I hear. Does everyone from those mountains and hollows drink moonshine and feud like those Hatfield and McCoy boys?"

We had a hearty laugh at that, and when we finished our talk I felt that Rucker was a man I could trust.

Next up was Myron Auxier, called "Ox" by the men. He was a burly, former high school football star from Knoxville. His demeanor resembled that of a Teddy bear, but underneath it all, he was a solid mountain man who everybody respected.

"Cpl. Auxier, please grab a seat," I told him as he walked into my office.

"I understand you're a sportsman of sorts. To be perfectly honest with you, I love sports, even played some baseball in school, too, but I was certainly no star like I've heard you were," I said.

"Well, sir, I played a little football, baseball, and basketball in high school, and I guess I must have been better at football, even offered a scholarship at the University of Tennessee, but decided to marry my high school sweetheart instead. I don't regret my decision one bit either; she's a doll, sir." he beamed.

"I signed up on December 8, 1941, with my wife's blessing," he continued.

Our conversation lasted another 15 minutes, mostly with loving and funny stories about his wife. Our exchange made me miss Sterre more than ever.

Murel Wilson loved cars and girls, in that order. He enlisted four years before the war started and was transferred to the 30th from the 501st Airborne Regiment a couple of years ago after he'd broken an ankle during a rough landing following a parachute jump. The 501st doctors declared him unfit for jump duty, and he could have been honorably discharged. After his ankle healed, however, he demanded a transfer to an infantry unit and his persistence paid off; his doctor and former commander finally agreed to his request.

He was a quiet guy but he got things done, and all of the men liked him. He'd been a coal miner back in Pennsylvania, but when one of his brothers died in a mining accident, he decided he needed to rethink his career path and became a soldier.

Sgt. 1st Class Bill Ford was one of the funniest men I'd ever met. He was always pulling pranks or cracking jokes, and he was well liked. He was a "lifer," a man who made the Army his career. Compared to the younger men, he was an older guy, 33 with a little gut. He'd been in the service for 15 years and was my most experienced non-com. He loved the Army, and I would need his experience.

McKnight and Winfree had been best buddies since grade school. Both had been high school baseball players and ended up marrying sisters. When the Selective Training and Service Act, nationally known as the "draft" was passed by Congress in September 1940, the two friends decided to join together instead of waiting to be conscripted.

Lanham and Edwards, unlike the other corporals, had both been drafted in November 1940 for one year, which was the service time requirement when the draft was reconstituted. Both were from Tennessee and wanted to be part of the 30th Division since it originally was organized and maintained as part of the Tennessee National Guard. In August 1941, the draft law was extended to 18 months of service. After Pearl Harbor, the Selective Service Act was extended for the last time and required military service for all draftees until the end of the conflict, plus an additional six months, if necessary. Those two became good friends because of their strong Tennessee connection.

The last non-com I met with was Stallard. He'd been a school bus driver before the war as well as a part-time painter during the summers. He was drafted in December 1940, stood about 6-foot-2, and wore a thin mustache that resembled Clark Gable's. The other guys joked with him all the time for calling everyone "buddy" because he couldn't remember names. When his pals got him flustered, out came the "buddies" from his sharp tongue, usually followed by a few choice words as well. He could be a hard ass at times, maybe even a little curt, but in a battle, you'd want Cpl. Stallard by your side.

All the privates assigned to my platoon were an odd assortment of unique characters, such as Burke, for example, who was tall and gangly with flaming red hair. So, naturally, his nickname was "Red." Krause was the polar opposite. He was short and bald by the age of 25. Holiday was short and slow, but very intelligent and a hell of a poker player, too. His nickname was, naturally, "Chunk." Green was cheerful, blond and blue-eyed, and could have passed as a Nazi poster boy. The men called him the cheerleader of the platoon. No matter what the task, "Cheerleader" was always up for it and encouraged the guys to jump in with gusto.

Frazier was sort of a goofy looking sort and that New England accent of his drove the boys from Tennessee crazy. They labeled him with what they deemed to be the appropriate, though disparaging, the nickname of "Daffy." Briles was the pretty boy of the platoon, always combing his hair or checking out his chiseled face in the latrine mirror. He liked to drink a little too much and would fight anyone at the drop of a hat. The men called him "Pretty Boy" when he was sober and "Asshole" when he was drunk.

Lastly, Puckett, who the guys called "Mole" because he mumbled and spoke with such a low tone that he could talk and sneak up on someone at the same time. His eerie laugh sounded similar to actor Peter Lorre's, the little Austro-Hungarian actor who appeared with Humphrey Bogart in a movie I'd seen recently called, "The Maltese Falcon."

Over the next few months, I got to know all of the men fairly well. My men loved to dole out nicknames. In addition to the odd monikers already described, we had a "Weiner," a "Dirty Butt," a "Stud," an "Old Man," a "Bojack," and a "Mad Phantom." During our dawn-to-dusk training, only the good Lord knows what they called me under their breath. They didn't give me a permanent nickname until later in the war.

Soldiers rapidly learned that transferring from place to place was routine while serving in the military. On September 7, 1943, the entire 30th Division moved from Camp Blanding to Camp Forest, near Tullahoma, Tennessee. Too near, I soon learned, to the whiskey distillery towns of Lynchburg and Cascade Hollow in which are brewed two of the south's best whiskeys, Jack Daniels and George Dickel, respectively. Most of the men came to enjoy both very quickly.

Just two months later, we moved again, this time to Camp Atterbury, Indiana, about 40 miles south of Indianapolis. Atterbury was only 215 miles from my parent's Illinois farm in Bloomington. The close proximity allowed me to make one last visit home for a few days before I had to ship out to go overseas.

I was happy to see my parents again, which allowed the three of us to spend valuable time together. But even though I was able to hide my emotions most of the time during my visit, my deepest inner thoughts were swirling around like a tornado. My heart was torn for several reasons: First, I was in the Army preparing to leave my country to likely engage in combat. Second, I was leaving my family behind not knowing if I would ever see them again. Last, I hadn't seen or heard from my girl in years and her fate was a constant worry.

The evening before I was to return to my unit was memorable. I leaned against a banister post on our back porch and stared aimlessly at the breathtaking yellowish-orange clouds as the sun burst through them, beginning to lazily settle over the western horizon. Mother gently pushed open the screen door and joined me in the peaceful moment, placing her arm around my waist before planting a kiss on my cheek.

"A penny for your thoughts?" she asked. "You know I heard you again last night. You were restless and talking in your sleep."

"Sorry, I didn't mean to wake you up, but I found myself tossing and turning," I replied.

"I worry about your health. I understand your predicament, but you've got to promise me that you will take better care of yourself, Zef, not only for me and Sterre but for your own sake," she said.

"Even with everything that's going on in my life, I can't seem to ever stop thinking about her," I told Mother. "I don't even know if she's safe and unharmed. That's not asking too much, is it?

"The not knowing part is what's eating at me. Is she still alive, Mother? If so, will we ever see each other again? Does she still love me?"

"Hush that kind of talk," Mother said in a tone intended to calm me. "Of course, Sterre is still alive, and, yes, she still loves you. She's a fighter, my son. She's OK. She's safe."

I pondered Mother's reassuring words as the sun continued its slow descent.

"Knowing the real answer to those questions is what keeps me on edge," I said. "You above anyone should understand how my long separation from her rips at my heartstrings. I realize you worry about your Uncle Karl. Not to diminish your concerns for his well-being, but Sterre's the love of my life. I don't know how to explain it, but there's this constant dull pain that keeps me on the brink of sanity and I can't seem to shake it off. You know, maybe I'm afraid to lose the pain for fear that I may have to give into the reality of our separation. I can't tolerate the thought of going through my life without her. I love her with everything I've got."

She turned to face me and began to speak while sternly raising her voice as she shook my shoulders to get my undivided attention.

"Look me in the eyes and listen good!" she said. "You're a man, a strong man, one who has never given up on anything, and you know damn well as I that you are not going to give up on Sterre either. You have the same love and worry for her that I have for you and Pops. I understand, my son. I know how you are feeling. You know without question that your father and I would never give up on each other or on you. Sometimes I cry myself to sleep over your plight, but I don't give up. I can feel your pain. Mothers have that special sense, you know."

Continuing to look into her eyes, I saw her warm smile and quickly came to the realization that what she was saying was true.

"Thank the good Lord that I'm blessed to have a mother like you. Even at my age, when I'm not 100 percent sure I can get through this ordeal, your encouragement reminds me that I can and will."

"It's that 'Dutch touch' you like to tease me about, Zef," she said with a chuckle.

"You will prevail, my son, you will prevail," she confidently assured me. "Besides, I can't wait to meet my little, yet unborn granddaughter, Rosalie, someday."

"Oh, I hear you, Mother. How could I ever forget dear Rosalie. I promise, even if I only have boys someday, that one of them will be named Rosalie," I quipped.

Feeling more comforted and without saying another word, she edged closer and kissed my cheek again as we both resumed looking into the distance at the beautiful, endless, flaming sky.

The next day I took the stoic and strong stance before saying my goodbyes. I didn't want to cause either of them any more heartache. Pops and Mother also tried their best to stay positive for me, but I could sense their pain. I will never forget the looks in their eyes when Mother gave me a last hug and kiss and Pops shook my hand before giving me a salute as I stepped onto my train. I returned to my unit in good spirits considering the challenges awaiting in the days to come.

After training for 2 1/2 months in Indiana, the men of the Old Hickory Division were loaded onto 14 trains and sent to Camp Miles Standish in Massachusetts. The freezing East Coast camp became our last stop on U.S. soil before our winter deployment across the cold Atlantic Ocean to England.

CHAPTER FIFTEEN

THE RESISTANCE

Everything changed dramatically in February 1943 after the German Sixth Army's crushing defeat at the Battle of Stalingrad in Russia. The Germans and their Axis allies suffered more than 700,000 casualties while their Russian counterparts counted more than 1,100,000 missing, wounded or dead. The horrific setback that destroyed the city on the Volga River not only left the Wehrmacht with massive losses of hard-to-replace veteran troops, but also the destruction of an enormous amount of military hardware, including thousands of airplanes, tanks, and field artillery pieces.

The painful defeat for the Nazis was compounded by American and British air forces, which, with their relentless bombing, inflicted major damage to the German Fatherland's industrial factories, cities, and infrastructure. Those setbacks along with other recent Allied victories, made the outlook for Germany bleak after the early winter of 1943. In North Africa, the British army under Field Marshal Bernard Montgomery defeated the Afrika Korps' German-Italian armies at El Alamein in October 1942. In the Pacific, there was the American naval victory at Midway over Japan, Germany's Asian Axis ally. The Russian army had been revitalized with thousands of new T-34 tanks and millions of fresh recruits from Siberia and areas east of the Ural Mountains. The deployment of the convoy system in the North Atlantic, along with better anti-submarine tactics, were devastating to the German Navy's U-boats that had enjoyed early successes in the war. The Nazi submarines were now the hunted.

Maybe the most devastating news of all was the industrial might the United States was employing to overwhelm Germany's output. The massive amount of war materiel that the U.S. produced, particularly warplanes, couldn't be matched by the Axis Powers. In 1943 alone, factories in the United States produced 86,000 airplanes. That provided the Dutch people with a ray of hope, and their German occupiers with deep concern that the Wehrmacht's once overpowering military machine might very well lose the war.

After the nightmare of Stalingrad, life in the Netherlands under iron-fisted German control changed dramatically for the Dutch, who had been living in fear and uncertainty since 1940. The hunt for Jews became more brutal and the NSB police acted more intrusively. Across Holland, food became ever more scarce. SS soldiers became more ruthless as Dutch saboteurs became bolder.

Having a ration card became the lifeblood of survival, and just being caught owning a radio could spell a death sentence. The dangerous game of hiding Jews or becoming a member of the resistance was viewed as a moral obligation and a symbol of national pride for the weary Dutch.

Sterre and her family became involved with the local Limburg underground by way of a surprise visit from a most unexpected envoy, Sister Truus from the Montforten Seminary of Saint Marie.

At 6:45 on the evening of November 13, 1942, a simple knock at the door of Sterre's home changed their world forever.

Sister Truus, Sterre's former mathematics teacher at Saint Marie Girl's Catholic School in Op de Bies, a Schimmert hamlet, came to the Tragses' house because she respected Sterre's father, Paul, and knew he could be trusted. Having known Paul her entire life, she understood that he loved helping people and was a solid family man who was passionate about his village and Limburg. Paul, she knew, could keep a secret and was a man of his word whose character was flawless. But, most of all, Sister Truus knew Paul was a loyal Catholic who lived by his faith in the Lord.

Sterre walked into the room where Sister Truus and her father were standing. The sister looked uneasy as Sterre warmly greeted her. The nun then glanced to gauge Paul's reaction to Sterre's presence.

"It's all right, Sister Truus. Anything you wish to say to me is safe to say in front of Sterre. You have known her since she was born, and you know her fine character, too," Paul assured the nun, urging her to continue.

"OK, of course, you're right. I should have known it was OK. Please excuse my apprehensions, but these days, you never know for sure who you can trust. But, Sterre, my dear, I would trust you with my life," Sister Truus said confidently.

"We understand, Sister," Paul responded.

"Paul and Sterre, I assume you have heard the rumors about what is happening to the Jewish people in our country," she whispered. "They are being rounded up and sent to camps in Germany."

Paul interrupted her before she was finished speaking and asked, "What camps? What do you mean when you say they are taken to camps? For what reason, Sister?"

"Priests throughout our whole nation have gathered verifiable information that the Gestapo, with help from the NSB and the Dutch police, are arresting and moving Jewish families to a transit camp at Westerbork in Drenthe Province," Sister Truus explained. "Most stay at Westerbork for only a few weeks before they are transported to the east on trains that leave the camp every Tuesday. Where the Germans are taking them, we do not know, but we do know once they leave the Netherlands, they never come back."

The camp at Westerbork had been originally constructed in 1939 by the Dutch government as a processing facility for more than 30,000 German Jewish refugees who had fled their country seeking sanctuary in the Netherlands between 1933 and 1940 after Hitler and the Nazis came to power. It was initially a short-term holding center where families could be fed and sheltered until more permanent residences and jobs could be located for them throughout the country.

After the Germans invaded Holland in 1940, Westerbork was converted by the Nazis into a temporary holding hub for people the Germans deemed as undesirables such as Dutch Jews, political opponents, captured resistance fighters, and German Jewish immigrants. After internment at Westerbork, they were loaded into hideously crowded wooden railcars and shipped to the merciless death camps in Poland and Germany -- Auschwitz, Sobibor, Bergen-Belsen, and Theresienstadt. Anne Frank, who wrote her renown diary while hiding in her home in Amsterdam, was the most famous Dutch Jew to die during internment. She perished at the Bergen-Belsen concentration camp just two months before the war ended in Europe.

"Of course, we have heard some terrible stories, too, but what can we do to stop that? Even if those rumors are true, we have no power to do anything," Paul replied.

"Oh, Paul, that is not true. There is much we can do to help those poor souls," Sister Truus earnestly said. "We can help hide them from those who would bring harm to innocent folks like them.

"Wouldn't you hope that if your family were in danger that some good people like yourselves would be willing to help you or your children? People like you, Paul, step up to protect them from dangers that lurk all around us in such times as we now find ourselves?"

"You know, Sister Truus, you can't expect me to put my family at risk without worrying about the consequences," Paul said. "I know you are well aware what the Germans are capable of doing, especially to those who help anyone in the resistance."

"Oh, Father, please allow Sister Truus to finish," Sterre broke in. "Please tell us what you expect us to do for you, Sister."

Sterre was polite but firm as she looked deeply into the nervous nun's eyes.

"My child, would the Trags family be willing to hide a scared teen-aged Jewish girl to keep her safe and protect her for only a few weeks until she can be moved to safety to the caves at Valkenburg or Saint Piertersberg?" she begged.

"This innocent child of whom I speak is from Amsterdam and fortunately was not at home when the Germans burst into her house and detained her parents along with her younger brother. Only by the loving hands of our Holy Savior was the girl saved from the same fate as her family," the Sister explained as she crossed herself.

"For the last two weeks, this girl has endured not only that heartbreaking and frightening experience of being separated from her family, but she's also been on the run during the night to avoid capture. She has been hidden by members of the resistance at eight different homes and comforted by a caring Dutch family, like yours. Oh, please, can the two of you help save this helpless child?" she pleaded.

"You spring this on us, Sister, when we, too, are just trying to survive this hell thrust upon us by the Nazis," Paul said. "Fortunately, my family is intact and we're all together. Remember, I lost my devoted wife and my children's dear mother only a few years ago.

"I must have time, Sister, to think long and hard about what you are asking us to do. I could be risking my family's future if I should say yes to your proposal."

After a brief pause and a troubled look, Sister Truus stared at his worried brow and softly spoke: "Paul, that's our dilemma. We don't have time. The girl is hiding in the trees across the road in front of your farm as we speak. She has no other place to go. She needs your help. We grew up together, Paul. You must know how tormented and desperate I am to ask you and your family to take such a risk. Because I know you so well, I could think of no better man than you to help this girl."

Sterre put her arms around her father's neck, and with a clear voice looked straight into his tear-filled eyes and expressed her feelings.

"Mother would want you to help this girl," Sterre told her father. "She knew better than anyone that in time of need, you were the one person she could always count on. Listen carefully to what Sister Truus is asking us to do. She is asking us to save a life, something that we could not do for my own dear mother, but this is something we can do for this poor Jewish girl.

Remember, she has lost her whole family, not just her mother, and she has no one to whom she can turn for help. Mother would want us to do this."

Paul looked into his daughter's caring blue eyes and slowly nodded his head, indicating his reluctant approval.

"OK, Truus," Paul whispered. "My sensible and compassionate daughter has convinced this old man to take this chance, but I'm still apprehensive about what might happen if we're caught. I am calling you by your first name and not by Sister Truus since I, too, have known you all of my life, ever since that day you threw that apple and struck me in the back of the head for calling you my girlfriend when we were seven or eight."

Paul calmly chuckled at the childhood memory and looked playfully into the nun's eyes.

"Oh, I remember that day. I should have used a rock instead, you stubborn ol' bull, and one of the best friends I have ever had. You are the man who I most respect and trust, uh, along with Father Peter," she said happily, giving the priest his due.

"Paul, once the skies become darker, the girl will be brought to your back door. Start thinking about places where she can hide. She will need some food, too, and a little love would not hurt either," the nun advised.

"Don't worry, Truus, I mean, Sister!" Sterre said confidently. "Don't forget I have known you all of my life, too, and don't worry, I will never throw an apple or a rock your way. Our family will protect this girl as we protect my brothers. She will be safe with us. Don't worry, Sister Truus."

"I have to worry, my dear, and may the good Lord be with you," the sister said as she walked out the front door and scurried down de Kling Road back to the nunnery.

Sister Truus' seminary had been built in Schimmert in the 1880s. The Catholic religious order was founded by Saint Louis de Montfort in France in the early 1700s as a sect devoted to schooling and developing priests for missionary work. The school was also considered preparatory for young girls who intended to become nuns. In the late 19th century, France became more intolerant of these missionary training schools, and some followers of de Montfort's principles took refuge in the Netherlands and established a small seminary and novitiate in Schimmert in 1883.

Maastricht's Saint Pietersberg caves along with those in Valkenburg boasted more than 250 kilometers of tunnels with 8,000 passages burrowed into the hillsides overlooking those ancient cities. The first caves were quarried by slaves during the reign of the Roman Empire 2,000 years before. They were a perfect hiding place for those needing refuge from the Nazis or the local NSB thugs. Inside the massive tunnel systems, Jews, downed allied airmen, Dutch resistance fighters, and others who opposed the German occupiers found well-organized support in relative safety.

In the confines of the caves, there were medical facilities, radio rooms, food and clothing storage areas, weapon repair shops, beds, kitchens to prepare food, and even rooms designated to train members of the resistance in the use of weapons and explosives. That training was critical throughout the war for Dutch patriots who participated in clandestine sabotage operations. They fought bravely for their country while greatly assisting the Allies. Printing presses located in the caves became an important lifeline for many Dutchmen because official government documents, such as identification papers and ration cards, could be duplicated by skilled artists and engravers.

Soon after Sister Truus left their farm, Paul and Sterre gathered the boys and explained to them the unsettling situation their family was about to undertake. The boys wholeheartedly supported the dangerous operation as something the Trags family needed to do. Both boys saw it as a way to defy the Germans. Soon after nightfall, the anticipated knock came at the back door and two men they had never seen before walked in. With them was an obviously timid and frightened Jewish girl.

The taller man spoke first: "My name is Wim and this is my brother Frans. We're with the resistance. The girl's name is Hannah. We will leave her with you for a few weeks, but we will come back to move her to another house or to the caves in Valkenburg. In the meantime, we suggest that you keep her out of sight. Don't let her go outside for any reason, and think about an escape route for all of you just in case things go awry.

"This is a good thing your family is doing. This girl has suffered more at her young age than most of us could imagine. Every Dutch family should do all it can to confront the Germans and those NSB bastards. We will leave you for now. Any questions?"

"Yes, I have many," Sterre's father said nervously "How do we contact you if we need to? Does the girl have any identity papers? Can we trust you to come back for her? Can you give us the exact time and day you will be back to retrieve her?"

"All good questions, my friend, but all I can assure of is that we will be back soon," Wim said. "If you need to contact us, leave a message under the largest rock at the right side of that little wrought-iron cross just down the road.

"The cross of Jesus on de Kling?" Paul asked.

"Whatever you call it, the one with the white image of Christ on the cross," Wim answered.

"Yes, we know which one," Sterre said.

"Someone will retrieve it, but I can't guarantee you when. Just make sure no one observes you leaving any messages. I just ask that you use good judgment at all times, be cautious and don't trust anyone," he warned.

"Why should we trust you?" Paul demanded.

"Do you trust Sister Truus? She brought us to you, and she trusts us, and I assume that should be proof enough for you, my friend. We will be back and good luck to you all," he said as they left and dashed into the brush.

The frightened girl was sitting at the dining table when Sterre sat down beside her, reached for her hand, and began to speak.

"Hannah, is that your name?"

"Yes," Hannah, Hannah Swope, the girl answered.

"Don't worry, my dear. You will be safe here with us. I will fix you something to eat. I know you must be hungry, and later we can get to know each other a little better, OK?" Sterre kindly said as she comforted her.

As Hannah finished her meal, they learned she was 16. Her father had been an accountant, and her mother managed a dress shop. She and her younger brother had been students before the Nazis occupied Amsterdam. For over two years, she and her brother were trapped in their home as virtual prisoners. On rare occasions, they would summon enough courage to leave the house for short periods of time, but only in their neighborhood. The day the German soldiers and NSB came for her family, she had ventured from her residence accompanied by a girlfriend to acquire some books at another friend's home. A trusted family from her neighborhood unselfishly gave her shelter until a Dutch resistance team smuggled her out of Amsterdam to the relative safety of the countryside.

She explained how difficult their family's life had been since September 1940. As Jews, they were required to wear a yellow Star of David armband on their clothing at all times. They were not allowed to ride buses, trams, or trains; their ID cards had a large letter "J" printed on them to easily identify them as Jewish; they were hunted and harassed by the NSB; they were not allowed to attend movies, use public telephones, or go to a public park; and they could only shop at non-Jewish shops from 3 to 5 p.m. They were permitted to get haircuts only at designated Jewish barber shops or salons and could not attend public schools.

After hearing her gloomy observations, Sterre appreciated the few freedoms her family had enjoyed as compared to Hannah's loss and trials.

Later that night, Hannah, who was invited to sleep with Sterre in her room, began weeping as she tried to sleep on a makeshift bed on the floor next to Sterre's bed. Saddened by her sobs, Sterre laid down beside Hannah on the floor. Sterre held the scared girl in her arms and comforted her by stroking her hair until she fell asleep.

The Netherlands managed to stay out of the First World War, but, as a precaution, Sterre's father and grandfather had constructed two hiding places for the family. One was concealed between two interior walls about a half meter wide, and accessible from Sterre's second-story room. A small, sliding door sat behind a large two-meter-high clothing chest. Through the lower section of the chest, one could slide the door open, and climb a small set of stairs to the attic.

The other hiding place was larger and more complex. It was built underground between the house and the attached barn so that a person could enter from either building. To gain entry to the hidden space from inside the house, a sliding door built into a bookcase was constructed to appear as if it were a permanent section of the wall. Once inside, there was a ladder to a basement area that measured five meters long and four meters wide and was located under the barn floor. From the barn, the secret underground space could be reached by a sliding door located between a wall that separated the area used as stalls for the animals. It, too, had a ladder to reach the safety of the basement hideout. The concealed spaces were never revealed to anyone outside the family.

As young children, Paul's kids loved to hide and play in that room, which stayed dry and surprisingly cozy with its concrete floor and stone walls painted white over stucco. Sterre's grandfather built four beds attached to the walls that could be pulled down for sleeping.

Soon after the Germans invaded, the family reopened and cleaned the secret sanctuary and stored enough canned food, supplies, a small heating device for cooking, and fresh water to last them for a month or so. The men had the foresight to add a small separate enclosure accessible from inside that room for a toilet with its own septic system. It was ingeniously ventilated through a crack in one of the stalls, so any odors would be attributed to the resident horses. It was a perfect hiding place for Hannah during the day. It was dark with the doors closed, but it was safe and difficult to detect.

Sterre's brother Jim made an immediate connection with Hannah as he was only a year older at 17. He kept a close eye out for any hints of potential danger and would rush quickly to her side if any appeared. The NSB, identifiable by the despised black shirts that they wore, was particularly worrisome.

Its members would frequently stop by the farm unannounced and always demand something, usually food, in return for not finding any violations.

They also wanted to reinforce fear or threaten the family with harsh penalties that would be imposed upon anyone for any hint of collaboration with the local resistance. Mostly, however, they left the Trags alone since they considered the family a low risk, and gave the NSB no reason to assume otherwise.

For three weeks, there was no contact from Wim or Frans of the resistance. On the 25th day, Jim, as instructed by his father, placed a small piece of paper under the rock at the little iron cross on de Kling Road with a message written in pencil by Paul using his non-writing hand.

It read simply: "When?"

As a precaution, Paul burned other sheets of paper that were similar to the sheet used for the note. Upon returning home, Jim entertained Hannah by engaging her in a discussion about his wide range of exploits. It was funny watching him awkwardly trying to impress her.

Speaking almost in a whisper, Jim said, "Hannah, a little over two years ago I rode my bicycle over 80 kilometers in one day. I went all the way to Roermond and back from Schimmert."

He beamed proudly as she displayed her amazement.

"Wow, in one day! That's so extraordinary," she marveled. "Why did you undertake such a long journey?"

"I just wanted to push myself to see if I could do it. My friends at school didn't think I could, so I had to prove them wrong, and I did," he answered confidently.

"Well, Hannah, let me tell you the rest of that incredible story," broke in Arjan. "What Jim failed to tell you was that one of his friends wanted him out of town so he could take a girl from the village who both of them liked to our town's annual Carnaval party. While crazy Jim was on this bicycle to Roermond, his friend took the girl to the party."

Everyone laughed as Jim gave Arjan a gentle rap on the head.

"Now, you understand how smart our Jim is, don't you?" Arjan said as he winked at Hannah.

"Oh, I think Jim can do anything he puts his mind to. I've seen how strong he is at shoveling in the barn, and lifting heavy bales of hay as he stacks them high, and he plays board games and card games with me daily to keep his mind sharp as a razor."

"Thank you, Hannah. At least someone around here thinks I'm special," Jim countered.

"I know you are special, Jim," Hannah replied as Jim's face turned beet red. The banter continued for another hour or so, as Paul looked outside to the rear of the house and Sterre kept a keen eye on de Kling Road from the front window.

Another night went by and still, no word arrived from the resistance. Paul was becoming edgier and more concerned for his family. He asked Sterre, once she was away from everyone's prying ears, "What if those men from the resistance have been caught?"

"If so, maybe we are trapped," he said worriedly. "Maybe we will be sent to Germany to work in their factories, or worse!"

"Papa, you can't keep doing this to yourself," Sterre advised him. "Everything will be fine. If the Germans or the NSB had suspected anything, they would have been here already for sure. Don't worry. The underground people will be in touch with us. If not, then I'm sure Sister Truus will let us know something soon."

"I guess you're right, Sterre. The Gestapo would have been here by now," he conceded.

Sterre quickly changed the discussion to a lighter topic.

"I think Jim is a little smitten by Hannah," she said, smiling at her father.

"Do you think so?" Paul responded. "I know she is a good girl. I can see it in her character and poise. Her parents did a wonderful job in raising her in such a difficult world, that I can tell for sure. She deserves more than anyone to be saved from the Nazis, and we will do all we can to help her, my dear Sterre."

About 10 o'clock on the night of Hannah's 29th day with the Trags there was a knock at the back door. Hannah was safely hidden in the basement. Sterre heard her father get out of bed and joined him at the back door. He opened the door slowly and recognized Wim's face.

"It's me, Wim," he whispered.

Paul asked him, "Are you alone?"

"No, I have a few people in the woods as lookouts," Wim said. "The Germans have been patrolling the area more than usual for the past two nights, driving by in a truck using a radio transmitter in an attempt to catch people listening to radios. That is why I have not come sooner for the girl. Where is she? Is she safe?"

"Yes, of course," Paul replied.

"Please get her now. We must leave here with her immediately!" Wim demanded.

"What will happen to her?" Paul asked.

"Don't worry, my friend. We will get her new identity papers, a new name, a new life. She will be safe with us, rest assured.

"For your trouble, here take this," Wim said as he handed Paul a small cloth bag filled with zinc guilder coins that were introduced in the Netherlands after the Germans invaded and confiscated all minted silver coins.

"I can't accept this money," Paul said. "I agreed to take Hannah to keep her safe, not to make money. Take the money or give it to someone who could really use it."

Just then Hannah walked into the room after fleeing the basement through the hidden barn passageway. She had that same frightened stare she wore on the first night she came into their home. Paul and Sterre went to her and wrapped their loving arms around her, stressing above her pleas that going with Wim was the right thing to do.

"The resistance has ways to help you avoid capture that we don't possess," Paul told her to comfort and give her hope as Wim nodded his head in agreement.

"If she is in any kind of danger or if she needs us at any time, please bring her back to us. We will care for this girl. She is one of ours," Paul said as he gave Hannah a warm hug and a kiss on her cheek. Hannah and Wim then disappeared hurriedly into the night.

A few days later, posters were hung on trees all around Schimmert warning that anyone harboring or colluding with or who had any knowledge of a traitor and criminal nicknamed "Wim the Butcher" must inform the authorities immediately or risk severe consequences from the Gestapo. The poster also asked for any photos of him. No one from Limburg came forward throughout the entire war with any damaging information about the infamous "Wim the Butcher."

Once safely inside the caves at Valkenburg, Hannah was provided a new ID card with a new photo and the required official identification stamps.

Using the appropriate official stamps that bore the emblem of the German eagle holding the swastika along with special paper and ink was of particular importance. The stamps placed on Hannah's ID card had been stolen weeks earlier by saboteurs from an NSB-controlled police station in Eindhoven. The official ID cards typically featured two types of postage-style markings: one was an ink stamp, another a paper stamp pasted to the page. The authorized certificate also included the holder's birth date, fingerprints, address, and signature. Hannah's new name was Trees Geerlings. Her place of residence was Maastricht.

The Dutch had no national resistance organizations. Instead, the country had many local groups that gathered information mainly about German troop strength concentrations and movements, including the locations of headquarters and infrastructure sites for fuel and supplies. The local resistance disrupted communications by sabotaging telephone, telegraph, and transportation systems. Once the Germans started to track down the Jews and punish Dutch citizens for hiding or helping them, more and more people joined the Dutch opposition ranks.

One of the leaders of the Valkenburg resistance was Pierre Schunck, who owned a laundry near the entrances of the caves in the town. He and many others were members of a resistance group called the LO, which was the Dutch acronym for Rural Organization for Help to the Hiding. That small group alone saved hundreds of lives, risking their own safety in the process.

The Dutch resistance numbers also increased after the German defeat at Stalingrad. After that disaster, Germany needed more men to work in its factories and on its farms. Many, including thousands of former Dutch soldiers, were rounded up from the Netherlands. They were used to fill vital positions, freeing up more German workers to fight on the Eastern Front against the ever-massive hordes of Russian combat troops.

More than 1,300 underground newspapers sprang up across Holland. Being suspected as a member of a resistance group could mean death by firing squad, deportation to a concentration camp, or imprisonment in a horrid jail. Under those circumstances, total secrecy was of utmost importance. One had to be fearful not only of the SS and the NSB but also of one's own neighbors, especially in the early years of the war when it appeared Germany might very well win.

Despite constant threats of retribution by the totalitarian authorities who controlled them, millions of Dutch citizens displayed several forms of passive resistance. They flashed a "V" sign with their fingers when they greeted a fellow Dutch sympathizer or wore jewelry made out of coins that bore the image of their monarch. On Queen Wilhelmina's birthday, they decorated their homes with carnations, one of her favorite flowers, to show their solidarity. Even the simple gesture of placing a postage stamp on the left side of an envelope instead of the usual right side was viewed as a form of defiance.

CHAPTER SIXTEEN
THE WEHRMACHT'S RETURN

One early morning just two hours before dawn, the Trags family was awakened by loud pounding on the front door. Four German soldiers, accompanied by several NSB thugs, harshly commanded the bewildered Tragses to gather in the front yard.

Drowsy and still in their bed clothing, the Tragses had little time to react. They slowly stumbled out of their doorway and stood in line as ordered.

Glancing at a clipboard he held, a Wehrmacht sergeant coarsely yelled a name that no one understood. As Paul Trags stepped forward and attempted to speak, he was viciously slapped and pushed to the ground by one of the NSB toughs.

"No one gave you permission to speak, old man," one of the black-uniformed Dutch henchmen screamed. Paul's children instinctively rushed to their father's aid.

"Stand back now or you will all be shot," an NSB officer commanded.

"Sterre, Jim, Arjan, please do what he says and step back, I'm all right," their father assured them as he dusted himself off and rose to his feet.

"No further resistance will be tolerated," the same officer insisted. "Is that understood?"

The family nodded their heads in agreement.

Informed by another soldier that he had previously shouted out an incorrect name, the German sergeant called out another on the list.

"Jim Wilhelm Maria Trags, age 18, step forward," he shouted. Then, he hastily started reading before Jim could move an inch.

"You are hereby ordered by the German occupation authorities to prepare for work as demanded by the ordinance so titled Duty for the Performance of Services enacted by Reichkommissar of the Netherlands Arthur Seyss-Inquart in the name of Reichskanzler and Fuhrer Adolf Hitler. Refusal to obey this directive will be punishable by death if violated by any perpetrator and will result in imprisonment for his immediate family," the sergeant intoned.

"You will be picked up within the hour in front of this residence and transported to Deutschland to be assigned to a work detail," he said. "Failure to appear for transport as ordered will subject you and your family to a sentence of death by firing squad. Appropriate clothing and food rations for three days will be required for all workers. Is that understood?"

"Yes, sergeant!" Jim said courageously without flinching to bolster his family's sinking emotions.

As the soldiers prepared to leave, one of the NSB hooligans walked over to Jim and spat in his face, then made a suggestively inappropriate comment to Sterre before driving away with his comrades.

Soon after the men left, the Trags family huddled in a circle still dazed by their horrifying dilemma but defiant in spirit.

"Don't worry about me, I can take care of myself," Jim reassured his stunned family. "I'll do whatever those assholes tell me to do and promise not to make any stupid mistakes. I know how ruthless they can be and I don't want anything to happen to any of you due to my misguided behavior. So, please trust my judgment and don't worry. I'll make it back alive."

"Jim, listen to me, my son," his father said. "If you get an opportunity to escape, promise me that you will do so. We Trags are not as foolish and afraid as those bastards think we are. That's our strength. We resist in our own way, but we always protect our family no matter how frightening the threats. Is that understood, Jim?"

"Father, what about Sterre and Arjan? If I try to escape, what about their safety?" Jim asked.

"Don't worry about any of us, we have friends in the resistance who will protect us in case of danger," Arjan said as Sterre emphatically nodded her head in agreement.

They all knew there was no option except to obey. Before the hour was up, Jim was on his way toward the German border, and his heartbroken family was left behind to grieve and pray for his safe return.

In the troubling days that followed, Paul, Sterre, and Arjan settled uneasily into their daily routines. There had been no heavy concentration of German troops stationed in the Schimmert area since the early months of 1941, and even then only a sporadic platoon or two. Still, the small complement of men was not housed in the village, but, instead, headquartered in the nearby town of Valkenburg. The bulk of the Nazi soldiers stationed in Limburg were strategically placed in much larger cities in the province, such as Maastricht, Sittard or Heerlen.

Beginning in the latter part of 1943, the Tragses' farm provided a temporary haven for downed airmen, escaping Jews, and runaway Dutchmen hiding from occupation authorities. Sterre carried secret messages that were sewn and hidden in her clothing to clandestine pickup points typically at or near the small chapels around Schimmert. Sister Truus was usually her contact. For security reasons, only a few partisans in the resistance knew the Tragses' identities or of their deeds.

Since May 1943, the Trags family had received no news concerning Jim. They had no way of knowing that he had escaped from a German farm just six months after being forced to work there. He was aided by the kind-hearted farm owner, Friedrich Abbermoski, who had been assigned as his supervisor but was sympathetic to Jim's plight.

The old farmer hated Hitler. He had lost three of his sons on the Russian front and told Jim that he felt it was his Christian duty to help him escape. The farmer was obligated by law to report to the nearest local police station if anyone under his care escaped. He waited almost a week, however, before informing the authorities, which allowed Jim a head start.

The German farmer was never suspected of any wrongdoing. He

provided Jim with some old Michelin roadmaps to assist in his dangerous trek. Jim eventually made his way back to Valkenburg and its secure tunnels and caves. Once safely there, he reunited with Hannah, or Trees as she was now known on her current identification card. Jim and Hannah became active in the resistance and experts at handling explosive charges used mainly to disrupt rail and communication lines.

Relieved by the news, the Trags family was informed weeks later by the resistance that Jim was safely back in the Netherlands and aiding in efforts to thwart the Germans.

Things changed dramatically, however, at the start of July 1944 when a large contingent of German troops was again housed in their midst. Sterre was distressed to learn that Cpl. Warner, the same arrogant, a sexually-charged German soldier who had harassed her in 1940, was among them. Back then, Capt. Welsch, Warner's commanding officer, had protected her from the troubled enlisted man's advances, but she feared she might not be so lucky this time around. She prayed Warner had forgotten her.

The Allied armies had successfully landed on the Normandy beaches in France during the first week of June 1944 and had been driving the Wehrmacht's combat divisions east and north toward Belgium. In response, the Germans deployed their troops closer to their western border in anticipation of an impending invasion of their homeland. With Schimmert located only a few miles from that border, it came as no surprise to the people of Limburg that German troops were returning to the area in large numbers.

Weeks earlier, Allied airplanes dropped propaganda leaflets to encourage the Dutch. The resistance printed and distributed underground newspapers and posted flyers. Queen Wilhelmina announced repeatedly, via her BBC Radio Oranje broadcasts, that the Allied armies were on the march and soon would be on their way to liberate her people.

The queen encouraged resistance groups, as well as individual citizens, to take any action necessary to disrupt German communication and transportation lifelines. Railways, highways, bridges, and telephone lines were favorite targets.

Since the start of the war, to assist the local resistance fighters with their dangerous sabotage missions, the British Royal Air Force and, later, the American Army's Eighth Air Corps, had been performing clandestine parachute drops, peppering France, Belgium, and the Netherlands with supplies, such as radios, weapons, explosives, and medical provisions. Due to the successful Normandy landings, partisan covert operations against the German's had increased significantly.

The demented Corporal Warner had forgotten little about the village and wasted no time trying to find the beautiful woman he'd once coveted, Fraulein Sterre Trags. One day shortly after dawn, two German soldiers riding bicycles they had confiscated earlier, appeared at the Tragses' farm. Sterre's father and Arjan were away assisting a neighbor with a cow that was in labor when she heard a knock at the front door. The visitors were a Pvt. Kurt Sluuder and the despicable Cpl. Max Warner, whom she recognized immediately as a past tormentor.

Warner was at best average in stature, with the arrogant nature of someone who thought himself more important than he actually was. The men in his squad did not respect him but feared his retaliatory tendencies. He had joined the army 10 years earlier and was never considered competent enough for promotion to a rank higher than corporal, which was telling, considering his military experience. He claimed his superior officers failed to recognize his combat leadership qualities. In fact, he saw very little, if any, direct battle action.

He quickly noticed the stunned look in Sterre's eyes, as her body stiffened, gripped with fear as he walked uninvited into the house. His narrow, cruel eyes became fixed, immediately revealing his lust.

"Goedemorgen, Fraulein Trags, you look so happy and surprised to see me. Well, aren't you thrilled to see me back in your quaint little village?" he smugly inquired in a sarcastic tone. "I must admit, you have been on my mind quite a bit during the lonely and cold nights that I have been away fighting our enemies in Belgium and in France."

As he stared and walked around her, he said menacingly, "Ah, I do remember those haunting blue eyes of yours and that perfectly sculptured striking face. Don't you agree, Private Sluuder? Like I told you, isn't she one of the most beautiful women you have ever seen?"

"Yes, Cpl. Warner," the private answered, nodding his head. "She looks exactly the way you described her to me."

Without warning, the corporal shoved Sterre against the wall and slowly turned her head to the left with his hand over her mouth and depravedly whispered in her ear.

"My last visit to Schimmert almost four years ago was interrupted by that vile Capt. Welsch, who, I assume, you remember. Well, my dear, that son-of-a-bitch is not here to protect you now. After I was transferred, I heard our brave captain was unceremoniously killed in France while running away during the heat of battle. A bullet in his back was exactly what the frightened little Prussian officer deserved.

"He was a traitor!" screamed Warner, angrily changing his tone.

After a short pause, he continued ranting.

"That asshole had eyes for you, too, but both of us realized back then he wasn't man enough for someone so enchanting as yourself. You need a real man who understands how to please a woman, and now, sweet Sterre, that man is standing right in front of you again. I first noticed you in front of the church riding that bicycle back in 1940. Do you remember our little-interrupted conversation then?

"I wanted you then, my dear, and I vowed to myself if I ever returned to this backward little village that I intended to have you."

Warner smirked as his hands roamed over Sterre's body to her revulsion and disgust.

She struggled and tried to resist, feeling so helpless that she began to weep. At that moment, her father and Arjan burst through the back door, startling the frenzied soldier.

"Stop!" her father Paul said harshly, and then lowered his voice as he pleaded. "Please. I beg of you, sir, please stop."

The corporal slowly stepped back and released her from his smothering grip. He then shouted at Paul to step back and swore that he would order Sluuder to put a bullet through each of their heads if they made any threatening moves.

"We were just having a little fun, your daughter and I. She was enjoying every minute of it, isn't that right, my dear?" he laughed as Sterre ignored him and rushed to her father's arms.

"Pvt. Sluuder, put down your weapon," the demonic Warner ordered. The private had been aiming his Mauser 98k 7.2-mm rifle at her father's chest.

"We will come back another day under more pleasant circumstances," Warner said. "In the meantime, I wish to inform you that in the near future all men between the ages of 18 and 45 will be required to report for work and will be sent to factories in Germany. For the well-being of the Fatherland, only men over the age of 45 will be allowed to remain to work his own farm.

"As a test run, all men over the age of 14 must report to Schimmert's Catholic Church with coats and identification cards in hand. You will be informed later of the date and time you will be required to appear," he barked.

Warner then walked over to Arjan and asked, "How old are you, boy?"

"Sixteen," Arjan replied, slightly shaken.

"Oh, the young man is just 16. Well, I guess we will have to keep you alive to age 18 when you will be strong enough to work for the Fuhrer when he calls again," the corporal said, mocking the boy. "As I recall, there was another brother who lives here. Where's he?"

"He's already working at a factory in Germany as of nine months ago," Paul quickly spoke up.

"Good. I see," Warner responded.

As tensions eased, both soldiers strutted out the front door without looking back. The corporal, however, rudely shouted that he was looking forward to spending more time alone with Sterre in the coming days and promised to return often to their farm.

Sterre stood there trembling as she held onto her father. They were frightened but determined to consider carefully what steps they might next take. They quickly agreed their limited options were either to go into hiding or to stay put and hope for the Allies to arrive soon. They made the latter choice.

For the next several weeks, Warner's superiors kept him busy. The one time he did return to the Tragses' farm, Sterre was able to avoid him by escaping to the basement's secret hideaway until he left unsatisfied. Without telling her father, she had already decided, if ever assaulted again by the corporal, she would sink a knife into his body at the risk of her own life rather than to give in to his wicked desires.

A week or so later, Warner and Sluuder were drinking heavily at a candlelit bar in Valkenburg, in spite of being ordered to report for patrol duty within a few hours. They shared a large corner table with four young women who appeared to be in their 20s, all most likely looking for male companionship, but not necessarily with the two of them.

The semi-intoxicated corporal was desperately trying to negotiate his way upstairs with one of the women. He was having little success. Around 8 p.m., three strikingly tall SS soldiers walked in wearing their Hugo Boss designer black uniforms. They looked prepared for a Nazi parade similar to the ones held in the mid-1930s in Nuremberg.

They came to the bar directly from a meeting attended by two Gestapo operatives and several thugs from the NSB. The women at Warner's table were obviously more impressed with the SS men than with him and Sluuder. They quickly made their preferences clear by consulting their compact mirrors as they began fidgeting with their hair and giggling.

Warner, himself a little in awe, decided to invite the SS troopers to join them. By doing so, he assumed his accommodating gesture would to make himself look more important to the star-struck maidens than he was in actuality. He hoped his association with the elite soldiers would help in his frugal attempt to secure a date with at least one of the young ladies before his patrol was to commence.

"Gentlemen, it would be our pleasure, and I'm sure it would be to the pleasure of these beautiful ladies, too, if you would be so kind to join us at our table for a drink," he said as the three SS men walked toward their table. Paying little attention to the corporal and the private, the SS soldiers immediately took command and quickly began their own maneuvers with the four charming, infatuated women. Though intimidated, Warner tried to regain favor by ordering drinks for his "brothers in arms," as he referred to them, in an attempt to wheedle a little respect from the three.

When the women excused themselves, Warner overheard one of the SS men share with one of his comrades his view of a conference they had just left.

"That meeting was a waste of our time. There was not one bit of important news, with the exception that the Fuhrer needs more workers for our factories," he said mockingly.

"And now the solution from the powers that be is to issue a new order to round up more Dutch workers between the ages of 16 and 60," one of the SS men replied sarcastically.

"What will be next, a new order for men and women from 8 to 80?" the last one asked followed by a hearty laugh from all three.

As soon as Warner heard the revelation that the new age requirement for factory workers had been expanded from the previous ages of 18 to 45, he asked, "When will this new order go into effect?"

"In two days, my naive little corporal," the SS man closest to Warner archly asserted. "The Third Reich will be invincible again because those new Dutch workers will help our factories manufacture millions of super weapons as promised by our Fuhrer. They will save us all from the Russians, the British, and the Americans."

The women returned to the table minutes later.

"Where is your headquarters and when will you be going back there corporal?" one of the SS men demanded.

"Schimmert, a small village about two kilometers from here, and we're headed that way now as a matter of fact," Warner replied.

"That's excellent, my good man. Do us a favor and drop off these proclamation posters, and inform your superiors that all of them are to be posted across the region by tomorrow afternoon. Doing this little favor for us will save us the bother of a long trip, for, as you can plainly see, corporal, we may be very busy with more important duties tonight," one of the SS men smugly remarked, winking at the women sitting willingly by their sides.

"We much appreciate your kind gesture, and I'm sure one of these beautiful ladies would be willing to reward you in the future for your good deed," the tallest SS man chuckled as the other two laughed in agreement.

Despite his tipsy state, the wheels of Warner's mind started deviously turning about how he might benefit from this new information. Sterre was again on his radar.

"No problem," Warner replied to the request. "We will make sure these posters are delivered as instructed." He picked up a packet of the heavy paper posters from the table and placed them under his left arm.

"Pvt. Sluuder, we must leave now as we have important work to do. We bid you farewell, ladies and gentlemen," Warner said and attempted a sloppy Nazi salute. He then grabbed his helmet and his carbine as he and Sluuder exited the bar. Outside, they hopped into their kubelwagen, a small, light-weight vehicle that was the Wehrmacht's answer to the American Jeep. It featured four doors, with an air-cooled, four-cylinder engine and a four-speed transmission.

Warner ordered Sluuder to head immediately back to their temporary headquarters in Schimmert as he neatly folded one of the posters and slipped it into his coat pocket. When they arrived in Schimmert, their inebriated state escaped detection since no officers were on duty at the HQ building that warm late August evening.

Warner and Sluuder were well acquainted with the sergeant in charge and engaged him in a banal discussion about some contrived problem they were experiencing with the kubelwagen. Knowing that the sergeant's civilian occupation was an auto mechanic, Warner, with Sluuder's nervous corroboration, easily managed to persuade him to take a peek at their vehicle to get his expert opinion about a repair. In addition, Warner dutifully handed over the stack of posters to the sergeant with instructions as ordered by the SS earlier.

Soon after the corporal, faking an urgent need to go to the toilet, offered to answer any incoming calls on the military phone while the sergeant attended to the vehicle. As soon as the sergeant was outside, the corporal dashed to a file drawer and removed the Trags family's personal information card, which had been completed by Paul and Sterre a few weeks after the invasion in May 1940.

Since Warner knew he was the only soldier in his current unit who had once been stationed in Schimmert at that time, he reasoned that only he knew anything about the Trags family. He wanted it to stay that way. With the personal information card in his possession, he envisioned it would provide him the leverage needed to put in motion his half-baked, sinister plot.

Ten minutes later, the sergeant instructed Sluuder to start the engine, which revved up immediately. The sergeant declared their mechanical problem solved.

Before they left, he took a telephone call and informed the two men they were to be in Borgharen, just north of Maastricht, by seven o'clock in the morning to pick up their commanding officer, who had been attending a planning meeting at Kasteel Borgharen. The 18th-century castle was an ideal meeting location. It was out of harm's way, complete with designer-quality rooms and parlors, and surrounded by a moat and a wall that made it easy to provide security.

"Make sure you're sober and on time," the sergeant ordered. "You both know by now how obsessed the major is about being prompt. He wants you to meet him at the front entrance of the castle, which is only 150 meters beyond the Kasteelstraat main gate. Remember, be on time and completely sober. We don't need any more of the major's shit. Understand?"

The two then sped directly to Sterre's farm. It was almost midnight when Warner started banging on the front door while yelling, "Schnell, steht auf! Schnell, Steht auf!" (Quickly, get up)

Startled, and barely awake, Sterre's father opened the door and was roughly shoved aside by Warner, who then commanded Sluuder to stand guard outside as he walked into the front room.

"Where is the woman?" he asked Sterre's father, as she slowly walked down the stairs wearing a robe. "Tomorrow, soldiers will be here looking for men between the ages of 16 and 60, who are to be transported, by force if necessary, to Germany and put to work in one of our armament factories or on a farm."

He pulled the stolen poster from his pocket and let them read it, line by line.

"Can this be true?" Sterre's father asked with a look of panic on his face. "I thought you said a few weeks ago the age range was from 18 to 45?"

"Of course, it's true. I just returned from a very important meeting where the details were discussed. That's why I came here immediately since you have a son who I know to be 16. Is that not so?" he demanded, stammering.

Paul and Sterre nodded in puzzled agreement.

"I know you both may be questioning why I, of all people, am standing here warning you of this terrible news in advance. But I have been soul searching of late and realize the Americans aren't so far away. They may be here sooner than we might like to think as the resistance likes to boast. Please don't look so surprised. I'm sure you must have heard these rumors, too!" he said, pausing for a response that he never received.

"If, and when, the Americans arrive here, helping a family in need couldn't hurt my chances if I'm captured or even if I decided to surrender to them."

They froze in silence at his suggestion but listened intently and cautiously as he continued.

"So, I thought, what a pity it would be for this poor helpless boy to be forced to go to Germany to work when, in fact, he can help the war effort just as easily by staying here and working on your farm," Warner said insincerely.

"I also have your information card in my hands," he said as he pulled the document from his pocket.

"With this card in my possession, no one but your closest friends knows that you have a young man here. The NSB rats are scattering like flies in total fear of reprisals from the resistance, and all of the German troops are new to this area except for me. So none of the authorities know the boy's age.

"This is my plan," he said addressing Paul. "Private Sluuder and I will take your son and daughter with us tonight for safekeeping. After the threat ends in a couple of days, we will bring them back here, and the boy can hide with friends or even someone with the resistance until the Americans come.

"I don't have all night to wait for your damn decision, you understand! I have four to five hours to save your son, at most, as I must be at Kasteel Borgharen by 7 a.m. sharp," he shouted, pounding his fists on the table.

"I have three questions!" said Paul, suspicious of the German's offer. "Why would you help us? Why should we trust you? And why would Sterre need to go with you?"

"First of all, what choice do you have?" the corporal responded. "Either you accept my offer or the boy goes to Germany, and most likely you will never see him again! Have you seen your other son since he went there?

"I need Sterre to go so she can be a lookout while the boy sleeps, and he can stand watch while she sleeps. I can't be there with them, you must understand. Proof that you can trust me needs to be no more than these documents I hold in my hand," he asserted as he again presented the poster and the stolen information card.

"Do you realize I could be shot for being here with these papers in my possession? I took a major risk to save your asses, and this is how I'm treated?" he angrily shouted.

"You realize by now that I must insist they come with me, not only to save your son but my ass as well, Mr. Trags. If asked, you must tell your closest friends that both of your sons are already in Germany working and that your daughter is either staying with a sick friend or working or something. Anything to throw them off. Without this personal information card, it's unlikely any soldiers will even come to inquire.

"With all of the confusion and uncertainty all around us now, why even the lowly Jews are not being hunted and deported from Limburg anymore. Especially with those American P-51 Mustang fighters strafing and dropping bombs on anything they deem to be of benefit to Germany's military forces."

Of course, he was lying. His story was becoming a jumbled mess, and the Tragses were not fooled in the slightest. The deranged corporal's ultimate goal was to seduce Sterre whenever he desired. He assumed he could guarantee that by threatening to send her little brother to Germany or by threatening to simply kill them all. The situation seemed hopeless for the Tragses.

Realizing that they didn't believe his story, which was full of holes, Warner pulled his Luger from his holster and pointed the pistol at Paul's forehead.

"Get your clothes on, you Dutch bitch," he angerly ordered, turning to Sterre, "and be quick about it or your father will get a bullet right between his eyes."

Warner's voice rose to a scream as he became more enraged.

Arjan awoke and walked into the room. The quick-tempered corporal ordered him to stand still as well or be shot. He ordered the boy to put his clothes on too, and then demanded the same of Paul. In a few minutes, all were fully clothed and standing at gunpoint before the crazed Aryan monster.

The drunken soldier became more erratic and began wondering if the Tragses' farm was completely vacated. He worried that his thinly veiled plan might possibly be discovered by the authorities.

Panicking, he muttered to himself, "What would happen to me if anyone even suspected that I was here and not on duty as ordered."

In his alcohol-addled state, he thought he might have boasted to a few others in his unit that Sterre was his to have and his alone and may have insisted that they keep away from his woman. So, he reasoned, if the Tragses were missing, he may become a suspect in their disappearance, and he did not want any questions asked about his loyalty, especially in such dangerous times like these when deserters, traitors, or anyone seen as assisting a foe was shot or hanged.

He yelled at Sluuder to enter the room. Once inside, Sluuder viewed the awkward scene before him. Warner's shouting had made Sluuder aware of the situation he now viewed with alarm.

"Cpl. Warner, what's going on?" he asked.

"Shut up, you fool, and listen to me. We're going to have a little fun tonight, my dim-witted friend. Here, take my pistol and if either of them moves even one millimeter, shoot them," he screamed, pointing to the men.

"You and me, sweet Sterre, we will be in the back room," he said suggestively as he looked straight into her eyes and put a sharp Solingen steel army dagger to her throat.

"I told you when I was here a few weeks ago, I would be back to take what I believe is rightfully mine, and if you don't cooperate to my satisfaction, I will have them killed," he threatened her.

"Father and Arjan, please don't move. Please promise me!" she cried out.

Helpless, and with few options, they reassured her.

As he pushed her into the back room, he said to Paul and Arjan, "I could simply have the good private kill both of you right now, but I want you both to hear your precious Sterre moaning in ecstasy."

Then, with an evil snicker, he promised Sluuder that he could later have his turn with her as well.

He closed the door behind him and pushed Sterre onto the bed. In defiance, she jumped back up. Angered by her action, he slapped her across her right cheek and ripped the dark blue dress she'd just put on from her fragile body. Completely nude, she resisted as he threw her down hard to the floor, and then picked her up and dumped her on the bed. She braced herself for the inevitable as he bragged to her that she was going to enjoy every minute of her time with him, just as her friend, Tiny Jergens, had when he was first stationed in their village a few years earlier.

To assure her capitulation, he ordered Sluuder to take the safety lock off the Luger.

"Sluuder," he yelled. "If I give the command, shoot her father and brother in the head," Warner shouted to remind her of the hopeless situation. Sterre reluctantly came to the realization that he would not tolerate any further resistance from her without violence. Suddenly, a calm silence enveloped the moment. Emboldened, he stood over her near perfectly shaped figure and undressed with a self-confident sense of power as he looked upon his frightened prize.

Now naked, he leaned over to join her on the bed. She was shaking and silently praying as he pulled her legs apart and smiled in delight at his anticipated conquest. He touched her breast as sweat poured from his scruffy face. She could feel his hot breath laced with the smell of beer as he fumbled over her body. Revulsion rose in her throat at the sight of veins swelling under the skin on his muscular arms and neck. As he lowered himself, her body stiffened against the inevitable pressure pinning her on the bed.

Without warning, the door banged open with the kick of a boot and a Mauser bayonet plunged deeply into Warner's back as Wim the Butcher lunged forward with a single throaty grunt. In seconds, Warner exhaled with a whoosh as blood bubbled from his mouth and his beady brown eyes rolled up in his head. He fell heavily onto Sterre's trembling body as her anguished screams pierced the air like sirens.

Her father and brother rushed to her side and wrapped her quivering frame with a blanket from the floor. All of them began crying and hugging each other as they came to the realization that they were all safe, at least for the moment. Wim did not flinch as he wiped the corporal's warm blood from his bayonet.

"Where did you come from?" Sterre screamed to Wim.

He told her that he and Frans happened to be nearby on a mission to retrieve an urgent underground message from the Catholic priest, Father Peter. They became suspicious and decided to further investigate the oddity after noticing a German military vehicle parked in front of the Tragses' home.

The two resistance partisans carried Warner's motionless body to the barn and placed it alongside Sluuder's, who had been killed by Frans just seconds before Warner. Sluuder had failed to fully close the front door when summoned by Warner previously, which allowed Frans his opportunity to sneak up behind the private to deliver a fatal blow to the back of his head with the butt of his Dutch Mannlicher M1895 rifle. Seconds later, Wim attended to the corporal.

Like clockwork, the poster and the Tragses' identification papers were removed from Warner's clothing and destroyed in the wood-burning kitchen stove. The floors were cleaned of all bloodstains, a process to be repeated in the morning by Paul and Arjan. The Tragses' lone remaining horse was used to walk repeatedly over the soldiers' vehicle tire tracks until all were erased. Within 45 minutes, no evidence remained to indicate that the German soldiers had ever been there.

Wim asked the Tragses if the soldiers had mentioned anything about their patrol route, which might help them figure how and where to dispose of the bodies. Paul remembered that Warner had divulged the two were supposed to be at Kasteel Borgharen by 7 a.m. With that information, Wim developed a plan.

The bodies were temporarily hidden in an old barn where Warner's nude corpse was dressed in his uniform, and Sluuder's boots were removed to complement some German uniforms the resistance had stolen weeks before. Wim and another resistance fighter wore those uniforms and drove the kubelwagen with the two slain soldiers in the back seat. After being splashed with brandy to fool guards at checkpoints, the dead soldiers would appear to be inebriated and passed out. But no roadblocks were encountered during the dangerous mission. The blood-stained sheets, a blanket, and a rug were gathered up by the Dutch fighters, taken to a remote area, and buried.

In darkness early that morning in Borgharen, the damaged kubelwagen rested upside down, partially sunken near the bank of the raging Maas River. Four days of near torrential rains had created the muddy deluge. The staged mishap gave the Germans the impression that the two unaccounted for soldiers, who had failed to pick up their commanding officer as planned, had wrecked their vehicle and were missing, possibly drowned. Their vehicle, it seemed, had slipped over a steep embankment and flipped on its canvas top and cascaded into the river at a curve on a dangerous, unmaintained road, just minutes from the Sluis Stuwcomplex locks that spanned the Maas.

To further support the ruse, two local farmers, who lived nearby and were sympathetic to the resistance, stated they heard the accident and dutifully reported it to the authorities. Three days later, Warner and Sluuder's badly battered bodies, still in uniforms that bore no holes, were discovered by a river barge operator. The Germans were floating about two kilometers downstream from the village of Oude Kanjelbeek, near a big bend in the river, just before reaching the mouth of the Kleine Geul River, which empties into the Maas.

That undeniable fact strengthened the appearance that an accidental drowning had occurred. As was the custom during wartime, the two dead soldiers were hastily buried in their uniforms without further investigation. The German squad that retrieved the bodies paid little attention to the fact that neither dead soldier was wearing his boots, assuming, perhaps, they had been washed away by the river's strong current. That curiosity most likely was dismissed as a result of heightened anxiety created by an American mechanized army fast approaching Limburg's western border just a few miles away.

CHAPTER SEVENTEEN
OVER THERE AGAIN

On February 12, 1944, the men of the 30th Division, the famed Old Hickory, boarded the USS John Ericsson in Boston Harbor and steamed across the Atlantic on the way to their first overseas port, Liverpool, England. Little on the naval troop transport vessel resembled the luxury German ship on my first excursion to Europe in 1936. The Ericsson had once been a passenger cruise liner owned and operated by the Swedish-American Line and christened MS Kungsholm. The steamer had been confiscated by the U.S. government after the attack on Pearl Harbor. Later, the Swedish vessel was purchased by the U.S. Navy, refitted as a transport ship, and renamed.

The rough seas made the crossing difficult. At several intervals, the ship rocked violently on the choppy high waves as the crew kept a close eye on the frigid Atlantic filled with countless small icebergs.

Diary: February 12, 1944
"Sterre, my love, I don't know if I can ever make sense of this war. As I look out my cabin window into the endless sea, I know my heart is by your side and my fate in God's hands. My men and I are trained and ready for action. The Yanks are coming!"

Once in England, the soldiers were happy to be on solid ground again. Most of them had suffered from seasickness while aboard the constantly rolling ship.

As we disembarked, we were met by the United Kingdom's Union Jack flag flying over the Port of Liverpool, but we had little time to take in the sights of our new surroundings. Wearily, the men of my regiment, the

117th, were quickly loaded onto waiting trains and moved to our initial foreign base at Petworth, about 40 miles southwest of London. The rest of the 30th Division was quartered in other nearby quaint villages spread around the quiet English countryside. Once the troops were safely settled inside either half-moon-shaped metal Nissen huts, drafty old hotels, or private homes, we looked forward to a long-awaited good night's sleep. We happily snuggled underneath our olive-green wool blankets and fell into our Army-issue cloth cots save for the lucky few who were blessed to have sturdy warm beds.

In the days that followed, we scouted our new temporary home and mingled with the locals. That brief luxury ended, however, as soon as we resumed our training with little reprieve, except for an infrequent furlough used mainly by the soldiers to visit the many nearby pubs. The setting led to several awkward encounters between our soldiers and the local population aggravated by the lack of young British men who were serving in their armed forces. Their absence, in conjunction with love-starved Yanks searching for female companionship, supplied the spark that lit many romantic rendezvous with lonely British women.

Most females in the United Kingdom were rumored to be very conservative and had little experience facing the brash and rowdy Americans who jockeyed for their affection. Frequent fights involving the rude Americans usually were preceded by an evening of drinking and bad behavior. The poor manners raised concerns among our English hosts who rarely witnessed such shenanigans on the part of their own relatively reserved citizens. For the most part, however, the British came to tolerate the fun-loving G.I.'s and welcomed us into their shops, pubs, and homes.

One particular embarrassing flashpoint was difficult for the British to comprehend. The American Army essentially consisted of two separate entities, with separate rules for both. Mainly, the combat troops and the officer corps were mostly made up of Americans of European descent.

The supply-and-support units were usually comprised of troops of African heritage although there were a few black combat units. That distinction sometimes led to trouble, especially when it came to women. The separation of races demanded by the American military, a result of centuries-old social and economic segregation, was odd and confusing to the British and fighting regularly broke out between white troops and their black counterparts.

Eventually, the tense situation was eased a little when the Army issued an order that required white and black troops to have separate days off for leave and free time, effectively eliminating most potential conflict. If the rigorous training schedule allotted time, black troops were granted passes on Mondays, Tuesdays, and Wednesdays, while white soldiers were given passes on Thursdays, Fridays, and Saturdays. For both groups, Sunday was set aside for rest. Even that relief could not completely stop the ugly fighting that still occasionally erupted, especially between the Negro soldiers and southern whites who were long-steeped in the Jim Crow segregation laws in place at home since the end of the Civil War.

When the southerners saw a black G.I. with a white English woman, it would most surely lead to confrontation. Predominantly, the English were very gracious and welcoming to our Negro troops, which was an odd behavior to witness for our more prejudiced Caucasian soldiers.

Unfortunate racial tensions aside, my men trained hard and were fast becoming combat ready. Learning about the English way of life and their peculiar customs was an eye-opener for many of the young, brash Yankees. Unfamiliar predicaments caused many awkward moments, from the funny ways we danced or ordered a beer to the instruction manual we needed to learn how to navigate and drive on the left-hand side of their narrow roads. Even though our countries spoke the same language, there were vast differences. The British had the tradition of afternoon tea, which we Americans deemed as girlish. On the other hand, the English laughed as our guys jitterbugged while the Brits did a slow, boring waltz, which, by the way, looked as if they were doing so with a board stuck up their asses.

The Army attempted to instruct our troops on British customs, terminology, and traditions and showed the visiting soldiers training films on the awkward, sometimes funny subject matter. One called "A Welcome to Britain" that featured Hollywood actor Burgess Meredith was hilariously juvenile. We were reminded to always be polite and courteous to our hosts. We were coached on how to make a purchase in a store and learned the differences in monetary values between our dollars, quarters, and dimes in relation to their pounds, shillings, and crowns.

The British found us a bit unique, too, and were quick to find clever ways to describe our brash soldiers.

"They're overpaid, oversexed, and over here," they said wryly in defining our presence in their country.

It was true. The American G.I.'s were paid on average five times more than soldiers from Great Britain and their allied Commonwealth servicemen, and British women seemed to adore all of the fun the Yanks brought to the table with that money. Therefore, the Yanks had the fiscal advantage and were able to capitalize on that fact by providing more amenities to their potential girlfriends that the native competition could not match.

The American men courted not only the local women but also their families. G.I.'s provided them with luxuries that were unaffordable or often unavailable to them, such as cigarettes, sugar, gum, soap, coffee, Coca-Cola, and, most desirable, nylon stockings for the women. The local lasses seemed to be especially flattered and spoiled by loads of attention paid to them by the friendly, overconfident men from the colonies.

Sexual liaisons were commonplace, with thousands of wartime romances leading to marriage. In fact, more than 50,000 British war brides married G.I.'s, and many of the women came to the United States to live after the war. On the other hand, countless children were born illegitimately due to liaisons between British women and an American father after short-lived relationships. In many cases, some of our soldiers left England never aware that they had even fathered a child. Unwed British women who gave birth to babies after a sexual encounter with a Negro serviceman were especially targeted for poor treatment. In many sad cases, some women, ostracized by their families, were forced to put their so-called "brown babies" up for adoption or into orphanages.

In early April, the 30th Division loaded up once again and trucked to Berkhamsted, a small town of 8,500 residents, 25 miles northwest of London. The town was most famous as the site of the English surrender to Norman raiders led by William the Conqueror in 1066. That capitulation marked the last time England was successfully invaded by foreign troops. That fact was true, of course, until the Yanks showed up.

We trained day and night, it seemed, as Major Gen. Leland S. Hobbs, commander of the 30th Division, insisted that our men had to be the best trained in the Army. After more than two years of constant drilling, our troops had no doubts that he had accomplished his mission. We all fully realized it was just a matter of time before our soldiers were going to be in fierce combat with our sworn enemies, the Germans, and we appreciated the general's attention to detail. But before that occurred, the men instead looked forward to a break in the difficult, constant training and prayed for a little R&R in nearby London.

The Americans took every opportunity to wine and dine the British females, but the practice was particularly true in England's capital city. Our soldiers frequented the many nightclubs that had sprung up all over bustling London. The clubs were perfectly suited to entertain the almost three million American troops who were stationed on the king's soil throughout the war.

Some of the best clubs had catchy names, such as the Poor Man's, Stoll, Rainbow Corner, Paramount, Red Cross, Embassy, Coconut Grove, the Monico, the Dance Hall, and one of the largest, the Covent Garden Opera House Club, which went from hosting distinguished patrons of the arts with opera and classical musical programs before the war to making way for jazzy swing bands and variety shows during the war. Guest stars included many of the finest bands and singers of the era, such as the British songstress Vera Lynn, who always sang her famous hits "The White Cliffs of Dover" and "We'll Meet Again," and fellow Brit performer George Formby, who played his ever-present ukulele. Some of America's best entertainers also captured the hearts of our servicemen and the British audiences alike.

Music lovers from around the globe were serenaded by America's top big bands, including the popular swing band of Glenn Miller. All the musical groups performed for free along with famous singers such as Bing Crosby and the beloved Andrews Sisters. When the sisters sang their hit single "Boogie Woogie Bugle Boy," the floors shook, and the applause was deafening.

The biggest comedians also came to London with Bob Hope and his cronies Jerry Colonna and Joe E. Brown leading the pack in Hope's famous "Road Show" variety extravaganza. To stir the soldiers' blood, Hope would usually bring along a few of the most alluring Hollywood starlets, who were very popular among the lonely servicemen.

One of his most famous lines always got a hearty laugh. Hope, in cahoots with one of his female stars, would point to one of the damsels who would flash him a suggestive stare usually followed by a wink. Then, Hope would declare to the crowd, "Now, I trust you guys understand what you're fighting for!" His jokes about Betty Grable's "Million Dollar Legs" or Rita Hayworth's sex appeal always brought down the house.

Lots of homesick soldiers visited London for a chance to see one of the most famous cities on the planet. Many of them enjoyed sightseeing more than drinking and partying the night away. They crowded the landmarks at Scotland Yard, St. Paul's Cathedral, the Houses of Parliament, and Buckingham Palace. They stood in awe in front of No. 10 Downing Street, home to one of the greatest political leaders of the western world, Winston Churchill. Some of the less adventurous enjoyed taking a spin on a double-decker bus, riding the Underground subway, or simply encountering an escalator for the first time.

Many of the most popular songs of the day blared from the dance halls, including two of my favorites, "I'll Be Seeing You" by the Ink Spots and "When the Lights Go on Again (All Over the World)" by Vaughn Monroe and his orchestra. The most famous wartime song, however, preferred by both Germans and Brits alike, was German-American actress Marlene Dietrich's rendition of "Lili Marlene." At the beginning or end of theatrical shows, at movies, or at many musical venues, the mixed crowd would join in unison singing "The Star-Spangled Banner" and "God Save the King" in a display of solidarity.

There was another side of London as well. The enlisted men would gather in droves at seedy night spots where female strippers regularly revealed their charms to the soldiers' delight. Prostitutes also roamed the capital's dark alleyways in search of easy cash for a one-night stand. American military policemen were constantly on the prowl as they unsuccessfully attempted to keep the two parties apart.

Wartime London was alive and busy with soldiers from Canada, France, India, Australia, New Zealand, Poland, Belgium, the Netherlands, Norway, and many other nations, in addition to the massive wave of enthusiastic Yankees.

One drab Thursday morning, all four lieutenants from Bravo Company, along with lieutenants Nathan Johnson and Scott Tabit from the 105th engineers, boarded the first early train and headed to London where we arrived at 10:45. We weaved our way through the huge Paddington Railway Station, which resembled a large airplane hangar. Inside the terminal, we immediately noticed an odd array of sights including a blood bank, several of the capital's red wooden phone booths, and, lastly, 10 or more posters plastered on the station's stark walls featuring Churchill flashing a "V" for victory sign. We were surrounded by smartly dressed men and women, many of whom were carrying gas masks, black umbrellas, or fire warden helmets.

As we strolled out of Paddington Station, we headed toward Hyde Park in the old city's center in an attempt to secure hotel rooms for our planned three-night stay.

"You've been in London before. Does it look about the same?" Nathan asked me.

"I was only here for five or six days back in 1936, so I didn't get an opportunity to see a lot, but so far it looks about the same except for the hundreds of boarded-up bombed buildings, the air-raid shelters, the thousands of broken windows, and the warning signs announcing, 'Danger! Unexploded Bombs!' that we saw on several street corners," I said sarcastically.

"Well, I guess that was a stupid question," Johnson said sheepishly. "Excuse me, I was just so happy to have a much-needed furlough, I forgot that the English have been at war two years longer than us. I know that London, in particular, suffered through the horrible Luftwaffe bombings during the 'Blitz' in 1940 and 41. Of course, it's different. What was I thinking about? Sorry about the dumb question, Joe."

As a subtle reminder of our upcoming mission, there were huge, hovering barrage balloons used to discourage low-flying enemy aircraft. Above them, we noticed some high-flying airplanes in the gray skies. It was a bomber squadron of B-17 Flying Fortresses of our own U.S. Army's Eighth Air Force, escorted by 10 or so of our finest fighters, P-51 Mustangs, on their way east for another daylight bombing run over Nazi-held territory. Later in the evening, the British RAF took the night shift and attacked Germany with their Lancaster bombers. Fast and nimble Spitfire fighter planes were always close by, providing air cover.

After checking in to our new digs for our weekend stay, we decided to spend Thursday afternoon doing a little sightseeing and getting the lay of the land. We discovered the city's historical hotspots with short visits to Westminster Abbey, Buckingham Palace, St. Paul's Cathedral, and the Tower of London. The Tower was infamous for its torture chambers and beheadings. As we left the Tower, we walked across the legendary Tower Bridge, which spanned the Thames River that cuts through the ancient city. Near dusk, we paused as we stood on the decking of the world-renowned structure.

"Can you guys believe this? We're standing at a place where Edward R. Murrow, the greatest newscaster ever, in my view, described the 'Blitz' during his CBS Radio broadcasts when London was being bombed by the Germans," Tabit excitedly said.

"That's right!" I replied. "He'd always open up his popular news reports in his commanding, smooth, booming voice. He would clearly announce a simple little three-word sentence with a slight pause," I replied.

"This ... is London!" Johnson said, imitating Murrow's delivery.

"I never thought I'd see the day that my tired eyes would be witnessing such a sight as this," Lt. Buffam said, as we all stopped to gaze at the old gray stone English castle we'd just visited with Big Ben's clock tower stoically standing in the distance.

As we continued our discussion, Tabit said, "It's such a shame that this magnificent city was on the brink of destruction just a short time ago"

Johnson said he learned from Murrow's news reports about women and children being sent to the countryside from London for their safety during the Luftwaffe's bombings of the city. Johnson added that he also first discovered by way of Murrow a much-maligned word used for food distribution in Britain and later in our own country: Rationing!

"Scott, maybe you should mosey over to the Speaker's Corner near the Marble Arch in Hyde Park and then stand and yell out in your best impression of Murrow, 'This ... is London!' " Johnson said, changing the tone of the conversation.

"Nathan, check this out," Tabit said quickly raising his middle finger at Johnson.

Lieutenant Michael Fenton, one of our regiment's quartermasters in charge of food transport and preparation, chimed in. "Over here, the

English would say, you just gave that bloke the finger, and told him, up my arse, you blimey ol' chap. How funny is that? In America, my big butt is nothing more than a little bitty ass."

"Yeah, exactly! I totally agree with your argument, mate. Here in jolly old England, both you and Tabit can both be asses and arses at the same time." Johnson quipped.

"Quickly changing the topic, did you guys notice that their policemen or bobbies, as they're called over here, don't carry a gun?" Fenton asked. "Also, did you notice the Women's Volunteer Service driving around in donated vans with the wording 'Gift of the American Red Cross' painted on them?"

"Life's too short to squabble, gentlemen," I declared. "I believe the mood calls for a good round or two of Britain's finest ale. What about you, fellas? Don't you agree?"

They all concurred, and we headed to Piccadilly Circus since it was known to be unusually loud and raunchy, and the guys wanted to witness the energy that resonated there.

We arrived at the popular destination in the late evening via the Underground or, as it's referred to by Londoners, The Tube, where we exited our semi-circular, white-tiled subway station.

We soon found ourselves standing at the intersection of Piccadilly and Regent streets. Finding the nearest bar was our first objective. Soon, my buddies and I were gulping down one pint of warm British ale after another. As we stumbled back to our rooms, well past three in the morning, I collapsed into a chair and sat alone with my thoughts, looking aimlessly out of my hotel room window at the moonlit skies.

Diary: May 12, 1944
"From my vantage point, I can clearly see the silhouette of London outlined perfectly against the backdrop of the light of a full moon. As I blindly gaze at the breathtaking sight, my most private thoughts are reserved for you, my darling Sterre. Love, Joe."

Wide awake around noon that next balmy spring day, we took in a little more of the city's sights, and by early evening we found ourselves again at Piccadilly. We went to the same bar as the night before. The guys preferred to grab a drink and chase the beautiful and charming British lasses. I, on the other hand, just wanted a great dinner, a little music, a movie, or a friendly game of darts before I settled into a nice warm bed for the night.

That night in London the description of American soldiers being oversexed and overpaid was on full display. Most of the British women, I gathered, didn't seem to mind all of the attention they received from the brazen, khaki-uniformed Yankees. My buddies were getting better acquainted with three English women named Alisha, Emily, and Audra, who was sitting near our table. The three sassy floozies were sisters, and I heard rumors from other men in the club that they were bar-scene legends. Sure enough, whether true or not, in the men's room, their names were plastered all over the walls with some rather taboo accounts of their talents.

While my friends stayed behind, enamored by the dicey trio, who to me seemed innocent of their improper restroom descriptions, I decided to check out a movie. The marquee we'd just passed down the street featured a gem that I'd been hoping to see. The war drama "Casablanca" starred two of my favorites, Humphrey Bogart and Ingrid Bergman, in the lead roles.

I walked into the crowded theater just as the credits were beginning. In the darkness, I could barely see but found an empty seat next to an attractive young lady.

When I sat down, she told me, "You haven't missed a thing yet. I've been waiting to watch this movie for months."

I responded in kind.

As we stared at the screen, I noticed about halfway through the film when Bogart's character Rick ordered the piano player to "Play it, Sam" that she started to whimper as the pianist began to play "As Time Goes

By." I felt sorry for her and offered her my handkerchief. She accepted with a grateful "Thank you" and without asking, rested her head on my shoulder throughout the rest of the movie. While we were strangers, it seemed perfectly normal under the circumstances in which we found one another.

As the ending credits rolled down the screen, she raised her head and looked straight into my eyes. I could see some dark pain in her sad brown eyes. She spoke softly as she fidgeted in her seat: "I'm so sorry, I must apologize. Please forgive me for my rude behavior!"

"No, no, it's OK," I responded. "I could tell the movie was having an effect on you, and, quite frankly, I think it had that same effect on me. Honestly, I think it was one of the best movies I have ever seen, but with Bogart and Bergman, what else can you expect?" I responded.

"My name is Karin with an 'i,' " she said as she held out her hand to shake mine.

"I'm Joe from West Virginia, and I'm in the American army," I said.

"So, you're Joe from West Virginia and an American, too. With your uniform, I had a good idea you were an American, but from West Virginia, I would have never guessed because I have no idea where that place is located," she smugly responded as we shared a smile.

"Well, Joe, it was a pleasure meeting you, and thanks for lending me your shoulder for the performance. Once again, please accept my apology for my intrusion," she said again as we waited for the audience to clear the aisles.

"Karin, please excuse my brashness, but, if you don't have further plans for the evening, I would be honored if you would consider joining me for a drink or maybe something to eat," I abruptly asked.

At first, she looked confused then softly whispered into my ear, "Joe, thank you for asking, but I'm not one of those women."

I slowly reached for her hand, gently nodded, and said, "Karin, I'm not one of those men."

Reassured, she accepted my invitation.

Outside, the streets of the British capital were humming, and the air was filled with the sounds of music and laughter. We ducked into a little pub, settled down at a table for two in the rear, and ordered drinks.

After just a few minutes of small talk, I blurted out, "Karin, I must tell you I have someone in my life who I love. I asked you to join me for no other reason than you appeared to be a nice person to talk to, someone other than my men, who only talk about the war, the constant training, or a woman back home."

"She sounds like a lucky lady, your woman back home in West Virginia," she said comfortingly.

"I wish it were as easy as that, Karin, but, unbelievably, the love of my life lives in a small town called Schimmert, in the Netherlands," I explained. "I haven't laid eyes upon her lovely face since July of 1937. I've had no written contact with my darling Sterre for over four long, maddening years, and even before that, I'd only gotten a few letters since her country was invaded. I don't even know if she is still alive, Karin."

Her eyes searched the wooden floors and then the ceiling above as she absorbed my story.

For the next hour and a half, our conversation went down a path I had never traveled. I spilled my feelings out to Karin and told her things I had never mentioned to anyone else in my life. She listened and held onto my words as if they were her own.

She excused herself for a moment as I admonished myself for pouring out my heart to a complete stranger. Karin sat back down in her chair, leaned closer to me, and slowly, in a voice not much louder than a whisper, revealed that she too had a story to tell.

She said she believed she could trust me and felt compelled to discuss her heartache with someone who, she believed, would understand. For the next several minutes, she described the love she shared with the only man in her life, her childhood sweetheart, George. His family called him George the V, as she also referred to him because he was his mother's fifth child. They had married just days before he shipped out to Belgium in 1940 to fight the Germans.

He survived that catastrophe and was rescued during the incredible evacuation at Dunkirk. He was redeployed to North Africa in 1942 and participated in the celebrated British Eighth Army's victory at the Battle of El-Alamein where General Bernard Montgomery led his soldiers to victory over Field Marshal Erwin Rommel and the German army's legendary Afrika Korps. Tragically, less than a year later, in July 1943, her husband George was killed in Sicily while fighting with the Eighth Army.

I remained motionless as she wiped away the tears that trickled down her flush, saddened face. At the same instant, haunted by our unfortunate reality, we both reached across the table searching for each other's touch. Warmly, we grasped hands and then gently locked our fingers together, forming a bond, as we looked deeply into one another's eyes. A few minutes later, we left the pub and stepped into a light drizzle on that dusky London evening. I hailed a taxi for the ride to her home in the Knightsbridge district and then walked her to the front door of her tiny third-floor flat. As we gazed into each other's eyes, spoken word was unnecessary, but three came to mind: Moment. Desire. Her.

We understood what was happening as we walked up the stairs and quietly locked the door behind us. War is senseless in every way; it shatters hearts, consumes souls, and creates torment and sorrow. Our situation was similar but less dramatic than the movie we had just seen. In one of the film's most memorable scenes, Bogart's Rick reflected on his tormented romance with Bergman's Ilsa in Paris years earlier. He reminded her of his undying love by simply saying, "We'll always have Paris." So it was with Karin and me. "We'll always have London." After that night, I never laid eyes upon Karin again.

Diary: May 14, 1944
My Dear Sterre, I have dishonored you this evening. I have no excuses
for my behavior. In a weak moment of betrayal, I took the company
of another. I can now only beg for your forgiveness!"

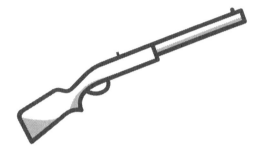

CHAPTER EIGHTEEN
THE HELL OF '44

For weeks, we'd been hearing rumors that any day we could be headed for the continent. On the night of June 5, we realized that gossip would soon become reality. The 30th Division had been moved to southern England near the port of Southampton and had set up what was anticipated to be temporary headquarters. Although terrified by the thought, joining the fight against the Germans was what we had been trained to do. I took comfort in knowing that my men in the 2nd Platoon were ready to enter the fray. All furloughs had been suspended, and no one was allowed to leave the base for any reason. All soldiers, whether enlisted man or officer, was expected to secure all of his gear, required to write letters home to families, and encouraged to get plenty of rest.

That cool night, all of the officers were ordered to attend a mandatory meeting at 10 p.m. at the largest Quonset hut on base. Gen. Hobbs spoke briefly, telling us the 101st and 82nd Airborne divisions would be in the air within hours. He revealed that each paratrooper was fully outfitted and armed, ready for a planned parachute drop behind enemy lines a few miles inland from a place in France called Normandy.

Operation Overlord, often referred to as D-Day, would be underway in just a matter of hours.

An excited yet somber mood fell upon the officers. A united sense of brotherhood was prevalent. All unit commanders were told to inform their men promptly. We fully understood that soon the soldiers of the Old Hickory would be thrust into the midst of a battle with the somber knowledge that some of us would never see our loved ones again. Later that night, we listened to the roar of engines and prayed as hundreds of our airplanes flew overhead. Sleepless and anxious, I wrote a long, loving, and reassuring letter to my parents.

The 117th Regiment departed Southampton Harbor on June 11, five days after the initial landings on the northwestern beaches of France. I was shocked when I gazed once again at the bustling, now immensely fortified, Port of Southampton. During my visit there in 1936, I disembarked at the English harbor in good cheer aboard a glamorous German steamship, the SS New York. This time, I realized within days I might be taking aim at some of the crew members who had served on her decks only a few years earlier.

Within hours after our ships left England, my platoon got the signal that we were headed ashore. Each of the men seemed consumed by an inner silence, lost in his own thoughts. Though at times the task that lay ahead of us appeared overwhelming, we were confident as we saw the French coastline for the first time. Our landing craft bobbed up and down in the salty waters, rocking with the sounds of the surf's cadence while the cool gray ocean waves lashed violently against her sides. As we inched ever closer to the wide sandy beaches, the unmistakable, deafening sounds of the Germans' 88-millimeter artillery shells could be heard exploding randomly in the distance.

"Kaboom! Kaboom! Kaboom!" the blasts reverberated after the shells screeched through the air.

As the landing craft's ramp tumbled into the foamy shallows, all 40 men aboard scanned the skies. The troops were on high alert, yet their faces bore few signs of panic. A few soldiers began to squirm while others prayed. Each man knew from the thundering roar that his training days were over. Francis Scott Key would have been right at home with the sound of the bombs bursting.

"You're at war's doorstep, boys!" Sgt. Rucker yelled.

"Grab your rifles, and move out!" I ordered as we waded through the water toward the destruction, the hell, and the war-ravaged confines that were Normandy's Omaha Beach.

The area where our soldiers stampeded ashore was relatively combat-free, save for the sounds of those artillery shells. The beach itself was filled with an array of military vehicles. Stacked wooden boxes filled with ammunition and supplies were mixed with countless pieces of scattered, war-torn debris.

Hundreds of our dead comrades lay silent, draped only by wet, olive drab tarps covering their mangled bodies. All across the beach, there were several makeshift hospitals where we could hear the screams of the critically wounded and the dying. The injured soldiers were being attended to in large tents identified by red crosses, receiving treatment from combat medics and doctors while awaiting evacuation to England. Their shrill cries chillingly echoed their suffering well into the darkness. To our shock, days after the first assault at the shore's edge where sand meets the surf, a few small pools of blood still floated on the stark water's surface, shimmering as it oozed and rolled over a few remaining half-buried, swollen corpses.

Simultaneously, "Kaboom! Kaboom! Kaboom!" The beat went on.

The 1st and 29th Infantry divisions had assaulted Normandy's coastline on June 6 and knocked out the concrete-fortified, heavy-gun emplacements and machine gun pillboxes located just a thousand yards away on the bluffs overlooking the beaches. After the initial bloody encounter, they had forced the German defenders to retreat from the wide, sandy shoreline days before we landed. The 30th was deployed to reinforce the forward divisions against an expected German counterattack, but our officers were more offensive minded: They hoped to assist in further driving the Nazis from the surrounding areas.

Establishing a fortified barrier around the Normandy beachhead was critical to the lasting success of the mission. The area was the linchpin for docking navy vessels and unloading the additional men and supplies needed to keep our troops in the terrible fight that lay ahead.

We learned only days after our arrival in France that London had come under aerial attack by a new secret Nazi "vengeance" weapon, the V-1 rocket, an unmanned, guided-missile, explosive device propelled mainly from launching pads in western France.

The 117th Regiment eventually gathered about a quarter of a mile inland, and after receiving new updates about the terrain and suspected locations of enemy strongholds, Bravo Company moved through the carnage to the countryside, which was overgrown with countless, man-made walls of hedgerows.

Over the centuries, French farmers had cleared their fields of rocks, trees, dirt, and brush and stacked them at the edges of their property creating large walls of debris that acted in essence as fencing. Those natural barriers provided excellent cover for enemy infantrymen, but they also formed impregnable obstacles for our tanks. Advancing through the narrow roads between the hedgerows was terrifying enough, but to be met by dead horses, bombed-out buildings, destroyed tanks, and an assortment of severely damaged military vehicles, both German and American, made it even more appalling.

The scene was foreboding for young, untested soldiers. The area was carpeted with suffocating, thick, black smoke from scattered fires that obscured our vision. Worst yet, lying strewn around us were hundreds of corpses, some missing body parts. It was a sobering experience to which even the strongest among us had trouble adjusting. Nonetheless, our focus remained simply to seek out our foes and hammer them into submission in order to obtain our ultimate objective, victory.

My operational goal was to lead my men to the best of my ability, keep them as safe as possible, and, with the help of our allies, destroy as many Nazi forces as possible. My personal goal was to reunite with Sterre at the first opportunity.

The platoon's first taste of combat occurred on June 15 a mile or so from the Vire River near the small French village of Isigny, when Bravo Company came under intense enemy fire by German machine gun crews and riflemen hidden among the despised hedgerows. Our company suffered several casualties including one death. The dead soldier was Cpl. Stephen Edwards of Tennessee. In the midst of battle, it was difficult to properly grieve, especially when enemy bullets and mortar shells were whizzing around us, but Steve's death hit me and my men particularly hard.

I was reminded by one of his dog tags, which I placed in my coat pocket, that an enemy bullet has no soul and neither did the duplicate tag that remained on his lifeless body. He was the most innocent among us, only 20, with a sweet smile and a kind disposition. I knew the letter that I needed to write to his parents would be the most difficult one I would ever pen.

Encouragement came with the news that the town of Saint-Lo, located 30 miles from Omaha Beach, had fallen due to the fighting men of the 29th Division with the 30th in support. The capture of that strategic point allowed our forces to continue pushing the attack forward, culminating with a break-out past the tangled traps of the hedgerows. Finally, that successful maneuver freed our tanks, allowing them to advance deeper into the French countryside.

The 30th learned the hard way that a raging battlefield can be a confusing place for friend and foe alike. Tragically, on July 24 and 25, units of the 30th Division were accidentally bombed by our own Army Air Corps, resulting in more than 800 casualties. None of the men of Bravo Company was injured or killed during the friendly-fire incident.

On July 28, the 30th was advancing slowly toward the town of Tessy-sur-Vire, 14 miles south of Saint Lo, when the Old Hickory came under heavy artillery and tank cannon fire from the German 2nd Panzer Division, which was attempting a counter-attack. Four days later, we took control of the French town on the Vire River, preventing the German tanks from causing more havoc, which led to their quick retreat. In less than three weeks of constant combat, our division had suffered more than 4,000 casualties. We received a few raw replacements, while the now battle-tested veterans hoped for a break in the action.

Instead, we were ordered to Mortain, another 30 miles south, and took up new positions. The 117th and Bravo Company found ourselves three miles north of the town at Saint Barthelemy with instructions to block the roads and set up anti-tank batteries.

Before dawn, I yelled, "Sgt. Rucker, are all of the men dug in?"

"Yes, lieutenant, they're all ready," he replied.

"Where are Wilson and Puckett?" I asked.

"They're over by that clump of trees, just to the left about 300 yards away with a .50-caliber machine gun. Chunk and Stud are just to the left of them, and Stallard, Weiner, and Cheerleader are behind that old brick barn with another .50-cal. The rest of the platoon is scattered about over there and behind that house," Rucker replied, pointing to their positions.

"What about the bazookas?" I inquired.

"We only have three, sir. I've got one and Winfree and Lanham have the others."

As we were walking toward Auxier and Pretty Boy's foxhole, we heard the blasts.

"Incoming!" I screamed as tree limbs splintered above us while we ran for cover. The barrage lasted 15 minutes or so, ahead of the clanking sounds of the enemy's tank treads gouging the road's hard surface.

We first saw the German infantrymen coming from the tree line about a thousand feet away.

"Hold your fire until they get closer," I screamed. "Wait for my order."

Just then their tanks let loose with another volley, and Pvt. Burdette and I were knocked to the ground. In a daze, I threw Burdette into a foxhole on top of Dirty Butt and McKnight, who were both taking aim with their M-1s, and shouted for a medic.

"He's dead, sir," McKnight said after checking Burdette's pulse.

As I rushed toward Burdette, McKnight grabbed me and threw me to the ground screaming, "He's dead, lieutenant, he's dead!"

I leaped from the hole dashing from position to position yelling, "Let 'em have it, boys! Fire! Fire!" as all hell broke loose and German bullets zipped around me as I ran. I dove behind a big rock and fired on our foes with my Thompson submachine gun, killing several Wehrmacht soldiers.

Within minutes, the Germans attempted another counterattack and we soon encountered advancing tank units of the 1st SS Panzer Division Leibstandarte SS Adolf Hitler. They quickly brushed aside our forward roadblocks but were heavily strafed by a low-flying squadron of our P-51s and some RAF Typhoons that repeatedly whizzed over the battlefield. Company B and the 2nd Platoon held their ground, fighting with all they had left. Our ranks were reinforced by a group of Sherman tanks and seven mobile light field artillery guns that arrived none too soon protecting our flanks. The added firepower provided the force we needed to repulse the fierce German attack. The Krauts eventually retreated, disappearing into the woods to our relief.

Rucker knocked out a Tiger tank with his bazooka while Wilson and Puckett provided protection with machine-gun fire. The combat became so ferocious that sporadic hand-to-hand fighting broke out. In addition to Burdette, another one of my replacements was killed when we lost Pvt. Johnny Nunley, a fellow West Virginian who had arrived only 10 days earlier. Lanham, Winfree, Holiday, and Krause suffered minor wounds. The brutal fighting had a dual effect on the men. For most, it strengthened their resolve and honed their combat skills. For others, it meant only fear and death. In recognition of halting the German advance at Saint Barthelemy, the 117th was awarded a presidential unit citation.

In mid-August, our division quickly rolled 125 miles northeast through France encountering light resistance. We chased the retreating Germans and crossed the Seine River near Paris. With little rest, we quickly moved another 200 miles northeast, just 20 miles south of Brussels, Belgium, where we halted, awaiting fresh supplies, fuel, and replacements before continuing our planned assault on the area around the Maas River on the southern Dutch border near the city of Maastricht.

Resting for a few days, my men and I slept in tents near the famous Waterloo battlefield where the Duke of Wellington defeated Napoleon in 1815. I remembered that back in 1936 I had quizzed Sterre about Waterloo when we visited the little Jewish graveyard in Schimmert. I never dreamed I'd be standing in that historic place under these horrible circumstances.

The morning before we moved out, I went to a small chapel nearby and prayed that Sterre was alive and safe. Before I left, an old, gray-haired Belgian woman took the seat beside mine and reached over and gently held my hand in hers. She said a few prayers in French as she gazed at an old battered wooden cross. Then, without uttering a word, she looked into my eyes and smiled before kissing my forehead and leaving the building. I sat there for a few minutes pondering the fact that this was only one of many times that she had to suffer through this hell. I wondered to myself, how many loved ones and friends had she lost during this madness and prayed again that I, too, would not lose any more of my men.

Many months later, I learned that during this bewildering period of the war in Limburg Province, the Gestapo and their NSB lackeys had become less concerned about capturing Jews and more concerned about saving their own necks. As a reflection of that fact, the number of hated oppressors still in the area rapidly dwindled.

At Jim's insistence, Hannah, now known as Trees Geerlings, had come out from hiding in the Valkenburg caves and settled in with his father at their farm in Oensel. With her new identity papers, she was supposedly Paul's niece from his dead sister and brother-in-law, Bep and Kevin Geerlings from Maastricht. Hannah stayed hidden during daylight hours in the makeshift basement sanctuary at Paul's farm. No one was too concerned that the enemy would discover her.

Most Nazi soldiers were now more concerned about avoiding the sharp blade of a British parachute-dropped Fairbairn-Sykes trench knife, preferred by the resistance fighters, than apprehending a Jewish girl in hiding.

In the midst of the confusion, the Germans were still rounding up Dutch workers to work in their factories forcing some of them to dig trenches or to string barbed wire in defense of their homeland near the Siegfried Line a few kilometers from the German/Dutch border. The heavily fortified defensive position boasted 3,000 pillboxes and was manned by thousands of fanatical veteran Nazi troops.

And that led to Sterre's misfortune. After Warner's attempted rape, Paul became concerned about her safety. He made contact with the LO resistance via his relationship with his friend, Sister Truus.

The sister rode her bicycle to Valkenburg almost daily to assist a local orphanage there. Unknown to the enemy, the crafty nun often carried clandestine messages for the resistance leaders hidden in the handlebars of her bicycle.

Through Sister Truus, Wim was notified and accompanied Sterre to the relative safety of the Valkenburg Caves. Once there, she was reunited with Jim. Like others seeking refuge from the Germans, she was provided with a new ID card, her hair was cropped, and she was given men's clothing, which she wore to better resemble a teenage boy of 17 with no facial hair. Her new name was Robbie Wieling. While in hiding in the caves, she frantically searched for the carving that Joe had made during their visit in 1936. She found it still intact. "Joe and Sterre, 1936." it read, placed there eight years ago, but still radiating the love she longed to again share with her Cowboy Joe.

Sterre decided to join the resistance, and one of her duties was to monitor BBC radio broadcasts, which often provided instructions to partisan groups across the Netherlands via certain phrases or words contained in the broadcasts. Many of the action messages were delivered by Queen Wilhelmina during the nightly Radio Oranje news program.

In late August 1944, only weeks after seeking shelter, just after dusk, Sterre was listening intently to the program featuring the queen. About halfway through the show, the queen uttered the odd phrase, "It doesn't cares me, Mr. Leers." Upon hearing the predetermined message, the resistance fighters knew the Allied armies would attack somewhere in South Limburg within days.

That provided Sterre and Jim the courage to inform their family of the long-awaited good news. In the early morning hours of August 25, they decided to rejoin their father, brother, and Hannah at their farm in Oensel. As Jim scouted the fields ahead, Sterre was spotted by German sentries stationed atop the Schimmert Water Tower and was quickly apprehended by a Wehrmacht squad searching for Dutch workers to send to Germany, She was forced into the rear of a large military troop transport truck. Tired and frightened, Sterre hunkered down next to an older man of her father's age, where she lay motionless and uttered not a word.

Initially, the prisoners were taken to an internment camp for a few days near the German city of Aachen. There, they were later sorted out and assigned to various work details. During this period, the frantic Germans forced many of the captured Dutch workers to help construct defensive emplacements around Aachen to ready the city for an expected Allied assault. At that camp, Sterre spotted John Weshovens, Uncle Karl's son and her lifelong neighbor, and Ralf, Uncle Wouter's son who had also been captured and forced into backbreaking labor.

A week later they were all assigned to work in a foundry near the German city of Solingen, made famous as the place where Nazi swords and knives were manufactured, including the infamous SS dagger worn by the elite Nazi black-uniformed SS soldiers.

The working conditions at the partially bombed-out foundry were appalling, and the food rations received by the laborers were barely adequate. Dysentery was a problem. All of the workers assigned to the foundry steadily began losing weight. But for Sterre, losing weight was a consolation and helped hide her feminine figure. Other Dutch captives soon realized she was a woman, but, as she hoped, they protected her secret and said nothing to the factory authorities or the guards. As best they could, John and Ralf stayed close by her side to offer what protection they could considering their dangerous and terrible situation. Frankly, during that confusing period, there were several captured Dutch women among the forced laborers. The desperate Germans needed workers, male or female, it made no difference to them.

On September 14, units of the Old Hickory Division took Maastricht from the Germans with little resistance. Maastricht was the first large Dutch city liberated by the U.S. Army. The city's citizens were grateful to see the Yanks marching through their cobblestone streets and enthusiastically welcomed them. Many Dutch and Limburg flags hung from windows intermingled with a few American ones. As in France earlier, Maastricht's women and girls kissed our guys, and the town's men and boys enthusiastically saluted or waved. Our men enjoyed the grateful affection and handed out chocolate bars and cigarettes to the gleeful residents of the long-tormented city.

On the same day, a cool and cloudy Thursday, American troops also reached the little town of Valkenburg but were delayed by Germans who had detonated pre-set explosive charges that blew up the bridges over the Kleine Geul River that flowed through the middle of the village. The enemy lobbed artillery shells from the plateaus, and roads that were nestled among the trees and hills that surrounded the small tourist town. German snipers and machine-gun teams were placed atop the bell tower of the Sint Remigius Church and the Water Tower in Schimmert.

The two tallest buildings in town were used as observation posts by German sentinels who could see for miles from their vantage points. The situation near Schimmert was extremely tense. As a precaution, most citizens had either scattered into the nearby countryside or hunkered down inside their homes in case of aerial bombardment or artillery attack that might destroy their village. Crackling, constant gunfire and loud exploding shells had been echoing throughout neighboring towns for several days. Rumors spread quickly that there were heavy casualties among soldiers from both armies followed by reports of hundreds of Dutch civilian deaths. The unsubstantiated news created more panic and increased anxiety among the region's population.

The local residents felt hopelessly trapped between the two powerful and bitter adversaries. During the night, leaders of the Limburg resistance sent their most experienced fighters behind enemy lines to gather any intelligence about the Germans deemed useful. Wim the Butcher and Sterre's brother Jim were among them. In Schimmert, other Dutch saboteurs attempted to reassure the townsfolk that the Americans were indeed only a few kilometers away.

Soon, Limburgers reasoned, the Yanks would finally relieve them of the horrors that they had been subjected to for the last 4 1/2 years. Still, that hopeful scenario was uncertain. Fear of the unknown was also their enemy. The last four days it felt as if they were being slowly strangled to death by the Germans with little hope of surviving the onslaught they anticipated would surely come. Vital food supplies were in short supply, and disease and sickness had taken their toll. A nervous tension added to the dreadful climate faced by the families of South Limburg.

Surely, many prayed that God would not abandon them now, not this close to regaining their freedom. Children were comforted by their mothers while the elderly prayed, and young men hurriedly plotted ways to assist the Americans and thought of methods to inflict retribution upon the Germans and their Dutch collaborators.

On Sunday, September 18, the village of Schimmert awoke to find the Germans preparing to flee. The Nazis abandoned many of their carts and wagons for lack of healthy horses to haul the loads. They left Limburg by the thousands on stolen bicycles and in old bullet-riddled vehicles, unlike the new ones they had confidently ridden as they had marched through town on those same streets in May 1940. Their sense of bravado and swagger had been replaced by doubt and uncertainty. They had boasted of occupying and ruling Europe for the next thousand years. Now, in disarray and demoralized, the Germans hastily deserted Limburg like the vermin they had shown themselves to be to the Dutch.

As the Germans fled, someone yelled from the church steeple that in the distance he had spotted the lead squad of a group of Sherman tanks of the U.S. Army. As the steel behemoths rolled cautiously closer to the town, several teenage boys began running down the dusty road to meet the Yanks. The Americans, understandably, brushed them aside and to the rear of their ranks, fearing there might be some sort of trap ahead. When the first units reached the village, the infantrymen brandishing Garand M-1 semi-automatic rifles and Thompson submachine guns began running rapidly through the streets. The American soldiers methodically approached each and every house with their weapons at the ready, searching door to door for any trace of the enemy.

In the meantime, Schimmert's suffering citizens dashed into those same streets cheering uncontrollably. Most were dancing and singing or jumping as high as they could in pure joy. Others merely cried or just knelt and prayed as they warmly greeted their still apprehensive but relieved American liberators.

As word spread, the roads in all five Schimmert hamlets became more crowded. The G.I.'s were mobbed by the women, both young and old, who greeted them with open arms. Some of the more adventurous women planted plenty of kisses on the passing soldiers' cheeks and lips. The citizens of Schimmert were at last free to cheer again. The merriment was a beautiful sight to witness, better than any Carnaval party Limburg was noted for celebrating.

Members of the Old Hickory Division, still in pursuit of the Germans, experienced the joy only momentarily as the now battle-hardened soldiers rumbled by with their heavy equipment, heading east toward the ever-closer German homeland.

In front of the Sint Remigius Church, soldiers who followed the initial assault unloaded a truck filled with much-appreciated canned food and handed out chocolate bars to the children, some of whom tasted that sweetness for the very first time. Dutch flags popped out from the windows of almost every house in town. The citizens were relieved and thankful but prayed that the rest of Holland would soon experience the same feeling. Thank God for that day and God bless the United States of America was the theme heard by many Yanks as they passed over Schimmert's tiny streets.

Although my platoon was not involved in the liberation of the village, as soon as I'd heard the news of its capture, I confiscated a Jeep and loaded it with food given to me by my friend, Capt. Michael Fenton, the officer in charge of the 117th Regiment's field kitchens.

As he walked nearer to me, I noticed he was wrestling with a large wooden crate he was carrying.

"What do we have here, Michael?" I asked as I made a casual inventory of the crate.

"Just some grub I rounded up for your journey. There are two cases of canned green beans and corn, four boxes of Hershey bars, powdered milk, six loaves of bread, three small bags of potatoes, a little salt and pepper for flavoring, and, of course, 12 cans of everyone's favorite, Spam," Michael said as he held up a can of the processed ham.

"I trust this will hold you guys over for a while!"

"Thanks, my friend, I appreciate your help," I answered.

"At least I'll know when you guys eat the stuff, you can't blame it on my cooks for the way it tastes," he chuckled.

With three men from my unit, I made straight for Oensel, hoping to soon be holding sweet Sterre in my arms. Schimmert looked little like the beautifully manicured farming community I had visited eight years prior and come to love. As I approached Paul Trags' farm, my heart was beating like a drummer playing to an upbeat Benny Goodman swing tune.

I hopped out of the Jeep while it was still slowly moving and burst into the front door of her home without a knock. The first person I saw was Hannah, the Jewish girl I'd never met. She, of course, had no idea who I was, either. Once I told her my name, she screamed in joy and started frantically yelling for Jim, Arjan, and Sterre's father to join us. Before they appeared, I raced up the stairs hoping she'd be there. Disappointed, I dashed outside.

I was devastated when Paul, who slowly stepped out from behind the barn, told me of Sterre's ordeal. My heart sunk to depths it had never reached before.

"She's not here, my son," Paul said over and over again, repeating a phrase I never wanted to hear.

My eyes filled with tears as did those of Sterre's family, which now surrounded me. We tightly held one other and wept in Paul's front yard. My men, who also got caught up in the emotional moment, rushed to where we were standing to offer their sympathy. They knew my story. It had become common knowledge among my men. They knew I loved Sterre and felt my pain as I sobbed uncontrollably for her. I took some comfort when her family told me how much she still loved me, and I held on to the promise that we would someday be man and wife, a hope that now looked overwhelmingly unlikely.

I spent the next few hours listening to stories of her bravery and kindness, and of her many trials. Jim told me about her capture, just weeks ago. Arjan handed me letters that she had written to me after that horrible day in 1940 when the Germans first invaded. They were stamped but never permitted to be mailed. Out of the blue, he also placed her diary into my shaking hands.

"Joe, I know she would want you to have this more than anyone," he said. "Out of respect, none of us has ever read a word in this book. It was only meant for Sterre's and your eyes."

In turn, I reached into my coat pocket, pulled out my own tattered brown leather diary, and handed it to Arjan.

"I place this book in your care," I told him solemnly. "Give this to Sterre when she returns. Our love story will not end this way. You tell her that Cowboy Joe will be back for her. You tell her that for me. Please, tell her that for me."

My appeal seemed to embolden her family as they continued their stories about our beloved Sterre. While conversing with them, my men unloaded some of the boxes of food we had brought and grabbed a few minutes of sleep in the barn.

For the rest of the war, over and over again, I read every word she lovingly wrote to me in her diary. Without question, it was my most treasured gift and provided me with a ray of hope. It was my only escape from the inner hell that I was experiencing.

As we pulled away in our Jeep, I ordered my men to drive to Uncle Karl's and Uncle Wouter's farms so I could check on them and drop off some food for their families before we had to rejoin our regiment. Both my uncles were OK but looked a bit haggard having heard nothing from either of their sons since the Germans took them away weeks earlier.

Before leaving Schimmert, I had to make one last stop. As we drove closer to a wooded area on a dirt road behind Uncle Karl's property line, I got out of the Jeep and slowly walked toward our fountain stone. I requested that my men stand near the vehicle to give me a few minutes alone. They respected my wishes.

When I reached our special place, I took a 1936 nickel out of my billfold that I'd been carrying throughout the war. Before dropping the coin into the standing water, I kissed it for good luck and said a few prayers for Sterre, and a few more for my men, hoping for her safety and wishing to find my darling girl safely at home in Oensel upon my return.

As I walked back to our vehicle, I spotted Sister Truus and the local priest, Father Peter, trudging thru the tall grassy field to greet me and my men. They were both aware of Sterre's and my love story and were pleasantly surprised to see me in uniform. Both were optimistic about Sterre and reassured me that she was a fighter and a believer, someone over whom God would surely watch. Their kind words of encouragement were cautious but helpful. They thanked my men on behalf of their people for liberating their village and offered us their prayers before we drove away.

CHAPTER NINETEEN
THE END
IS IN SIGHT

The 117th moved 15 miles east to Kerkrade with the rest of the 30th Division and prepared for more action. Kerkrade, a Dutch city with a civilian population of almost 50,000, was located on the southeastern border the Netherlands shared with Germany. While there, I met Hoop Michel Wachelder, a Dutch music teacher who taught piano and guitar before the war. He was a kind gentleman who also was fluent in German and English. He was hired as an interpreter for the 30th Division. Wachelder's wife, Phyl, was a German national. They had married in 1938 and had a two-year-old daughter named Joseme. Marriage between the Dutch and Germans had been commonplace for generations especially for those who lived near their common border.

But soon after the 1940 invasion of the Netherlands, Wachelder and his family were forcibly separated by the German authorities. As a result, his wife and daughter were required to reside on the German side of the border fence.

Normal communication among the family was forbidden. But on rare occasions, when the NSB guards or their German counterparts were absent, the family would secretly rendezvous along the forbidding six-foot-tall fence that ran down the middle of Nieuwstraat and Akerstraat separating Kerkrade from the neighboring German town of Herzogenrath. There, they could exchange information while they briefly touched each other's fingers or stole a kiss through the fenced barrier.

Soon after the Old Hickory liberated Kerkrade, Wachelder and his family were reunited. but they learned the hard way that subjugated people do not readily forgive. Though Wachelder had been loyal to his country, his marriage to the woman he loved had brought his family harassment from a few vindictive Limburgers. Despite the fact that he and his wife, Phyl, had been forcibly estranged by the Nazis, they were still regarded with suspicion. Nonetheless, Wachelder became a good friend to me and my men while we were temporarily bivouacked in the Dutch city.

The relative peace the 30th experienced in Kerkrade did not last. On October 2, 1944, our artillery units started a barrage on the city of Aachen, the heavily fortified German town just a few miles southeast of the border. The town was well protected by intricately connected strands of barbed-wire and surrounded by rows of concrete barriers appropriately called dragon's teeth. Aachen was the first major battle for the American Army on German soil. Our infantrymen and tank crews slugged it out toe to toe with the Germans, who were armed with their overwhelmingly powerful 88-millimeter guns. In addition, Panzer tanks, minefields, Panzerfaust anti-tank weapons, and deadly machine guns zeroed in from fortified pillboxes, all backed up by soldiers wielding lethal hand grenades, flamethrowers, and mortars. For almost three horrific weeks, the Wehrmacht fanatical soldiers fought fiercely in defense of their homeland before surrendering the city.

Axis Sally, the despised German radio propagandist, endlessly spread lies over the airwaves, telling our troops that we had no chance of victory against Hitler's elite divisions. She claimed the Fuhrer's superweapons were destined to be deployed at any moment and would be used to utterly destroy our armies. Our soldiers paid no attention to her fiction, as we rolled back the depleted German defenses that in many cases were manned by old men and young boys. Most appeared unwilling to die for their witless leader. Some teenage fanatics from the Hitler Youth, however, fought furiously to the bitter end.

We were encouraged by the fact that our fighter planes and bombers had complete control of the skies. Our own Sherman main battle tank was no match for the Tiger or Panzer tanks used by the enemy, but the sheer number of Shermans we could bring to the fight ultimately proved to be overwhelming. Even with such firepower, much of the action in Aachen was staged between two determined enemies fighting in barbaric hand-to-hand combat.

We advanced from building to building in the smoke-filled streets littered with chunks of blown-up concrete, bricks, and broken glass on top of a sea of mud. It was the brutal face of war at its most horrifying and savage. Indiscriminately, thousands of innocent civilians including children were trapped in the middle of the ghastly carnage unable to escape the horrors of Aachen.

Eventually, white flags of surrender sprung from almost every window as our soldiers finally took command of the battle-scarred city. The cries heard from behind the piles of rubble and inside burned-out buildings that had once been their homes were hard to stomach. We had a strong sense of compassion for those innocent, suffering civilians. Even in victory, our troops understood we are still human beings.

I witnessed a few of our soldiers weeping in sorrow for the destruction and pain we had inflicted upon our enemies. But in the face of the devastation, we were reminded of the task at hand: focusing on our jobs and protecting each other's backs. Defeating these long-oppressed people left us few options except to finish our brutal task.

Sleep and silence are a soldier's best friends, but I couldn't seem to ever be blessed with enough of either. My empty heart was breaking, and my restless mind wondered nearly every minute if Sterre were still alive. The good Lord knows I'm not normally a praying man, but I pleaded for her safety and prayed that she was not alone or buried deeply somewhere under a wasteland of debris. I feared that without some guidance from above to make some sense of the terrible madness, I might drive myself beyond the breaking point of sanity. For the safety of the men under my command, as well as for her, I knew I had to remain focused and stay in control of my emotions.

Capturing Aachen took a terrible toll on Bravo Company as four more of my men died, including three, Auxier, Burke, and McKnight, who had been under my command from the very beginning at Fort Blanding. I was wounded when several shards of shrapnel tore into my left arm and back when I attempted to pitch, without luck, an incoming enemy grenade out of a foxhole. Before I was able to reunite with my platoon, I spent 16 days in an Army field hospital while my wounds healed. As I lay in bed, Rucker and Ford visited me and told me the men had given me a new nickname: "Duke," after the Hollywood actor, John Wayne. I wore my silly new title with pride, and I smiled a lot at the thought, but I was certainly not on par with Mr. Wayne.

While in the hospital, I received a Purple Heart commendation in recognition of my combat injury along with an unexpected promotion to the rank of captain.

With my higher rank, I was named the new commander of Bravo Company. I understood my role and was pleased after learning that my old platoon was now under the supervision of 2nd Lt. David Boyd, who just months before graduated from West Point. He had been assigned to Bravo Company just two weeks after we landed at Normandy. By the time of Aachen's surrender, he was battle-tested, and the men of my old platoon respected him.

While recovering, I read Sterre's diary over and over and discovered on some previously unexamined back pages a few entries that I had overlooked before:

Diary: September 3, 1937
The pain is almost unbearable. Last night I vomited constantly. I think I need to see a doctor in the morning.

Diary: September 4, 1937:
Instead of a doctor, I went to see Sister Truus and told her of my condition, and she immediately asked if I was with child. I knew it was a possibility but assumed her theory was false.

Diary: September 10, 1937
Lord, forgive me, but I had been bleeding and met Sister Truus and
another nun who assisted me during my miscarriage. They swore
their secrecy and no one else knows of my sorrow. I regret not telling
you, my love. I beg for your understanding.

My heart sank at the revelation but was I somewhat relieved knowing my child had been spared the devastation that now existed. Oddly, I was thankful that I did not know of her pregnancy until then.

Upon my return to duty, our division learned we were headed south and back into Belgium to counterattack a surprising German winter offensive through the Ardennes Forest near a little town in Belgium called Bastogne.

After receiving our orders to move out, I turned to my men and shouted, "Grab your gear, boys. There are still some Krauts out there who need to feel the sting of a little American-made steel."

We never made it to Bastogne. Instead, the 30th fought a savage battle about 30 miles north at a place near Stoumont, Belgium, only 50 miles south of Schimmert. We were credited with stopping an armored counterattack made by the 1st SS Panzer Division. We'd fought that elite unit at Mortain, France, a few months earlier. The entire battlefield from Bastogne to where we fought was about 40 miles long and later came to be known as the "Battle of the Bulge." We stayed in that freezing hellhole until the first part of February 1945. Sadly, we learned 84 of our comrades had been gunned down by the Nazis at Malmedy after surrendering. The men in Bravo Company learned quickly that nothing about war is fair and the victor may end up being the last man standing. Our intent was to be that man.

Also in February 1945, after several months of slave-like conditions and 16-hour workdays, the steel foundry where Sterre was forced to work was suddenly abandoned after a heavy RAF bombardment destroyed most of the factory. John Westhovens was killed during the air raid.

Ralf Schrijnemaekers received a small cut on his left arm that required no medical attention, and Sterre escaped unscathed. The survivors were rushed south near Cologne and put to work reinforcing the battered city's defenses.

At the beginning of March, Cologne city proper, west of the Rhine River where Sterre was located, came under heavy air and artillery assault by the Americans. Sterre, Ralf, and 10 other Dutchmen escaped during the confusion and took refuge in an old abandoned building on the outskirts of the city where they huddled beset by fear and starvation. Two days later, the building collapsed when struck by a powerful artillery shell. Ralf suffered several minor injuries to his face and hands, but Sterre was buried by the building's debris and thought to be dead. Scrambling for survival, those who were able fled the confused scene; Ralf refused to leave. He stayed to search for Sterre, his lifelong friend from Schimmert, hoping to find her alive.

A day later, Ralf heard a faint sound that he immediately recognized as Sterre's voice. He could reach her fingers through a small opening, but the concrete on top of her was too heavy for him to lift. With German soldiers all over the area, all he could do was wait and plot his next move. Exhausted and hungry, he stumbled upon two cans of green beans and a half-loaf of moldy bread in the rubble and pilfered a canteen full of water from a dead German soldier. At night, he was able to widen the hole over Sterre and provide her with enough food and water to keep her alive.

From the end of February until the end of March, the 30th Division engaged the enemy in the Roer River Valley between Aachen and Cologne, 25 miles further west. With heavy equipment in tow, our men waded through mud and high water after the Germans flooded the river valley in a desperate but unsuccessful attempt to slow our advance. Once the high water subsided, we easily rolled past the Roer Valley and by the end of March, our regiment was crossing the Rhine River just south of Cologne.

The British and Canadians were fighting and liberating territory in northern Holland and attacking Germany's Baltic ports from the west, and the Russians were threatening Germany in the east as the Nazis' warmongering days looked as if they might soon end.

Ralf was glad to finally see the Americans, but before he could make contact, he was knocked unconscious by the concussion from a blast by an attacking Sherman tank.

Minutes after, near Ralf's seemingly lifeless body, sat eight 2 ½-ton U.S. Army trucks at the edge of town on the side of a muddy road with their Negro drivers taking a well-deserved rest break. One of the soldiers, Cpl. Amos Goolsby walked to a bombed-out building that had been partially reduced to rubble to relieve himself when he thought he heard a muffled sound. Excited, he screamed to a buddy nearest to him.

"Bernie, did you hear that? Come over here. Quick!" Goolsby shouted. "Listen, do you hear that?" he repeated as he put his hand to his right ear so he could hear better.

"I don't hear a thing," Bernie responded.

Just then, a louder moan emanated from a pile of debris.

"I heard that," Bernie said as he moved closer to the sound. Both men began to rip into the cluttered pile, tossing scraps of wood, glass, and metal as they frantically dug into the rubble.

"Guys, a couple of you grab some shovels and come over here now!" Goolsby ordered as he glared at three other men leaning against one of the trucks, sharing water from a canteen. The men ran toward him with shovels in hand and started digging feverishly into the mound. The moans became louder followed by unmistakable screams from a woman. Suddenly, they noticed a dirty hand barely moving. Carefully, the men dug deeper until they had uncovered an arm sticking out from under a massive concrete slab.

"She's alive, she's alive!" one of the soldiers yelled as they dragged her bloody, near-lifeless body from under the last obstacle. Sterre had been rescued.

Quickly, the men placed Sterre's limp body on an impromptu cot created by using the soldiers' blankets as an improvised mattress. She was then carefully positioned on the wooden rear floor of one of the trucks. Pvt. Bernie Rexroad, the first soldier summoned by the corporal, drove as quickly, and cautiously, as he could to the nearest Army field hospital located five miles away, just west of Cologne. Ralf, whose condition was never checked by the Negro soldiers, had been only one hundred feet away from Sterre but was lying face down, unconscious.

Alone and left for dead, Ralf awoke a few hours later, began muttering to himself, and stumbled aimlessly until he was discovered by a squad of American soldiers. He received medical attention and food but refused to leave the area as instructed, insisting instead, in his broken English, that his rescuers help him search for Sterre. He took them to her tomb-like enclosure but found no body. He was told by the troops that she must have been rescued, or he was mistaken. Ralf had no idea where to begin looking for Sterre and was himself in desperate shape. Once he was strong enough to travel, he started his trek homeward walking westward with thousands of other displaced survivors.

Sterre lay helpless in her hospital cot. She had lost a significant amount of blood, and her condition was perilous. She had a severe concussion from her head wound and suffered from dehydration, exposure to the elements, and had several minor cuts on her arms and torso which caused terrible bruising.

After a week of treatment in the hospital, her condition was still touch and go.

"Nurse, what's her condition today?" Capt. John Bill Feltner, one of Sterre's doctors, asked as he approached her bed.

"It's the same, sir," Lt. Alexis Addie replied. She is barely able to squeeze my hand and occasionally tries to speak. Addie rarely left Sterre's side. She had taken a special interest in her vulnerable patient and checked hourly on her vital signs.

The doctor then examined his patient and agreed with the nurse's opinion.

"She's a very lucky woman. I think she's going to make it. For now, she's in the best place and in the best hands right here with us," Feltner declared.

"I agree, sir. I hope when she wakes up she can speak some English. I would love to know how she got that American nickel we found in her sock," Addie said.

"She was carrying an American nickel?" the doctor asked, clearly puzzled.

"Yes, that one on the table beside her pillow. It's a 1936 Indian head five-cent piece. We also found that cross and chain, too," Addie said as she pointed to both.

"Having that nickel is odd. There must be a story behind that coin. I hope she recovers soon, too. I'd be interested in knowing how she got that coin," the doctor said as he turned to his next patient.

Hundreds of our wounded combat soldiers were treated at the field hospital. Among them were many civilians, sadly most, of whom, were women and children, who had either suffered injuries or were diseased. One of the hospital's brick-and-mortar buildings housed several temporary operating rooms, including one where I visited one of my men, Sgt. Murel Wilson, who had surgery for his wounds after fighting near Cologne during the early spring of 1945.

As we continued moving eastward, the main roads were clogged with thousands upon thousands of starving refugees. Among them were surrendered German troops, abandoned foreign workers as well as recently released former captured soldiers from countless nationalities. It was an array of misfortunate souls who helplessly roamed through the scarred countryside scrounging for something to eat and searching for any place that provided safe shelter.

Too few vehicles were available for hauling such massive numbers of people, and most horses had long been devoured by the starving masses. Small wobbly carts and wagons pulled by the throng were loaded with innocent, hungry, young children or the sickly and old, all with sunken eyes and wearing blank looks of trepidation and doom upon their pitiful faces. The sorrowful sight of war's human carnage tore at the hearts of our men, many of whom fought back tears as they sped on tanks and trucks past the tormented masses. G.I.'s on foot offered what rations they carried to help the war-stricken refugees.

As we drove on Germany's once magnificent Autobahn, we were met by thousands of surrendering Wehrmacht soldiers. Their ragged lines stretched for miles as they plodded past in a dazed state. The defeated German troops were not marching to a flag-waving, celebratory victory parade, but rather to a hastily-constructed, barbed-wired internment camp for interrogation.

Our commanders had to decide what to do with them. Ultimately, they would have to be processed and interviewed to help determine who among their ranks were former Nazi Party members and sympathizers, and who were just ordinary soldiers fighting for a despicable cause led by the most hated tyrant and murderer the earth had ever known.

The defeated enemy slowly trudged along in the grassy middle space between the lanes of their battered, but not totally destroyed four-lane highway system, once hailed as a construction marvel. Defeated and exhausted, a few with their heads bowed, held small homemade white flags. Our soldiers showed little sympathy and gleefully harassed their former adversaries with obscene verbal taunts and extended middle-fingered hand gestures as our military vehicles passed by them.

Our battle-hardened men looked down upon their beaten foes with their emotions ranging from sheer glee to abject disgust. Discarded enemy weapons and abandoned military gear littered the roadways. During fueling or rest stops, our guys hunted for what they deemed to be priceless war souvenirs. The men wanted to present the captured, hard-earned victory trophies to their girlfriends or relatives back home.

At one such stop, I walked toward a German captain who looked tidy compared to most of their soldiers and ours. He'd just searched his coat pocket and pulled out a small, silver cigarette case when he was approached by two of my men, Cheerleader, and Weiner.

"What do we have here," Cheerleader asked the German as he jerked the cigarette case from the captain's hand.

As I looked on about 20 feet away, I heard the German say in English, "That case belonged to my grandfather, and I would like to have it back, corporal."

"Hell no, you asshole," Weiner screamed.

"What's going on here, guys?" I asked as I walked over to investigate the disturbance.

"This Kraut wants this case back. He probably took it off some dead body, but he says it belonged to some dead relative," explained Cheerleader.

"I'll bet my life he's lying, Captain Fisher," Weiner said in support.

"If I may, from one officer to another?" the German said to me. "If you look at the case, it has the name Welsch inscribed on it. My name is Welsch."

"Give it back to him, Cheerleader," I calmly ordered.

"But, sir, my father would love to have this. It's real silver. I can tell from the color," the corporal pleaded.

"That may be, but it belongs to the captain. Give it back now," I ordered more sternly as the corporal placed the case in my hand and walked away.

"Here," I said to the German officer. "If I were you, I wouldn't display that case again if you plan to keep it for very long."

I handed it to him along with a Lucky Strike cigarette.

"Thank you, captain. I appreciate your intervention," he replied.

"It's a pity about war," I said, curious about his story.

"No, it's not a pity. It's senseless. War is pointless, captain. We Germans were deceived and came to believe our own misguided propaganda," lamented Welsch.

"I must admit, captain, it's baffling to me how an accomplished and well-educated nation such as Germany could have been so easily duped by the foolish promises of a madman and his henchmen. I agree with your observation. War is senseless."

"I only pray that all Germans will not be judged by the actions of a few, but I fear we will be," he said. "My cousin, for example, was a U-boat torpedo mechanic. He was a minister of the gospel before the war, and never was it his intention to harm anyone. But he, like all of us, will be viewed as a Nazi."

Welsch, sadly pondering the future, gazed into the distance at the once-proud, but now haggard German troops as they slowly trudged past.

Changing the mood, the German said, "I'll tell my daughter, Daisy, about your kindness, captain, when I give this case to her someday."

"Daisy, that's not a German name," I said.

"No, it's not, but it's funny you mention that. I once had a conversation with a lovely lady from the Netherlands about my daughter's English name. She was also curious," the Wehrmacht soldier reminisced. "She was very beautiful and so kind, the type of beauty that a man never forgets."

"Are you talking about Daisy or the woman from the Netherlands?" I quipped.

"Both," said the German with a smile. "I can't wait to see my wife and daughter again. With all of the bombing in the north where I live, I'm worried about their safety. Do you have a wife waiting for you, Captain Fisher?" Welsch asked.

"Sadly, no. The love of my life ironically is also from the Netherlands, and I haven't seen her in eight years. As soon as this war is over, I hope to find her if she's still alive," I replied just before our brief conversation ended.

"Capt. Fisher, we're moving out," Sgt. Rucker yelled.

"All right, I'll be right there. Get the men loaded up, and let's end this war so we can all go home," I answered as I tipped the brim of my helmet to Capt. Welsch.

After a parting handshake, he instinctively responded by clicking his heels and started to offer a Nazi salute before he realized who he was addressing. Then, he simply saluted me in the customary fashion.

"Have a safe journey and good luck finding your Dutch woman," he said as he nodded before walking away.

Once the small towns and villages were secured, our guys waved, blew kisses, and flirted with the local frauleins. But the war was not over yet. Pockets of Nazi fanatics still took potshots at my men as our Army rolled ever closer to the Elbe River.

The men of the Old Hickory thought they had seen it all until we encountered tens of thousands of still more refugees from countries all over devastated Europe. They seemed to simultaneously hit the road on their desperate trek to find their homes again. Every day I heard at least 10 different languages, all of them searching for answers.

Constantly, it seemed, we had new problems to tackle, but none was worse than the one we confronted when we learned about the terrible concentration camps. Millions of innocent people had perished in gas chambers, were beaten to death, used in medical experiments, or just plain shot or starved. Sadly, more than six million of the victims were Jewish.

We had the misfortune to see one of those awful places at a small internment camp near the Polte Ammunition factory at Magdeburg, Germany, on the Elbe River. In the camp, which had been liberated by tank units of the 30th Infantry in April 1945, dead bodies were stacked like cordwood. Those lucky enough to be alive stared at us through eyes sunken deep into their skulls, their bones covered by a thin layer of skin devoid of proper nourishment.

The smell was appalling, and I wondered in utter disbelief how any man could do such a thing to his fellow man. The biggest job was simply feeding the starving and providing the survivors with humanitarian aid. Daily, our doctors and nurses were overwhelmed by the ghastly conditions. Their skills were challenged by the sheer massive numbers of sick and malnourished patients. It was a horrible scene. I doubt I shall ever be able to forget that abominable sight.

CHAPTER TWENTY
THE ROAD TO LOVE

In late April 1945, our forward units linked up with Russians on the Elbe River. Hitler committed suicide on April 30. Germany officially surrendered on May 7, 1945. Thank God, the war was over in Europe. The soldiers of the Old Hickory Division were delirious after 282 days of nearly constant combat.

To my chagrin, before that final capitulation, I was once again wounded, at Magdeburg, just days before meeting up with our Russians allies who had been fast-approaching from the east. The sniper who shot me had been hiding in a concealed position behind a pile of rubble in the middle of the street where we had been cautiously entering and searching buildings. My shooter was a 12-year old member of the Hitler Youth who had me squarely in his gun site seconds before preparing to blow off my head. Luckily for me, his quick-thinking German sergeant who realized taking another life was futile, attempted to stop the frightened boy from firing, but to no avail. However, the sergeant's sudden interference caused the young rifleman to misjudge his aim, which, no doubt, saved my life. Just minutes after I was shot, I learned the details of my life-saving encounter from the old veteran sergeant after he and his men surrendered by hoisting white flags atop their rifles.

Angered, my men wanted to kill them both before I stopped them from doing so. I didn't want the sergeant and the young boy's demise to haunt me or any of my men in the future. Killing them would have been senseless. They too, I reasoned, had a mother and a father who loved and worried about their safety.

The bullet went through the outer fatty flesh of my right thigh. Thankfully, none of my bones were broken. The wound was more annoying than incapacitating requiring only minor medical attention, but necessitated my use of a pair of crutches for three weeks. I received my second Purple Heart for my inconvenient little injury.

Just three days before the war ended, I was promoted to major. My commander, Colonel Pachol, said it had been in the works for weeks, but I couldn't shake the notion that the timing seemed peculiar, particularly in light of my minor wound.

After mopping up some scattered resistance and helping to restore some semblance of order, the next mission called for a rapid transfer of the 30th Division back to the U.S. by summer's end. Once home, the entire division would have a short rest while being refitted. The Army intended to send the Old Hickory to the Pacific to continue the fight against the Japanese.

Colonel Pachol knew I wanted to go back to Holland to search for Sterre. He pulled some strings and got me assigned to another division that was staying in Europe a little longer.

Before my reassignment, each regiment received an honorary tribute in front of the general staff. A military band played, speeches were delivered, and awards were presented. I appreciated the event more because it gave me a chance to say farewell to the men who so faithfully and courageously served with me throughout the war.

Later that clear, moonlit night, we got together in a partially bombed-out building that had been hastily converted into a dancehall. The large structure featured several makeshift pubs where we unwound over beer, wine, and vodka. We started the party as fellow soldiers but ended it as good friends enjoying a well-deserved celebration. Some of our unit's nurses also joined in the fun as we partied, relieved and joyful that the terrible fight was, at least for us, over in Europe.

At first, I didn't plan to attend but was persuaded to go by Sgt. Rucker.

The place was buzzing as we walked through the front entrance door, which was pocked by bullet holes. Men from our military band had hurriedly formed a musical combo and were doing their best to play a few impromptu popular tunes of the day. A couple of gals and guys were singing along with them on an improvised stage made from old boards nailed together on top of what was once a loading dock. To illuminate the space, about 25 light bulbs were strung together and powered by mobile generators.

The enormous room was humming with laughter, music, and conversation and filled, not only with our guys, but also with hundreds of Russian soldiers as well. Rucker and I made our way through the crowd to a corner spot where men from our company had gathered against a wooden wall that featured a large, crude, hand-painted portrait of Hitler. Earlier, someone had taken the liberty of celebrating the Führer by plunging a bayonet right between his eyes where it remained.

Throughout the evening's festivities and to everyone's amusement, both the Americans and the Russians took turns giving Hitler's picture the middle finger or mooning it as they dropped their trousers to their knees. Each performance was followed by laughter and a toast as the drunken audience approved either by thrusting their thumbs upward or with their applause.

When I reached our unit's table, fashioned from big wooden barrels and a battered old door, it was soaked with spilled beer and littered with wet cigarette butts. I was by greeted by a sloppy "a-ten-hut" instead of the usual "attention." Captains Johnson, Fenton, and Buffam yelled the pathetic order simultaneously as each man staggered, but stood erect while holding beers in both hands.

"At ease, you bunch of drunken sailors," I shouted back to them as Rucker shoved a mug of warm beer into my outstretched palm.

"What a party, Capt. Fisher, oh, I forgot, I mean Major Fisher, sir," Sgt. Wilson bellowed to Sgt. Ford's approval. They both put their arms around me while from behind, Mole Puckett pulled my hat over my eyes and hugged my neck. Cheerleader and Weiner were on the dance floor acting like a couple of long-lost lovers dancing the waltz, surrounded by their buddies who were egging them on. Weiner had a leather knife sheath in his mouth pretending it was a rose stem while Cheerleader tried occasionally to dip his partner. Military rules and discipline took the night off, and no one cared.

"Look at those damned Russians dancing," 'Old Man' Gary McClure, my company clerk, shouted.

"What the hell is that, I wonder?" Captain Demler chimed in as we watched the Russians performing a traditional Cossack dance. The movements seemed almost impossible as they lowered their torsos down with their butts just inches from the floor. Then, while moving, they kicked their legs out in front of them while holding their arms firmly across their chests. Of course, it didn't take long for the Americans to attempt to copy the difficult maneuver as everyone howled in delight.

To say the least, my men had a little too much to drink that evening, but it was an honor for me to be in their company. Before I left the room, each man saluted me and offered kind words about serving under my command. Those heartfelt tributes meant more to me than any medal I could ever receive. The back slaps and toasts flowed freely, and I was encouraged by all of them as they wished me good luck in my quest to find Sterre.

I was fortunate to have had the opportunity to talk with every one of them that evening and shared my gratitude not only as their leader but instead as good friends. I will never forget that night. I heard my nickname spoken over and over, and I hoped they knew that Duke was appreciative. Before I left them for good, I told my men to be safe and that I planned to rejoin them in the future to fight against the Japanese. They knew better and encouraged me instead to find my girl.

The 30th Division was shipped home but never had to fight in the Pacific. Japan surrendered on August 15, 1945.

I didn't know it then, but while I was preparing to leave my men for the new assignment, Sterre was still battling for her life in the Army hospital near Cologne.

I learned later that for six weeks she had been unresponsive, and only two days earlier had awoken but was still dazed and suffering from temporary memory loss.

"Where am I?" she asked Lt. Alexis Addie, her nurse, as she opened her eyes to the morning sun.

"You're in a hospital, my dear. You're safe here and doing much better. You had us all worried for a while. Here, take a drink of water, and I'll get you something to eat," Addie said.

"Where are Ralf and John?" Sterre demanded.

"I don't know either of them, but let me assure you that you're going to be OK. However, you do keep calling for someone named Joe. Who is he?" the nurse asked.

"Joe? I don't know anyone named Joe. Where's my father? I want my father. Please get him for me. Where is he?" she pleaded.

After Lt. Addie motioned to another nurse to keep an eye on her patient, she told Sterre, "I'm going to get you something to eat, and I'll be right back." She gave Sterre another drink of water and left.

Confused, Sterre stared intently at the ceiling and listened to the radio playing over the loudspeaker. The radio was tuned to the BBC, and singer Vera Lynn's rendition of the song "I'll Be Seeing You" was playing.

I was reassigned to the 63rd Infantry Division of the 7th U.S. Army and stationed with a unit near Oettingen in the southern German state of Bavaria. The picturesque town was located on a meteor-cratered plain 100 miles northwest of Munich. The town vaguely reminded me of Schimmert. Later, the 63rd moved to the city of Stuttgart and then to Würzburg.

For 39 days, I was stationed in Oettingen where I was in charge of Charlie Company. My men were handing out rations of food when I met the wife of a German soldier who had fought in Russia and had not yet returned home to his wife and their two-year-old daughter. The girl had never seen her father. The woman's last name was Reulein. Looking at her sad face, I was reminded once again that the brutality of war affects not only soldiers, but innocent noncombatants alike. The look of sweet innocence on her child's face conflicted with the pain that I felt for them. However, that wholesome look offered a ray of hope, something that I desperately needed at that time.

I had been distressed about Sterre, and meeting that smiling little girl lifted my spirits. I needed a plan to return to Schimmert and to my complete surprise, I found a way, courtesy of my old friend George Alfred Obermeyer III, who located me after trying for months to track me down. He was an Army captain assigned to the press corps and wrote articles for Stars and Stripes, the military newspaper published in London for our troops in Europe.

I couldn't believe my eyes when I spotted him coming out of a tattered, recently reopened bar.

"Oh my God, I can't believe it's you!" I screamed. "Of all of the places in the world who would ever guess we'd end up together again in this two-bit town."

After our heartfelt hug, we laughed in unison at the thought.

"Al, you're the last person on earth I expected to see here!" I said.

"Yeah, you ol' hillbilly, I feel the same way about it. I had a helluva time finding you. Luckily, I got a call thru to your old commander, and he told me where I might find you, and unbelievably, here we stand."

"What's the name of this place, anyway?"

"Oettingen!" I said.

"Man, all of these German town names are tongue-twisters aren't they?" Al chuckled.

"Anyway, what in the hell are you doing here other than looking for me?" I asked shaking his shoulders.

"Joined up in 43' after I promised Ruth Ann that I wouldn't be in any danger working as a reporter, but wouldn't you know it, Uncle Sam lied about that. I took a Kraut bullet in the leg at Bastogne, and the funny thing about that was I wasn't even supposed to be there. My commander ordered me to write some stories about the 101st Airborne and to my shock, I got trapped there with those guys when the Germans counterattacked us last winter," Al explained.

"You were stuck in the middle of that Belgian hell hole?"

"Yelp, Joey, and I was damn scared as hell too, but we didn't have time to think about dying, we were too busy fighting and trying to keep from freezing to death. We were just doing all we could to stay alive, you know."

"I understand your fear, I've been through some hell myself. My Division was a few miles north of Bastogne when the Krauts and their panzers opened up on us."

"So, you've seen plenty of action, too?"

"Too much, my friend, and I hope I never have to see anymore."

"I get it, ol' Buddy, the crazy thing about it all, when the fighting at Bastogne was over, I was awarded a Purple Heart. Can you believe my luck? For a minor wound, I get a hero's medal for being in the wrong place at the wrong time. I'm a reporter for God's sake, who gets a medal for doing that?" He pondered.

"Well, look at it this way, you're not just a reporter now, you're a decorated reporter. It's an honor all newspaper scribes long to achieve," I joked.

"Still the funny boy aren't ya, you silly hillbilly," Al shot back with a zinger.

"My long lost friend, let's grab a beer at that bar you just left so we can catch up on things," I said as we walked arm and arm towards the little establishment.

Our conversation continued at our table.

"Patton got credit for saving our asses at Bastogne, but the 101st Airborne really deserved most of the credit for holding back the Nazi's. I was there my friend. I saw what happened. I even met a battle-hardened hillbilly from West Virginia there. His name was Stewart, Sam, I think. He was short and stocky, but without a doubt, the fiercest man I'd ever seen. He fought as a man possessed. He was wounded but brushed it off as a mere scratch. But, from the terrible blood-soaked arm that I bandaged, I knew he had to be in horrific pain. There must be something in that mountain water that you West Virginian's drank as children." Al guessed with a smile.

"It's not the water, Al; it's the moonshine, my friend. It's the moonshine," I declared.

Right on cue, Al countered, "Bartender, my friend and I will take another round of beers!"

Later that evening, I shared the story of my search for Sterre, and Al, always a step ahead of his superiors, concocted a plan for a perilous journey to Schimmert. Within two days he set his plot in motion. He commandeered a Jeep, some food, five jerry cans of gasoline, and some outdated road maps. Al provided his his and my commanding officer with a cockamamie story that he needed a Jeep to travel to different units to interview some of the top brass for the newspaper. He also managed to convince my C.O. that he needed another experienced writer, me, to come along. To support the ruse, one of his buddies, pretending to be an aide to Allied Supreme Commander Gen. Dwight D. Eisenhower, called my C.O. to request reporters for the deceptive assignment.

"Don't forget your rifle and ammunition. We don't know what kind of trouble we may find ahead," Al warned me.

"I never go anywhere without my Thompson, and don't worry, she's fully loaded," I answered, patting my submachine gun.

"Hopefully, we can get to the Netherlands in a couple of days, maybe sooner. We've got plenty of gas, but if we run out, we should be able to bum a gallon or two from other Army units along the way. I've packed two boxes of Hershey bars, plenty of canned food, two cases of booze, and 11 cartons of Camels," Al said confidently as he took inventory.

"Camels? We don't even smoke, Al," I reminded him.

"I have the Camels for insurance, my friend. We may need to barter our way out of a jam," he announced, hopping into the Jeep's driver's seat.

"Ready, Joey?" he asked. "Let's go find your girl."

"Hallelujah, you bet I'm ready. Slam that pedal to the floor, soldier," I commanded as we sped off.

Inspired, Al started singing a tune by one of our secret crushes, Doris Day,

"Gonna take a sentimental journey ... Gonna set my heart at ease ... Gonna make a sentimental journey ... To renew old memories."

After a hearty laugh, Al handed me a photo of an infant as he dodged potholes that dotted the road.

"You're a father?" I asked in disbelief.

"Yep!" he proudly confirmed. "I've never seen my son in person."

"What's his name?" I asked.

"Joey. Joey's his name," Al shouted. "I named him after you, you hillbilly. I couldn't think of a better godfather. Yes, you're Joey's godfather, too."

I could not have been happier as I looked at the photo of little Joey, six months old, wearing my name embroidered on his outfit, as his dad and I headed west toward Schimmert.

After the war ended, our soldiers took on an array of duties. They acted as policemen, prison guards, road and bridge repair workers, food distributors, supply truck drivers, interrogators, and water plant operators. But mostly they assisted with humanitarian aid.

Even though the fighting was over, Germany was still a dangerous place. The roads were in horrible condition. Many bridges had been blown up or were in need of urgent repair. Driving through Germany, we saw lifeless bodies and dead animals littering the highways and streets. In almost every village, houses and buildings were destroyed. Damaged vehicles, bombed-out tanks, and broken glass were everywhere. Looting and people fighting for food and shelter were routine sights. Brutal reprisals and extrajudicial partisan trials that led to death and humiliation for Nazi sympathizers were rampant. Rape, unfortunately, was also commonplace.

The entire country required order beyond what could be sufficiently provided by the conquering Allied armies. During the chaos and confusion, former German officials, including many former Nazi Party members, were desperately needed to help bring some sort of order to the war-torn population of defeated Germany.

Disinfectants were used to stop the spread of diseases. Dysentery posed a particular concern, the result of a lack of fresh drinking water, and sanitary sewage disposal was almost non-existent. Just feeding and housing the demoralized millions was an almost impossible task. It was difficult to truly comprehend the devastation, but somehow the citizens and soldiers ultimately fought through the terrible ordeal together, no longer as enemies but instead as human beings.

On the morning after our first day of travel and following a restless night in our pup tent, I wheedled a month's old copy of Stars and Stripes from a fellow soldier passing by in a supply unit convoy. As I excitedly scanned the front page, a headline grabbed my attention. It read: "German Ocean Liner SS New York Sunk by British." The story described the grand ship capsizing during an attack by the Royal Air Force on April 3, 1945, off the coast of Kiel in northern Germany.

I realized that the last time we saw the SS New York was when we stepped off her deck back in June 1936 in Southampton Harbor. We remembered with sorrow that only nine years ago the great ship was filled with laughter and music. She was a beautiful lady who could not escape the horrors of war and its tide of destruction. The magnificent ship was sunk just a month or so before the end of the war in Europe. Later, I learned that her sister steamer, the SS Deutschland, on which Al and I had sailed home from the Berlin Olympics, met the same fate on May 3, just four days before peace was declared. She went down during another RAF attack in the Bay of Lubeck in the Baltic Sea.

Even though Limburg and roughly half of Holland had been liberated in September 1944, food shortages and malnutrition remained dire problems there. Butter and meat products were almost impossible to find.

In the Netherlands during the last bitter winter months before the war's end, Queen Wilhelmina called for a nationwide railroad strike in a revolt against the Nazis, who had demanded that her countrymen be taken against their will to Germany to work in armament factories. In retaliation, the Germans withheld fuel and food especially in the northern and western provinces of the country, which, at the time, had not yet been liberated. The people of the Netherlands scavenged for food and survived on red beets, potatoes, and bread mixed with sawdust. More than 20,000 Dutch citizens died during what was called the "Hunger Winter."

Until the end of the war, Dutch Jews were hunted and deported to death camps where many of them suffered the inhumanity of Zyklon B gassings and cremation. Even though the Jews had the sympathy and limited protection of the Dutch resistance movement and the support of the Catholic and Protestant churches, their agony was endless. The Netherlands experienced the highest percentage of Jewish deaths among all Nazi-conquered nations: more than 100,000 fatalities out of a prewar Jewish population of 140,000.

On our second day of travel, we spotted a soldier standing beside a Jeep.

"Another roadblock. How many does that make now?" I anxiously asked Al.

"I'm not sure, but we can't afford to give out all of our cigarettes and booze just yet. We've still got 150 miles or more to go. That last captain charged me three bottles of Johnny Walker for 10 measly gallons of gasoline. That's highway robbery, you know!" Al said in disgust.

"Let me do the talking this time, OK?" I suggested.

"What's the holdup, sergeant?" I inquired. "Everything looks clear ahead."

"Well, sir, I don't rightly know, but we were just notified by walkie-talkie that there's some type of commotion about two miles up ahead," the sergeant replied. "I heard some gunfire myself just five minutes ago. It's probably some die-hard Nazis still trying to cause a ruckus. I was personally instructed by the General to stop all traffic regardless of rank and not to let anyone pass until he gives the all-clear order."

"Sergeant, I can tell that you are without question a fine soldier. Doesn't he strike you as such, captain?" I said, surreptitiously winking at Al to get his agreement.

"Well, yes, I can see that. Yes, I noticed that trait as soon as we pulled up here," Al said, playing along. "What's your last name, please?"

"Shanklin is my last name, sir."

"Thanks, sergeant, we'll need that for our accommodation report," I told him. "Where are you from, Sgt. Shanklin?"

"Mississippi, sir. Hattiesburg to be precise, and before you go any further, sirs, I'll be happy to let you both pass for a carton of those Camels and two bottles of Jack."

"What?" I said.

"You heard me, sir. I'm not going to stick my neck out for anything less. My final price is once again a carton of Camels and two Jacks," the veteran noncom said, clearly not budging from his demand.

"You ungrateful rebel. I ought to have you arrested and court-martialed for bribery," I threatened.

"You should, sir, but you won't. We both need something, and I just offered you a pass. I'm the one taking the risk with the General here and, with all due respect, gentlemen, I think it was a fair offer."

"Give him want he wants, Joe. Next time, I'll do the talking," Al laughed as we handed the sergeant his extortion fee and headed down the road.

We passed through the "trouble" area and soon realized there was no General or any disturbance, only a good ruse. The audacious sergeant had tricked us.

"As the saying goes, all is fair in love and war," I said to my pal.

Al and I reminisced during the 350-mile, two-day drive.

"It's too bad that Roosevelt died before seeing the war end," I said with regret.

"Yes, I wish he'd made it, too. I'll never forget the date of his death, April 12, 1945," Al said. "So many people have died unnecessarily, and for what!"

"It seems like a tragic nightmare doesn't it? I mean it's a different world, thinking back from now to our innocent youth in 1936," I reflected.

"It's hard to relate the promise of that time to the devastation of today," Al answered sadly.

We recalled the young girls we'd witnessed marching and singing in Berlin during the Olympics. We assumed they'd become armament factory or farm workers or had taken on civil service duties or served with fire crews, or manned bomb shelters or searchlight batteries. Many, we guessed, had become nurses or served in other humanitarian capacities, but we feared many had perished as members of the home guard or died with a weapon in their hands.

We went from Würzburg to Frankfurt through a small German town also called Limburg. At the time I'd incorrectly confused the little town in Germany with the Netherlands' province of Limburg. Oddly, Al remembered the name of the town from years ago when it was mentioned by Agnes, the girl he'd met in Berlin during the Olympics. It was her hometown. Both of us happily reminisced a little about Agnes and hoped she too had survived the war.

Leaving the battered town, we continued toward Cologne where the world-renowned medieval cathedral was still standing even though it had been badly damaged. But the massive Hohenzollern Bridge had been destroyed and had fallen into the Rhine River. We drove past the ruins of Aachen to the Netherlands border at Kerkrade, through the streets of Heerlen, and finally made it to our destination, Schimmert.

CHAPTER TWENTY-ONE
THE SUN ARISES

Sterre had been fighting for her life for more than two months while receiving medical treatment in a U.S. Army hospital near Cologne. She'd lost more than 25 pounds during her perilous ordeal but was steadily regaining her strength after a miraculous recovery. Initially, she remembered very little, but as her stamina improved, so did her memory. Her doctor and her devoted nurse, Lt. Alexis Addie, were ecstatic by her progress, but still very concerned about her precarious predicament.

Shortly after the war's end, the makeshift hospital staff was ordered to release all civilian patients who were strong enough to walk. Although Sterre's full memory had not yet returned, physically her health was much improved. Over pleas from her nurse who feared for her safety and objected to her release, Sterre was selected for discharge. Once the order became a reality all Sterre could do was properly thank her caregivers and reluctantly say her goodbyes.

As a favor to Nurse Addie, the officer in charge of a truck convoy that was headed back to Belgium's Port of Antwerp for supplies, allowed Sterre to hitch a ride with his unit. The good nurse had gathered, through recent conversations with Sterre, that she was from a small town called Schimmert. On that slim hunch, Lt. Addie correctly assumed Sterre's hometown must be the same one near the Dutch city of Maastricht as shown on a large map hanging on the wall of the hospital's headquarters indicating open roadways in Belgium, western Germany and Limburg Province in the Netherlands.

As the 2 ½ ton army truck began to move, Sterre found herself alone and huddled under the tarp-topped rear corner of the vehicle. She covered herself with an old woolen coat provided by her nurse friend. She was still strikingly underweight and wearing a blank stare on her stark face. As the miles started to add up, the somber mood of the soldiers riding with her in the truck's bed changed abruptly as one of the men started singing an old cowboy tune, "Tumbling Tumbleweeds," made famous by the western country musical group, the Sons of the Pioneers.

Sterre, too, became more at ease as the music provided a welcomed release. The guys shared food and drinks with her along the way and she enjoyed listening to the music as the men joined together and sang a few of their favorite melodies.

One song, in particular, struck a chord when she recognized and heard one of the guys singing Fred Astaire's movie hit song, "Cheek to Cheek."

Immediately, past images of me flashed through her mind.

"Joe, Joe!" She cried out.

Over and over, she screamed, "Joe, Joe!"

Frantic by her cries, two of the soldiers rushed to her aid to help calm her fears.

Overcome and weak, she passed out, sleeping for roughly two hours.

Later, she was awakened by movements of her body bouncing against the wooden railings caused by the truck constantly swerving and hitting potholes on the unrepaired war-damaged road. As the evening's light faded away, she was listlessly gazing through the truck's wooden slats when she suddenly recognized a sign illuminated by the truck's headlights.

"Maastricht," she muttered to herself.

"Stop the truck, please stop! This is my home, I'm home. Please stop the truck!" She pleaded.

One of the men banged on the truck's rear window and the driver pulled over to the right side of the road.

"Are you sure this is your home, lady?" one of the men asked.

"Yes, I'm sure, It's my home," she said happily.

With her constant assurances, the soldiers helped her off of the truck, handed her some food and water, wished her well and sped away into the moonless night.

She was 10 miles from Schimmert but had no clue how to get there from her current location. For two hours, she walked in the darkness before exhaustion overcame her. Too weary to continue her journey, she fell to the ground passing out in the tall weeded overgrowth just a few feet from the narrow gravel road.

Early the next morning, a boy riding his bicycle noticed her lying in the grass and alerted his father who luckily recognized her. With his son's help, the man loaded Sterre onto his horse-drawn cart and took her to her home to Oensel where she eagerly reunited with her family who was happily relieved to see her alive.

Days later after regaining some of her strength, Sterre patiently listened intently to everyone's enthralling stories about the liberation but was more interested in hearing of my demeanor and actions while I was there last September frantically looking for her. Until her return, she had no idea that I was in the Army serving as an infantry officer. Thereafter, she begged for information from every American soldier she met for any scant details as to the whereabouts of the Old Hickory Division surmising I had to be no more than a few hundred miles away from her. She was reassured that I still loved her after reading my diary entries and prayed constantly for our speedy reunion.

She was excited to see Ralf Schrijnemaekers and was consoled by the fact that he had returned home unscathed, but mourned the loss of her lifelong friend and neighbor, John Westhovens. She felt guilty about their sacrifices, knowing she would not have survived her forced-labor ordeal without their constant protection. Ralf and John had shared their meager rations with her and sheltered her during their captivity, in addition to keeping her identity secret as she posed as a male. Without question, their devotion and sacrifice saved her life.

My long anticipated return to Schimmert was less fraught with peril. As we turned onto de Kling Road at Oensel that afternoon, only the unusually hot, sultry 96 degrees temperature caused me any grief. The suffocating heat caused beads of sweat to form on my brow sending salty streams onto a direct path into my burning eyes. It was so hot in fact that the chain on which my dog tags dangled created a thin line that colored the skin on the back of my neck green. To avoid baking my bare chest, I wore my metal identification tags numbered 77888023 T42 43 O on the outside of my shirt.

I hadn't showered for days, and the heat not only added to my discomfort but surely rendered me unfit for companionship. None of that seemed to matter as we pulled our Jeep within a few feet of Sterre's house.

Without knocking, I opened the door and shouted her name.

"Sterre, Sterre, Sterre," I yelled as I searched the house for any sign of her. Frantically, I rushed to the barn, where I was met by Paul and Hannah, who was shocked by my sudden appearance. I uncharacteristically ignored their welcome and repeatedly asked about Sterre.

"Calm down, Joe," Al said as we both heard Hannah say with glee that Sterre was safe, and had walked toward a clump of trees as she pointed the way. Immediately, I began running in that direction. I could feel my heart beating, realizing with extraordinary anticipation that every stride took me nearer to my love. I knew that soon all of my torment would be replaced with pure elation.

I could see in the distance that Sterre was clearing away the brush that had grown up around her stone wishing well. For the past five years, her life had been a nightmare filled with fear, hunger, and despair, but now she only dreamed of a brighter future with her Cowboy Joe.

Lost in her thoughts, I saw her drop to her knees and dip the tips of her fingers into the fountain's cool water from showers the previous night. While peering into the little pool, she noticed a coin lying on the bottom. She smiled as she retrieved it. It was the 1936 nickel that I'd placed there months earlier. Carefully, she examined the five-cent piece that matched the one I'd given to her when I'd first proposed nine years earlier.

Before my darling stood, she again kissed the cherished coin she'd been holding, before dropping it back into the fountain. As she slowly arose, she was stunned by the sound of my voice calling her name.

"Sterre! Sterre!"

She turned in anticipation, teardrops coursing down her pale cheeks, her mouth open and flashing a wide grin but not answering.

"Sterre!" I shouted once more, exhausting my last breath but still able to throw my hat in the air.

She leaped into my outstretched arms and pressed her lips to mine. We held each other for several minutes, kissing and smiling, crying and laughing, all at once, never wanting our long-awaited, astounding daydream to end.

"My darling, I have never stopped loving you," I said with joy, lifting her off her feet. Her trembling hands pulled my face closer for another kiss.

Laughing, I told her I saw her toss a coin into the fountain.

"They say if you put a coin in that well, it will bring you good luck!" I said. "I believe that saying must be true now."

"Sterre, my love, I told you I would come back for you. Nothing was ever going to keep me away. I'm here, my darling. I've returned and I'll never leave you again."

She was still in shock after seeing me standing in front of her in uniform.

"Joe, I know I'm not the same care-free girl you fell in love with back in 1936. I know my looks have changed, but my love you for has never wavered."

Yes, her features had changed. She was painfully thin, so thin that her blue eyes seemed too big for her lovely face. Her beautiful, long brown hair that I so fondly remembered was now cropped short and brittle. But Sterre's radiant smile, caring personality and unflinching resolve were still there, making me realize once again how much I loved her.

As our foreheads touched and our eyes met, all I could focus on at the moment was her. To me, she never looked more beautiful, and I never loved her more as I held her tightly never wishing to surrender our embrace.

"I love you more than ever. I never lost faith, my darling," I gushed.

Shaken in disbelief, she lowered her head and began to tremble before speaking in a low soft tone.

"Joe, I have a sad secret that I've been hiding from you ever since I came back to Schimmert after leaving you in America," said Sterre tearfully. "No one except Sister Truus knows of my sorrow. I betrayed you and disgraced both you and my family. I was pregnant with your child. I lost our child, Joe."

"Oh, my darling, I know about our child. I read it in your diary. Please don't cry, Sterre. There is no need to feel sorry. You did nothing wrong."

"I have felt so guilty about not having the strength to tell you. I am so ashamed that I failed you," she blurted out in distress then awaited my reply, seeming to expect some displeasure for holding onto her secret for so long.

"Knowing about our child has kept me alive throughout the war, I truly believe that. We will have more children, but I only want one woman, and that woman is you, my love," I reassured her.

"Joe, how did I ever meet such a wonderful man like you?" she tearfully said as she raised her head relieved by my answer.

"There will be no more secrets between us, Sterre. Since we're being honest, I must tell you about an encounter that has been torturing my soul. I, too, have been burdened by a dark secret. I was with a woman for one night when I was in London last year. I've tried to convince myself that the war was to blame for my indiscretion, but in reality, I have no credible excuses. I dishonored you during a time of emotional weakness. I'm sorry. Please forgive me!"

"Joe, it doesn't matter. I know your heart. All that really matters to me is that we've found each other again. I chose you, Joe, only you," she earnestly replied.

It was difficult for either of us to comprehend that the long-awaited moment could be happening at our special place, on that sacred ground. As we continued looking into each other's eyes, we screamed in joy as I swirled Sterre around. She firmly hugged my neck as if never intending to let go. At the same time, we started to laugh and cry uncontrollably in our joyful moment of sheer contentment.

"Is this a dream, Joe? Please tell me this is not a dream!" she asked as we held one another tightly.

"I prayed so long for this day, my darling! Thank God that you are now safely in my arms! I have loved you from the first moment I saw you. Promise me that you will never leave my side again," I lovingly pleaded, as she nodded her head in agreement.

With a blissful gaze, she eagerly replied, "I promise to be with you until I stop breathing. I knew you would come back for me. I prayed nightly with confidence that our Heavenly Father would never sacrifice our souls to those madmen," she said as she wiped her teary eyes with a handkerchief.

"That's right, my darling! You are right!" I said.

"My prayers have been answered a thousand fold. The Good Lord sent you here for me and me here for you, and now, our hearts can beat as one again," Sterre said.

Without pause, I got down on one knee as I had done nine long years before. In my right hand, I held my grandmother's ring between my thumb and index finger and asked her the one question I had long dreamed to say again.

"Will you marry me?"

"Yes!" she said without hesitation.

"I cannot live another day without you, my love," I told her.

She gently put her arms around my neck, and then in a voice that broke, began to sing, "Heaven, I'm in heaven ... And my heart beats so that I can hardly speak ... And I seem to find the happiness I seek ..."

Excitedly, I joined her in singing the last line, "When we're out together dancing cheek to cheek." Another long kiss then followed our embrace.

Together at long last, we slowly walked through the tall grass with her head leaning against my shoulder and my right arm around her waist. Gratefully, we both realized our emptiness had been forever replaced by love in its purest form. We looked deeply into one another's eyes, and we both understood from that moment on that we would never be alone again.

Later, after talking with Sterre about our wartime experiences, I learned by sheer coincidence, that I had been at the same Army medical facility in Cologne where she had been treated in the spring of 1945. I was visiting one of my men, Sgt. Wilson, who had suffered severe shrapnel injuries to his legs and buttocks after fighting near Cologne. Of course, at the time I was unaware that Sterre was hospitalized there, too. She was bedridden in a building located just yards away from where I had been standing.

Not willing to take any more chances, two days later our hastily arranged wedding took place. First, the official formal state ceremony was held at the courthouse in Beek followed by a more traditional religious ritual at the Sint Remigius Church in Schimmert. When I saw her entering the church's sanctuary through the big wooden doors wearing the hand-made dress she adored, the same one so lovingly crafted years before by Sister Truus and her friend Kelly, I beamed with pride as she walked towards me as I stood at the altar smiling from ear to ear. She was a vision of perfection as she walked arm and arm with Paul as he escorted her down the aisle as a proud father would, offering her hand to mine as witnessed by friends and family, blessed by Father Peter.

Ours was the first wedding to take place at the church after the war's end. St. Remigius was packed with well-wishers, friends, and family members. Al stood by my side as my best man and was on his best behavior. Sterre's friend, Kelly, was the matron of honor. It was a joyous event. Finally, after nine frightful years, I placed Oma Renee's ring on the finger of my new wife's left hand. Mother had insisted that I take the ring with me once we knew that I was going to be stationed in Europe. I kissed the love of my life, my beautiful bride, Mrs. Sterre Maria Francien Fisher-Trags. My only regret was not having my parents in attendance.

Regretfully, Al and I were only able to stay in Schimmert one day after the wedding since we had to report back to our unit to avoid a court-martial. It gave Sterre and me precious little time for an improvised honeymoon. We spent the night at Uncle Karl's house while he chose to sleep in his barn for the evening.

On our first night as a married couple, we slept in the room where my mother was born, which seemed oddly appropriate.

On August 21, the entire 63rd Division, including yours truly, shipped out for the United States and home. Though I was forced to leave her once again, we both knew this time it was only temporary. After debarking, I took a train home from New York but didn't contact my parents in advance, choosing to surprise them instead.

When I reached Bloomington, I discovered that my parents were not at home and soon realized all of the doors were locked. The grass had been freshly cut and a healthy crop of corn blanketed our fields. I fetched a door key that we kept hidden on a wooden ledge above the right front window, but once inside, I found the electricity had been disconnected.

I walked over to the Mangus farmhouse next door. As I got closer, their girls, who had been swinging on the front porch, quickly ran into the house. I was met by Mr. Mangus and his wife who, by then, was standing on the porch looking forlorn as their children peered nervously from their living room windows.

"Welcome home, Joe. We're all so very happy that you made it home safely," Mr. Mangus greeted and congratulated me while reaching for my hand.

"Thank you, it's good to be home again. But do you have any idea where my parents are?" I asked.

After a slight pause, Mrs. Mangus started to quietly weep, then without warning her children pushed open the screen door and rushed to her side. All were in tears.

"Joe, there is no easy way to say this, son, but if you have to hear it from someone, I'm glad it's from me, from someone who cares. Like I said before, there's no easy way to say this. Son, your parents are dead. They were killed in a car accident two weeks ago," he said with his voice quivering.

In silence, I closed my eyes and fell instantly and uncontrollably to my knees in shock at the news.

"This can't be true; I can't believe what I'm hearing. Please, stop!" I said in heartbreak as I covered my ears attempting to block out the sound of any more painful words Mr. Magnus might say. In anger, I punched my fist into the rich black soil leaving knuckle imprints in the soft dirt. For a second, I remained motionless as I dipped my head and watched my tears drop to the ground beneath me.

As the pressure subsided, I felt the calming touch of a gentle hand. Mrs. Mangus put her arm around my shoulder, both of us in tears.

"We tried to contact you several times through the Red Cross, but I can see by your reaction that you never got our messages or letters," Mr. Mangus said.

"No, I didn't, but that's understandable. I'd been transferred to another division at the war's end and had been moving from one place to another amid all of the confusion over there," I mumbled to them as I attempted to gather myself.

"Of course, we understand," the good neighbor said.

"Your folks were wonderful people. We considered them our best friends. We all loved them, especially our children. Your mom and dad were like a second set of parents to them. Their passing was such a tragedy, and the outpouring of love for your parents by the community was overwhelming. We will never forget them, Joe," Mrs. Mangus said.

I somehow managed to stand up and compose myself as I had done many times during the war. I had grown accustomed to death, but this unforeseen news struck the hardest blow of all.

"Your parents were fine people and beloved by everyone here. Why almost the whole county came out for their funeral. Your mother's co-workers at State Farm took up a collection and raised enough money to pay for all of their funeral expenses. There was even enough left over to pay the property taxes on the farm for the next few years," Mr. Mangus said with pride.

"Everyone knew they loved that farm, Joe, so we felt it was only proper that they were buried near that stone that your mother loved out back of your farmhouse. We prayed that it would be OK with you, Joe," she said.

"Yes, thank you both. I can think of no better final resting place for Mother and Father," I agreed.

"These are for you. I know they wanted you to have these," Mrs. Mangus said before reaching into her pocket and handing me a small red box containing my parent's wedding rings along with an unopened letter from my mother.

I thanked them for being so kind and for their friendship as I slowly walked away stung by more pain than any I'd suffered during the war.

As the tears continued to roll down my face, I walked immediately to my parent's gravesite. Standing alone under sunny skies with a steady easterly breeze, I opened Mother's last letter and read it aloud to myself while gazing at two wooden crosses. While reading her letter I was reminded once again how blessed my life had been to have had such wonderful parents. Their loving guidance was the cornerstone of my existence.

"My dear Zef, your father and I received your letter today, and we were thrilled to hear that you were reunited with Sterre. Raymond fell in love with her the day he met her and I long before you even knew her. After meeting her, we both knew she was the perfect partner for you. The description you wrote us about your touching wedding brought loving smiles to our faces. You know we were there with both of you in spirit. I know how much you love being an American, and, of course, we share that love, too. But I know that Schimmert will always have a special place in your heart and that makes me happy. Remember, I always told you that someday a good decision will change your life forever, and marrying sweet Sterre will do just that. We can't wait to put our arms around you once again when you come home to us. We know you will still have more decisions to make about your future, but always remember, we will always support your choices. We will always love you, my precious son! Love forever, Mother and Pops."

Ironically, her last letter to me was dated on the very day of their fatal accident.

I spent several melancholy weeks in Bloomington arranging the sale of my parents' farm to the Magnuses, and sorting through their personal effects. Much had pained me over the past decade, but dealing with those sad tasks constituted the most grueling period of my life.

The ocean passage back to Europe seemed exceedingly slow, owing to the fact that I missed Sterre so much and was eager to see her once more.

On the mantle of our home in Schimmert lovingly stand two prized keepsakes I brought from Illinois. I made the oak frames for both of them from wood taken from our barn in Bloomington. One frame holds the last letter penned by my mother and the other features a black-and-white photo of my parents' tombstone.

I had purchased the gray marble grave marker before I sold the farm to the Magnuses, who I knew would care for Mother and Father's gravesite. I had the headstone engraved with their names, their dates of birth and death, and had a single tulip carved at the top. The bottom bore only a simple phrase, "Returned to the Silence of Schimmert 1945."

The post-war years in the Netherlands passed serenely for me and Sterre, but our greatest gift arrived not long after I returned from America. Rebekka Rosalie, a beautiful daughter, was born and gave our lives, even more, meaning and joy. Along with Dutch influences, we raised her to appreciate American values as well.

One beautiful morning, after listening on the radio to the Andrews Sisters' "Rum and Coca-Cola" song, which was her favorite, our precious four-year-old, Rebekka Rosalie, ran past me heading in the direction of our family's most special place at the back of our property. She was clutching in her right hand a single red tulip that she had just plucked from our flower garden. Her long, curly golden locks bounced freely as she sprinted through our meadow.

Sterre reached for my hand, and I hers, as we watched our little sunshine frolic happily and carefree in the lush green grass. Sterre wore my Oma Renee's ring on her right hand and on her left my mother's wedding band. Her mother's crucifix necklace dangled on a chain around her neck. I carried in my billfold for good luck two coins, a 1936 US nickel and a Dutch 10-cent piece dated 1945 and proudly wore my father's wedding band on my ring finger.

As we gazed out into the open fields, all around us were lush pastures ablaze with colorful tulips in full bloom. Hearty crops flourished in our fertile fields, ready for picking. It was a wonderful sight, especially knowing that only a few short years ago those same fields had been the scene of the terror of war. Music and laughter had replaced the sounds of gunfire.

During that serene moment, I was reminded once again of the simple beauty of my tranquil surroundings. I came to the conclusion that I had made the best decision of my life when I returned to Schimmert for the fifth and final time.

Just then, the bells atop the Sint Remigius Church started chiming while teenage children laughed as they scurried past our little farm on their bicycles. Over our barn door, I beamed with pride at the oaken plank from West Virginia on which my father had carved the word "Schimmert" for my mother. On the distant horizon, I could see the blades of the Sint Herbertus Windmill circling in the wind.

As I turned and watched our little Rebekka Rosalie tenderly place her lone red tulip upon our family's precious fountain stone, a gratifying contentment filled my soul. For the first time in my life, I could now clearly see Schimmert through the eyes of my loving mother.

As I slowly raised my eyes toward the clear blue heavens above, I softly whispered to myself, "Dear Mother, we are home again at last."

EPILOGUE
THE LAST
ROAD TRAVELED

The war left much of Europe's industrial base, residential areas, railroads, communications apparatus, and large cities in ruins. Basic infrastructure was severely disrupted or left in shambles. Agricultural production was dramatically hampered, and fears of famine and starvation spread across the continent. Millions of people were displaced or made homeless, and millions more were in urgent need of medical and humanitarian assistance.

The only major economic and military power spared the war's devastation to its industrial and agricultural base was the United States. As a result, in 1948 the American Congress enacted the Marshall Plan, which provided more than $13 billion in economic aid to Europe. The money was earmarked to assist in the reconstruction and recovery of the continent's war-ravaged economies.

The program was named after Gen. George C. Marshall, who had been America's overall military commander and the main architect of the country's wartime strategy as chairman of the Joint Chiefs of Staff. After the war, Marshall was appointed Secretary of State by President Harry Truman and helped create the economic revitalization plan named for him.

The Netherlands received more than $1 billion in direct financial assistance from the United States under the recovery aid program. The first and largest beneficiaries were food production companies. Later, money was given to assist the textile, steel, electric generating, and railroad industries. In Limburg, funds went to Eerste Nederlandse Cement Industrie to help the company increase its cement production capacity in order to rebuild the country's infrastructure. Other key projects in Limburg included assistance to restart water projects, financial aid, and technical assistance that helped the Royal Dutch State Mines (DSM) resume its mining and chemical operations.

Direct monetary aid was also provided to help families rebuild their homes and to assist farmers in re-establishing their agricultural operations. Farmers were provided the funds needed to purchase new equipment, tractors, and steel plows manufactured by American companies, such as John Deere and International-Harvester, both headquartered in Illinois.

In the years after the war, I learned to speak better Dutch and Limburgish. My Uncle Karl Westhovens died, and in his will as his sole surviving relative, he left me his farm in Oensel. In addition to farming, I took a job in Limburg Province as an administrative envoy for reconstruction under the Marshall Plan. My job was working with companies to determine which were eligible to receive financial aid. Once funding was secured, my duty was to ensure that the money received by the different entities was spent properly until the projects were completed.

Limburg slowly settled back into its calm, day-to-day lifestyle. Wilhelm De Beau, the brave wartime resistance fighter known as "Wim the Butcher," became, in fact, a well-respected meat cutter and operated his own butcher shop in a little Limburg village called Meers, located on the Maas River near the Belgian border.

Wilhelm married and had three wonderful, accomplished children of his own. To honor the American soldiers who had liberated his beloved homeland, he gave all three of his children Americanized names. Five years after the war, Wilhelm was awarded the Verzetsherdenkingskruis, the Dutch Royal Memorial Cross, in honor of his bravery and service to his country while fighting with the resistance during the war.

Wilhelm's brother, Frans, who had been by his side throughout the war had been severely wounded during a failed Resistance railroad bombing operation. He is currently living in Meers and has recovered, married and has two fine sons. Wilhelm's father, also named, Frans and his mother, Anna Maria, who I met on several occasions, lived in the same little village throughout the war and were fortunate to make it through the struggle unharmed. They did, however, have the misfortune of giving birth to nine naughty and unruly children named, Peter, Francien, Paul, Tiny, Math, Wim, They, Marjo and Frans. The family's small house in Meers had one small bathroom and bench seating at their kitchen table, but the children were blessed by having incredible parents who loved them all in spite of their rowdy nature. Their hard-working father, Frans, raised horses and enjoyed milling about in his garden. Anna Maria cooked, cleaned and attended to her children with a warm, loving smile.

Sister Truus took a sabbatical assignment to the Dutch South American Protectorate of Suriname where she was credited with saving hundreds of people during a terrible cholera epidemic that plagued the territory and lasted for several years. For her unselfish humanitarian service, she was rumored to be on the Vatican's short list of sure-fire candidates being considered for sainthood. Although one is not normally elevated to that lofty status before death, if she receives the final nomination, according to Schimmert's Father Peter, her election by the Vatican would be just a formality.

The good Father Peter was instrumental in the reconstruction of Limburg by encouraging and sponsoring fundraising events to help support local construction companies in their rebuilding and repairing of damaged homes and businesses. He also assisted the homeless by helping them find temporary shelter, and he and his flock helped with food distribution.

Jim Trags married his sweetheart, Hannah. They are expecting their first child and live happily on his family's farm with his father and younger brother, Arjan.

Arjan, by the way, learned to be quite adept at playing basketball. I taught him the game. We used an old bicycle rim nailed to his barn as a makeshift rim. Even though his skills are still developing, he swears that someday he'll be the first European invited to join the world famous Harlem Globetrotters basketball team.

Kelly van Dyke, Sterre's dear best friend, is also with child and expecting

SCHIMMERT: JOURNEY TO SILENCE

her baby next May. She married a local engineer, Loek, who she met while working together.

After the occupation, life in Schimmert was incredibly difficult for Tiny Jansen, the girl who was impregnated at the beginning of the war by the German corporal Warner and later aborted the baby out of desperation. For befriending and supporting the Nazis during and after the invasion, her family was ostracized by the locals. Tiny's long blond hair was cut off and her head was shaved by members of the resistance in retribution after the Germans were expelled from Limburg in 1944.

Uncle Wouter and his children all made it through the war without physical harm. His son, Ralf, became a truck driver, son Math became a banker, and youngest daughter Kiki enjoyed making and selling teddy bears for children. Lastly, his daughter Judy became a national personality who became famous as the country's premier chef, noted primarily for preparing a Dutch entré called the "Frikandel Speciaal."

Herbert Engel, one of the brothers who Al and I met on our first ocean voyage, stayed in touch. Both he and his brother, Jonathan, joined the US Navy and became fighter pilots in the Pacific and took part in one of the largest naval-air battles during the war. The epic battle was fought in the Philippine Sea and famously called the "Great Marianas Turkey Shoot." During the battle, the Japanese navy lost three of its carriers and over 600 airplanes. Sadly, Herbert's brother, Jonathan, lost his life during the fight when his plane was shot down. His body was never recovered.

My buddy Al Obermeyer writes to us regularly, and we're expecting a visit from him and his family in a couple of years. He promised to come over as soon as his three boys, Joey, Thomas, and Finney, are old enough to travel. He now works for a little American company called IBM.

Most Sundays, I visit with my fellow soldiers now peacefully interred at the American Cemetery at Margraten where 8,301 of my comrades in arms are buried. There are also 1,722 other U.S. soldiers and airmen whose names are forever memorialized on Margraten's marble walls, many of whose final resting places are known but to God. Most of the men buried at Margraten were cut down in the prime of their youth.

Though grieving American families lost their sons, husbands, brothers, and fathers, I hoped they take solace by knowing those sacrifices were not in vain. They fought and died for freedom, the greatest cause of all. Countless Europeans, including German citizens, are enjoying that priceless gift today partly because of the brave sons of the New World who are buried here, along with countless other Allied soldiers who are laid to rest all across Europe.

We can take comfort, though, in the fact that grateful Dutch Limburgers will never forget those liberators interred forever in peace at Margraten. In honor of our fallen heroes, each soldier's grave has been adopted by a thoughtful Dutch family that has lovingly attended to its care since the end of the war. Every holiday, every birthday, even on days for no special reason, the Dutch faithfully express their appreciation for their adopted sons, our loved ones. Their self-appointed care for our young men is not considered by them to be a burden or a duty, but instead as a heartfelt privilege, so much so that there is a waiting list of Dutch families to continue the service once current caregivers are no longer able to perform their honorable task.

I will never forget them and, I know, neither will the Dutch.

Made in the USA
Middletown, DE
19 February 2019